RIDING
FOR THE
FLAG

RIDING FOR THE FLAG

JIM R. WOOLARD

PINNACLE BOOKS
Kensington Publishing Corp.
www.kensingtonbooks.com

PINNACLE BOOKS are published by

Kensington Publishing Corp.
119 West 40th Street
New York, NY 10018

All Kensington titles, imprints, and distributed lines are available at special quantity discounts for bulk purchases for sales promotions, premiums, fund-raising, educational, or institutional use. Special book excerpts or customized printings can also be created to fit specific needs. For details, write or phone the office of the Kensington sales manager: Kensington Publishing Corp., 119 West 40th Street, New York, NY 10018, attn: Sales Department; phone 1-800-221-2647.

PINNACLE BOOKS and the Pinnacle logo are Reg. U.S. Pat. & TM Off.

ISBN-13: 978-0-7860-3481-9
ISBN-10: 0-7860-3481-5

First mass market paperback printing: September 2015

10 9 8 7 6 5 4 3 2 1

Printed in the United States of America

First electronic edition: September 2015

ISBN-13: 978-0-7860-3482-6
ISBN-10: 0-7860-3482-3

CHAPTER 1

Dismounted and afoot, they crept from the darkness, the barrels of their weapons glinting in the pale light of the late September moon. Hardly breathing, Judah Bell studied them through the cracked door of the horse barn. His uncle's prediction had come true. Captain Hunt Baldwin and his volunteer Yankee cavalrymen were honoring their dire threats: They weren't suffering another public insult from the acid tongue of pro-slaver Temple Bell, not without treating him to a loss he'd regret forever.

What Captain Baldwin and his night-stalking cavalrymen sought filled the stables of the barn and the paddock behind it. Temple Bell's stock of Denmark Thoroughbreds was the envy of every horseman within a hundred miles. And the burgeoning conflict between Rebel and blue-belly armies made them easy prey as "spoils of war."

The night stalkers' boldness shocked Judah Bell. They were intending to make off with marked and registered animals belonging to a highly respected Scott County, Kentucky, horse breeder. It made him shudder that with the coming of the war nothing would ever be the same again. Decades of respected and trusted laws were being cast aside like winged seeds dispersed by the wind.

Straw rustled and Judah felt the heat of Asa Barefoot's body. Old Asa, half-black and half-Cherokee by blood and solid as seasoned wood, was always nearby, watching over Temple Bell's favorite nephew. Like Judah, he held a Navy Colt revolver and was fully alert, though it was their fourth straight night on watch. Asa Barefoot was without a doubt the only mixed-blood slave in Kentucky whose white master trusted with a gun. And he was an excellent marksman.

Keenly aware that others might be approaching from outside his range of sight, Judah counted six shadowy forms in the wan light. He rightfully feared bloodshed. Rifle at the ready, his uncle was stationed in a blackened second-story window of his frame home, a structure sitting to the north of the barn at right angles. Hunt Baldwin and intruders had no clue they were sneaking into a potentially lethal crossfire, and Temple Bell wouldn't hesitate to pull the trigger, if necessary, to protect his prized possessions.

Judah wiped the sweaty palm of his shooting hand on his trousers, waiting for his uncle to challenge the would-be thieves. When it came, Temple Bell's shout carried far beyond the barnyard:

"Take another step and one of you is a dead Yankee. You have them in your sights, Nephew?"

Judah's hasty response from the front of the barn was equally loud. "Yes, sir."

Heads turning toward the unlit house, the shadowy figures halted in unison, their chance of surprising their victims evaporating in less time than a spitting of tobacco required. Judah stared at those he could make out, wondering which one would be the first to move or break the overwhelming silence.

The thickest of them spoke, undeniably the gruff, throaty voice of Captain Hunt Baldwin. "There's too many of us, you secesh-loving son-of-a-bitch. You might kill some of us, but you can't kill the eight of us. Not before we have a go at you and your family."

Judah winced when his uncle let his temper get the best of him and further pinpoint his position. "You're a bunch of shit-sucking Yankees, Baldwin, attacking at night like your kind always does."

Any prospect of avoiding the shedding of blood vanished in a moment of outright madness spawned by the long-standing feud that had solidified a hate between Temple Bell and Hunt Baldwin that made backing down a fate worse than death. Eschewing good sense at the risk of his life, Hunt Baldwin screamed, "Shoot the secesh bastard," leveled his rifle at the second story of the unlit house, and fired.

Ignoring any threat from the barn, three of the Baldwin men raised their weapons and loosed a round in the same direction. Bullets tore into wooden siding with sharp *whaps* amid the rolling thunder of the shots. A gun boomed from within the house. A red streak of burning powder bolted toward the sky, not toward a target on the ground, and Judah's ringing ears heard a heavy object bounce with a loud clatter on the metal roof of the porch below his uncle's perch.

Asa Barefoot clutched Judah's arm. "Mastuh hurt or dead. We save you."

A stunned Judah gripped his pistol so hard his knuckles throbbed with pain. "We can't run," he blurted. "They'll burn him and the house."

"Mastuh say he die, you live. Come," Asa Barefoot said.

Hunt Baldwin yelled, "Judah's at the front door of the barn," just as hinges squealed at the opposite end of the runway separating the stalled horses. Asa Barefoot spun and fired.

Judah heard a shrill yelp of pain, and an intruder stumbled in the middle of the rear doorway and collapsed.

Without hesitating, the half-breed turned about, aimed, and shot at a moving target in the barnyard to freeze Hunt Baldwin and those flanking him in place for a few precious seconds, grabbed Judah by the shoulder before he could trigger his cocked Navy, and yanked him toward the rear entryway. "After me, be ready."

Bullets thudded into the front door of the barn, imparting the need for quick movement, and Judah, resigned to the fact nothing could be done for his uncle unless they evaded Hunt Baldwin's vengeful temper to fight another time, clung tightly to Barefoot's heels. Just inside the rear door, the half-breed slowed, rapped the butt of his revolver against a stall door, yanked his hat from his roached head, and with his opposite hand whirled it into the darkness awaiting them.

A musket roared, the ball whanging the door frame in front of Barefoot, and then they were clear of the barn running between milling horses and scaling the planked fence of the paddock like scampering monkeys. Barefoot was fast on his feet for his age, and Judah was sucking wind when they reached the fringe of the narrow meadow beyond the paddock. As they plunged into the woods beyond it, a volley of bullets snipped the leaves above and around them.

Their destination was a ravine that straddled a never-dry creek. Abiding by Temple Bell's wishes, Judah and Barefoot had stashed two horses, riding gear, a supply of grain for the animals, and a poke of human vittles in the ravine four days ago in case flight was necessary. Judah marveled at his uncle's foresight. A veteran Mexican War officer deserving of his rank and medals, Temple Bell never underestimated the enemy, and he never allowed that enemy to take him by surprise or cut him off from a means of retreat. It had made no difference to Temple Bell that his sprung knee made it impossible for him to personally flee on foot. The patriarchs of the Bell family were expected to sacrifice whatever was required to sustain the family bloodline, and did so without hesitation.

Deep within the covering woods, Asa Barefoot dropped the pace to a fast walk. The half-breed negotiated the dark, winding pathway as if it were high noon. Judah seized the opportunity to fill his starved lungs with fresh air. His limbs were shaking from the sheer excitement of what he'd experienced in five short minutes, and it took several deep breaths to steady himself.

Judah mouthed a silent prayer of thanks. Had Hunt Baldwin stationed more of his cohorts behind the barn, the outcome would have been very different. Even then, if not for the shooting skill, decisiveness, and cleverness of Asa Barefoot, Judah knew he'd be lying dead on the barn's dusty floor.

Yes, he thought with a nod and a sigh, he'd survived, but sadly, everything that had brought him to Kentucky two years ago had amounted to naught. The laming of the sonless Temple Bell had left him in need of trusted help, and Senator Clay Bell had dispatched his middle son from Ohio to assist the senator's older brother. Until this fateful night, the arrangement had satisfied all parties, especially the horse-crazed Judah, for it had provided him with a legitimate excuse to avoid the career in the practice of law with its vast book learning that his father wanted for each of his sons.

"Will they follow us?" Judah asked Asa Barefoot in a near whisper, concerned, though it was impossible, that he might be overheard.

Without missing a step, Barefoot glanced over his shoulder. "They be after us in the morning."

That left the question of what was next for Judah and Barefoot the rest of the night?

After the formation of the Confederate States of America in February 1861, support for the Yankee cause had grown steadily in the immediate environs of Temple Bell's horse farm, and lingering in an area dominated by Yankee sympathizers who had once been friendly, tolerant neighbors to Temple Bell was no longer a wise choice for either Judah or Barefoot.

A widower, Judah's uncle had relented once the growing tension between Kentuckians erupted in armed violence and shipped his daughters to Judah's Ohio home for the duration of the war. But given the perils of traveling roads heavily patrolled by homegrown Union cavalrymen such as Hunt Baldwin, Temple Bell had decided to stay put and defend his Denmark Thoroughbreds on familiar ground.

Those same roads would be doubly dangerous for the fleeing Judah and Barefoot. Judah suspected Hunt Baldwin would claim that Temple Bell had fired on his men first, and he was certain the Yankee felled by Barefoot's bullet hadn't survived. The devious Baldwin would pin the blame for that death on Judah, making him a Yankee killer and subject to Union military justice.

So, if he'd been branded a secesh Rebel with no say in the matter, in which direction should he travel to save his hide? North to Ohio and his true home was too distant and required him to pass through too many miles of territory where every Union patrol would be on the lookout for him once Hunt Baldwin leveled murder charges against him with his superiors. From reading the local newspapers, Judah was aware that Confederate forces controlled areas of southern Kentucky and northern Tennessee. Those Rebel forces were recruiting heavily, and he knew their cavalry commanders wouldn't turn down a nephew of well-known secessionist Temple Bell who could provide his own top-notch horse and weapon. South it was then, without delay.

And Judah needed to keep on the move.

The harsh shock and pain of abruptly losing an uncle he loved like his birth father hadn't struck him yet, but when it did, he didn't trust his ability to hold the grief at bay and maintain his composure. Mourning had to wait.

A snort and a whinny greeted Judah and Barefoot at the clearing. "That Jasper, he talks more than a flighty girl," Judah said, drawing a chuckle from Barefoot.

The sorrel stallion's red hair was so bright it had a dull sheen even in faint moonlight. Judah gave Jasper the expected rubbing of nose and pat of the neck, slipped a bridle over his head, saddled him, tied a bedroll consisting of canvas tarp and blanket behind the skirt of the saddle, and draped a set of saddlebags across the sorrel's withers, his work quick and efficient from long practice. As he expected, Barefoot matched his speed in outfitting his saddled mare with the cotton sacks containing their camping gear. Judah had never found Barefoot lacking in his handling of horses, guns, and knives.

Judah had correctly assumed that, if all hell broke loose, Barefoot would travel with him. With Temple Bell gone, the half-breed's sole loyalty was to the nephew of his deceased master. Judah really didn't think it necessary, but he felt compelled to make certain he and Asa Barefoot shared the same page about how they must conduct themselves on purely Confederate ground, where folks believed the eternal obedience of slaves was inviolate and granting them their freedom was against the will of God.

"Asa, we're headed south," Judah said. "We're going to locate Captain Morgan and his Lexington Rifles and pray he'll let us ride with him," Judah said.

A frown wrinkled Barefoot's deep brown features. "You sure that's best for you, Mastuh Judah? I heard Mastuh Temple say your daddy back in Ohio wouldn't have no truck with no Rebels, not now, not ever."

Judah's answer was swift and firm. "After what we've been through, I couldn't fight beside any man wearing blue, not now, not ever. A soldier true to his flag doesn't spill the blood of those not in uniform, not if he can avoid it. My uncle didn't deserve what happened to him simply because of what he believed. I can only pray Father will understand how I feel."

Judah paused, then said, "One last thing, much as I hate to ask it of you, you'll have to play Old Asa every minute."

His destiny decided, Asa Barefoot flashed Judah a knowing grin. He understood the difference between the world of the Bell horse farm and what happened beyond its fences from decades of negotiating a careful path through the labyrinth of white disdain for those of another color. The absence of whip scars on his sixty-two-year backside was a stark testament to his acting skills.

"Never you worry, I be your head-nodding, do-as-you-asked, do-as-you-told Asa Barefoot till the Lord calls me home," the half-breed said in a meek drawl, ending his impersonation—with a sweeping bow—of a humble servant who always knew his place.

"I swear, by all that's holy, tamer than a week-old puppy dog," Judah said with a knowing smile of his own, fisting Jasper's reins. He bounced on his left foot and swung into the saddle.

Asa Barefoot mounted his brown mare and Judah said, "We'll follow the ravine to the east, top out on Bishop's Hill, and track south down Hanford Creek until we're past Grayson. I'd just as soon avoid any more shooting."

"Yes, sir, Mastuh Judah, you the boss."

Judah took the lead. They crossed the ravine's shallow creek and wound along the far bank. The walls of the ravine started shrinking within two miles. At a spot where a washout allowed them to exit the ravine, they located the narrow track that coursed over Bishop's Hill. On the crown of that elevation, Judah spied a bright red glow amid the trees on the western horizon, a sight that riled his guts something awful. The wishful child in him had hoped Captain Hunt

Baldwin wasn't a total bastard. But the roaring fire meant he was burning Temple Bell's house and his body with it.

There would come a day, Judah vowed, when he would look Hunt Baldwin in the eye and put a bullet in his cold-blooded heart.

How revenge could be sweet was an emotion that had eluded him until now.

The thought of tasting it warmed his soul.

CHAPTER 2

A chill September breeze swept up High Street, ruffling the collar and skirt of Jacob Bell's knee-length duster as he hustled through the front entryway of the Bishop House. At least he would be warm for the coming confrontation with his father. Twenty-two-year-old Jacob had never before gone against the wishes of State Senator Clay Bell on a matter of great importance to the Bell family. But he had now, and the consequences of his decision might cost him the love and goodwill of his father, which he cherished.

Jacob removed his duster and leather-billed cap and crossed the lobby of the Bishop House. Chillicothe being a fair distance from the Capital Square in Columbus, State Senator Clay Bell occupied the same commodious rooms at the Bishop House through the week whenever the Ohio Legislature was in session, a comfortable morning buggy ride away.

Jacob halted before the door of his father's room. He could hear voices from inside. Senator Clay Bell wasn't alone. Jacob's arrival late in the evening, dressed in cotton twill shirt and trousers, and knee-high riding boots with a linen duster draped over his arm, would signal he had arrived on horseback from Chillicothe. His sudden appearance without prior notice, however, would perplex and quite possibly anger his father. Senator Clay Bell was renowned for his disciplined approach to public and personal matters, and he detested surprises.

Tomorrow wouldn't be any more favorable to Jacob's cause than this moment.

No one entered Clay Bell's private quarters without knocking, company or no company. Jacob bucked up his courage, swallowed a deep breath, and rapped on the oaken door loud enough to awaken half the Bishop House's clientele. He cursed his nervousness and waited for someone to respond.

The high-pitched voice that acknowledged Jacob's knock was that of Ramey Knowlton, his father's senior legal clerk. Ramey opened the door and stepped aside, his thin face showing his shock at greeting Jacob of all people. Clay Bell's oldest son seldom left the family's Chillicothe law office and came to the capital city only by invitation; Ramey knew none had been forthcoming.

Fifty-six-year-old Senator Clay Bell was dressed in a silken sleeping robe and seated in an overstuffed chair next to a marble-topped table. A writing board holding an inkwell and a stack of documents, awaiting his signature, lay across his knees. The door to the senator's left provided access to his bedroom. Glowing coals in a small fireplace heated the sitting room. Made by a Cincinnati weaver from a pattern specified by Senator Bell, a woven rug displaying the head of a golden eagle against a royal blue background filled the middle of the sitting room's wooden floor.

Senator Clay Bell's older peers in the legislature envied his broad shoulders, deep chest, and tucked-in belly. He was more fit than most men half his age. Whenever Jacob peered at his father, he felt like he was staring into a mirror. Senator Clay Bell had bequeathed his three sons coal black hair, brows, and eyes; a straight nose; high cheekbones; solid jaw; dust-hued skin; and a mouth full of good teeth, features Grandmother Bell partially attributed to an infusion of native redskin blood back some generations. Many females of the current Bell generation, however, dismissed that contention as whimsical nonsense.

The sighting of his eldest son in the yellow glow of the sitting room's whale-oil lamps did not wring a smile or a warm word of welcome from Senator Clay Bell. While no one knowing him personally disputed his love for his offspring, in Clay Bell's mind only a family tragedy justified spur-of-the-moment night rides on horseback, and he responded accordingly. "What's happened, Jacob? Has your dear grandmother passed away? Have one of the girls or your brother Jarrod been injured?"

"No, sir, none of that."

Clay Bell's brow lifted and his black eyes snapped, clear signs that his patience was worn thin after a taxing day on the floor of the Ohio Senate. "Out with it, lad. What could be worse?"

Jacob knew that it was imperative he own up to what he'd done. He had to trust that his father's love of the unvarnished truth would keep his temper in check. It took every ounce of willpower he had to look Senator Clay Bell square in the eye and say, "I've enlisted in the First Ohio Volunteer Cavalry."

The fiery outburst Jacob expected with his admission didn't materialize. His father slumped down into his chair, motioned for Ramey to remove his writing board, and said to the clerk, "Pour me a glass of our nice red wine, would you please?"

Jacob stood stiff as a statue with his mouth clamped shut while Ramey removed the writing board from his father's lap and fetched the requested glass of wine from a sideboard in the bedroom. Worried the excuse for his sudden decision without prior consultation with his father might sound childish and foolhardy, Jacob needed to know how Senator Clay Bell felt before speaking again. A wise bird didn't foul his own nest in haste and diminish any chance of forgiveness and understanding.

Senator Bell sipped wine from his thin-stemmed glass and stared at the ceiling. When his hard gaze fastened on Jacob once more, Jacob swore his father was fighting tears, a possibility beyond his imagination. "I'm not disappointed with the decision you've made to enlist. I'm disappointed that you let your impatience overcome your better judgment."

Straightening in his chair, Clay Bell cleared his throat, sipped more wine, and said, "I believe we discussed military service as part of the adjutant general's office or Union staff headquarters where we thought your law degree and experience with court documents could best be utilized. Didn't we rule out the frontline cavalry and infantry, or am I that forgetful these days?"

The slope on which Jacob was poised grew slipperier than water on ice. Determined to keep his composure and not falter, he quickly said, "No, sir, your memory isn't faulty. We did rule out arms-bearing duty."

"And why did we do that?" Senator Clay Bell said just as quickly.

Jacob's nervous twisting of his cap bill threatened to rip it apart. "You said we don't know what happened to Judah after Uncle Temple was killed, and you weren't inclined to put another son at risk, if it could be avoided."

"And how then, may I ask, with all the intelligence the Lord gave you and your penchant for detail could you possibly forget our understanding and proceed in the opposite direction?"

It was hold his ground for Jacob or fold his cards like a beaten gambler. "I don't want to miss out on the fighting. I'm afraid the war will end before I can be a real part of it. I'm tired of sitting at a desk week in and week out. I want to taste the heat of battle the same way you and Uncle Temple did in the Mexican War."

An acute sadness washed over Clay Bell, and his head lowered. This was the payback for Temple and his answering the questions of curious male offspring about their service in the Mexican War with depictions of cavalry charges replete with thundering hoofs, barking pistols, and excitement that threatened to tear your heart from your chest. Charges that ended with the exalted thrill of watching the stars and stripes rise into the sky above enemy entrenchments with not a dry eye in the American ranks.

They had unwittingly portrayed the fleeting joy and addictive danger of combat as eternally rewarding, not mentioning out of respect for young tender ears the dreaded scenes that gave them nightmares for years afterward—comrades with wounds spurting rich red blood, others staring at nothing with blank eyes, and downed horses screaming in agony. No mention was made at family gatherings of their whispered thanks afterward that they had by divine intervention or sheer luck, which did not matter, survived intact for yet another wild ride smack into the teeth of the enemy, wondering where they would find the courage to launch the next charge.

His thoughts sobered by resignation, Clay Bell lifted his chin. "What's done is done and can't be undone, and given the passion this regrettable conflict has aroused in men I once considered reasonable by nature and instinct, to renege on your oath would besmirch your name and that of the family."

The tension that had Jacob's nerves on edge slackened and he settled back on his heels. Voice quavering with excitement, he vowed, "I will not disappoint or shame you, Father . . . or my country."

Clay Bell drained his wineglass. "You have always been dependable when it comes to discharging your personal and business responsibilities, Jacob, and I have no doubt that you will attend your military duties in a similar way."

Placing his empty wineglass on the marble table beside his chair, Clay Bell rose to his feet. The black brows of Ohio's most powerfully connected Republican senator bunched together. "Now, before we part company, I have a request to make of you. I know you young bucks craving military fame want to do everything on your own accord without any help or interference from old fossils such as doting fathers. Nevertheless, I would like permission to write the colonel of your regiment an introductory letter on your behalf. Contrary to the common belief that this will be a short fight, I believe it will be many long months, perhaps years, before the issues are resolved by a contest of arms, and, in my humble opinion, it would behoove you to start your service with a leg up where your regimental commander is concerned. Will you permit me to do so?"

Knowing he had but a few seconds before he must answer, Jacob ran through his mind what was likely to result from such a letter of recommendation. If the colonel of the First Regiment of the Ohio Volunteer Cavalry was amenable to receiving unsolicited endorsements of a new recruit, it could be of benefit to him. Of course, Jacob's colonel might decide Senator Clay Bell's letter was merely another example of an elected official using the power of his state office to promote his own son and trash it, hopefully with no harm done.

Jacob's greatest concern about such a letter was negated by his knowledge that his fellow Company M enlistees from Chillicothe and Ross County were to choose their officers by ballot after their muster at Camp Chase west of the state capital. Therefore, no matter how flowery the letter, there was little chance Senator Clay Bell's pen could exert undue influence on what promised to be a highly spirited election. A number of Company M recruits with high aspirations were already campaigning for votes prior to their arrival at Camp Chase, and Jacob didn't want to start off on the wrong foot with any of them.

"Please forward your letter, Father. I appreciate your support and thoughtfulness," a smiling Jacob said, totally satisfied with events since his knock at the door.

"Fine, that's just fine," proclaimed Senator Clay Bell, extending his hand to his eldest son. As Jacob shook his father's hand, he again spied that misty look in the senator's black eyes. He had not anticipated how difficult it would be for his father to accept his enlistment in an active battlefield unit.

Senator Clay Ball clung to his son's fingers. "And perhaps if the First Ohio Cavalry campaigns in Kentucky, you could inquire after Judah. Union officials may have word of him."

"I will most assuredly make that inquiry, Father," Jacob promised with utmost sincerity. "I love Judah as much as you."

With that declaration, a solitary tear escaped the corner of Senator Clay Bell's eye and his oldest son, astonished by his father's public anguish over Judah's disappearance, and wanting to spare him further embarrassment, nodded good night and backed hurriedly from the room.

CHAPTER 3

A crouching Asa Barefoot lifted his hand and pointed three fingers at Judah Bell.

Seated on the opposite side of their small campfire, Judah peered at Barefoot's craggy, flame-lit face over the rim of his tin cup and raised a questioning brow. Barefoot touched his lips with the same three fingers, and the curious Judah kept quiet.

Judah strained his ears but made out nothing except the snap and pop of burning wood. If someone or something was out there in the dark, either one was too quiet for him to detect.

The half-breed slowly opened his four-button coat wide enough to gently tug his Navy Colt from behind his belt and motioned for Judah to do likewise. Judah's senses came to full alert. Until Barefoot determined otherwise, the half-breed considered whatever he had heard or seen a danger to the both of them.

"Hello, the fire."

The soft hail drifted from the trees and brush at the bottom of the hillside behind the startled Judah. Near as he could tell, it sounded like a young male had spoken. He resisted the urge to look over his shoulder and watched

Barefoot, his Navy Colt pressed against his thigh, slowly rise to his feet, take a step backward, and disappear into the black woods.

Judah mouthed a silent, "Thank you, dear Lord," when no shot rang out.

He was surprised that he and Barefoot had been discovered so easily. They had chosen the two-acre meadow bisected by a meandering stream and surrounded by hills on three sides as it was a campsite well away from the road that offered fresh water, ample graze for their horses, and a large deadfall that screened their fire from the valley's open quarter. Yet someone had somehow crept around behind them.

With the hidden Barefoot covering him, there was nothing for Judah to do except call the stranger out. "No need to be shy or afraid. The coffee and meat and beans are hot. We have an extra plate and we ain't contrary to feeding a guest," Judah said, talking more than necessary in case Barefoot needed time to gain a better vantage point for what was to follow.

"But," Judah warned, "if you have a weapon, it better have the hammer down and the barrel aimed at the stars or the ground when you show yourself."

"I ain't got no gun and I haven't eaten for a night and two days," the youthful voice said. "My stomach would be right grateful was you to favor us with a small serving of your vittles. Steady meals morning and evening of branch water and sassafras root wears thin right quick. Tell your man in the trees yonder to keep his finger off the trigger of that pistol he's holding. I ain't aiming to be shot when I mean no harm to you all."

"No cause for you to worry lest you rile him," Judah said. "Step out real slow with your hands up where we can see them."

Judah didn't move or turn his head. He waited patiently while their uninvited guest circled around him and confronted him the across the fire with his backside aligned with Barefoot's Navy Colt.

A young male returned Jacob's searching stare. Judah estimated his age to be about fifteen or sixteen. Of slender build, he was dressed in baggy pants, loose-fitting cotton shirt, and oversized coat, all rough sewn with uneven seams. Flat-soled brogans adorned his feet. Closely cropped auburn hair, lively blue eyes, straight nose with slightly flared nostrils, cheekbones dusted with freckles, sun-tanned skin, and a somewhat delicate chin fit together in what Jacob would deem a handsome countenance, one capable of snagging the attention of any female on the hunt.

"What's your name?" Judah inquired.

"Aw . . . Ben Langford."

The hesitation in answering was long enough that Judah suspected the young man was lying.

"Where you from?"

"Did you say you had an extra plate?"

Judah grinned and nodded. Was the abrupt change of subject a delaying strategy to prepare the next lie?

Reaching into the cotton bag resting at his hip, Judah retrieved a spare tin plate, spoon, and cup. "Help yourself."

His late-evening guest accepted the plate, cup, and spoon with alacrity and served himself from the small kettle and coffeepot resting in hot coals at the edge of the fire. Between mouthfuls and sips, the supposed Ben Langford asked, "What happened to your friend?"

Judah drank from his own cup. "Barefoot's making certain you're alone. One fright per night suits us just fine."

"Mighty careful, ain't you?"

"Uproar Kentucky's in, the careless die the quickest."

Young Ben Langford chewed awhile, swallowed, and said, "I can't argue with that. I only travel at night myself."

Judah tried a different tack. "Where are you bound?"

Intense blue eyes fastened on Judah and stuck tight. "South until I'm out of the reach of the Yankees," Ben Langford said, tone suddenly harsher than a growling dog's. "I aim to wear gray and kill every blue-belly bastard my savior puts in front of me. I'm looking to acquire a horse and fight with the grayback cavalry."

Intrigued and fascinated that the blurted intentions of his campfire intruder matched his own, Judah asked, "Pretty big ambition for someone young as you, isn't it?"

"You're not that much older than I am," a defiant Ben Langford said. "I'll be eighteen years old before I reach Tennessee and I can ride and shoot. Long as I can stay in the saddle, some Rebel company will have need of me."

"It's a long walk to find the nearest graybacks, and to get there you have to pass through Nicholasville and then avoid the Yankee forces at Camp Dick Robinson north of Lancaster," Judah cautioned. "Wolford's First Kentucky Cavalry are stationed at Camp Robinson. I heard tell before we left Scott County that Wolford's troops are a wild bunch of homegrown Union boys just as anxious to kill the enemy as you are."

Judah's grin had a touch of the devil about it. "Besides, you don't even know my name or where I stand on this war. How do you know I won't turn you over to the First Kentucky?"

"Because I was hiding along the road up yonder and saw you and your friend scoot out of sight into the brush so that Yankee patrol didn't spot you," Ben Langford countered. "Ain't any reason to act thataway lest you're sneaking away south same as me."

That response piqued Judah's curiosity. Ben Langford

wasn't lacking intelligence and possessed a modicum of common sense. Always given to thinking ahead, Judah realized the next logical step for young Langford was to ask permission to accompany Barefoot and him, and Judah wasn't interested in a traveling companion that had to share one or both of their horses. On top of that, having been reared in the household of a prominent Ohio lawyer, Judah couldn't quell his instinctive feeling that some person, most likely a true parent or legal guardian, would most certainly come chasing after a healthy young male like Ben Langford. Youthful runaways, Judah had witnessed living with his uncle Temple, seldom fared well in Ohio and Kentucky courts, for free, cheap labor was highly prized, skin color notwithstanding.

Asa Barefoot's approach was soft as drifting smoke. His Navy Colt rested behind his belt again, sure sign that nothing threatened their safety at the moment. The half-breed dropped into his familiar loose crouch an arm's length from Ben Langford and sat silently, waiting for Judah to take the lead, just what would be expected of an old servant or slave.

Young Ben Langford was buying none of that. "You're the first darkie I've ever seen carrying a pistol," Langford said. "You must be downright trustworthy."

"He's a freed slave and travels with me," Judah said by way of explanation. "I've never had a better man covering my backside. You have a problem with that, you can light a shuck soon as you finish eating."

Abashed, Ben Langford raised a placating palm. "I was just remarking on a situation new to me. No offense intended."

Young Langford's swift apology wrung a crooked grin from Asa Barefoot, who recognized a nifty feat of personal diplomacy when he heard it. It was a skill that had served him well when dealing with strange folks in touchy situations where trouble could bloom faster than the strike of a snake.

Barefoot's grin and the kindly look in his baggy, sunken eyes told Judah the half-breed had taken an instant liking to Ben Langford. Judah wasn't prone to disappointing others unnecessarily, but his mind was set regarding Langford. He didn't want anyone tagging along that could endanger Barefoot or him with a wrong impression or a wrong word. The road to Cumberland Gap was perilous enough already without adding a person with an unknown history.

"Langford, you can spend the night with us, and after breakfast, go your own way," Judah proposed. "We've a considerable distance to ride tomorrow."

Young Langford couldn't hide his disappointment. His jaw sagged and Judah thought tears were certain to flow. If they did, he missed them, for Langford lowered his head and silently finished his meal.

Langford's chin eventually lifted, and after a cup-emptying slurp of coffee, he studied Judah carefully, as if measuring what he was about to say against how stubborn Judah might prove. Judah wasn't pleased when Barefoot flashed him another crooked grin. The half-breed seemed to be calculating in concert with Langford. Was he that easy to read?

Ben Langford glanced at the dying fire—gathering courage Judah guessed—fixed his gaze on Judah, and said, "I don't want to burden you, but I need your help. I aim to find me a town and have me a horse."

Judah snorted. "How? Steal it? Horses are mighty expensive, lest you settle for a worthless nag. How much money are you carrying, anyways? Can you even afford a weak-kneed swayback that will give out on you in less than a quarter mile, if not sooner? Well, can you?"

Eyes widening, young Langford's body wilted under Judah's questioning blast. Judah felt a twinge of regret before Asa Barefoot, he of obedient tongue and demeanor, flabbergasted him by winking slyly at him and saying, "Can't be but twenty miles or so to the next town. Wouldn't be too hard on the horses to allow him to tag along that far."

The occasional pop and snap of the fire separating Judah from Asa and young Langford was louder in the ensuing quiet than a church choir striking peak notes. Buttressed by Barefoot's support, Ben Langford's backbone straightened and Judah swore he saw a meager, tentative smile on his face that lasted less than a second.

Damn the half-breed, he'd put Judah in a bad spot. If Judah refused, he appeared a mean-spirited bastard selfish enough to abandon a young, unarmed runaway in dangerous country for fear his spindly frame might tax their horses if he had to ride double with Judah and Barefoot for most of a day.

Judah felt his dander swelling, but he quickly clamped his teeth together, temper cooled in a whipstitch by the thought of Barefoot's mysterious behavior. For the half-breed to boldly oppose his master in front of a stranger, there was something about Ben Langford that Judah was missing. What, he couldn't fathom. Nonetheless, it was there and he decided to follow Barefoot's inclinations until he could talk to him in private.

Judah loosed a deliberate sigh. "This clear weather holds, I guess the horses can manage riding double on dry roads. But the next town is it, Langford. Without a horse and a gun, you won't be worth much the hundred or so we may have to ride after that, and I'm believing there's a goodly chance Barefoot and I won't make it to where we're going without a running fight with the Yankees. I won't have the blood of a young whelp on my hands that can't defend himself. You follow what I'm saying?"

"Yes, sir," a relieved Ben Langford said with a bouncing nod of his head. "We part company at Nicholasville. That's the next town of any size. Only I'd like to know your names first, you don't mind."

"I'm Judah Bell from Scott County. The old stag sitting next to you is Asa Barefoot."

"Pleased to meet the both of you," Langford said, rising to his feet and extending a hand to Barefoot. Circling the fire, Langford did the same with Judah, his shake strong for his age.

"Are you related to the Bell family of Scott County that breeds those Denmark horses every man has a craving for?"

"Yes, that would be Temple Bell, my uncle."

Taking his seat again, Langford said, "Judge Stubbs of Paris, Kentucky, races his Denmark stallion at the Bourbon County Fair. That stud draws huge crowds. I'd dearly love to ride him around that track one time at full gallop."

Judah saw an opening. "Is that where you're from, Paris, in Bourbon County?"

"I was," Langford admitted, "but no more. I ain't got no family, and I won't take handouts or hand-me-downs, so I set out to become a soldier and be my own man . . . beholding to no one."

Judah doubted that was the whole truth, but if he pushed for more details, he figured young Langford would become evasive and waste time best spent sleeping. And what did it matter anyway? Wouldn't his temporary charge be someone else's concern come tomorrow evening?

Pushing himself off the ground with his arms, Judah came upright. "Asa, let's scatter the coals and turn in. You need to visit the woods, Langford, pick your tree. I'll loan you a blanket. One will be suffice for me on a warm night like this."

While young Langford beelined for the woods behind the fire, Judah stepped to the shallow bank of the stream and scoured their tin plates and spoons with sand, washed them off, rinsed their coffee cups, and dropped the dinnerware into a cotton sack. By then, Barefoot had separated the dying coals from the live, leaving a few of the brightest clustered together to hopefully spark a morning breakfast fire.

Judah dropped the cotton sack beside his blanket. Young Langford was nowhere in sight. "Damnably shy, isn't he?"

"Shouldn't surprise you," Barefoot responded.

"What do you mean?"

"He's no boy. Mister Langford is a woman dressed like a man."

Asa Barefoot's assertion Langford was a female shocked Judah so deeply the tap of a child's finger would have knocked him from beneath his hat. But when he thought on it, he saw young Langford in a different vein. He'd attributed Langford's rather high voice to his not being old enough for his voice to deepen as those of young males did when they matured, and there was no denying he was handsome enough to pass for a girl. Plus, females of Judah's acquaintance shunned closely cropped hair. Perhaps the biggest giveaway was Langford's complete absence of facial hair.

Judah chuckled. Barefoot had spotted everything he'd missed. Yet, while her simple disguise had fooled him completely, he found that learning her true sex greatly enhanced his opinion of her. He'd never met a female audacious enough to strike out on her own with no man to watch over her and having no means of defending herself except her speed afoot. Even more daunting was her intention of joining the Confederate cavalry.

Just who was she he wondered.

Maybe, on second thought, it was best he never found out. A female determined to bear arms in a male uniform might ignite feelings and situations too explosive to contemplate.

Judah touched Barefoot's shoulder. "It's good we'll be rid of her before she causes any trouble for us."

Fortunately, for Judah's peace of mind the balance of the night, he didn't spot Asa Barefoot's last crooked, knowing smile, a portent of things to come.

CHAPTER 4

Jacob Bell halted before the Sibley tent housing the headquarters of Company M of the First Regiment, Ohio Volunteer Cavalry. Corporal Lee Winters, his escort from the office of Colonel O. P. Ransom, the First Regiment's commander, saluted the sentry on duty, parted the front door flaps of the Sibley tent, stuck his head between the flaps, and requested permission to announce Sergeant Jacob Bell. Permission received, Corporal Winters held the front flaps aside and announced Jacob.

Jacob handed his horse's reins to Corporal Winters, gathered himself, and stepped into Company M headquarters. Two lanterns on the folding desk at the rear of the Sibley cast yellow light on the canvas walls and the faces of the two officers present. A smirking, slab-jawed first lieutenant with single bars on his shoulders standing at the side of the desk said, "Captain Logan, I believe our missing sergeant has finally found us."

The cleft-chinned officer with wavy brown hair behind the desk glanced up from the paperwork in front of him. "Took him long enough by damned, Shavers."

The casual disrespect shown Jacob by Captain Cameron Logan and Lieutenant Shavers fit the disconcerting tenor of his arrival at Camp Chase. Nothing had gone as he'd anticipated, and a new surprise seemed to rear its head at every turn. First, there had been his encounter with Colonel Ransom's adjutant at regimental headquarters. The exacting adjutant hadn't recognized Jacob's name and had informed him that Colonel Ransom wasn't available when Jacob asked to see him.

Attempting to establish his identity and move things forward, Jacob asked the adjutant to check the latest roster for Company M. The adjutant did so, and his pen halted abruptly near the top of that document. "Here you are, Sergeant Jacob Franklin Bell."

Puzzled as to how he had been granted a non-commissioned officer's rank without his knowledge that he hadn't sought, Jacob had asked, "Sir, are you certain that's what it reads?"

The adjutant had bristled and said, "No one ever questions the accuracy of our paperwork. If you are shown on the official roster as sergeant, Company M, that's what you are. Weren't you present for the election of officers?"

"No, sir, I reached camp late this evening from Chillicothe. I forwarded a letter to Colonel Ransom explaining that I would report for duty on this date, 10 October 1861, due to legal matters pending before the county bar that required my personal attention."

Tone crisp and devoid of sentiment, the adjutant had said, "The colonel did not see fit to share your letter with me or any other personal information concerning you. But, he obviously had no objection to your reporting on this date. That he would have made known to me. In the absence of orders to the contrary, please report at once to the captain of Company M. Corporal Winters will serve as your guide. He will see you to your destination. Good evening, Sergeant Bell."

Corporal Winters led Jacob across the far western

quadrant of Camp Chase. The six-man A-frame tents of the 1,002 troopers of the First Regiment, Ohio Volunteer Cavalry, lined the northern end of an open parade ground. Troopers surrounded dinner fires in the open lanes between the tent rows. In the eastern quadrant of Camp Chase behind Jacob, lamplight shown in the windows of the wooden barracks housing the Fortieth and Forty-Second Regiments of the Ohio Volunteer Infantry. Just south of the infantry barracks, additional wooden buildings of the same size within a separate stockade housed forty-two hundred Confederate prisoners of war.

From reports appearing in the *Chillicothe Gazette*, Jacob knew thirty-four hundred plus Union cavalry and infantry were currently undergoing training at Camp Chase. The quiet of the early evening hours was deceiving. Jacob suspected a flying bird peering down on Champ Chase during the heart of morning and afternoon drills would spy what resembled hundreds of freshly kicked anthills.

When Corporal Winters pointed out the Sibley tent serving as Company M headquarters, a curious Jacob had asked, "Who's in command, Corporal?"

"Captain Cameron Logan, sir. He's from Ross County, same as you."

That name was a jolt from the blue and didn't necessarily bode well for Jacob's career with the First Regiment of the Ohio Volunteer Cavalry. He and civilian Cameron Logan had been rivals and at odds with each other since childhood. In fact, Jacob had come to blows with Cameron Logan on two separate occasions in the past, once over a point of honor and once over a woman.

The rumor circulating in Chillicothe three weeks prior to Jacob's departure for Camp Chase had claimed Cam Logan was still trying to raise his own volunteer infantry company. That obviously unfounded piece of information,

Jacob should have realized then, was out of character for the son of the wealthiest horse and cattle breeder in Ross County. Cam Logan was a bold, would-be cavalier of considerable swagger who craved the public eye and pretty much expected the world to cater to his personal whims. Jacob could easily imagine him in a splendid uniform with saber in hand atop a charging stallion. The opposing picture of the son of Brice Logan, Senator Clay Bell's chief political rival in Ohio politics, leading an infantry assault afoot was foreign to Cam Logan's belief that he was destined to be a shining hero for all to witness and adore through the ages.

Numerous appearances before the judges of Chillicothe and State of Ohio courts had refined Jacob Bell's ability to mask his personal feelings. And now, standing in the light of the Sibley tent's lanterns, that skill enabled him to hide his disdain for Cam Logan except for a slight, imperceptible narrowing of the eyes. Jacob Bell saluted his new captain and said in a firm, unruffled voice, "Sergeant Jacob Bell reporting for duty, sir."

The handsome face every eligible female in Ross County wantonly admired clouded over, and the full mouth those same gals longed to kiss bunched at the corners, revealing Cam Logan's fury that he had once again, though he clearly held the upper hand, failed to rattle the composure of the man he detested.

"It's good, Sergeant Bell, that you have at last managed to divorce yourself from the law and now desire to devote time to your country," a glaring Cam Logan stated bluntly. "I hope your belated commitment to the Union doesn't falter and cause problems for my company or the regiment. I expect and will demand total obedience of my orders. My word is the law here, not your precious *Blackstone*. Understood, Sergeant Bell?"

Well, Jacob thought, *so much for any possibility of our burying the hatchet until the war is over.*

Captain Cam Logan rose from his canvas chair and squared his shoulders. "Lieutenant Shavers will provide you a copy of *U.S. Cavalry Tactics* and show you to your tent. Corporal Fritz Howard of your mess has spare blankets and a gum poncho for you. The "General" call is at five o'clock. We are not yet in possession of our horses and are presently conducting the School of the Trooper, Dismounted. You need to catch up with the rest of the company during drills and study *Tactics* day and night. The training and the knowledge of a sergeant must be superior to that of the corporals and troopers reporting to him. I will not stand for anything less. That is all, Sergeant Bell. Show him to his quarters, Lieutenant Shavers."

Cam Logan hadn't welcomed Jacob to Company M. Neither did he return Jacob's departing salute. Jacob regretted that civility and military regulations had fallen victim to personal hate and the lust for revenge, emotional harbingers of further discord. Henceforth, he must consider every move he made beforehand and be careful of every word he uttered. Nothing would please Cam Logan more than to break him to the rank of private, or, better still, have him cashiered out of the cavalry altogether. Jacob believed wholeheartedly that, if bringing either of those options to fruition required a bending of the truth, it wouldn't prove a problem for Brice Logan's son. He had learned early in his school days that devious souls such as Cam Logan have no scruples no matter the circumstances.

Lieutenant Shavers handed Jacob a bound copy of *U.S. Cavalry Tactics* and Jacob followed the slab-jawed trooper into the darkening evening. He hadn't seen any reason to mention to either Cam Logan or Shavers that the leather bag he toted contained a copy of those same *Tactics* along with his razor, bar soap, Bible, daily journal, ink bottle, and steel pens. While he had missed portions of the training for the dismounted trooper, he'd practiced the individual commands with an unloaded revolver and a saber into the wee hours of the morning in his Chillicothe law office. And not knowing what his role or rank would be, he had studied the duties assigned both commissioned and non-commissioned officers as well. He was, by damned, the issue of a decorated Mexican War cavalryman who constantly preached the virtue of as much preparation as possible before undertaking any endeavor.

Jacob's belated reporting had left him vulnerable to circumstances beyond his control, and personal questions of vital importance nagged him as he trailed after Lieutenant Shavers. Who had nominated him for sergeant? Who had voted for him? How did his subordinates regard him? Had anybody objected? In particular, how had Cam Logan reacted? Fortunately, as luck would have it, he would shortly find himself face to face with the very person who could answer his questions.

Lieutenant Shavers led Jacob down the street between the rows of tents directly behind Company M headquarters. "The evening roll call has been completed and the men are enjoying a final cup of coffee before turning in," Shavers said over his shoulder. "Taps will sound in about thirty minutes. That will give Corporal Howard time to introduce you to your messmates."

Jacob spied cooks banking supper fires amid huddled troopers. His passage garnered little attention. What conversation he overheard centered on the regiment's lack of weapons, uniforms, and horses. "We ain't nothing but harmless stick soldiers," one disgusted trooper lamented, spitting coffee on dying embers. "Those kids watching us from the Broad Street after school think we're funnier than crazed squirrels and darned if I ain't starting to agree with them. I didn't enlist to fight with no tree branch gun against sabers and bullets."

The wry logic of that contention wrung a grin from Jacob. Recruiters had been a little too free with the truth in guaranteeing their new charges that the necessary garb, equipment, and proper horses needed to be a mounted cavalryman awaited them at Camp Chase. A solid six weeks of weaponless drill afoot was wearing a tad thin with the frustrated cavalry enlistees and adversely affecting morale, not a particularly good omen for an officer fresh to their ranks who had yet to hear their complaints.

Lieutenant Shavers halted at the last pair of tents bracing the lane. In the fast-dwindling daylight, Jacob noted that the troopers lounging in front of the tents wore loose-fitting cotton trousers and shirts, short coats, boots or brogans, and slouch hats and caps if they had them, clothing commonly seen on farm boys and field hands. Their unshaven cheeks were mostly fuzz covered, with beards and mustaches a rarity, a solid indication of their youth. Except for one or two of them, Jacob didn't think any of the rest was much past the legal enlistment age of eighteen. If they had proper uniforms based on their previous military experience, green would be the most appropriate color.

Though he was but a step way from the relaxing troopers, Lieutenant Shavers shouted, "Corporal Fritz Howard, front and center."

Jacob saw the open dislike for Shavers and his curt manner on the faces surrounding them. A slight five-foot-four-inch figure separated himself from his messmates, stepped forward, came to attention, and saluted. "Here, sir."

"Well, by God, Howard, for once you followed the correct procedure when addressing a superior officer," Shavers snapped as he saluted in return.

Though born two years apart, Corporal Fritz Howard and Jacob's youngest brother, Jarrod, shared a mutual love of horse racing and mischief and had been inseparable before Fritz's enlistment. Their bond had deepened after fellow horse lover and co-conspirator, Judah Bell, moved to Kentucky. Jacob suspected that Fritz and Jarrod would be together again when Jarrod turned eighteen next summer, a likelihood that wouldn't please a certain state senator fearing a prolonged war might leave him without male heirs.

Jacob had found Fritz Howard to be an astute and quick-thinking lad, and he smiled behind Shavers's back when Ross County's legendary young jockey nodded and said, "Thank you, Lieutenant Shavers. We plowboys never mean to disappoint our leaders. It's just that knowing your left from your right every minute wasn't so blasted important back home, and neither was calling anybody by anything other than their first name. 'Sir' was something we only used when addressing our pa or the preacher. But I promise you'll be proud of us by the time we break camp."

"Sir, damn it, sir!" Shavers corrected vehemently.

A seemingly sheepish Fritz repeated the word "sir" with lightning speed, saluted again, and asked, "What is it you want from me, sir?"

Lieutenant Shavers motioned for Jacob to step beside him and, voice dripping with exasperation, said, "This is Sergeant Jacob Bell, your new superior officer, the officer the bunch of you voted for. You will introduce Bell to the other members of your mess, Howard. I can only hope he can make you into something other than what you still are after six weeks of drill—clod-hopping upstarts I wouldn't trust with slingshots let alone sabers or loaded rifles. Carry on, Corporal, I believe even you can handle the simple chore at hand."

With a parting, "Good night," Shavers saluted, about-faced, and huffed up the street toward Company M headquarters.

"You best be careful, Fritz. Don't ever taunt him when no

one else is around," a beet-complexioned trooper advised. "His skin wasn't overly thick before he joined this here army and lately a blade of straw can draw blood where he's concerned."

Corporal Fritz Howard chuckled, and still mocking the departing Shavers, came to attention in slow motion and saluted Jacob in the same fashion. "Welcome to our mess, sir. We're delighted to have you join us."

Jacob knew full well that baiting and degrading superior officers in public and in private was disrespectful behavior normally subject to harsh discipline, conduct he could not permit once he assumed command. But he thought it best not to mar his introduction to his new messmates by lecturing them on the finer points of military regulations and proper conduct while they were joyfully savoring Fritz Howard's command performance. That could best be done in the morning after he gleaned as much information as possible from Fritz regarding his perceived status with his new command and what they were expecting of him. A favorite axiom of Grandmother Bell's held that a wise man got his moorings before jumping into the boat with his fishing pole.

Jacob smiled and saluted Fritz Howard. "And I'm delighted to be here, Corporal. Please make your introductions or you'll be naming shadows instead of troopers."

"Yes, sir," a sobering Fritz Howard said, beckoning for the watchers to come closer. "Gather 'round, boys. Don't be bashful. The Bell brothers had a proper upbringing. They don't bite lest you provoke them, and their word can be trusted."

Jacob silently thanked Fritz Howard for that complimentary introduction. He sensed the mess held Fritz in considerable regard, and his open endorsement would hopefully hold the doubters and naysayers at bay long enough for Jacob to show the most solid and dependable among them what kind of sergeant he intended to be and why they should follow his lead.

"Please nod and step forward as I call the roll," Howard ordered. "We'll start to the left, Sergeant Bell. The first two in line you can't tell apart except for the size of their ears are twin brothers, Hugh and Aaron Spencer."

Fritz Howard hadn't exaggerated. Both brothers had straw-colored hair and brows, tawny eyes, button noses, plumb cheeks, sloping shoulders, and oversized feet. "These two boys have had trouble at drill, sir. Their natural stride is three furrows wide, and shortening their step to match the rest of us has been mighty difficult for them. Lyle Tomlinson next to them is a preacher's son who's not allowed to bring out the good book except on the Sabbath."

Corporal Howard introduced the next three troopers with a ticking finger. "Nate Bush, Frank McCarran, and Luke Purcell hail from the Bainbridge area and admire a finely built girl same as they do a purebred bull."

After the hooting died out, Fritz Howard continued, "The gent standing beside them is Tom South. He's the son of a pig farmer, the solitary one in the whole company. He traded his slop pail and butcher knife for a horse and saber. 'Course, he ain't seen either yet . . . but then neither has anybody else."

Jacob laughed with his new charges, but, at the same time, he was busy committing names and faces to memory. Calling any trooper, particularly a subordinate, by the wrong name was demeaning and ruffled feathers hard to smooth out later.

"Next is Sam Kite. He's the orphan my pa boarded at our livery stable after the ague took his parents and his sister. The last two troopers at the end of the line are Isaac Wood and Lawton Anderson. Isaac claims he owns the best pack of hunting hounds in this part of the country. As for

Lawton, he's forever hunting a whisker to shave off with the spanking-new razor his lover gal gave him."

Fritz Howard turned forty-five degrees in a left oblique, saluted Jacob, and said, "That's our mess, sir, all present and accounted for. Would you care to address the men?"

During Fritz's introductions, Jacob had made a physical assessment of each individual trooper and his findings proved insightful and encouraging. To the man, they were younger than their new sergeant and appeared to be in excellent health. Their height ranged from Fritz's five feet, four inches to the five feet, nine inches of the Spencer twins. None of them exceeded the twins' 170 pounds in weight and there wasn't an ounce of fat in sight. The recruiters had chosen carefully, picking those of the size and weight that would burden a hard-ridden horse the least. And given their origin and rearing, they undoubtedly recognized one end of a horse from the other. He suspected some, if not most, of them were comfortable and confident in the saddle.

Jacob realized the young men watching him so attentively were the finest Ross County had to offer and he spoke to that. "I place no credence on what has transpired in the opinion of other officers before my arrival. We will start with a clean slate. I believe you have the makings of professional troopers, and I will do everything in my power to help you succeed. I will not ask you to perform any duty I wouldn't perform myself. We are in this fight together and must trust and support each other. You will find I am a fair man by instinct and habit. But I will brook no insubordination or slackening in the traces. Our mission is to preserve and reunite our divided nation, and the enormity of that task demands our best effort every hour we are on duty. All of us will not survive this conflict, but we need not sacrifice any life needlessly due to insufficient training. We must leave Camp Chase properly equipped, fully schooled in the art of mounted warfare, and prepared for any eventuality. It is that goal to which I will devote myself day and night and I will ask the same of you. We must do our country, our state, and our families proud without fail. Are you with me?"

"Yes, sir," Tom South blurted with the gusto of a braying donkey. "Until the last Johnny Reb drops dead at our feet."

Tom South's fierce declaration opened the floodgates, and Jacob was certain the cheering that followed carried to company headquarters. He let the troopers' enthusiastic response run its course, and when they quieted, he said, "I will hold all of you to that. We best retire for the night. I believe 'Taps' will sound shortly. Corporal Howard, I would like a word with you privately, if you please. Gentlemen, you are dismissed."

As the mess made for their A-frames, Fritz Howard suggested, "We can talk in our tent, sir. The Spencer brothers prefer to sleep in the open whenever the weather allows. Sam Kite shares our tent, too, but we can trust him to keep a quiet tongue."

A bugler blew "Taps." Private Kite took the far end of the A-Frame and Jacob and Fritz Howard settled on their blankets and ponchos near the front entryway. The late evening air was warmer than usual for early October, and Jacob removed his jeans jacket and laid it aside.

"It would be helpful, Fritz," Jacob began, "if you would tell me how I became a sergeant while I was off in Chillicothe?"

"I hope you won't be angry with me, but I'm responsible," Fritz Howard admitted right off. "Colonel Ransom called a meeting of Company M and asked for nominations for officers. Cam Logan had been rounding up votes with promises and his father's money from the moment we entered camp, and he was elected captain by a large margin. He nominated his bosom pal, Tor Shavers, for first lieutenant. He won big, too. Then six sergeants were nominated and elected."

Fritz Howard's tone sharpened. "That was when our mess got their backs up, as every officer elected to that point was a crony of Cam Logan. Well, we knew you had enlisted before we left home and I knew from a letter of Jarrod's that you were still intending to come to camp, so we nominated you. Cam Logan objected, claiming you had to be present to be elected. Colonel Ransom nixed that. He said you had his permission to report late and were well qualified for the rank of sergeant. With Colonel Ransom's ruling, you were a lock."

The foreknowledge of Colonel Ransom told Jacob the regiment's commanding officer had received both his letter and his father's and explained why Ransom had intervened on his behalf. While grateful for the colonel's stamp of approval, Jacob was equally grateful that his nomination had emanated from the ranks, for he considered the use of money and popularity to curry favor insulting. Deep down, he was too straitlaced and high-minded to ever walk in the boots of a Cam Logan. He took great pride in working hard to judge others on merit, not by what they could do for him. He found nothing uplifting in taking advantage of men of lesser stature and means. His preference was a place at the table for everyone.

It was a philosophy that had caused haughty Marissa Stewart to spurn him for Cam Logan, but Jacob was sleeping peacefully at night. He couldn't help wondering in his dreams, however, just how far down the throat of Marissa's bodice those rose-tinged, enflaming freckles of hers wandered in the flesh.

Worried by Jacob's prolonged silence and unable to read his expression in the dark, Fritz Howard asked, "You ain't mad at me are you, Jacob . . . I mean, Sergeant Bell, sir?"

Sergeant Jacob Bell let Corporal Fritz Howard off the hook straightaway. "No need to worry. I want to experience the fighting firsthand, not from behind a desk. I'm not too proud to serve as your sergeant. And never fear we'll succeed no matter how much guff we have to take from the likes of Cam Logan."

Jacob folded his jacket into a pillow. "Corporal, I've studied the *U.S. Cavalry Tactics* and I'm fairly well versed in individual and company drill. I will be ready to take command by the afternoon tomorrow. The men are yours until then. Be advised, I meant what I told them earlier. We'll relax when it's permitted. The balance of the time, our training and education are our paramount concern without exception. I'm counting on you to reinforce my orders and help me get to know our messmates. I trust I can count on you."

"Yes, sir. We'll be the best mess in the regiment."

Jacob had no problem taking Fritz Howard at his word. After all, Jarrod's soul mate was practically a member of the Bell family. He stretched out on his blankets, comforted by the fact that a trooper he trusted offered a second pair of eyes to watch over the members of the mess, for given the animosity of Cam Logan and Tor Shavers and their power within the ranks of Company M, there would most assuredly be rough waters to sail before the First Ohio Volunteer Cavalry departed Camp Chase for the real war.

CHAPTER 5

Judah Bell came awake with a start when Barefoot clasped his arm. Judah pushed himself into a sitting position, and a damp burst of air brushed his cheek and scattered the ashes of their cold supper fire. Dark clouds had replaced the moon and the star-laden sky he'd seen upon retiring.

Asa Barefoot warned, "Big storm coming with much lightning and rain. We best seek shelter."

The half-breed possessed an uncanny knack for predicting the weather that Judah didn't dare ignore. They needed to be in the saddle jack quick. There was no cover the way they had come yesterday for at least six miles except for a piddling, long abandoned shack far too small for two men and a wayward female. Judah doubted the tiny structure still had a roof over it. The way ahead was their best bet to find dry quarters of some kind, hopefully for both travelers and horses.

"No time for breakfast," Judah said. "Fetch the horses to the fire. I'll roust Langford out and we'll pack the camp gear."

"I'm awake," young Ben Langford or Whatever-her-name-might-be said across the blackened fire pit. "I can handle the gear. You help with the saddling."

The fetching and saddling required scant minutes, and by then Ben Langford had rolled and tied blankets and tarps, packed Juddah's saddlebags, and strung together the cotton sacks for looping over the withers of Barefoot's mare. Much of what Judah had learned to that point about their mysterious female was suspect, but she had definitely spent enough time out of doors to learn how to break camp in a hurry.

Saddlebags and bedroll tied before and aft his saddle, Judah swung aboard Jasper, cleared a stirrup for Langford's foot, gave her his wrist to grab, and hoisted her up behind him atop the bedroll. She was lithe and nimble, and when seated to her satisfaction, locked both arms about his waist.

"Don't need to be told I walk if I fall off. My brothers made me walk home more than once."

Judah was on the verge of challenging her earlier statement that she had no family. He decided instead to let well enough alone. They had a dangerous storm to contend with and she would be lying to a different man soon, if not today, then surely tomorrow. Much as he was coming to distrust her, he'd ride a hundred miles in the rain to make that happen. And, if push came to shove, he'd pay a kindly person to take her off his hands.

They crossed the meadow and its bisecting stream at a trot and struck the southbound road whose dirt and stone surface was wide enough to accommodate two farm wagons passing hub to hub and not an inch more. The wind picked up in a rush and autumn leaves swirled around the legs of the horses. Both veteran saddlers ignored them. They were too well trained to be distracted from answering the rein.

They rode for a solid hour. "Should spot a house or barn or town soon," Judah shouted above gusts of wind. "It's been nigh onto twelve miles by my reckoning since we snaked around Versailles yesterday."

Another mile and the road angled upward to clear a high rise of ground, and there below them stretched a sizable valley. On the valley's northern fringe loomed a ten-window, two-story frame house with a roofed porch and a sizable barn with a front ramp that accessed its second-story haymow. The dormant fields in the center of the valley comprised two hundred acres of tillable soil. The owner was a man of substance, lest he'd backed the wrong flag in the dispute threatening to rip Kentucky in two and suffered property and monetary losses.

Large dollops of rain pelted them during their descent from the swell. Thunder boomed beyond the horizon. Lightning flashed and zigzagged high in an ever-darkening western sky. Judah touched Jasper with his spurs and the stallion broke into a gallop. Barefoot's quick-footed mare had no trouble matching the stallion's gait across the quarter-mile lane leading to the fenced yard of the farmhouse.

The storm was in full force, rain sloshing off the drooping brim of Judah's hat when he halted Jasper and found the gate of the picketed fence closed and latched. The faint yellow glow of a lamp shone through the glass surrounding the front door of the farmhouse. Someone was home.

"Hop down, Langford," Judah ordered.

Soon as Langford was clear of Jasper, Judah dismounted and handed her the stallion's reins. "Wait here with Barefoot. I'll say our hellos and see if we're welcome to occupy the barn."

Judah lifted the gate's latch, pushed through, and walked up the stone walkway to the steps of the roofed veranda, unbuttoning the middle button of his coat to allow access to his Navy Colt. He wasn't expecting trouble, but the unwary had filled graves for centuries.

His boots thumped on the plank floor of the veranda and

the front door opened a crack, an opening wide enough to allow a few inches of a shotgun's barrel to jut out.

Judah froze.

A no-nonsense, not-to-be-trifled-with, deep-throated male accustomed to exerting authority said, "My name's Dayton Farrell. I've two sons fighting with Wolford's Cavalry. My other two boys are here in the house with me and they're armed. We'll kill anybody who tries to invade our home. You are welcome to hay from the barn and water from the well. Damage our house or barn or steal from us and we'll hunt you down and make you mighty sorry for what you done. I don't much care whether your politics favor blue or gray. Storm passes through, you hightail it down the road. Is anything about what I said difficult for you to understand?"

Judah whistled softly and said, "No, sir."

"Good, because the next thing I want is your butt staring at me on your way out of my yard . . . and latch the gate behind you."

Judah swore he heard a female giggle exiting the veranda. It was possible Dayton Farrell had a daughter in his home he didn't want to put at risk with strangers. He latched the gate with deliberate care, motioned for Langford and Barefoot to follow him, and scooted for the barn to escape the continuing deluge. A disturbing thought crossed his mind: *The roads would be a sorry mess for days after the rain let up.*

Figuring the Farrell family livestock was housed in pens and stalls on the barn's lower level, Judah opened the rolling door at the top of the ramp accessing the upper-level haymow and storage bins. He peered inside, discovered open space adequate for his companions and their horses, and waved Langford and Barefoot inside, rolling the door to the midpoint behind them. He wanted a clear view of the Farrell farmhouse and the family's shotgun-wielding patriarch until they departed.

Hair plastered to her head from the heavy rain, What-ever-her-name-might-be revealed an awareness of the strategic value of horses by tending to Jasper straightaway on her own. Ground tying the red stallion's reins, she untied and set aside Judah's saddlebags and bedroll, freed cinches, and removed the stud's saddle. The weight of the saddle no problem despite her slight stature. She dried the stud's neck, chest, and legs with the saddle blanket.

The observing Judah watched Langford help herself to a blanket from his bedroll and step behind the stallion where only the top of her head and lower legs were visible. Her coat and shirt fell to the floor of the barn, and then her head disappeared below Jasper's backbone. A minute later, Whatever-her-name-might-be rounded Jasper's rump with soaked coat and shirt in hand and the blanket wrap-ping her body from waist to neck. Though her thin ghost-white arms were comical sticking from the thick folds of the brown blanket, Judah begrudgingly admitted that she was damn clever about maintaining her privacy, and, if you weren't careful, equally clever at worming onto your good side.

The rain varied in intensity but never stopped. Thunder kept the darkly clouded sky booming, and spiderwebs of white lightning cracked and sizzled. Ignoring his sodden clothing, Barefoot saw to his mare and settled at the barn door to keep watch. Judah supplied the horses with read-ily available hay and, not concerned with his privacy like a certain other person present, stripped to the waist and dried off with a blanket. Seated bare chested next to his saddlebags, he checked his Navy Colt and that of Barefoot for damp powder.

Whatever-her-name-might-be dried her hair with the loose ends of the blanket encasing her upper torso. Then, digging into the cotton sacks containing Judah and Barefoot's vittles, she located a slab of smoked ham, which she proceeded to slice into pieces with a short-bladed knife produced from somewhere on her person—Judah forever wondered where—and served the three of them a makeshift breakfast that warmed their bellies and dulled their hunger. No conversation was required, and the sole noise in the barn was that of their horses munching hay.

"We've got company," Barefoot announced in his usual terse manner. "Three men on foot, two of them armed with long guns. Nobody you'd want for friends."

Judah jumped to his feet. "Get dressed, Langford. Roll up the blankets. We may be leaving here in a hurry."

Whatever-her-name-might-be grabbed her drying shirt and coat and disappeared behind Jasper. Judah handed Barefoot his Navy Colt and donned his own damp clothing. Judah's haste and caution were genuine. He wouldn't have trusted a messenger from the Lord that morning, not after the demise of his uncle at the whim of Captain Hunt Baldwin, Langford's ambushing of him and Barefoot the previous evening, and the menacing barrel of Dayton Farrell's shotgun. You had but one life and it wasn't to be sacrificed cheaply.

Judah positioned himself far enough into the barn so he couldn't be spotted from the Farrell farmhouse, but where he could witness what transpired there. Dressed in black broadcloth and black stovepipe hat, the tallest of the three strangers advanced on the Farrell veranda. His companions assumed a casual stance at the yard gate with their weapons slanted across their chests in a position that allowed for a quick throw to the shoulder. Given their powder horns and shot pouches, Judah surmised they carried black powder and not percussion long guns, something worth remembering since the reliability of the flintlock during and immediately after a rain was questionable, even if its lock was kept covered.

Stovepipe Man and someone in the Farrell house exchanged heated words, most of which Judah couldn't understand. The tall stranger's head spun about and he stared in the direction of the barn. With a parting comment, Stovepipe Man crossed the veranda, stomped down its steps, and barged past his flintlock-wielding companions, making no attempt to close and latch the yard gate. When one of his fellow travelers sought to do it for him, Stovepipe Man's brusque "Don't bother" carried to Judah's ears.

Judah saw hints of pending trouble as the three strangers approached the barn. Stovepipe Man's stark red features marked the depth of his anger, and the butt of a holstered revolver swelled beneath the broadcloth coat he was slowly unbuttoning. He had clearly taken what Dayton Farrell had said to him as a personal insult and was not intending to suffer further indignities from the occupants of the barn.

Then there was Jasper and Barefoot's mare, healthy horses that would look mighty attractive to men on foot; furthermore, the strangers' food stock seemed to amount to the contents of a smallish cloth bag tied to the waist belt of the shortest of them, a sack too small for campfire cookware. These men, whoever they were, were not long on means and in a hurry to be someplace.

"Stay out of sight, Langford. Asa, we'll not be robbed, and these three aren't shedding our blood."

Judah was positioned directly before the door some twenty paces inside the barn. Barefoot was beside the door to his left. Langford was hiding behind Jasper and the mare

fifteen paces to his right, which put her out of the initial
line of fire, if any shooting were necessary.

Stovepipe Man had his coat open and pushed aside
when he stepped through the haymow door. His probing
eyes took in Judah and the half-breed and their horses in
one sweeping glance. His companions tried to flank him,
but Barefoot's presence kept the stranger on his right
behind him.

"I'm Reverend Smite Hardin," Stovepipe Man haughtily
proclaimed in a deep, overbearing, near shout, "and these
are my sons, Levi on my left, and Colin at my rear. And
who might I be addressing?"

While normally an easygoing, friendly soul, Judah took
an instant dislike to the Reverend Smite Hardin. The reverend was broad in the body, gray-haired, and grizzled,
with blood-shot blue eyes, an acorn-shaped nose, and
sallow flesh. In addition, a four-knuckles-wide chin coupled with a twitch in the corner of his thin-lipped mouth
pulsed in rhythm with his speech and gave him little manly
appeal. His clothing was mud stained and his boots worn
at the heel. He smelled of intolerant fire and brimstone and
a self-serving Gospel interpretation preached to the advantage of the Hardin family over the welfare of whatever flock
he might assemble.

Reverend Smite's features stiffened when his son, Levi,
blurted, "That's one fine red stallion he's riding, Pa."

Levi Hardin was a perfect replica of his father physically
except for the absence of a facial tic and his high-pitched,
whiny voice that grated on Judah's nerves something awful.
While his father had briefly held Judah's attention, Levi,
thinking Judah wouldn't notice, had rested his black powder
rifle in the crook of his arm and slipped the cowhide cover
from its lock. But Judah had noticed and the shifting of

Barefoot's feet told him the half-breed had caught Levi's readying of his gun.

An impatient Colin Hardin squeezed past his brother and took up station between Judah and the horses. Judah thought Colin had to be the family misfit. Short in stature and slightly humpbacked with dark skin, shaggy brown hair, a pug nose, protruding lips, and vapid pale blue eyes, Colin's gaze flitted in several directions at once as if he were trying to confirm where he was and who he was with. Colin was flighty as a pecking barnyard chicken, but his flintlock also rested in the crook of his arm with its lock uncovered.

The behavior of the Hardin clan told Judah they had confronted men in lesser numbers before. The sons knew what the reverend expected of them and did so without verbal orders. Judah believed they would bring their weapons into play the instant their father reached for his revolver.

Judah was holding his Navy Colt against his thigh. He was sure both Levi and Colin were aware from where they stood that he was armed, and probably their father, too. Asa Barefoot was a different story. He was positioned to their right in the shadows by the door with his Navy Colt out of sight.

Judah's hopes soared. The last thing the Hardins would imagine on this earth was the thwarting of their devious desires by the intervention of an armed black man. It was that element of total surprise that Judah was counting on to swing the forthcoming nastiness in their favor and spare their lives.

"Yes, Levi, I've never laid eyes on a more handsome animal, either," Smite Hardin agreed. Then, addressing Judah, he demanded, "You gentlemen have names?"

Judah saw no disadvantage in identifying himself. "Name's Judah Bell."

"And the darkie?"

"Old Asa. He cares for my horses and cooks if his limbs aren't hurting him too much," Judah said, making Barefoot seem docile and harmless.

"We're bound for Camp Dick Robinson," Smite Hardin offered, demeanor softening and tone suddenly dripping with honey. "My mission is to bring the word and guidance of our heavenly father to the loyal troops defending the unity of our great nation. If you're riding that direction, perhaps you'd care to accompany us?"

A clever ploy, Judah thought. He'd been backed into a corner that left him no option except to identify where his true loyalties resided. If he lied, he might avoid a show-down with the Hardins for a while, but he was convinced he would merely be postponing the inevitable.

Judah could guess what Smite Hardin was thinking without any difficulty. Wouldn't the maker of men prefer that the bearer of his word arrive at Camp Dick Robinson astride a magnificent steed rather than sore footed in muddied boots? Smite Hardin had no reason to believe Judah would willingly part with a valuable possession like Jasper. So, in his lofty thinking, if a killing was required to implement the will of the Lord, was that not what was meant to be?

A steely coldness gripped Judah's heart. He had to make his move and trust Barefoot to do his part, for not every-one was leaving the barn alive.

"I'm afraid my destination is Tennessee and a different color uniform, Reverend. Do you want to shoot us this morning or later down the road? It's your choice, but either way you won't be riding my stallion anytime soon."

Awed by Judah's blatant audacity, Smite Hardin flashed

him a hateful, dismissing smile and nodded sharply, his
hand snaking sideways to his holstered pistol.

With all the speed he could muster, Judah raised his
Navy Colt, catching movement by Colin Hardin out of the
corner of his eye. Asa Barefoot shot the youngest Hardin
as Judah centered the barrel of his Navy Colt on Smite
Hardin's chest and clawed at the hammer with his thumb.
To Judah's amazement, the reverend's revolver was already
cocked and aimed at him.

"You're a dead man, Pa!"

The shrill yell from the farside of the haymow surprised
Smite Hardin enough he hesitated before pulling the trigger, and Judah's bullet drilled him square in the heart.
Smite Hardin toppled backward, his trigger finger finally
tightening. His errant shot gouged a harmless hole in the
wooden floor of the haymow.

Then steel snapped harshly against steel and Asa Barefoot shot a second time. Judah turned toward Levi Hardin
and found Levi frowning at the lock of his flintlock, grasping as he died on his feet that damp powder had caused
his long gun to "hang fire" and save Judah at the cost of his
own life.

The smoke of spent powder made Judah's eyes water. A
shaking of hands and legs beset him the more it dawned on
him how close he'd again been to death. Without Langford
yelling out and Levi Hardin's misfire, he'd be sprawled
stone-cold dead with the reverend and his two boys.

Ben Langford ran past Judah and began kicking the face
of Smite Hardin with her hard-soled brogans, screaming at
the top of her lungs, "You bastard, you'll never lay a hand
on me again. Never, you hear me?"

The reverend's nose and mouth had morphed into a
pulpy mash of torn flesh and blood before Judah recovered
his wits, grabbed Langford by the arms from behind, and
wrestled her beyond kicking distance.

"Stop it," he ordered. "He's dead, for Christ's sake."

Tears wet Judah's clutching hands, and after a futile attempt to free herself, Whatever-her-name-might-be sank to the floor in a heap, her sobs echoing through the haymow. Having no experience in consoling an overwrought female, Judah let her have a full-blown cry.

Dayton Farrell and his sons would be wondering who had survived the gunfire in their barn loft. They would likely assume that the three Hardins had won out over a single white man, an unarmed black man, and a young squirt riding double. When none of the Hardins showed himself, Dayton Farrell's curiosity would trump his inclination to hide behind locked doors and he and one or more of his sons would venture out to learn who was still standing and how much of a threat they remained to the Farrell household.

With Barefoot's assistance, Judah collected the bodies of the Hardins and laid them side by side at the rear of the haymow. Since the Hardins no longer had a use for their personal belongings, Judah helped himself to Smite Hardin's belt, cartridge box, and holster for his Navy Colt and thrust the reverend's .58 caliber Remington revolver behind the belt of his trousers. The flintlock rifles with their shot pouches and powder horns were too cumbersome to fuss with, so he left them for the Farrell sons. He was too squeamish about touching the deceased any more than necessary to root through their clothes, and he doubted they were carrying things of much value anyway.

Whatever-her-name-might-be, however, had no reservations. Still drying tears with her fingers, she shoved Judah aside, unbuttoned her father's shirt, and removed a gold locket and chain from about Smite Hardin's neck, not the least bit bothered by the damage her brogans had wrought to his face.

Pocketing the chain and locket, Langford stood and said

by way of explanation, "They belonged to my mother. He didn't deserve to have them. He beat her, too."

While Judah allowed she undoubtedly had a family history that would challenge a holy man's allegiance to the Lord, it wasn't one he had either time for or the inclination to hear. He could see via the door of the haymow that the rain had ceased, the sky was clearing, and the wind had slackened to an occasional bumbling gust. They must move before the Farrell clan came nosing around.

"If you can quit crying long enough, climb down that ladder over there on the far wall and find out how many and what quality of horses Dayton Farrell feeds."

When Langford peered at him without moving, Judah added, "You can either walk or ride. Which will it be?"

With that question, Smite Hardin's daughter hustled to the ladder and disappeared from sight. Judah caught Barefoot's raised brow. The half-breed abided by Temple Bell's stern observation of the commandment, "Thou shall not steal," every waking minute.

Judah said, "I'll pay Farrell for the horse if she finds one that suits her."

The half-breed's brow threatened to kiss his hairline. "She's coming with us?"

"We agreed to travel together to Nicholasville and no farther, and I'll hold her to it. She can sell the horse and provide for herself until someone will take her in."

Barefoot rubbed his nose with his fingers to hide the mischievous grin he couldn't avoid and thought, *if she'll stand for that.*

Whatever-her-name-might-be hove into view, dry-cheeked, and brimming with information. "I saw a draft horse team, pair of gray buggy horses, and a six- to seven-year-old bay gelding thick in the neck, but he has a long hip and strong pasterns."

"Any horse gear handy?"

"Saddle and bridle are hanging on the wall of his stable."

"Can you reach them?"

"Yes."

"Saddle the gelding and lead him out behind the barn. Stay there until I yell for you."

Langford ran to the ladder, and Judah said, "Saddle our horses, Asa, and load our gear. Then wait here while I talk to old Farrell."

At the barn door, Judah halted long enough to tug a leather wallet from his coat pocket and count out a number of gold coins. Wallet pocketed again, he eased through the barn door with his hands held above his head. He walked slowly to the unlatched fence gate, gained the veranda, and halted a few steps from the front door.

"Mr. Farrell, you there?"

"I am," Dayton Farrell answered, "and I'm still holding a shotgun on you. What do you want?"

"The three men who followed us into your yard tried to steal our horses. They're laid out in your haymow. We need a horse ourselves. I'll pay you forty dollars in gold coin for your bay gelding, ten dollars for a saddle and bridle, and another ten dollars to bury the three bodies. What say you?"

It was more solid money than Dayton Farrell would see in two or three years. That sum would also make a dent in the stash of money Temple Bell had given Judah the day before Hunt Baldwin's night raid. But Judah was inclined to take Farrell at his word about tracking down anybody that damaged his property or stole from him, and he didn't want to sleep with one eye open the balance of the war. Bad blood was a burden he preferred to nip in the bud, what with old Farrell and his sons being downright headstrong and familiar with firearms.

Dayton Farrell sounded like he was biting off the words when he spoke. "Leave the money in front of the door. You've five minutes to be out of my sight or we'll keep your money and kill you for the hell of it. The ground's soft and we can bury six as easy as three."

Judah staked three Double Eagle twenty-dollar gold pieces on the floor of the veranda and skedaddled, latching Farrell's all-fired gate behind him. Short of the barn he yelled, "Barefoot, Langford, on the double, right now."

Barefoot led Jasper and his mare from the haymow. Langford came around the corner of the barn atop Dayton Farrell's bay gelding with a smile brighter than sunshine plastered on her face. Judah was intrigued by how fast she seemed to have overcome the loss of her father and brothers. Just how bad had life been under the same roof with Smite Hardin?

Cursing his lack of concentration, he accepted Jasper's reins and swung into the saddle. Ignoring the stirrup, Asa Barefoot sprang off both feet and landed astride his mare. It was a feat Judah had ceased trying to master after realizing he might not mature into a fully equipped male if he persisted.

They crossed the barnyard with Barefoot's mare bringing up the rear and angled into a lane thick with mud. Judah touched Jasper with his spurs and they departed Dayton Farrell's acres at a gallop with nary a glance over a shoulder.

The road was clear in both directions and they galloped about half a mile before Judah switched their pace to a trot. As he rode, the deaths of Smite Hardin and his two sons preyed on his mind. While he regretted taking his first human life, he found he harbored no guilt or sorrow over shooting Smite Hardin and wouldn't lose any sleep tonight. It had been kill or be killed, four shots with three men dead. The Hardin sons had followed their father's path and suffered a similar fate.

Judah had learned from two separate incidents that a soldier might have to kill when he least expected it. Random confrontations with an enemy not in uniform were as much of a threat as battles fought in line with flags flying and cannon roaring. He saw as clearly as he was seeing Jasper's ears that survival in either case was a matter of courage and luck. A soldier could only hope he was blessed with a stock of both and that neither ran short before the last shot was fired.

Given all that was unknown about his future, maybe, just maybe, he should seriously consider resuming the nightly prayers Grandmother Bell had hammered into his stubborn young soul from birthing bed to schoolyard. He shook his head in disbelief. Be damned if stern, austere Nadine Bell wouldn't make him a Christian yet.

Langford appeared at his elbow on her gelding, jarring him loose from his own thoughts. "May I have my father's revolver?"

Judah tugged lightly on Jasper's reins and eased him into a walk. "You have much experience with a gun?"

"I'm right handy with a pistol, rifle, or shotgun. I beat my brothers at target shooting till they wouldn't let me have powder and ball. I'd feel safer if I could defend myself. Besides, that .58 caliber Remington belongs to my family."

Her awareness of the specific make and caliber of revolver her father had been carrying swung Judah's opinion in her favor. He passed her the Remington and observed how smoothly she unbuttoned her coat and slipped it behind her belt. The Remington resembled a cannon on her hip, but she seemed comfortable toting it.

Judah couldn't resist asking, though he anticipated more evasion on her part, "Just exactly what is your real name?"

She proved him partly wrong. "Ben Hardin."

"Hardin, not Langford?"

"Yes, Langford was my mother's maiden name."

Though they'd probably established a correct family name, Judah was certain she was lying yet again about her first name. But if she wanted to keep on pretending she wasn't a female, he'd play along for now. If push came to shove, the truth might work to his advantage at some juncture.

Slight body and wild swing of emotions aside, Whatever-her-first-name-might-be Hardin was attractive and appealing, and Judah found it difficult to avert his gaze. There was a boldness about her and a capacity for deep feelings that set her apart and heightened his interest. Those same traits warned him to stay clear of her and not put his feelings at risk.

Judah swore under his breath and glued his eyes to the road ahead of them. He was bound for the Confederate cavalry and had no time to waste on a turbulent, deceptive woman who might make demands on him he couldn't meet. He had unknowingly killed the father she hated and bought her a horse. That was as far as he was willing to stick by her.

Nicholasville couldn't loom on the horizon any too soon.

CHAPTER 6

Happy as a schoolboy having finagled his way out of a paddling, Corporal Fritz Howard saluted Sergeant Jacob Bell smartly and said, "Sir, we got horses at last."

Jacob's coffee cup stopped short of his mouth. "You actually saw four-legged animals on the grounds of Camp Chase?"

"Yes, sir, they're leading them into that big field they fenced to the west of our parade ground."

"How many?"

"Bunches of them, sir. Word is those horses were driven over the roads and more will be arriving by train later this morning. The quartermaster received a shipment of saddles and bridles last night. We should have guessed Colonel Ransom meant business this go-round when he had us unload all those hay wagons earlier this week."

Jacob flexed his sore shoulders and arms. His mess has been assigned to pitchforking and stacking that hay for three solid days. The arduous hay stacking was an example of Cam Logan and First Lieutenant Shavers's deliberate effort to insure Jacob's mess consistently received the heaviest and least desirable fatigue assignments. Their hours spent filling in old slit trenches and digging new ones totaled more than any other mess in Company M, prompting Private Lyle Tomlinson, the preacher's son, to remark that he knew the slit trenches by heart and could marry two turds with a shovel in the dark of night and emerge with clean boots.

Pig farmer Tom South had pooh-poohed Lyle's complaint by assuring him that if he ever had the privilege of spreading hog manure on a field under a blazing hot sun, he'd realize the putrid slit trenches actually had a flowery whiff to them. No one challenged Tom South's opinion, but Jacob wrote in his journal afterward that in a cavalry training camp where water was scarce for bathing any bodily appendage and everybody had a rank, distinct odor to him, there seemed to be a tad more open space on each side of the pig farmer at mealtime.

News of horses and saddles and bridles in large numbers ignited spirited conversation over the breakfast fire of Jacob's mess, for those saddlers were the final step toward the Ohio First Volunteer Cavalry becoming real mounted troopers. The first step had taken place two days after Jacob reported for duty with the introduction of sabers. Though manufactured in the Prussian style with long, straight, heavy blades, the sabers allowed the entire regiment to burn their tree branch guns and swords and boosted morale enormously. Saber drill on foot was difficult to master, and Jacob had the mess stand in a single line at nine-foot intervals per regulations, which prevented serious injuries for he'd no clue in advance how many ingenious ways the atmosphere could be sliced until the rudimentary exercises of the moulinet had been digested.

Saber drill on foot was becoming old hat when the regimental quartermaster made good on a lengthy string of broken promises and issued uniforms and revolvers. The farm clothes of the recruits composing Jacob's mess had dwindled to tatters, and the rural lads had used cornhusks to plug the holes in the bottom of their shoes. To them, a United States Cavalry uniform consisting of dark blue, canvas-lined jacket, a blouse, heavily reinforced trousers with yellow leg stripes, a change of underclothing, shirt, stockings, boots, and a forage hat ornamented with crossed sabers was luxurious military apparel they had previously associated with soldiers guarding presidents, kings, and members of royal families. The sole hitch to every member of the mess being in proper dress was the necessity of acquiring boots from a Columbus cobbler large enough to house Hugh Spencer's and Aaron Spencer's gargantuan feet.

Regulations regarding firearms for a United States trooper specified a carbine and a revolver, gun tools, holsters for revolver and carbine, and two cartridge boxes. Jacob's charges were delighted with the initial distribution of an Army Colt, holster, and a single cartridge box. They were now missing only the cherished four-legged animals denied the envious, footslogging infantry.

A light breeze fanned the flames of the breakfast fire. The weather had been remarkably clear, dry, and warm for days on end during the Ohio autumn of 1861, sparing those training at Camp Chase the cold spells, rain, mud, and damp ground that made tenting in the open downright miserable. That fine weather also helped offset the morning monotony of coffee, fried meat, beans, and bread trimmed with a knife to expose its fresh core; Spartan fare that had Jacob and his subordinates dreaming of the vegetables, fruit, pies, milk, and butter that graced the poorest of tables back home.

"How will the horses be assigned?" Sam Kite asked Corporal Fritz Howard, the mess gossip and newshawk whose rank bore the responsibility of delivering the morning roll call prepared by his sergeant to company headquarters.

"The horses will be assigned to the companies, and

company commanders will create matching numbers, tie one to the horse's halter, and put the other in a hat. Each trooper will draw a number when it's his turn and then hunt up his horse on the picket line. Word is they'll start the whole shebang in lieu of afternoon drill and inspection."

Lyle Tomlinson said, "Sounds like a fair divvying up to me. Do you have any recourse if you're not satisfied with the horse you draw?"

"You can trade with any trooper willing to do so," Fritz Howard responded.

Jacob felt there was little chance even a few bad animals would be foisted upon the regiment. He had reviewed the standards for the selection of horses with his fellow non-commissioned officers during their evening training sessions at company headquarters. The officers doing the examining would not accept any horse if he was less than five years old and would handily reject those with obvious defects. It was anticipated that the mounts brought to camp would be of excellent quality, as few cavalry horses had been purchased in that section of Ohio to date.

The buzz and excitement of the breakfast fire did not interfere with morning fatigue or drill. The mess undertook the saber exercise and manual of the pistol flawlessly, hoping in their hearts all future drilling would be done with their booted feet in stirrups and not on bare earth. Jacob was positive his charges would appreciate on some distant battlefield Colonel Ransom's contention that the prolonged absence of horses had forced the regiment to learn to maneuver and fight afoot in small details and as a company, skills that would save a number of their lives before peace reigned.

With the sun high overhead, the trumpeters blew "Dinner Call" and Fritz Howard returned from a visit to the parade ground on behalf of Sergeant Bell and reported that a separate drawing among companies had been held in the interest of fairness, and Company M's mounts were second in line. They gulped their boiled beans and ham and were ready and waiting when a beaming Lieutenant Shavers, a shocking visage for those accustomed to the dour temperament Shavers had inherited at birth, came to fetch them on a handsome black bay.

An orderly confusion awaited them at the picket lines. Captain Cam Logan stood at the near end of the second picket line of tied horses with a slough hat held in front of him. Company M troopers drew their numbers in the same sequence their mess tents were aligned behind their commanding officer's tent, which meant Jacob's mess reached into the hat last. Schoolboys half their age couldn't have matched the speed and excitement of horseless troopers scampering off to claim their mounts.

Jogging along behind his messmates with number in hand, Jacob surveyed the waiting horses and found his expectations regarding quality had been met twice over. While of different colors and bloodlines, their conformity in height and size and physical characteristics was close to remarkable. He saw no ewe-necks, high withers, short backs, weak muscled hindquarters, or sprung knees. He had no means of foretelling the length of his future service with the First Ohio Volunteer Cavalry, but he knew instinctively that he would never see a finer lot of cavalry horses than these.

The numerals on the halter of a chestnut with one white stocking, a hint of the Denmark Thoroughbred in the shape of his head, and large, clear, intelligent eyes matched Jacob's number. Talking softly, he slowly grasped the chestnut's lead rope and gently patted his neck. The chestnut didn't shy and continued to stand rock solid in the midst of running bodies, his skittish four-legged fellows, and chattering troopers. Jacob deemed him a keeper then and there.

Corporal Fritz Howard waved in Jacob's direction and

shouted, "Sergeant Bell, Private Hugh Spencer wants to speak with you."

Leaving the chestnut tied to the picket line, Jacob crab-stepped sideways in the crowded pathway between rows of horses until he reached the corporal and private. Hugh Spencer held the reins of a blue roan with big ears, a narrow forehead, and a dish face, features true horsemen judged unsightly. Other than his ugly head and the fact the roan was two hands shorter than practically every other animal on the parade ground, the gelding was equal to the best horses Jacob had observed.

"Do we have a problem, Corporal?"

"Yes, sir, Private Spencer says the roan is too small for him."

Jacob was on the verge of chiding Hugh Spencer from the standpoint he should be thankful to have a serviceable horse of any kind instead of bitching about his lack of size, but he held his tongue. He was Private Hugh Spencer's superior officer, and when any subordinate complained about something important, he deserved his sergeant's time and consideration.

Hugh Spencer was five feet, nine inches tall, extra long in the thigh, and his feet were oversized. When Jacob pictured Hugh astride the undersized roan, he understood the problem: Hugh's feet would be near to touching the ground as if he were a child riding a pony. Replacing the plain, coarse clothing Private Hugh Spencer had worn since childhood with a spanking-new United States Cavalry uniform had fostered a strong personal pride in his appearance. He didn't want that image tarnished by being seen on an ugly-headed, undersized mount, a sight that would subject him to a razzing by the balance of the company and the regiment at large as surely as ice melted in fire.

Recognizing a well-configured saddler like his brother Judah, Jacob hated to part with the chestnut, but he was sympathetic to Hugh Spencer's situation and he doubted many troopers would be willing to trade for the roan. Hugh Spencer and Fritz Howard were inseparable friends during off-duty hours, yet five-foot-four Fritz had brought his sergeant into play rather than solve Hugh's problem by simply swapping horses with him.

Tom South overheard Hugh Spencer's misgivings and rescued Jacob. Private South was taller than Fritz Howard by the width of a tomcat's whisker. The pig farmer's son had drawn a rangy seal-brown gelding that stood a hand taller than Jacob's chestnut. "I'll trade horses with you, Spencer. I like my stirrups closer to the ground," Tom South said. His offer and wide, tooth-baring smile put the matter to rest. The exchange was made *post haste.*

Jacob was developing a deep respect for Private Tom South. He was trustworthy, obeyed any order given him, and was more concerned about the welfare of his messmates than his own. When Tom South said he was prepared to make any sacrifice necessary to help win the war for the North, he meant it. He was, Jacob judged, the kind of steadfast trooper you wanted next to you when the bugler blew "Charge."

Once every Company M trooper had claimed a horse and taken possession, Captain Cameron Logan, riding Tor Shavers's black bay, assumed command. "Water your horses at the creek north of camp, lead them to the stables built by the local contractors, and see that they are fed," Cam Logan called out. "The stall numbers match those of your horses. The next call will be for supper. Tomorrow morning, you start mounted drill under our new regimental training officer. Move your hides, gentlemen."

The evening took an unexpected turn after supper. The lieutenants of each company summoned their sergeants and marched them to the large tent housing Colonel Ransom's headquarters. There the lieutenants and sergeants joined the colonel's entire staff and the captain of each company. Lanterns strung above head height from supporting pole to supporting pole illuminated the tent's interior. Gray-speckled hair and muttonchop whiskers neatly trimmed, Colonel Ransom and his stickler of an adjutant occupied an elevated wooden platform at the rear of the tent. Commissioned and non-commissioned officers stood shoulder to shoulder in what was close quarters, all eyes locked on Colonel Ransom. Large-scale regimental meetings may have occurred before Jacob reported to Camp Chase, but this was a first for him.

Coming to attention at the adjutant's barking command, the assembled officers saluted their leader. Colonel Ransom returned their salute, putting them at ease and wasting no time, as was the custom, in conducting the evening's business. "Gentlemen, now that at last we have horses, I thought it appropriate that you meet Major Dance Walker, who will take command of your mounted drill at reveille. Colonel Walker, would you please join me and address your new charges as we discussed."

A whip-thin officer climbed the steps of the platform, his progress hampered by a gimpy leg. His hat was under his left arm, and the sweat on his baldpate glistened in the lantern light. He was clean shaven except for a waxed mustache parted in the middle. The parted mustache, the metallic, buckshot eyes, the flat planes of his cheekbones, and the iron jut of the officer's jaw lent him the ferociousness of a wood's panther poised to attack. The officer's tailor-made, brass-buttoned uniform was immaculate. The shine on his black boots hurt the eye, and his spur rowels were the size of Jacob's palms. The holster on his right hip held a revolver with ivory grips. Here was a deadly serious soldier, not to be trifled with, crossed, or insulted. All told, he made Jacob shudder a bit. His tenure at Camp Chase had struck an entirely different chord.

When the officer spoke, his voice had the deep thrum of a croaking bullfrog, as if a giant were talking. "My name is Major Dance Walker. My task is to mold you into honest-to-God cavalrymen who can shoot and thrust from horse-back with no quarter given our enemies. I won't abide poor horsemanship or the neglect or abuse of a single animal. It's best you consider the horse beneath you your lover, your mother, and your sister. He's more important to you for the duration of your service than the three of them to-gether. Consider yourself married to him. Lose him and you're lost to me, your comrades, and your country."

Major Walker's audience was spellbound and he played it to the hilt. "You will learn in a rush that horse cavalry service is no soft snap. The foot-slogging infantryman has his rifle to care for and keep in proper working order, just as you will your carbine. But you also have a revolver, saber, and horse equipment to keep in order and a horse to water, feed, and groom every day. On campaign, the in-fantry will stack their arms, have their supper, seek their blankets, and are soon sleeping . . . but not you. A picket line must be strung and your horses watered and fed. If there is no forage immediately available, a trooper must search the countryside for it, even if it means walking a mile or two. Then you can unsaddle, have your coffee and vittles, groom your mount, and finally rest after the in-fantry has been snoring merrily away for an hour or two."

Hooking a thumb behind his holstered revolver, Major Walker continued, "The next morning will be no different. If you are to water and feed your horses properly, and you must, reveille will be blown for you an hour before that of the infantry. On the march, you will finally have an advan-tage on those walking, but you will find marching in the saddle forty, fifty, sometimes sixty miles a day no easy task and hard on your crotch, hams, and innards."

Major Walker's upper body leaned toward his rapt audience. "On horseback, you will be prime targets for the enemy. I can best teach you how to kill Rebels from the saddle. I'm not called 'Dance' by accident. Some might make light of my name, but the Injuns, Mexicans, and Rebel trash whose graves I've danced upon regretted doing so. If you want to survive this fight, make your life a prize more precious than everything in the Lord's realm except the life of our Maker himself. I can't carry a gun and saber for you. I can, and will, swing the odds in your favor. It's time for you to make victory your sole reason for wearing that uniform. Never forget that the army who wins the war has the most soldiers standing at the surrender."

Placing all his weight on his good leg, Major Dance Walker paused for a long moment and then turned to Colonel Ransom. "Shall I dismiss them, sir?"

At Colonel Ransom's nod, Major Walker visually scanned the tent, his gaze seeming to focus on each trooper. His smile was knowing and confident. "Gentlemen, your orders are to visit the stables before retiring and kiss your wife good night. You're dismissed."

Major Walker's dismissing salute was as precise as everything else about him. Outside the tent, First Sergeant Dan Clutter, walking between Jacob and Lieutenant Tor Shavers, observed, "That old boy reminds me of my uncle Toussaint. He was never off the mark. What he promised came to pass as surely as a few girls are prettier than the others. Won't be nothing bad about having Major Dance Walker backing you when the shooting starts."

Tor Shavers snorted and spat. "Captain Logan says Dance Walker ain't no good in the field since his leg was hurt. He'd be of no account after a long march or in a skirmish afoot, so they assigned him to the drilling of recruits to make him useful. Rumor is that he favors the bottle overly much whenever whiskey can be had. Captain Logan's wondering how long it will be before Walker gives Colonel Ransom reason to send him packing."

Neither Jacob nor Dan Clutter commented on Cam Logan's assessment of their new drill instructor, as reiterated by Shavers. After Shavers veered away toward Logan's Sibley tent, First Sergeant Clutter and Jacob swung into the street dividing Company M's A-frame tents.

Dan Clutter lowered his voice to keep their conversation private and said, "Jacob, we've never shook hands or jawed much, but your law office kept Cam Logan's father from carving up our family acres in the Paint Creek Valley against our wishes. My family and I owe you a heap, and I aim to repay some of that debt. I'm the oldest recruit and non-commissioned officer in the regiment, and I've been 'round the bend in the road more than once. You got to know Cam Logan's no friend of yours. What you may not know is if every cut he makes on you with the rest of the company outside your mess were done with a knife, you'd bleed to death in a fortnight. It isn't any of my bees wax why, but Logan's out to ruin you. Most of the men are afraid of him and rightly so. He doesn't give a dog hair about a single one of us. Whatever feathers his nest with the colonel is first and foremost in our captain's thinking. He'd order a senseless charge against the Johnny Rebs that could get us killed to the man, if it would bring him a promotion."

First Sergeant Clutter freed a big sigh. "I'm probably not telling you anything new. I just felt you needed to know we company sergeants are aware of how much of a threat Cam Logan's leadership poses to each of us, and you in particular. You lead by an example we admire. We know how much the men of your mess trust you. We sold ourselves awfully cheap at that election. If we had a say now, you'd be our captain."

Jacob walked quietly a little ways. "Dan, I appreciate what you've told me, and though they're a mite overblown, I appreciate the compliments. But we took an oath. Cam Logan is our captain, and we don't dare forget that, period. Any hint at disobedience or report of an open word against him, and Logan will have our scalps. The colonel would have no choice except to back him or risk undermining his entire command. Maybe Logan's loose talk about Major Walker and his other superiors will catch the right ear and sink his ship. It's our best hope for the moment."

They halted in front of Dan Clutter's tent. On a sudden impulse, Jacob extended his hand and Clutter shook it vigorously. "I'm glad we had this chat, Jacob. It ends here. I consider what we said a private a matter between us, not to be shared about."

"And thanks to you, Dan," Jacob said, "I'll be extra diligent about watching out for me and my men. Good night."

True to the words of Major Dance Walker, the daily lives of the First Ohio Volunteer Cavalry at Camp Chase adopted an equine orientation the next morning that began well before daybreak when the fourteen company buglers blew "Reveille" in unison. As soon as the troopers were dressed, each company formed two lines on its company street and the sergeants called the roll. The "Stables" call for the grooming and feeding of the horses came next; the feed being issued by the company quartermaster sergeant. Once the feeding and grooming were completed, troopers were allowed a brief respite to wash up before the "Breakfast" call rang out. The first "Water" call followed the morning meal, and the men rode their horses bareback at a walk to the nearest stream, pond, or trough. Watering of the horses accomplished, it was time for "Sick Call," "Fatigue Call," requiring the policing of the horse lines, company streets, and camp. Then came "First Call for Guard Mount," which dispatched five or six pre-assigned men from each company to compose the regiment's daily guard detail.

The balance of the regiment responded to the "Drill Call." The first sergeant of each company gave the orders "Saddle Up" and "Lead Out," formed the company, and turned it over to the captain. The captain, in turn, issued the commands "Prepare to Mount," "Mount," and "Form Ranks" and led the company to the drill ground where morning training commenced.

After answering the "Recall from Drill" call and enjoying the noon meal, afternoon drill put every man back in the saddle and ended with the second water call of the day. The grand finale of each day was a dress parade of the entire regiment before Colonel Ransom, followed by the evening "Stables" call, supper, "Retreat," and the nightly calling of the roll. The days from Monday through Saturday started near five a.m. and drew to a close about nine p.m. with the blowing of "Taps."

Sunday was intended as a day of rest, there being no "Fatigue Call" and no drill, yet the horses had to be fed, watered, and groomed, the guard had to be mounted, and following breakfast came a company inspection of stringent thoroughness and severity. Divine services were then held with the balance of the day free time given over to visits by families and friends, letter writing, card playing, storytelling, and various other entertainments ranging from singing to staged debates. To Jacob and his messmates, Sunday always seemed the shortest day of the week.

After training on horseback was initiated, Jacob quickly realized mastering the knowledge required for a regiment, company, or detail to succeed in the field challenged the best of officers and horsemen. The boys of the First Ohio were in the main familiar with the horse and his peculiarities. They had started riding at a young age when they

possessed a dose of recklessness and were devoid of fear
and timidity, and over time, they had developed confidence
in their ability to control a horse. But now they were
mounted on strange horses as green as their riders at performing precision exercises with other animals in close
proximity to them.

Green, skittish horses meant a number of troopers were
thrown, kicked, or dragged the first few days of drill and
broken bones, aches, and bruises proliferated. The number
of injuries declined rapidly after the intractable horses
were withdrawn for service. Jacob counted each day a
success if his entire mess was upright and present at morning roll call and still standing in the evening. His patent
response to any physical complaints from his charges
was, "You wanted horses, didn't you?" That refrain quickly
spread through the regiment and was employed by non-
commissioned officers if a trooper so much as grunted
in pain.

Morning drill was devoted to individual skills with pistol
and saber while mounted, and platoon and squadron ma-
neuvers. Company drill, and later, regimental evolutions
and practice marches filled the afternoon hours. As Jacob
anticipated, Major Dance Walker gradually imposed his
indomitable will and relentless energy on the First Ohio.
His scalding tongue cured an initial plague of men crowd-
ing in the ranks, getting out of place, and struggling to
regain the right position, and pushing forward and drifting
backward or sideways. Jacob watched troopers improve to
where they successfully guided their horses through the
mounted drill with only their left hand on the reins, and
basked in the approving smile of Dance Walker.

On the second Saturday of November, the hour having
arrived for the first grand review before Colonel Ransom,
Major Walker marched the regiment to the parade ground
and the company captains formed their commands in an

acceptable line abreast. The colonel then gave the order to "Draw Sabers!"

The men obeyed and the rattle and clatter of a thousand sabers being drawn from metal scabbards and waved over the heads of their mounts created enough sudden noise and visual distraction Jacob feared the horses would surely panic. To his utter amazement, other than a shiver of a shoulder and a hoof pawing the ground here and there, not a single animal broke rank.

The line held fast again when Colonel Ransom's complimenting of Major Walker spurred lengthy, top-of-the-lung cheers from every throat, except those of Captain Cam Logan, mounted to Jacob's right. Logan's cheers were half-hearted at best.

Center stage and glory or disappointment and boredom, Jacob thought.

Rival or not, sworn enemy or not, it saddened Jacob to reflect how hollow life would be if a man was never once fully committed to a cause greater than himself.

CHAPTER 7

By Judah's reckoning, they reached the outskirts of Nicholasville late on a Saturday afternoon. He preferred that hour to high noon on the busiest day of the week for bankers, merchants, and sundry businesses. He had hoped their passage would attract minimal attention, but the sheen of Jasper's red hair in bright sunshine and his near perfect conformity mitigated that possibility the closer they came the center of town and the street filled with people.

The stallion turned heads in horse-loving Bluegrass Kentucky like they were on swivels, and once people started gawking, Judah knew they would next take note of him and his attire. Dressed in a flat-brimmed planter's hat, Kentucky jeans jacket and trousers, and tall riding boots, and armed with a Navy Colt, he appeared a man of some worth. His finely tooled saddle and saddlebags and silver decorations on Jasper's bridle added to that moneyed image.

While dressed in home-sewn coats, cotton trousers, and slouch hats, his companion travelers were both mounted on quality animals and, following his lead, appeared to be his servants. Asa Barefoot's virtually new riding boots probably seemed out of place on a half-breed to some onlookers, but the supply sacks hanging across the withers of his mare reinforced his presumed servile status.

Nicholasville was a substantial city. By the time Judah turned into the alley beside the Crown Hotel, guided by a sign and arrow on the side of the building indicating a blacksmith and livery stable were located to its rear, he'd counted four church steeples, a bagging factory, a walk for turning hemp into rope, two mechanic shops, a public school, and a female academy. On the main square he also noticed a courthouse, three merchant/grocery stores, four lawyer and physician shingles, a butcher shop, a news-paper office, a post office, and three taverns. Nicholasville was the terminus of the Kentucky Central Railroad, and the depot was visible a few blocks beyond the square. Judah had passed through Nicholasville fifteen months earlier bound for the Seven Walnuts racetrack in Clinton County smack on the Tennessee border where Uncle Temple's Denmark Thoroughbreds had beaten all comers.

Huddleston's blacksmith and multi-stalled livery was a half-block establishment with an attached office. Bush-bearded Elam Huddleston, the owner, a beanpole-thin man dressed in a black suit, grease-stained blue shirt, and string tie, popped from the attached office, dust-colored eyes sparking with excitement. The livery proprietor had a habit of confronting those he deemed paying customers with the swiftness of a diving hawk pursuing a skittering rabbit.

Judah stepped down and Elam Huddleston said, "That stallion is maybe the best saddle mount I've seen in a decade. How can we serve you, sir?"

"Grain and water for the horses and a little talk in pri-vate would suffice," Judah said.

"Have your people lead your horses through the barn to the watering trough out back," Huddleston said, glancing from Judah to Ben Hardin. "Tell Stub Early you have my say-so. He'll fetch grain and nose bags."

Addressing Judah again, the livery owner said, "Come into my office, sir."

A paper-strewn desk, two slatted chairs—one behind the desk, one in front—a dirt-hazed window, and a spittoon reeking of old chews and spotted with countless brown splatters, some on target, some not, constituted Elam Huddleston's office. Fussy was not Huddleston's forte. Profit was.

Huddleston plopped into the slatted chair behind his desk, pointed at the empty guest chair across from him, and with a condescending smile, said, "Talk away, Mr. Bell."

Judah was stunned momentarily. "I don't believe we've met. You must be mistaken."

"It's true we've never been introduced. I was in the crowd that gathered outside Hamish McDonald's tavern the day you and your uncle took a meal there on your way to the summer races at Seven Walnuts. Those two Denmarks were the talk of this town for weeks. How is your uncle?"

The truth was out of Judah's mouth before he knew it. "He's dead. Killed by the same skulking blue-belly cavalry that confiscated his Thoroughbreds."

There was a protracted silence while Elam Huddleston digested what he'd been told during which Judah fretted he may have insulted a Union man whose cooperation he was about to seek. "We heard rumors to that effect," Huddleston said with a nod. "It set us to thinking the same thing could happen to us that favor secession if we don't watch each other's backsides."

A relieved Judah said, "Mr. Huddleston, what's the situation south of here? Do you have any idea where Captain John Hunt Morgan's Lexington Rifles are encamped?"

"Latest word we have that might be accurate was that he was bound for the Confederate stronghold at Bowling Green, Kentucky, southwest of here. Seems to me a man clever enough to smuggle his rifle company and two hundred guns out of Lexington in the dark of night under the noses of the Federals would scoot for the strongest point in our lines. That's what Tell Conner was thinking when he left Nicholasville to hunt up Morgan two weeks back. I take it you intend to do the same."

"Yes, sir, I plan to enlist in Morgan's company, if he'll have me."

"I wouldn't expect that would be a problem. Like every other Confederate officer, Morgan is desperate for bodies, horses, and dependable weapons. It looks to me like you and the young man with you offer all three."

Judah straightened in his chair. "Ben Hardin's the reason I wanted to talk privately with you, Mr. Huddleston. He's only fifteen. Too young yet to join the fight."

Lying about Whatever-her-first-name-might-be's sex and age seemed appropriate. There was no need to make things more complicated than they already were. "Ben's parents are gone and his two brothers were killed recently. The only remaining relative he has is an uncle who may still be somewhere in or around Nicholasville. I'm hoping to find him and ask him to take Ben in."

Judah was playing a long shot made possible by the Hardin gal during their ride from Dayton Ferrell's farm to Nicholasville. When Judah asked if she had any surviving family members, she'd blurted she had a distant uncle, her father's brother, whose last known postal address was Nicholasville and then clamped her mouth shut, as if she'd regretted divulging that tidbit of personal information.

Judah had dropped the subject immediately. Show too much interest and she might refuse to consider what he was contemplating. Given her past history of abuse in one

Hardin household, the prospect of living under the same roof with another adult male relative might have less appeal than a rattlesnake den; though it was difficult for Judah to accept the idea that any brother of Smite Hardin could be an equal bastard. Preacher Smite had redefined the meaning of that word.

"This uncle's name is Hardin, too?" Elam Huddleston inquired.

"Yes, he'd be about fifty years old, I'd say."

Elam Huddleston ran fingers through his bushy beard, studied the ceiling of his office, and ruminated. With a decisive rap of his knuckles on the top of his desk, he fixed his dust-colored eyes on Judah, and said, "Can't be anybody besides Stokely Hardin. He and his boy have a place on the Danville Road, the same direction you'll be traveling, by gum."

"His farm a decent property?"

"I'm told it is. If his wagon and team are any indication, he isn't prosperous, but he's surviving out there. I heard he lost his wife to the fever a couple of winters back. They only ever had the one boy, no girls. Like any man trying to keep his nose above water, he could use another pair of hands and a willing back. His place is three miles from Nicholasville. Barn and house are both painted red. House has white shutters and doors."

Judah was feeling better about his situation by the minute. Maybe he and Asa would soon be off the hook with Missy Hardin. It would be hard for a blood relative to turn away a young woman who could help with chores, cook, and clean. And no matter where she boarded, Missy Hardin would have to earn her keep.

"Mister Huddleston, what's the best route to Bowling Green from Nicholasville, if I want to meet the fewest Yankees in blue uniform possible?"

"You're in luck, Mister Bell. I was born in Glasgow,

thirty-five or so miles to the east of Bowling Green, and I'm going to give you the same advice and directions I gave Tell Conner. Take the Danville Road south out of Nicholasville. After you cross the Kentucky River, take the west road from Bryantsville to Harrodsburg. That route will add some miles to your ride, but it will keep you well to the north of the Union forces at Camp Dick Robinson. From Harrodsburg, take the road running southwest through Perryville, Lebanon, Campbellsville, and Greensburg to Glasgow. When you reach Glasgow, inquire after my brother, Granger. He operates a gristmill, sawmill, smithy, and hardware store at the end of Main Cross Street. Granger is mayor of Glasgow and keeps an ear to the ground for what's happening. If anybody knows where Captain Morgan is, he will. Tell him I sent you."

Taking note of Jacob's concentrated frown, Elam Huddleston opened a desk drawer, removed a piece of paper, laid it on his desk, dipped a pen in a glass inkwell, and started writing on the blank sheet. "Excuse me, Mr. Bell, I forgot that I wrote everything down for Tell Conner to keep from confusing him."

In a few short minutes, Jacob held a set of directions spelled out in bold, legible handwriting. "Mr. Bell, you have a ride of some one hundred and forty miles ahead of you. Take my advice and travel at night. Buy what supplies you need at a corner store in some small hamlet or from a farmer. Don't tarry in any of the towns I've listed for you. The next person you dare trust is my brother."

Judah stood, fished five small coins from the wallet in his jacket pocket, and passed them to Elam Huddleston. "For the grain and the information, and I'd like a ten-pound bag of grain to take with us. You've been most helpful, and I sincerely thank you."

Elam Huddleston accepted the coins, pocketed them,

and extended his hand across his desk. "I'm glad I could be of some assistance."

Outside the cramped office, Judah said, "Believe I'll treat young Ben to a meal at Hamish McDonald's Tavern. I'll leave old Asa here with our horses, if you don't mind."

"Fine by me, Mr. Bell. One thing I'd like to know, if I'm not prying where I don't belong, how did you come by that red stallion with your uncle being a Denmark breeder through and through?"

"A gentleman at the Fayette County Fair dared my uncle to run his Lexington Beauty stud against his Jasper with both horses going to the winner."

Elam Huddleston's head shook. He laughed and said, "An addled brain can empty a racing stable in a hurry."

Whatever-her-first-name-might-be Hardin was delighted with the idea of dining at Hamish McDonald's tavern. She practically skipped crossing the town square, remarking how the tavern's green door fit the Irish origins of its owner. The statement was another indication that this abused daughter of a fire-breathing spellbinder had been exposed to considerable book learning and had missed nothing of what happened about her.

Hamish McDonald, a brawny Irishman with tufts of hair on his ears, a large mole on one cheek, a beard that curled on the ends, and a gold front tooth, served them in person, boasting incessantly—in a brogue straight from a Sir Walter Scott novel—of the quality of the fare he brought to the table. Judah had to admit the thinly sliced fried pork, boiled potatoes, pork gravy, spiced stewed apples, and cornbread hot to the touch was a right tasty combination, and the hard cider laced with whiskey Hamish offered Judah was as easy to swallow as brown silk. Neither he nor his dining companion put any restraint on their appetites.

By the end of the meal, Judah was aware that three

roughly dressed individuals with holstered pistols and sheathed knives at a table near the front door had been staring in his direction for some minutes. Each of the bearded men had a long gun leaning against the arm of his chair. The drooping brims of their slough hats hid their eyes. All told, they appeared a menacing trio capable of violent mischief.

When Hamish's body shielded Judah from the trio's view while the tavern owner refilled his mug, he softly asked, "Do you know the three with long guns near the front door, Mr. McDonald?"

Without looking to confirm their identities, Hamish McDonald said, "They would be the three Douglas cousins. The one in the middle is named Bagnell. They other two follow him like pet-starved puppy dogs. They're mean, hard on women and anyone weaker than them, and steal whatever suits their fancy. Rumor says they're bosom friends of Champ Ferguson from Clinton County. Champ's acquiring a reputation for Yankee killing. They're a bad lot whichever side they take up with. If I were you, I'd keep a sharp watch on that red stallion folks are yapping about. They'd slit the Lord's throat to throw a leg over him."

Judah said, "We'll ease past them to the door. I don't want to cause you any grief, if I can help it."

"There won't be any trouble from them in here. That shotgun hanging behind the bar is loaded and Willard has taken it down in a hurry before. I have a revolver stashed inside the kitchen door, too. The Douglas cousins know that. Mind my word, the two of you and the half-breed need to stay alert once you pass the city limits."

Always the consummate host, Hamish McDonald then inquired, "Do you need food for the half-breed?"

It was a generous offer from a tavern keeper who didn't dare serve anybody with the taint of black skin at his bar or tables. While Barefoot could eat a portion of the food left in their travel stash, the half-breed had a fondness for fresh pork and Judah saw a chance to please him. "He would sincerely appreciate some of that fried pork."

The speedy supper had allowed little time for conversation. Judah had considered telling Ben Hardin he'd located her uncle, then decided against it. He couldn't predict how she would react with any certainty, and a heated public disagreement would draw attention to them they didn't need. Though he felt somewhat of a coward, it appeared best to tell her when they neared Stokely Hardin's farm. Perhaps she would accept staying there as the inevitable consequence of her destitute situation. If she didn't and protested, he had devised a means of making it impossible for her to follow after him and Barefoot.

Hamish McDonald returned from the kitchen with a cloth-covered wooden trencher. Ben Hardin took charge of the trencher and Judah paid Hamish their bill from his wallet. The Douglas cousins studied the far end of the room and ignored the departing Judah and Ben Hardin. Three saddled horses were tied to a hitch rack in the alley beside the tavern. Judah was betting they belonged to the cousins and that the other patrons inside had arrived on foot.

Near the end of the business day there were fewer horsemen, wagons, and pedestrians populating the street in the waning daylight. A group of seven riders dressed like the Douglas cousins but armed with just flintlock rifles trotted past and disappeared up the street running north from the public square. Given their lack of recognizable military uniforms, Judah pegged them as Home Guards belonging to one of the local militia companies raised in various Kentucky counties to defend those loyal to the Union against the likes of Champ Ferguson and the Douglas cousins as well as the Confederate Army should it make an appearance. Judah decided then and there without a smidgen of doubt that the safest pursuit for a rootless man in Civil War Kentucky was enlistment in an organized army—whether blue-belly or Rebel—where he knew and could trust the loyalty of those next to him.

Hanging lanterns lit the broad entryway of Huddleston's livery barn. The door of Huddleston's attached office was closed and padlocked. An older chap with a dragoon mustache and lantern jaw was seated in a chair just inside the barn's open entryway with an over and under shotgun across his lap. He said to Judah, "I'm Stub Early, the roustabout and night guard. Mr. Huddleston asked me to tell you it's okay if you want to bunk down in the tack room. I'll be here all night. Like I told your boy with the trencher, this is the only door to the barn, the smithy, and the corral out back. Anything untoward happens I'll yell good and loud; that is, if I don't shoot first."

Stub Early spat a stream of brown tobacco juice into a bucket beside his chair. "Your half-breed is watching the corral anyways. Guess he didn't believe my claim we ain't never lost a horse to thieves."

"Don't take it personally, Mr. Early, Barefoot is always that cautious with our animals," Judah assured the night guard.

Jasper's head jutted from the last stall at the far end of the barn's center runway. The stallion nickered and Judah paused to pat his neck. A lantern by his hip, Asa Barefoot was seated on a bench inside the livery barn's rear opening, conversing with a thick-shouldered Negro who wore a leather apron and had the oversized right forearm common to blacksmiths.

Miss Whatever-her-name-might-be told Asa Barefoot to make a lap, sat the trencher on his thighs, and removed its cloth cover. The smile that creased the half-breed's cheeks exposed a childish joy. Hamish McDonald had sent along a virtual pile of pork slices and wedges of cornbread.

Kindhearted Barefoot patted the bench beside him. "Sit, Tobias, this is too much for a single old half-breed."

Once the two men were chewing vigorously, Judah knelt in front of them. "Tobias, has Mr. Huddleston gone home for the evening?"

"Yes, sir."

"Do you sleep here?"

The blacksmith swallowed and said, "No, sir, I sleeps at my brother's place."

Judah nodded. "That's helpful, I don't want you shot by mistake."

Barefoot deposited a bite of uneaten cornbread on the trencher and swiped his mouth with the edge of his hand. "We're expecting trouble, Master Judah?"

"Not one hundred percent certain, but I caught three cousins named Douglas armed with revolvers, rifles, and knives staring at us in the tavern and Hamish McDonald thinks they might try to steal Jasper."

Tobias's eyes bugged. "They are bad men," the blacksmith blurted. "Mr. Early told me they got mad and cursed Mr. Huddleston in the tack room last spring. They said he wanted too much money for his saddles. They threatened him, but didn't come back."

Judah asked, "Are there bunks in the tack room, Tobias?"

"Yes, sir," Tobias answered.

Curiosity and disbelief growing simultaneously, Whatever-her-first-name-might-be said, "Are those cousins really foolhardy enough to attempt stealing a horse from a guarded livery barn in the middle of a crowded town? Wouldn't it be easier to follow us tomorrow and sneak up on us when we're camped for the night and then hightail it with all of our horses? Any one of our horses is from better stock and in far better shape than the three we saw tied at the side of the tavern."

Damn girl reasons like Jarrod and me, and might be smarter than our lawyer brother, Judah thought.

"Done properly, stealing Jasper tonight wouldn't be that difficult. The barn is open on both ends with no doors. They'll leave their horses in an alley down the street a block or two, come up behind the livery, and scale the corral fence. While one cousin locates Jasper, the other two do the rest. One of them barricades the tack room door since they'll expect we're sleeping there if they keep watch on the alley beside the hotel. The final cousin sneaks up on Stub Early, who won't be all that alert in the middle of the night. He ties him hand and foot, and gags him. Then they quietly lead Jasper to their horses and skedaddle. While they're escaping, we'll be trapped in the tack room until Elam Huddleston appears in the morning and wonders why Stub isn't guarding the livery."

"So, suppose they put the sneak on us, what do you want us to do?" Ben Hardin demanded.

Judah looked at Asa Barefoot and found nothing funny about his bemused countenance. He didn't understand why, but the half-breed was enthralled by the forward manner of Smite Hardin's daughter.

"I'll sleep in Jasper's stall," Judah said. "Asa will hide outside the tack room. If Tobias is agreeable, he'll stay the night and make sure Stub Early isn't taken by surprise."

"And what about me?"

"You sleep in the tack room and stay out of harm's way. That's all we need from you."

Whatever-her-first-name-might be didn't like being set aside like a child good for nothing other than making noise. She grabbed Judah's blanket and gum poncho and stomped off up the barn's runway with her brogans raising puffs of dust behind her and backbone stiff as a ramrod.

"Master Judah, you surely have the charm of the leper when it comes to womenfolk," Asa Barefoot said.

That wry comment made Tobias squirm. The blacksmith wasn't accustomed to chiding his betters from his lowly station. He relaxed when Judah shot back by reminding the half-breed that nobody, ugly or pretty, had shared his bed for years.

"Tobias, like I mentioned earlier," Judah said, "you can go home to bed if you like."

"No sir, that was right tasty pork and cornbread. Believe I'll keep Mr. Early awake like you wants."

"Then let's hope we don't have unwanted visitors and can share a peaceful night."

Judah heard the scrape of a boot sole against gravel and saw a shadow against the moonlight pouring through the rear door of the livery. He shook sleep from his head, drew his Navy Colt, rose to a crouch in the rear of Jasper's stall, and clasped the stallion's nostrils with his free hand. He wanted nothing to warn the nocturnal intruders.

A whispering voice said, "Why can't I take care of that snickering bastard Stub Early, Bagnell?"

A slightly louder, and cross-toned voice said, "Keep quiet and do as you're told for once. Count to fifty and then lead that stud up front."

More boot scraping was followed by absolute silence except for a yapping dog somewhere behind the livery. Judah breathed evenly and kept a tight rein on his nerves. When the situation exploded, things would happen with amazing rapidity, the same as they had in Dayton Farrell's barn.

A hatted head appeared above the gate of Jasper's stall. Judah had tied the stallion to an iron bolt on the back wall of the stall to force any would-be thief to come to him. The latch bar on the stall's gate moved, the gate slowly opened, and a whispering voice said, "Easy, big boy, easy."

The shadowy figure toting a bridle placed a hand on the stallion's rump near his tail, a touch Judah knew Jasper wouldn't tolerate. Luckily for him, the thief recognized the danger in the slight dip of the stallion's hindquarters and lunged sideways. Jasper's kick missed the cursing thief's body by mere inches.

With the distracted Douglas cousin directly in front of him, Judah made his move. "Freeze or I'll blow a hole in you."

Judah missed the sweep of the thief's arm for half a second, and the headpiece and curb bit of the lashing bridle caught him square on the ear and cheekbone. He lost his grip on his revolver and reeled backward.

Judah thought for an instant that his attacker, knowing he was armed, would flee. The determined Douglas cousin charged instead. They met shoulder to shoulder, and Judah found himself pinned against the wall of the stall with one arm trapped behind him.

With the sudden burst of strength that spares men in desperate straits, Judah found the wherewithal to thrust his head backward, landing a blow on his attacker's nose, and push off the wall with his free hand. Though his opponent was the stunned contestant now, he managed to wrap Judah in a bear hug with both arms.

Judah struggled to stay upright and keep his feet moving, afraid that if he didn't the Douglas cousin clinging to him would bring his knife into play. They bounced off the flank of the excited, prancing Jasper out into the runway of the barn. When the Douglas cousin tried to wrestle him to the ground, Judah ceased struggling, turned in the air as they fell, and landed atop him, breaking his attacker's hold.

Judah scrambled to his feet, fists balled and ready, and

a rush of fear engulfed him. The would-be horse thief had lost his revolver in their tussling, but with the moonlight now shining from behind Jacob, the blade of the longest knife he'd ever seen glinted with wicked menace. Common sense told Judah to yell for help or run. But the obstinate streak that had gotten him into trouble from childhood to the dismay of his parents and older brother held him in place.

His crouching opponent, blood flowing from his broken nose, knife poised, edged closer, and said, "My friend, it will be a pleasure to stick you in the belly."

"Hey, you!"

The knife wielder shuffled his feet and glanced over his shoulder. The thud of the wooden plank against the top of his skull matched the blunt strike of a sledgehammer. The knife slipped from his fingers and the Douglas cousin's legs failed him. His broken nose hit the gravel bed of the runway first.

With his opponent flat down and unconscious, Judah had a clear view of his rescuer: It was none other than the smiling, smug daughter of the deceased Smite Hardin.

"Bet you're glad I came to check on you, huh? Think where you'd be if I'd followed your orders."

The same obstinate streak that kept him from fleeing to save his life negated an outright "thank you" on Judah's part. "What about the other two cousins?"

Ignoring Judah's bullheadedness and failure to acknowledge that she'd spared him a stabbing at the least, Whatever-her-first-name-might-be said, "Bound and gagged. What are our plans now? Turn them over to the law?"

Judah rubbed his sore ear and jaw, glad he didn't feel any wet blood there. He'd just as soon not deal with questions from her about any wound he had suffered. "Forget the law. We aren't hanging around for a court trial. We've enough fixings for another few days. Come first light, we're headed south before this town is up. Stub Early can cut the cousins loose after we have a good head start."

Trying not to show any excitement, and then appear disappointed afterward, Ben Hardin asked, "Does that mean you're taking me with you?"

Judah's answer was truthful, but knowing what lay ahead of them, he did honestly feel like a cur dog saying it: "For now."

Stokely Hardin's farm didn't match Elam Huddleston's kind description. The half-open gate on the narrow lane leading from the public roadway to the small one-story house and dilapidated barn hung from one hinge. The barn and house bore red paint and the house's doors and shutters were indeed white, but every painted surface of both structures was faded and peeling badly. Knee-high weeds filled the yard of the house. The barren truck garden beside the house seemed small for feeding two grown males. A few scrawny cows nipped at sparse vegetation in an overgrazed pasture. The horse team sharing the pasture with the cows was lean-hipped and unshod.

Hard scrabble poor at best, Judah thought.

Whatever-her-name-might-be booted her bay alongside Jasper. "Why are we stopping here? Shouldn't we be putting miles between the Douglas cousins and us?"

Judah took a deep breath and said, "This is your uncle Stokely's farm."

Judah kept a close watch on her out of the corner of his eye. The puzzled expression that he saw initially slowly turned into disbelief. Her mouth started to open, then her jaw clinched so tightly it wouldn't have surprised him if he'd heard bone snap.

"I'll get the gate," Judah said, dismounting.

They advanced up the narrow lane with Judah in the lead, followed by Ben Hardin and Barefoot. Halting Jasper short of the sagging steps of the roofless porch, Judah yelled, "Hello, is Mr. Stokely Hardin at home?"

After thirty seconds that seemed a year, rusted hinges began squealing and the windowless front door crawled open. An emaciated white male with a gray beard that extended to his waist and hair that touched his shoulders emerged with a squirrel gun missing its lock, a useless weapon, held across his chest. "I'm Stokely Hardin. What you want with me?"

Given the crusted dirt on the exposed skin of Stokely Hardin's face and hands, he'd obviously become allergic to soap. His cotton shirt and trousers hadn't been washed in eons, either. Black nails protruded from the toes of his worn shoes.

"What you want with me?" an impatient Stokely Hardin repeated.

While Judah couldn't deny he was fast developing misgivings about what he intended doing, he couldn't shake the dread gripping him that, if he let Whatever-her-first-name-might-be trail after him into the war, he would ultimately be responsible for her death, and he didn't want female blood on his hands.

Turning in the saddle, Judah said, "This is your niece, your brother Smite Hardin's daughter. Smite and your nephews were killed and this young lady needs a place to live. Can you take her in?"

Stokely Hardin gaped and said, "I'll be double damned. You must be Brianna. Last time I laid eye on you, you was in a crib."

Well, kiss the donkey on the behind!

In the most roundabout way imaginable Judah had finally learned her elusive first name. He had to admit "Brianna" rolled smoothly off the tongue.

Stokely Hardin danced a jig and yelled, "Dawg, come meet Brianna, your first cousin."

The second being to emerge from the Hardin house conveyed the image of half dog and half something else. His nose and chin flowed together in a long muzzle befitting a hound. Closely spaced beady eyes peered from beneath a wide forehead. Hair covered nearly every inch of his skin. His speech sounded like the yip of a small dog. "Howdy, Brianna, howdy. You gonna live with us, huh, huh?"

Judah had to be gone in a hurry or he would cave. "Get down, Brianna."

Stone-faced and showing no emotion, Brianna Hardin dismounted and handed the bay's reins up to Judah. She knows, Judah marveled. She knows I'm taking her horse so she can't tag after us. She wasn't happy, but she was too smart to fight what was inevitable. He sincerely wished they could have parted under more amiable conditions.

With a nod good-bye, he motioned for Barefoot to follow him and rode for the gate and the Nicholasville-Danville Road, holding the pace to a walk, concerned that departing at a gallop might insinuate he was dying to be out of her sight and further hurt her feelings.

They were down the roadway far enough a copse of hickory trees hid the Hardin farm when two shots rang out in rapid succession behind them. Judah tugged gently on Jasper's reins and halted in the middle of the road.

What the hell had gone wrong so soon? How could anything have gone wrong where firearms were involved? Stokely Hardin's squirrel gun couldn't be fired. Then he remembered he hadn't disarmed Brianna, and she had her father's .58 Remington and kept it loaded except for the cap under the hammer.

Had she murdered both Stokely and Dawg? Judah groaned aloud. Given a reasonable excuse, or one less than reasonable, he'd do likewise as surely as the hound chased the fox.

Gripping the reins of her bay, he spurred Jasper back the way they'd come with Barefoot's mare chasing after them. Judah had no clue what awaited them.

Brianna Hardin met them in the lane just inside the listing gate, Remington revolver banging against her thigh with each stride, her eyes lightning hot with anger.

Judah blocked her path, and asked, "Trouble?"

"The minute you were out of sight Stokely Hardin tried to wrestle my Remington away from me while his son pinched my breast."

"And what did you do? I don't see either of them in the yard."

"I was too quick and slippery for them. I got free and shot at the ground in front of both of them and told them if I could see any part of them after I counted to ten I'd kill them. They were in the house before I got to five."

Judah steeled himself for the coming storm. Despite having the best of intentions, he'd wronged her, and then come back for her, and unless he wanted to abandon her a second time, he had no choice but to endure her wrath. He ignored Asa Barefoot. One more knowing smart-ass grin from the half-breed and he'd be tempted to shoot him more than he was Stokely Hardin and Dawg.

Newly named Brianna Hardin got off to a roaring start. "I misjudged you, Mr. Judah Bell. You're a black-eyed bastard, and the only thing you truly give a damn about is fighting the war. Any man with an ounce of compassion in his soul would never leave a girl with that old coot and his dolt of a son. What were you expecting to happen? That is, unless you're too stupid to figure it out on your own. You know my family's history. My father and his brother believed women had no more say than rabid foxes, and their lot was to do as they were told no matter how much it hurt and tired them, or suffer a whipping. My uncle and Dawg would have raped me after they disarmed me and locked me away for their future pleasure or worked me to death, one as easily as the other."

Sticking her revolver behind her belt, Briana continued, "You needn't worry any more about my being a burden to you, Mr. Judah Bell. Trust me, I won't let the next under-handed son-of-a-bitch I might meet decide my fate again. I don't want to walk back to Nicholasville and give the Douglas cousins a chance to lay their hands on me. After last night, they might prove worse than my family, if that's possible. If you have a smidgen of decency in you, which I have reason to doubt, you'll let me use that bay horse until we reach the next town. After that, I'll make my own way without you and your damn horse."

Placing her hands on her hips, Brianna Hardin, gaze still blazing hot, sucked in air and said, "Well, Mr. Judah Bell, do I ride or walk? If I ride, I'll stay well behind you and Mr. Barefoot. You won't know I'm there."

It was the worst dressing down Judah had ever endured, and his father was an expert when it came to that endeavor. She'd left him with no excuse for his behavior, no meaning-ful way of saying he was sorry, and not a single shred of dignity. She had branded him the sorriest red worm at the bottom of a tall pile of horseshit, and he deserved it.

Even if the stinging hurt of what he'd done to her wore off over time, he suspected she might never be able to stand being near him, and to his astonishment that hurt more than anything she'd said in her tirade. His old axiom that no matter what caused him to lose out with any pretty girl, he needn't be concerned for a prettier and more will-ing girl would shortly fall into his lap wasn't as confidence boosting as it had been in the past. He had always scoffed at brother Jacob's contention there was but one right woman for every man. To his surprise, he found himself thinking his attitude in that regard was perhaps as wrong headed as a fool claiming a single bucket of water could douse a large fire.

Stamping her foot, Brianna Hardin asked in a near shout, "Well, Goddamnit, Mr. Judah Bell, do I ride or walk? Those Douglas cousins are narrowing our lead every minute."

Unwilling to chance a fiery retort by uttering a solitary word, Judah leaned from the saddle, passed her the bay's reins, spun Jasper, and made for the beckoning quiet of the Nicholasville-Danville Road at a trot.

Whatever confronted him during the balance of the war, it had to be more manageable than the disaster of his own creation he was fleeing.

CHAPTER 8

The whole convoluted affair ignited after the dinner meal on a bright clear Sunday. The sight of Corporal Fritz Howard running toward him, head down and arms pumping, stopped Jacob Bell's second cup of coffee short of his mouth. Howard skidded to a halt and, without bothering to salute, said between gulped breaths, "Sergeant, you best come quick. Trouble, bad trouble is brewing."

"What's this about, Corporal?"

"The Forty-Second Infantry drew guard duty this morning at the gate next to the sutlers' wagons. The Fortieth Infantry's tents are the closest to the wagons, and the Forty-Second guards won't let those boys pass through the gate and tempers are turning mighty raw. The sutlers have a fresh stock of goods on hand and the Forty-Second guards feel both infantry regiments should be allowed to buy from the sutlers at the same time to keeps things fair."

"How does that concern us?"

"Some of our First Cavalry boys have permission to call on the sutlers today and they're not happy, either."

"If the guards can't handle the situation, regimental headquarters is nearby. Someone from there can summon support for the guards."

"Remember, sir, Major Walker and the commissioned officers of the entire regiment are in town at the Neil House Hotel to meet Colonel Ransom's guests from Washington City. The colonel's adjutant is in charge in his absence. I saw boys from all three regiments making for the sutlers' wagons. So was First Sergeant Clutter."

Mindful of the barroom brawls he'd witnessed at Gentry's Tavern back home in Chillicothe, Jacob took time to belt his holstered revolver about his waist. Officers were expected to maintain and restore order, and he needed to prepare for any eventuality. He couldn't imagine the Forty-Second guards firing upon their Yankee counterparts, and that awareness coupled with the absence of the regiment's highest-ranking officers made the chance of a riot more likely. Who could swear later exactly what had happened in a no-holds-barred free-for-all involving scores of men over sutlers' supplies cherished by every man in camp.

"Corporal Howard, follow me," Jacob ordered. "You other men stay put. No sense in your risking a spell in the guardhouse."

Jacob held his pace to a brisk walk despite the urgency he felt, not wanting to be out of breath when he reached the area of the sutlers' wagons on the far boundary of the parade ground. Curiously, the door to the colonel's headquarters tent on the near boundary was closed and unmanned. Jacob heard shouted profanities as he approached the crowd gathered in front of the gate guarded by sentries from the Forty-Second Infantry.

The din swelled to a lung-bursting volume, a body sailed into the air, and a punching, gouging, kicking, and tackling melee erupted among three hundred plus men. Jacob spotted blue-striped infantry trousers and yellow-striped cavalry pants, Fortieth and Forty-Second Infantry insignia hats and forage caps adorned with the crossed sabers of the

First Ohio. A corporal caught between contesting bodies was screaming "Attention" repeatedly to no avail.

Near as Jacob could tell the undersized First Ohio boys were not faring well against infantrymen who in the main were taller and outweighed them. The alignment of bodies indicated the First Ohio and the Fortieth Infantry were tussling with members of the Forty-Second, which made logical sense based on Corporal Howard's recent report.

A rock struck Jacob's cheekbone under his left eye with enough force to stagger him. He shuffled his feet and managed to stay upright. His probing fingers came away blood-smeared.

The pain galvanized Jacob. He drew his revolver, aimed at the sky, and fired, and then fired three well-spaced shots, figuring one shot wouldn't grab everybody's attention. Whether men were standing or on the ground, by the fourth shot all eyes were looking at Jacob over heads, from between bodies, or through legs. The sudden quiet was downright eerie.

"Form line by regiment," Jacob shouted, "and come to attention. Now!"

Swiping with his fingers to keep blood from dripping off his chin, Jacob hurried them along with another shot at the sky. A chorus of moans and groans arose from those with broken bones, bloody noses, cracked ribs, missing teeth, and sprung knees while they formed lines with their proper regiments. Some of the injured needed help from their comrades to stay erect. The disjointed attempt of the hurt and disabled to come to attention and salute him was so ludicrously funny Jacob bit his tongue to keep from laughing aloud.

Bruised lip fattening like rising bread, First Sergeant Dan Clutter stepped up beside Jacob. "We best disperse them. They'll bash each other's heads, but they won't rat on each other. That means whatever punishment Colonel

Ransom metes out will be on the regimental level. You have the situation under control. No point muddying the water by diverting their attention elsewhere."

Jacob holstered his revolver and said, "Gentlemen, take your fallen comrades with you and return to your tents and barracks. You have permission to escort any man requiring medical assistance to the camp hospital. Move along. You are dismissed."

Jacob and Dan Clutter kept watch until the last rioter stumbled off on his own accord. An alert sounding at the camp gate on Broadway drifted to them. "Must be the colonel and his entourage," Clutter speculated. "I'll report everything to him as I was the senior officer present. I'll have to include your discharging a firearm in the line of duty. He may well want to discuss your actions with you in person."

"I'll make myself available whenever he sends for me," Jacob assured the first sergeant.

Dan Clutter poked at his swollen lip and winced. "We must look like two drunks that lost a bar fight. You best have that cheek tended to. Who hit you anyway?"

"Nobody. It was a rock from I don't know where."

"I'll be damned," Dan Clutter said. "Never known the boys to stoop that low before. Better shake a leg for the hospital. The colonel is headed this way. That horse's ass adjutant of his is running to give him an earful after hiding in the headquarters tent till the trouble was over."

With a farewell nod, Jacob proceeded to the hospital, a white-painted frame building located adjacent to the Fortieth Infantry Regiment barracks smack in the middle of Camp Chase. He survived the rough hands and wavering needle of a wheezing military physician and emerged an hour later with a harshly scrubbed face, three stitches under his eye, and a headache that worsened with each minute. The walk to his tent lasted an eternity. He couldn't miss the curious stares and amused grins he garnered from onlookers lounging on both sides of the company street. Word swept through Company M with the lightning speed of salt passing through a goose; augmented, of course, by Fritz Howard's expansive mind and wit.

The dedicated rumor hawk and former Ross County jockey greeted Jacob with a freshly brewed cup of coffee and news he didn't particularly want to hear. "Lieutenant Shavers brought word you're to report to Colonel Ransom straightaway. I promised him I'd give you the message soon as you returned."

Jacob finished his coffee and set off. His cheek below the stitches was enlarged and throbbing, and the black eye to follow would be a sight to behold. He was probably the only man involved in the riot that hadn't landed a single blow of his own and earned a trek to the hospital for doing his duty.

A two-seated buggy with a fringed top pulled by a team of Roman-nosed geldings was tied to a hitching post beside Colonel Ransom's headquarters tent. Sighting them made Jacob forget his headache. What was his father's buggy doing here? He'd received no notice that Senator Clay Bell was scheduled to visit Camp Chase, and such visitations by politicians were always planned in advance with a written advisory issued to regimental staff and the commissioned and non-commissioned officers commanding companies. Colonel Ransom left little to chance when treating with outsiders.

Jacob saluted the armed privates guarding the door of the tent and stepped inside with considerable trepidation. The colonel's adjutant was on the lookout for him and accosted him immediately. "Colonel Ransom wants you brought straight to him. His esteemed visitors and the colonel's staff wish to discuss the sutlers' riot with you."

A tiny alarm bell chimed in the back of Jacob's mind.

The last thing Colonel Ransom would want was for the riot to become public knowledge before he had a complete grasp of what had occurred, and why, and had decided how much of that information was best kept within the camp stockade. Jacob's curiosity mounted. Who might be present besides his father, if anybody, and what was it they wanted?

The regiment's captain and lieutenants were standing at ease in the front portion of the tent, conversing quietly. The adjutant led Jacob to a small group of officers and civilians in a cordoned-off area before Colonel Ransom's desk. The party was composed of the colonel, Major Dance Walker, Captain Cam Logan, First Sergeant Dan Clutter, Jacob's father, a well-dressed, older gentleman Jacob had never met, and the most beautiful young woman he had ever seen in person.

The second Jacob spotted her, every male present, no matter how important or powerful, faded into the background. She nearly matched his height, and her red dress and flowered jacket couldn't hide the curves of a full-blown mature female body. Her hair was the color of caramel candy, her eyes cornflower blue, her nose slightly fluted, her lips rose-hued and full, and her dimples swimming in skin white as alabaster. The tiny cleft in her chin invited the tap of a finger where her delicate ears invited a kiss. Jacob did not know her name, her age, her taste in men, or anything else about her, but, pure and simple, he had to have her. It was a spur-of-the-moment decision, uncharacteristic of a man taking pride in careful, reasoned deliberation before acting. But he knew with absolute certainty it was irreversible: This was the woman for him.

He resisted the urge to brush his uniform sleeves and straighten his collar. He was thankful he'd had a cold-water bath in a stand-and-wash tub the previous evening and had shaved and had Fritz Howard trim his hair that morning. He could only pray the unsightliness of his stitched cheek and the darkening flesh around his entire eye didn't repulse her. Maybe she didn't put much store by first appearances. But then, maybe she did.

Colonel Ransom spied Jacob. "Here's the man we want to talk to. Welcome, Sergeant Bell, let me introduce our visitors. Your father needs no introduction. This august gentleman is James Henry Denning, the principal partner in the renowned Denning, Denning, and Denning law firm here in the capital."

James Henry Denning wore low-cut boots, an austere black suit, starched white linen shirt, black string tie, and a vest of red silk. A watch chain studded with tiny gold rifles stretched across his protruding belly. Thickets of gray-white hair surrounded his clean-shaven chin and upper lip. His eyes had a watery cast, and a tracery of tiny red veins on the skin below them hinted at a man who tipped the glass whenever the social occasion permitted, and often when he was alone. Diamond rings on the hand he extended Jacob oozed prosperity.

James Henry Denning exerted all the power he could with his clasping fingers, perhaps to override the blatant softness of his body in the presence of trim military officers and the physically fit Senator Clay Bell. Undaunted, Jacob matched Denning's exaggerated grip ounce for ounce. He'd endured enough male bravado and silliness for one day.

"And this, Sergeant Bell," Colonel Ransom continued, "is Mr. Denning's daughter, Felicia."

Felicia Denning's smile was warm and revealed perfect white teeth. She stepped closer to Jacob and offered a gloved hand. Grandmother Nadine Bell's "training of the graces" as she called it came to the fore. Jason bent at the waist and kissed her knuckles, straightened, stepped closer yet to her, and leaned forward so his lips were almost touching her ear. She didn't shy or pull back when he whispered, "You're the lovely creature every man dreams of meeting."

With the noisy clearing of his father's throat, a warning sign in the past that it was time for Jacob to cease and desist, he stepped away from Felicia Denning. There wasn't a trace of blush on her cheeks. The mischievous glint in her cornflower eyes told a different story. If nothing else, he'd sparked some interest in her, however fleeting it might prove.

Jacob's flamboyant behavior amused the other military men. From where they stood, Dance Walker and Dan Clutter thought he might have also kissed Felicia's ear and they marveled at Jacob's boldness. Jacob did catch a fleeting scowl on Cam Logan's features over her shoulder. Her father's benign expression indicated he was accustomed to men fawning over his daughter.

The impatient, business-at-the-expense-of-all-else Colonel O. P. Ransom actually chuckled, establishing a historical first. "Sergeant Bell, Sergeant Clutter has provided a detailed accounting of the misguided behavior of some of our cavalry and infantry earlier today. I regret your injury and wish you a speedy recovery. I understand you found it necessary to discharge your weapon to restore order. I find no fault with that and wish to commend your conduct in an ugly situation and thank you for sparing additional injuries to our troopers."

Veteran Dan Clutter seldom missed an opportunity to stroke the cat for a fellow non-commissioned officer he admired. "Slickest pulling of the bung I ever witnessed, sir. The first couple of shots didn't do the trick, but the next two put a serious note in the air and horse-collared the whole shebang. Every man there realized the show was over. The last shot gave a real tug to the injured to fall in line no matter how much it hurt."

"Sergeant, I can't condone what happened," Major Walker said, "but you're making me sorry I missed out on the fun. A good brawl in the middle of a long stretch of training is to be appreciated. It tunes a trooper up right smart. That's allowing you aren't among those still in pain a week later or wearing a cast."

Once again his deadly serious self, Colonel Ransom said, "You're correct, Major, we can't condone what transpired and that begs the question of how punishment should be administered. Since individual culprits would be nearly impossible to ferret out, that leaves us with making the entire regiment pay for the misdeeds of a few of their comrades. We need a punishment that tells the guilty as well as the innocent that it wasn't worth lighting the candle again. Gentlemen, I'm open to suggestions."

Major Dance Walker's smile was that of the cat holding the mouse in his paws. "Colonel, I've fought in wars on three continents, and the paramount dread of a mounted trooper is to lose his horse and find himself afoot. Walking is for the cussed infantry, not the horseback warrior. A ten-mile hike fully armed and toting their saddles and bridles without any water should make them think twice the next round. And the march must include a trip through the streets of both infantry regiments at the finish. Over the years, I've learned parched throats, blistered feet, and wounded pride are more effective than the ball and chain."

"Excellent suggestion, Major. We were planning a practice march for the entire regiment this coming week. I believe the punishment should follow the crime as quickly as possible. We'll issue the orders this afternoon. Officers will ride, and troopers will walk."

Now, it was Colonel Ransom's turn to play the cat.

"Those orders, however, will make no mention of the absence of horses. We will allow breakfast, and then proceed to morning drill on foot carrying the specified arms and equipment. Sergeant Bell, you will ride in the van with Major Walker and First Sergeant Clutter. You've earned that privilege."

Jacob was so enamored with Felicia Denning his gaze had drifted back to her and he almost missed Colonel Ransom's announcement regarding him. A mere company line sergeant riding in the van was a rare event. Jacob guessed before he looked that Cam Logan had been taken by surprise and would be greatly displeased that a privilege had been granted to a subordinate of his without his being consulted in advance, which was standard protocol, a protocol the colonel had disciplined his own staff officers for violating.

Given Cam Logan's clenched jaw and stern expression, Jacob's guess was right on target, and he didn't doubt there would be repercussions awaiting him down the line, for Cam Logan having to swallow what he perceived to be an insult to his authority was akin to rubbing salt in an open wound. It bugged Jacob how fate always kept Cam Logan and him on opposite ends of the stick.

At that juncture, the colonel's adjutant called for order and the tent quieted. Colonel Ransom excused himself and mounted the small wooden platform his staff had placed between his party and the conversing regimental officers. "Gentlemen, we will undertake a march out the National Road in the morning in lieu of regular drill on site. Orders will be forthcoming within the hour. You are dismissed."

A buzz arose among the departing captains and lieutenants. They had assumed they'd been kept from returning to their respective companies so they could be told what punishments resulted from the riot at the sutlers' gate.

Instead, they'd been left clueless and uncertain if any participant would be held accountable, which puzzled them in light of their colonel's penchant for the swift disciplining of negligent and wayward infractions. Had their colonel lost his edge? Was he to be trusted? Had age and hard service finally taken its toll on him?

A discerning young lieutenant from Company H saw things on a different slant. "You boys wait till tomorrow. Colonel Ransom keeps his cards tight to his chest. He plays them at his whim, not when we want him to."

While the headquarters tent emptied, Colonel Ransom's guests became his major concern. Rejoining them, Ransom said, "Senator Bell, I believe you and your friends wanted to tour the camp, did you not?"

"Yes, we did, but perhaps we best postpone our tour until another time. I would offer that your men have had the day they have to themselves each week disturbed enough without two old goats rambling around staring at them. You have any objections, James?"

James Henry Denning answered, "None whatsoever, Senator; I'm never one to intrude when I might make people uncomfortable. We'll come again when the men have plenty of notice. I thank you for honoring our request the best you could, Colonel."

"I hope you're not disappointed, Miss Denning," Colonel Ransom inquired.

"No, I'm not, Colonel. Like Father, I never want to impose. Perhaps my coming along wasn't a good idea anyway."

"Nonsense, Miss Denning, there will never be an occasion when ladies aren't welcome in our camp," Colonel Ransom assured the Denning daughter. "Please come next Sunday and I'll escort the three of you personally."

Colonel Ransom's invitation was music to Jacob's ears.

He'd been madly calculating how he might pay a visit to Felicia Denning before the First Ohio entrained for Cincinnati and a new post somewhere in Kentucky. Even a brief stop before his tent during her tour in a week was better than nothing.

Jacob was disappointed when Cam Logan was a beat faster than him offering to see his father and the Dennings to their waiting buggy. Felicia's father accepted readily and the matter was closed.

Or was it?

The female offspring of Lawyer Denning turned her back to the others, leaned toward Jacob, and whispered, "We'll meet again, Sergeant, somehow, will we not?"

The stunned Jacob thought a hammer had hit his heart. He recovered enough to smile wryly and mutter, "That we will, I promise."

With an inviting smile that sent Jacob's blood racing, Felicia Denning turned away and said, "If I may have your arm, Captain Logan, I'd be pleased to accompany you."

Jacob was staring after the Denning father and daughter and missed Colonel Ransom's calling of his name. A louder calling jarred him down to earth. "Yes, sir," he responded, hoping his embarrassed blush wasn't too obvious.

"I was reaffirming with your father and Major Walker here how well I believe you acquitted yourself today," Major Ransom said. "Sergeant, let me be frank. You are not a stranger to me. Major Walker has been very complimentary regarding your performance in all aspects of mounted training, the respect you receive from the ranks, and your ability to command men. Going forward, Major Walker and I may call on you to perform certain tasks beyond the scope of your current assignment on detached duty as part of my headquarters staff. You would, of course, hold the rank of Acting Lieutenant at such times until a promotion is warranted. Would that type of service interest you?"

Jacob had no prior clue that Colonel Ransom and Major Walker had paid such detailed attention to his performance. It made him wonder what his father's letter had told the colonel about him. For the major to sort out a solitary sergeant from among a thousand troopers was hardly an accident or random fate; some prompting from higher up the chain of command seemed likely.

There wasn't much deliberation needed for Jacob to answer the colonel. Having met Felicia Denning, the possibility of future promotion was suddenly quite attractive to him. He could shamelessly admit that, if an enhanced military status could help him win her love, whatever the price was, he would willingly pay it twice over. He was desperately trying to come to grips with how much she had stirred his emotions and inflamed his manhood. An unusual tightness in his chest was both uncomfortable and enjoyable.

Was his brain melting?

Shaking his shoulders in an attempt to clear his head, Jacob said with utmost sincerity, "It would be an honor to serve on your staff in any capacity, sir."

"Excellent," Colonel Ransom said. "Senator, I believe your son can make a significant contribution to this regiment's effort to help win the war, and we will afford him every opportunity."

An unmistakably proud Senator Clay Bell responded, "He can be trusted in any circumstance. He will not fail you for lack of trying."

"Rest assured, Senator, we'll hold him to your high standard," Colonel Ransom said, glancing at the front door of his tent. "Gentlemen, if we delay any longer we may insult those waiting to depart, and the major and I have orders to write. Sergeant Bell, please see the senator to his buggy."

Walking beside his father, Jacob asked the question that had been on the tip of his tongue since his arrival. "Any word of Judah?"

Senator Clay Bell's deep sigh said it all. "Nothing to date. In response to my letter, General Buell reported he had inquired through the appropriate Federal military channels in Scott County as I had requested and found no trace of him. The general did confirm Judah didn't die in the fire that burned Temple's home. Only your uncle's body was found. I doubt we will ever learn the truth of what happened that night or what became of Judah unless he tries to contact us. I refuse to admit we've lost him. Your brother is a very resourceful individual like you, and Temple would have done everything in his power to get Judah clear of trouble of his making."

The haggard ridges on his father's face told Jacob how much the potential loss of his middle son was weighing on him. Jacob regretted his inability to do anything at the moment to ease the strain his father was under and offered what solace he could. "I promised I would ask after Judah once the First Ohio is stationed in Kentucky, and I will. I'd like to know, too, who has Uncle Temple's Denmark Thoroughbreds. Horses like that don't just vanish. Have you tried writing to Uncle Temple's neighbors or someone in Buffalo Stamp?"

Nearing the tent's front door, Jacob's father answered, "I wrote to a couple of men I remember, and Frank Masters, the Buffalo Stamp postmaster, who may be retired or dead, but heard nothing back. Your nieces wrote to their friends to no avail. Your uncle was living in the midst of ardent Union sympathizers and they may well have decided Temple got what he deserved and washed their hands of him. I left Kentucky twenty-two years ago, son, and returned only once to march off to fight in Mexico with Temple. Much has changed in the Bluegrass since then, and the war has thrown the balance into a cocked hat. Separating friend from enemy there is as full of surprises as it can be back home in Chillicothe."

They stepped out into bright sunlight. Captain Cam Logan was standing next to Felicia Denning with her father watching them from the front seat of Clay Bell's buggy. Skirt-chasing Cam was exuding charisma and charm, his face alight and animated, his stance formal but as tight to Felicia as proper decorum permitted. The sight was a familiar one to Jacob. Cam Logan was a gifted actor with a honed ability to make females appear the center of his universe without their realizing he was spinning a web of deceit so as to have his way with them. Brice Logan's son had the mesmerizing power of the cobra rising from his basket. The intriguing question for Jacob was whether or not Felicia Denning was worldly enough to discern the real Cam Logan.

Senator Clay Bell paused and said to Jacob, "Every man jack in Columbus wants that young lady on his arm and in his bed. So far, they've all been left panting with their tongues hanging in the dirt. Don't get me wrong. She's a fine upstanding girl. I just enjoy the sideshow. Her father frets over her constantly. He once thought about sending her off to a female academy to protect her virginity. That idea lasted about as long as it takes a stallion to kick his farrier."

Jacob was accustomed to such blunt, humorous obser- vations and assessments from his senator father. Clay Bell had raised his sons with an open book regarding male and female relationships. Women were to be respected and treated as equals, but they were not all pure of heart and intention the same as men weren't. It was a man's respon- sibility to sort the wheat from the chaff and decide which female was an appropriate partner for him and a mother for his children. Taking advantage of or abusing a female was cause for banishment from the family circle with the offender's name stricken from the family Bible.

"You must admit, Father, it would be a fun chase while it lasted," Jacob said, "and the right hound is going to cross the finish line and claim the prize."

"Given the look in your eye and the tone of your voice, let me wish you luck at what I presume is the starting line."

Father and son shared a good laugh and interrupted the conversation at the buggy. A man who preferred to do for himself, Senator Bell untied the snubbing rope of the Roman-nosed geldings. With a hearty and expectant sounding "Good afternoon," Cam Logan offered Felicia Denning his hand and helped her into the rear seat of the canopied buggy. Senator Bell boarded, took up the reins, backed the team clear of the headquarters tent, and turned it to the south. Jacob and Cam Logan watched the buggy until it had circled the parade ground and was bound for the Broad Street gate. Felicia Denning did not deign to wave or call "Good-bye."

She had seemingly appeared and disappeared at the same speed, leaving Jacob wondering if he had viewed a mirage. But the scent of her gloved hand, the white teeth between sumptuous lips, cornflower blue eyes that made a man want to inch ever closer, her whispered hope for a future meeting, and the swish of her skirt were real. He could feel solid ground beneath his boots, could he not?

Cam Logan always had a spear at the ready and stifled Jason's romantic speculation with a solid thrust. "Be interesting, Bell, to find out if she'll choose a sergeant that can't leave camp without his captain's permission over his captain who can request and receive leave, won't it?"

Jacob stood mute. The enjoyment of the day was past history. This was the first occasion upon which he'd been entirely alone with Cam Logan since entering Camp Chase, and Jacob reminded himself that Logan was the superior officer and he was his subordinate. Lose his temper and land a blow and he was at a fault, period.

"Attention, Sergeant Bell," Cam Logan snapped.

Unfortunately for Jacob, the headquarters' sentries were too far away to overhear Cam Logan, and he braced himself for the coming degradation. "My pa and I have never trusted a Bell, no matter the age. You turds have a knack for hogging influence and seizing political power wherever you pop up. Sure as the moon shows on a clear night, you'll be Colonel Ransom's pet errand boy before we break camp. Maybe I can't prevent that, but mark my words, no matter how careful you are, I'll have my chance to break you before you're out of my reach."

Jutting his nose into Jacob's face, Cam Logan said, "And don't bother daydreaming about Felicia Denning. She'll be putty in my hands same as your dear little Marissa Stewart was. You aren't man enough for the likes of Felicia Denning. She'd make a lap dog out of you and lead you anywhere she wants. You'd be the laughingstock of the First Ohio."

Jacob didn't move a muscle. He stared at Cam Logan, his ire under a hard rein. Risky or not, he couldn't resist a dab of retaliation. "We're ever truly alone without witnesses again, bring a gun. I remember correctly, you couldn't win out with your fists the last time and there won't be a woodpile handy, either."

They had fought bare-knuckled at the age of twenty behind the Hancock Bank on Water Street on an icy, windy, snowy evening that kept the bulk of Chillicothe's residents indoors. Jacob was well bundled with a muffler tied over his ears, walking with his head down and shortcutting through back alleys—homeward bound after a Saturday evening of card playing at Gentry's Tavern. Cam Logan had jumped him from the dark and sent him flying headfirst into a snow bank. A snow-spitting Jacob had managed to hold Cam Logan at bay with a stiff arm long enough to regain his feet.

Cam Logan's rage stemmed from Jacob's having caught him cheating at poker an hour earlier. Not wanting trouble over a dime-a-hand game, Lars Gentry politely asked Cam Logan to retire for the evening, and Brice Logan's son had complied without protest and then staged an ambush of his accuser.

Once Jacob was upright, the fisticuffs commenced in earnest. A tally of the blows landed counted a split lip and bloody nose for Jacob and a cut above the eye and three cracked teeth near the hinge of Cam Logan's jaw. The blow that cracked his teeth had sent Cam Logan reeling against the rear wall of the Hancock Bank. Jacob had stormed in for the finish and taken a blow to the side of his head from a length of firewood Cam Logan snatched from the bank's woodpile.

Jacob's consciousness had dissolved in a sea of stars. He came around fifteen minutes later with a lump the size of a small egg above his left ear and honest-to-God seeing two banks, two alleys, two woodpiles, and two scruffy-bearded, wide-eyed, bulb-nosed clown faces that frightened him out of half of his remaining wits. The more his vision cleared, the fogginess clogging his senses had faded away and he realized the single clown face before him belonged to Uzziah Stallworth, the city's foremost tavern sweeper and trash picker. Though his coat was virtually see-through thin, his scarf a rag, his pants holed at the knees, and his shoes held together with twine lashings, Uzziah—a teetotaler immune to cold weather—roamed at night searching for food scraps or discarded items of use to him. Recognizing Jacob, Old Uzziah had helped him to his feet, provided a shoulder for him to lean on, and guided him home, enduring their staggering gait and frequent tumbles into the snow without complaint. For Jacob, the only good outcome of the fight in the snow that blustery winter night had occurred the following Monday when Senator Clay Bell hired Uzziah Stallworth to clean the building housing the Bell family law offices at a weekly wage sufficient to feed him twice a day, a heavenly sum to a former tavern sweeper and trash picker.

Jacob's dab of retaliation wounded Cam Logan's prickly pride. Jacob watched Cam's nostrils flare, and then an angry welt of red stained his cheeks and his chest swelled when he took a deep breath. But Brice Logan's son had matured since the fight in the snow and demonstrated why he was even a more dangerous adversary by slowly letting his lungs empty and forcing his hate for Jacob back into its cage.

"I stand where I said. I'll have the Denning girl plus your career or your life, whichever is the easiest for the taking. You are dismissed, Sergeant Bell."

Jacob's walk back to his Company M mess was a mixture of joy and melancholy. The compliments from Colonel Ransom, the privilege of riding in the van during tomorrow's march, the colonel's extending of a path to promotion, and the encounter with Felicia Denning were marks in the positive column of the ledger. They were offset, however, by the lack of any news about Judah and the stark realization that a confrontation with Cam Logan was truly destined to happen and might have tragic consequences for one or the both of them.

It was a mighty full plate for any two men.

Grandmother Nadine Bell's nightly prayers wouldn't go begging in the days ahead.

CHAPTER 9

Judah Bell's sister, Elizabeth, wasn't prone to casual conversation, but Liz was a blabbermouth compared to an angry Brianna Hardin. The first five days of their ride after departing Nicholasville, Smite Hardin's daughter didn't bother herself saying good morning or good night. She rode behind Judah and Barefoot, stood apart when they were dismounted, and retired to a blanket placed well away from their cooking fire.

She took the news that she was free to accompany them to Glasgow, where Southern sentiment predominated, a concession Judah made in light of her as yet unexplained hostility to the Northern cause, straight-faced and without so much as a nod of thanks.

As they wended to the southwest through Perryville and Lebanon toward Campbellsville, Brianna picked the pinkish fruit of persimmon trees and gathered black walnuts. She cracked the nuts open with a stone, removed the kernels with her knife, and brought fruit and nut meat to the fire a hat full at a time, adding significantly to their meager breakfast meals. She again ignored the thanks of Judah and Barefoot and watched the horses munch late-growing grass in the chill air of early November while she ate her share of the morning's fare seated on her distant blanket.

They camped at first light on the sixth day north of Campbellsville beside a fast-flowing creek, intending to pass through the village after sunset that evening, and Brianna finally ended her silence. She addressed the astonished Judah in a no-nonsense voice brimming with authority. "I'm going upstream, treat myself to a bath, wash my clothes, and let them dry. I'd strongly suggest you two do the same before they smell you coming a mile from Campbellsville. If I see a face before I return, I'll shoot it."

With that piece of sage advice, Smite's daughter picked up her blanket and marched upstream out of sight. Judah was somewhat placated by the fact she had the wherewithal to take her revolver to her bath. And damn it to hell, he did stink like a sun-cured skunk. He stripped, walked into the stream, and washed the best he could with an empty cloth bag Barefoot thoughtfully tossed to him.

The water was cold and he didn't linger to wash his clothes. He had donned his shirt and was pulling on his jeans when the shot rang out upstream, the report indicating a rifle, not a Remington revolver, had been fired. He grabbed his Navy Colt, motioning for the alerted Barefoot to cross the creek and follow the far bank until they discovered the source of the shot.

He found her crouched in the creek with water up to her neck, staring at the opposite bank. Over there the body of a dead deer lay half-in and half-out of the creek, and standing on the lip of the far bank behind the downed buck were two young white boys no older than fourteen dressed in farm clothes and slouch hats. One boy was holding a flintlock rifle. They were returning Brianna's stare with lifted brows and gaping mouths.

Nice surprise, eh, boys, Judah thought. *You bag a deer*

and the Lord throws in a shockingly naked female taking her morning bath in the middle of nowhere.

The taller of the deer hunters fiddled with his flintlock, and Judah trained his Navy Colt on him and said in a voice loud enough to carry across the creek, "Gentlemen, if you'll look at me, you'll see that I'm armed and have you in my sights. Let's not do anything hasty and get someone hurt."

The boys' heads slowly turned in Judah's direction and they experienced their second shocking sighting of the morning, for a black-haired stranger was holding a pistol at the end of an outstretched arm that was indeed aimed squarely at them, and both boys had no doubts about his ability to kill with it at such close range.

Out of the corner of his eye, Judah saw Barefoot putting the sneak on the two deer hunters and thought, *And the Lord our God threw in a third fright for good measure.*

The oily click of Barefoot's Navy Colt cocking carried to Judah's ears. The boys' heads swiveled and they were now staring at a half-breed with a craggy face that showed no emotion whatsoever. Judah admired their courage. Most boys their age would have cast the flintlock aside and run. They had to be scared, but neither youngster was inclined to flee.

The taller lad slowly pushed his hands away from his body. He knelt on one knee, gently laid his flintlock rifle on the bank, and stood. Doing his best to grab the clouds far above him with those same hands, he said, "Me and Brady didn't mean her no harm. We tracked the buck here. We popped out of the trees and there she was."

"It ain't our fault she wasn't wearing nothing but the skin the Lord provided her," the shorter Brady chimed in.

A sputtering arose in the middle of the creek. "Well, are you fool men going to stand around like fence posts and watch a girl freeze to death or let her have the privacy you so rudely interrupted?"

Judah ignored her for the moment. In his thinking, how the balance of the day played out depended in large measure on the political loyalties of the deer hunters' father. As soon as they were out of Judah's sight, how likely was it the two lads would run to local authorities of perhaps the Union persuasion and report that two armed strangers—one a half-breed to boot—were hiding along the creek in their father's woods?

Judah solved his dilemma with a quick question. "You have a father or brother off toting a gun in the war?"

"Yes, sir," Brady said. "Our pa, our uncle, and our older brother."

"What color uniform are they wearing?"

"Gray, sir."

Judah lowered his revolver and said, "It's your deer, Rebs, but I'd surely love to roast meat off of it for breakfast."

"Seeing as how you're on the same side of the war as Pa," the relieved taller lad said, "I don't reckon he'd be upset were we to share with you."

In five minutes, Brianna Hardin had the privacy she desired, and in twenty minutes, deer loins were sizzling downstream on stout sticks propped over a fire with stones. To the astonishment of Jeremy and Brady Clawson, Asa Barefoot ate the deer's raw heart and liver, blood dripping from his fingers and chin. The horrified Clawsons' offspring politely declined Asa's offer to share what for him was a native delicacy. Judah chuckled and said, "It's an acquired taste. Never had a hankering for it myself."

"That's a handsome red stallion you're riding. Mr. Bell, if I ain't being too nosy," Jeremy Clawson said, "are you headed for the Confederate stronghold at Bowling Green?"

Judah decided these two youngsters could be trusted

and might have something to contribute regarding what awaited them farther south. "I'm hoping to meet up with Captain Morgan's Lexington Rifles."

"My pa mentioned Captain Morgan while he was home for a day a week ago," Jeremy Clawson offered. "Pa's in General Johnston's quartermaster corps. He was hunting for horses to buy for regimental officers."

"And what did he say about Captain Morgan?"

"He said Captain Morgan is acquiring horses and guns for his company with money from his own pocket. That's why Pa knew of him."

"Did he say where Morgan is located with any certainty?"

"I think it was Woodsville or Woodsonville. Whichever it was, it was somewhere around Glasgow."

That information heartened Judah. The odds were greater now that Granger Huddleston might be able to pinpoint Captain Morgan's exact location. They had so far successfully navigated miles of country without an incident that brought them gun barrel to gun barrel with a unit of the Union army or a county home guard. All the while, the future of Brianna Hardin was always foremost in Judah's mind no matter how much it frustrated him. He couldn't countenance abandoning her a second time, and he was even more desperate to find her a situation in which she would be comfortable and provided for.

The problem was he had not a single clue as to how he could bring that about. But come hell or high water, she wasn't accompanying Judah and Barefoot to Morgan's camp. This morning's fiasco over her wanting a bath was a clear warning as to the difficulties a strong-willed female could ignite traveling with just two friendly men aware of her sex and meaning her no harm. Magnifying those potential difficulties by taking her into a military encampment posing as a male was tantamount to lunacy, and there by damned, he would draw a line that wasn't to be crossed, period.

Judah, Barefoot, and the Clawson brothers feasted on venison until they were stuffed, and cooked extra for the road. After learning the Clawson home place was a half mile to the east of the creek, Judah had the brothers tie the gutted deer carcass on Barefoot's mare, and with the boys riding double on Brianna's bay gelding, they forded the creek well below her bathing site, wound through a shallow stand of trees, and then crossed fallow fields to the family barnyard. The Clawson mother and the brothers lavished Judah with profuse thanks.

Upon Judah's return to their camp, Brianna was eating venison and drinking the last of their coffee. Her clothes and hair were damp. Barefoot was nowhere to be seen. Judah knew the light-sleeping half-breed would be stationed near the road they were traveling, and the slightest hint of activity on or near that hard-packed surface would awaken him instantly.

Brianna finished her coffee, peered at Judah, and said, "I suppose those two boys had fun describing what they saw when they surprised me."

Unable to resist an opportunity to goad her, Judah dismounted and said casually over his shoulder, "They didn't mention you again. Maybe nothing about you was worth remembering once their surprise wore off."

Fortunately for Judah, the empty coffeepot missed her target—the back of his head—and struck his shoulder a glancing blow. "You must sleep with the devil, Judah Bell," Brianna swore. "No one else can stand your company."

He turned around and she was stomping toward her blanket. She flopped down and pulled the blanket over her, hiding her face from him.

Judah stood rubbing his shoulder, a tad ashamed of

himself, but the prospect of another quiet, restful day quickly assuaged the smidgen of guilt.

There were eight of them by the shivering Judah's count. The air of the dark night was sharp and biting, and Judah's ears and fingers felt numb. Seven members of the Yankee detail were standing about a fire in the center of the small meadow, eating on their feet. The eighth was guarding the quartermaster wagon parked closer to the crossroads flanking the fire. Bunched horses grazed at the wagon's tailgate. Enfield rifles stood in two stacks beside the wagon's front wheel, facing the fire.

Barefoot had smelled meat cooking short of a bend in the road, and they had left Brianna with their mounts, short-cut through the bulging woods, and discovered the detail enjoying a late evening repast. After a long gander, Asa whispered, "Might be best to leave them alone."

"We would except for those overcoats they're wearing. They're the wrong color, but they would serve a man well on cold nights like this, blue wool being as warm as gray."

"Seems risky to chance a life over a warm coat."

"Let's pull back and talk a while."

Judah was pleased Brianna had held fast and kept the horses quiet. Reins in hand, they knelt by the berm of the road. "We're bound southwest for Greensburg. By the direction that Yankee supply wagon is pointing, my guess is they're bound southeast with supplies for the blue-belly encampment at Columbia the Clawson boys told me about, the one I read about in the Lexington papers back home."

Warming a cold ear with a vigorous tug of his fingers, Judah continued, "We'll wait until they've bedded down. Asa, you'll put the sneak on that sentry. Once he's out of the commission, we'll hide their Enfields in the woods and draw down on those sleeping around the fire. We'll pick out the coats we want and throw a shovel full of coals into their supply wagon to give the Yankees something to worry about besides us."

"And what am I to do, wait her here like a good little girl that can't be trusted?" Brianna inquired with a touch of sarcasm.

"You be ready when I yell for you to bring up our horses. Ride around behind the Yankees, their supply wagon, and the horses grazing behind it. When I yell 'Now,' fire a couple of shots to scare their horses out onto the road, and then look for us. We'll be coming to you in a hurry."

Judah considered his strategy dangerous, but workable. The key elements were Asa Barefoot's stalking skills and the disarming of the Yankees. Barefoot had expressed no serious objections to his plan and would follow orders. Judah was acutely aware of how much he was asking from a seventeen-year-old girl. But she could handle a revolver and was mature for her age. She had seen her father and brothers shot dead, had no fear of the sound of gunfire, and bore an abiding hatred for anybody wearing blue. Lastly, if Asa Barefoot had any reservations about her in tight spots, he would have made them known long ago.

Judah fought the excitement welling inside him. He was risking three lives, and too much nervous enthusiasm could cloud his thinking and squander the element of surprise and decisive action their ambush required. One slip could prove deadly.

The five-hour wait for the Yankee camp to retire and settle into their blankets seemed to stretch a length of time equal to one running from Judah's birth through each event of his life until he signaled Barefoot to put the sneak on the head-drooping sentry. There was no moon and the quiet reigned except for Yankee snores and the sigh of a light wind. A shadow flitted across the empty shafts of the supply wagon. The sentry's head snapped backward and his body disappeared behind the bed of the wagon. He was bound and gagged before he could recover his senses.

Moving with great care so as not to alert the sleeping enemy, in a span of five minutes Judah and Barefoot hid the stacked Yankee rifles at the edge of the woods, behind a deadfall overgrown by vines. Judah doubted the Yankees would find them in anything less than full daylight.

At that late juncture, Judah realized the darkness was no longer an advantage to them. He needed light to insure the awakened Yankees could clearly see him and Asa. Judah wanted them to comprehend that they had been taken prisoner and follow his orders, and Brianna needed enough illumination to ride around the supply wagon and run off the Yankee horses.

Surprisingly, the delay didn't fray Judah's nerves or strain his patience. The embers of the Yankee fire were still glowing with heat, and Judah helped himself to the plentiful supply of dry wood gathered earlier by the blue-bellies and calmly stoked up a blazing fire while Barefoot kept a close eye on the soon-to-be-startled enemy.

Satisfied with the height and intensity of the flames, Judah positioned himself on the opposite side of the fire from Barefoot, drew his Navy Colt, sucked in a deep breath, and fired off a round. Two of the Yankees erupted from their blankets like goosed rabbits while most of the others came up on an elbow, curious about what had disrupted their sleep. At Judah's nod, Barefoot fired into the roaring blaze and the last sleep-sated Yankee surrendered his dreams.

"Freeze where you are, if you want to live," Judah commanded, his tone brutally harsh and threatening.

One of the upright Yankees thrust a hand inside the overcoat he'd worn to bed. Without hesitation, Judah put a bullet in the left leg. The sound of yet another gunshot and the sight of a fellow trooper collapsing with a yowl of pain drained the will of the remaining Yankees before they could muster the courage to resist, and they froze to the man as Judah wished.

"Gentlemen, listen up. We've disabled your sentry and hidden your rifles. We intend to fire your supply wagon and run off your horses. But first, we want some of those blue overcoats. That's all we want from you. Understood?"

Before Judah could shush him, an obviously hot-blooded Yankee wearing nothing but trap door long johns muttered, "Jesus jump, he shot a man for a coat."

Judah promised to kill the next man to say a word, surveyed the staring Yankees, chose one roughly his size, and pointed at him with his free hand. "Real slow now, crawl over here with your coat."

Judah accepted the coat, and, trusting Barefoot's covering revolver would discourage any rash moves by the Yankees, slipped it on over his jeans jacket. "Your turn, Asa."

Once Barefoot was outfitted in warm blue wool, Judah picked a third Yankee the size of Brianna and took possession of his coat in like fashion. He draped the coat over his arm and said, "Pick a Yankee, Asa, and have him shovel some hot coals into the bed of that wagon behind you."

The Yankees grumbled but watched helplessly as Judah's orders were carried out. Not really caring if the wagonload of supplies ever actually caught fire, Judah yelled, "Bring up the horses," at the top of his lungs.

Brianna Hardin had to have been fully alert and ready to come forward, for she appeared on horseback faster than the snap of a finger, leading Jasper and Barefoot's mare. She swept past the tail end of the supply wagon, paying no attention to the status of those circling the fire. Three shots rang out and neighing horses bolted for the crossroads. They could soon be heard pounding down the southeast pike connecting with Columbia. A thankful Judah grudgingly conceded that Barefoot was right about one thing: Brianna could follow orders when she wanted to.

When Brianna emerged from the dark night the second time, she came from behind Judah. Barefoot circled the fire and joined them. Judah handed up Brianna's new overcoat, and with his Navy Colt still trained on the Yankees, mounted Jasper.

Barefoot jumped aboard his mare, and Judah, smiling at the Yankees, said, "Gentlemen, your hospitality and generosity are much appreciated. We bid you good evening."

Judah turned Jasper, spurred him into a gallop, and the overcoat thieves raced for the southwest road leading to Greensburg. Judah heard the faint bark of a revolver, but after a quick glance to his rear confirmed that neither Barefoot nor Brianna had been hit, he dismissed it as an errant shot.

Daylight would render a different conclusion.

CHAPTER 10

They rode through the night, Judah alternating gaits between bursts at a gallop and a mile-eating trot, outrunning any possible pursuit by boiling-mad Yankees lucky enough to find their rifles and corral some of their loose horses. Thinking back, he reckoned he was mistaken in not throwing the blue-belly rifles on his fire. In the future, given the choice, he wouldn't allow the enemy any opportunity to re-arm.

Just before dawn, he sought a secluded campsite with graze and water. They were, by his estimation, two nights' travel from Glasgow. He passed over a couple of potential sites until they came upon a scalloped dip in the road containing a shallow creek knee-deep on Jasper and overhung with trees. He turned Jasper up the middle of the creek, advanced a hundred and fifty yards, encountered a cut bank high enough to shield an early morning fire, and just beyond that an open glade on the opposite bank with sufficient grass for their three horses.

Defying custom, Brianna Hardin left the unsaddling to her male companions and sought a level stretch of ground under the cut bank for her blanket. Judah thought she was simply tuckered out from the excitement of the Yankee ambush and a hard night in the saddle until Barefoot sidled over next to him. "She's hurt and doesn't want to tell you."

"What do you mean hurt?"

"Bullet wound in the left arm. I saw her flinch and grab her elbow at the same time we heard that shot back at that Yankee camp."

Suddenly angry with Barefoot, Judah snapped, "Why didn't you tell me earlier?"

"I got her attention and she waved me off. I figured as long as she could stay on her horse, it was none of my business. She's not easy to argue with, Master Judah."

His temper cooling, Judah sighed and said, "No problem. I've no cause to question your judgment. But we need a look at that wound."

"It's yours to try. I've been scratched enough times by women already."

Judah didn't refute Barefoot's contention, but if the rumors concerning the half-breed's fondness for females and theirs for him were true, those scratch marks were most likely located on his backside or his shoulders.

"Wish me luck."

Barefoot flashed his orneriest smile. "Prayer might hold you better stead."

Brianna, of course, saw him walking in her direction. Her freckled features were smooth and somber as polished stone, and her mouth a straight line. Her eyes were clear, showing none of the redness associated with the shedding of tears. She did nothing to welcome his intrusion on her morning rest.

Boxed in, Judah took the direct approach. "If you've been hit by a bullet, I want to examine the wound. You can disrobe and show me where you're hurt, or I'll remove your clothes for you. Either way makes no difference to me."

"I bet you've ripped the clothes off a girl before, haven't you?"

Patience fading rapidly, Judah countered, "No, lest my memory is failing me that was always done willingly by the gal I was with."

With a disgusted snort, Brianna Hardin sat upright and removed her four-button coat, having shed her Union over-coat before retiring to her blanket. Dried blood covered the left arm of her cotton shirt from near the shoulder to below the elbow.

Judah was trying to concentrate on her wound, but he was surprised how well her baggy cotton coat and shirt had hidden female attributes of admirable proportions. The breast beneath the oversized shirt wasn't overly large. Yet it was shapely and the nipple sharply pointed.

The very mystery of her heightened her physical appeal. This was the closest he'd been to her since the shooting in Dayton Ferrell's barn, and he hadn't noticed her smell then. It was a combination of peach and apple blossoms, a scent he found both intriguing and enticing. He suspected she had enhanced the fragrance somehow after her bath, for she had more secrets for a plainly dressed female with mere pockets than a witch of the moors with a fancy wagon.

Delicacy was too time consuming for Judah. He grasped the seam connecting the shirt and sleeve, and, with a hard yank, he separated the sleeve and pulled it free over her wrist in one piece, hearing of her sharp gasp of pain.

His examination produced additional gasps of pain, but he was able to determine that the Yankee bullet had plowed a furrow in the flesh on the outer portion of her arm be-tween the shoulder and elbow, missing both bone and artery. The bleeding had stopped some time ago. She was one lucky young woman. An open wound meant no frag-ments of the bullet or tiny pieces of her shirt were lurk-ing beneath the skin, giving her an excellent chance of avoiding the suppuration and proud flesh that had killed so many of Temple Bell's fellow soldiers in the Mexican War.

Still, what had to be done for her wasn't pretty and was damn painful. "Give me your other arm," Judah ordered.

Brianna's mouth opened, but on second thought, she held her tongue and allowed Judah to help himself to her other shirtsleeve. She watched him tear the empty sleeve in half, then tear one part into strips and wet the other in the creek. From the creek, he proceeded to Barefoot's hastily built fire, waited until flame was licking away at dry wood, secured a long knife from Barefoot, and stuck the blade in the heart of the blaze.

Brianna shuddered. Though she couldn't remember the precise word for the cauterization of flesh, she had witnessed the application of hot steel to an open wound as a child and had never forgotten the sickly burning smell it produced. She ground her teeth together. She would not resort to screams and tears no matter what. While she had suffered from the asinine attitudes and prejudices of her heritage regarding women, she'd never surrendered the pride the Hardin clan took in their personal courage and toughness.

A grim but purposeful Judah passed the heated knife to Barefoot. The half-breed inserted the blade in the fire again and Judah returned to her blanket. He handed her a stick and said, "Clamp down on this with your teeth. It will keep you from biting your tongue."

Then everything occurred in a flurry of quick movement. Judah washed her wound the best he could and wasn't concerned that he induced fresh bleeding. He called for Barefoot and the half-breed hustled over from the fire. Judah straightened her arm, exposing her wound, and Barefoot applied the hot blade.

The pain overwhelmed her. She tasted the woody tang of the stick as her body stiffened trying to ward off the hurt. A red film covered her eyes, she screamed inside her head, and a black cocoon of nothingness blinded her. She gladly let it take control of her senses and floated into a dark void where she was safe from further harm.

They entered Glasgow after a short morning ride two days later. Judah felt it wise to confirm which national flag was flying within the city before revealing their political leanings, so they wrapped their Yankee overcoats in their blankets well short of the city's outskirts. Glasgow boasted of whiskey distilleries, wagon factories, shoemaking and tailor shops, grocery and dry goods merchants, and an apothecary. A ladies millinery sat adjacent to a two-story dwelling advertising rooms for rent by the day, week, and month, and there was a combination barbershop and public wash house, gunsmith shop, and large tobacco warehouse, welcoming them to a thriving city unscathed to date by the war. Judah breathed a tad easier when he sighted no flags displaying the Union's star and stripes. So far, Elam Huddleston's observations had panned out.

They turned onto Main North Cross Street and their destination was visible from three blocks away. The upper story of a gristmill dominated the skyline, painted green with tall white letters reading HUDDLESTON'S MILL & STORE, and in smaller letters, GRANGER HUDDLESTON, PROPRIETOR. The street was busy with wagon, horseback, and foot traffic. Jasper seemed to draw less attention here than in the Bluegrass horse country of northern Kentucky, which didn't displease Judah. He was hoping for a quiet visit with no complications involving horse thieves, firearms, and bloodshed.

Huddleston's Mill was a conglomeration of discordant noise. Millstones ground grain into meal, saws cut lumber, and smithy hammers pounded and shaped red hot metal. The anchor building was a general store, marketing everything from bagged cornmeal to window frames and window glass to wooden scarecrows.

While Mayor Granger Huddleston had his brother's dust-colored eyes, his cheeks and jowls were clean-shaven rather than full bearded. He was built string-bean thin like Elam, but his round, protruding belly made him appear pregnant. As Judah anticipated, Mayor Huddleston shared his brother's brusque penchant for getting down to business straightaway.

"Who might you be, young man, and what is it you want from me?"

"I'm Judah Bell from Scott County. Your brother, Elam, advised me to seek you out as to where I might find Captain John Hunt Morgan and his men."

Elam Huddleston's brother studied Judah with a harsh stare until he started to squirm in his boots. Judah didn't avert his gaze and give Granger cause to suspect he might be lying. He understood Granger's caution. Snap judgments regarding strangers in wartime often led to unwanted grief.

A contrite grin revealed Granger Huddleston's stained wooden dentures. "Excuse me for staring. I've grown too touchy dealing with strangers lately. I'll allow my brother has never dispatched an enemy to my door, and that includes your companions."

The customer counter was at the front of the general store, affording the proprietor a view of North Main Cross Street through plate glass windows bracketing that entryway. Asa Barefoot was standing at the head of his mare with his face impassive and seeming to lack any interest in his immediate surroundings. Brianna Hardin was lounging in the saddle, watching the comings and goings of local folks out and about conducting their personal affairs, which frequently brought them into Granger Huddleston's domain.

Farther down the counter, an elderly, grizzled clerk, wearing a cloth apron and leather garters on his sleeves, was totaling purchases and taking payment or crediting accounts. "Old Mitch can handle things for a while," Granger Huddleston said. "He's a hard man to cheat. Come along to my office where we can talk in private."

The hardware office had a window overlooking a gated storage yard surrounded by the sawmill, gristmill, and the smithy. Judah spied a green-painted barn with a fenced paddock containing six draft horses to the south of the blacksmith shop. Granger Huddleston's enterprises made a piker of his brother.

Taking a chair behind a desk on which ledgers and paper documents were organized in neat stacks, Granger Huddleston pointed to a leather-covered chair beneath the office window. "Have a seat, Mr. Judah Bell. That coffee on the stove should still be hot if you care to indulge before we conduct our business."

Judah poured coffee from the enamelware pot atop the small potbellied stove into a clay-fired mug and seated himself. The coffee wasn't piping hot, but that didn't distract from its rich deep flavor. It was the best coffee Judah had ever tasted.

Leaning back in his chair, Granger Huddleston said, "I apologize beforehand, but I'd like to learn a little about you, Mr. Bell, before I supply you with the information you're seeking. I'm extra particular about the armed men I send to Captain Morgan."

Judah had no objection, and in short, terse sentences, he identified his uncle, described the circumstances of Temple Bell's death at the hands of abolitionist Yankees, and related how his wish to join Captain Morgan's Confederate company had brought him to Glasgow. He made no mention of having met Smite Hardin and the Douglas cousins along the way or the night raid on the Yankee detail outside Campbellsville out of a concern they might raise a multitude of unnecessary questions.

A nodding Granger Huddleston then asked, "Your companions? Who might they be?"

Identifying Asa for a pro-slavery Confederate was no problem. "The half-breed belonged to my uncle. He serves me now."

Curiosity lifting his brow, Huddleston inquired, "And the boy that's old enough to tote a pistol?"

Judah sipped his coffee. Brianna Hardin needed shelter in Glasgow and a means of providing for herself, and after exhausting his feeble brain for days, a solution dawned on him that had been right there in front of him all the while and would be as easy to implement as picking a boll of cotton. He would simply pay for her keep, and he had the means to do that in his wallet.

"The boy's name is Ben Hardin. His mother's gone and he lost his father and two brothers in a skirmish above Nicholasville. He has no living blood relatives, and there was no one handy to take him in, so Barefoot and I let him travel with us. Problem I have is he was wounded in the arm while we were eluding a Yankee patrol two nights ago. He needs a place to mend and rest up. Do you know who runs that boardinghouse next to the ladies millinery on Main Street?"

Granger Huddleston straightened in his chair. "Yes, I certainly do, my missus operates both the boardinghouse and the millinery, and she has rooms available. I must warn you, though, she won't take anyone unless they can pay in advance."

Judah returned Huddleston's broad smile. The sole thing better than a boardinghouse for his purposes was a boardinghouse governed by a female. Though he had yet to meet her, he couldn't imagine the missus of Glasgow's mayor and wealthiest citizen taking any guff or sass from her boarders.

"Money won't be a problem," Judah assured Huddleston. "I'll gladly pay a month in advance, more if your wife prefers."

"I'll let you make the financial arrangements for Ben Hardin with Maud. She keeps her own ledgers."

"You may also be able to help me in regard to the bay gelding Ben's riding. He belongs to me, and if you have a stall free, and you're agreeable, I'll hire you to grain and graze him and store Ben's saddle and gear. Once Ben's on the mend, he can muck out the bay's stall and ride him occasionally so he won't go soft on us."

"I'll board your gelding for ten dollars a month, Mr. Bell. Maud keeps a riding horse in the barn with my freight teams, and maybe she and Ben could ride together on Sundays. That were to happen, I'd worry less about Maud venturing outside Glasgow on her own. Maud can be somewhat muleheaded and keeps her own counsel whenever the whim hits her."

Jacob couldn't keep from thinking, *Just like Brianna Hardin.*

Granger Huddleston's mercenary smile vanished, and he propped his elbows on his desk. "Now, Mr. Bell, let me tell you where Captain Morgan's company is camped."

Granger Huddleston's directions were straightforward and foolproof. Captain John Hunt Morgan and his company were a fifteen-mile ride away at Bell's Tavern in a small hamlet named Three Corners where three county roads came together. To ensure Judah was well received by Captain Morgan or another officer in his absence, Huddleston offered, and Judah accepted, a short letter of introduction. Pocketing the letter, Judah thanked the mill owner and paid him a month's boarding fee for the bay gelding.

"We'll leave the bay with you now. I'll settle up for Ben with your wife as you suggested. I want to reach Morgan's camp before dark."

"Cairo will take the bay to the barn," Huddleston said, standing and offering Judah his hand. "And don't worry, you'll find your horse and the young boy as you've left them when you return."

Judah exited the hardware store aware the toughest task of the day awaited him. He was hoping Brianna would decide without making a huge fuss that the arrangement he had made for her was best for the time being for all concerned parties. He was treading on thin ice, but hope was all he could do, short of tying her to a bedpost at Maud Huddleston's boardinghouse.

Her attention was riveted on him the second he stepped out onto the plank sidewalk of the store, and she wasn't a bit hesitant in asking, "Well, did you find out where your esteemed Captain Morgan can be found? You were in there long enough to get directions to the moon."

Judah gave her the hardest no-nonsense stare he could muster and said, "Get down."

Brianna frowned at his harsh tone. She dismounted, wondering what was in store for her, and a little panicked by the thought her glib tongue might have finally exhausted his patience with her. She'd learned in the days she'd spent with Judah Bell that he was first and foremost a man who stuck to what he was about and didn't welcome or condone distractions. She wished now she'd been less of a bother to him.

She had no hold on him. He could walk away and there was nothing she could do to stop him, and she had no one else in the whole world to turn to. She took some consolation in the fact he hadn't abandoned her to the disgusting touch of her uncle and her half-crazed first cousin. She couldn't bring herself to believe he would stoop that low again. She crossed her fingers and mouthed a silent prayer in which she vowed she would harness her temper and for once think like an adult female instead of an immature girl shaking inside with fright and trusting no one.

As Judah mounted Jasper, a bald black man with snow-white sideburns dressed in denim coveralls approached him. "Give Cairo your reins, Ben," Judah said, freeing a stirrup, "and climb up behind me. Asa, why don't you water and hay your mare and the bay while I tend to business down the street?"

Judah Bell didn't consider himself a coward. In this instance, however, he was glad Brianna was seated behind him. He wouldn't have to watch her reaction to what he was about to say. "I have something important to tell you, so listen up. One word from you and you'll find yourself alone in the middle of the street. Understand me?"

She wrapped her good arm around his waist, snuggled against his backside, and he felt the heat of her breath on his ear. "Yes, sir, you won't hear a peep out of me."

"I've arranged a room for you at Maud Huddleston's boardinghouse. I want you to rest there and let that arm heal. I will pay your room and board and provide you money for decent clothing. I don't know how long I'll be gone. I intend to offer my services to Captain Morgan as a scout. That should give me some leeway about coming back to check on you."

He felt her shudder through his jacket. She was silent for three whole blocks. Judah was pleased that she wasn't crying or objecting to staying in Glasgow for a while. He knew it was a relief for her to learn he wasn't abandoning her altogether.

When she spoke, her voice was steady and respectful.
"Can I talk now?"

"Yes, you can, but don't try to change my mind."

"Did you sell the bay gelding and his saddle?"

"No, I paid his board for a month. He'll be available for
you to ride as long as you don't light out after me.
Huddleston will expect you to help muck out his stall once
your arm permits that."

Brianna's sigh equaled a sharp gust of wind on the back
of Judah's neck. He had no difficulty reading her mind. If
he hadn't sold her horse and saddle, the odds were even
greater that he was really serious about keeping in touch
with her. She faced an uncertain, unsettled future, the same
as he did, but for now she had enough anchorage for a few
weeks to keep her spirits from failing her completely.

He wouldn't have her hurt again by people taking advantage of her if that were at all possible. He didn't think
he was in love with her, but that didn't mean she hadn't
wormed her way into his heart a hefty distance. Leaving
her behind wouldn't be as easy for him as he'd expected.

A willowy, sweet-smiled black female of an indetermi-
nate age greeted them at the door of Maud Huddleston's
boardinghouse and led them to a large kitchen in the rear
of the two-story building. Dressed in a green dress and
yellow apron, Maud Huddleston was flattening strings of
egg and flour noodles with a rolling pin on a table covered
with old newspapers. Judah wasn't sure how he had expected her to look, and his surprise was genuine. Maybe
Maud's sturdy hips and shoulders, muscular arms, brown
hair tied in a tight bun, tawny eyes, blunt nose, firm jaw,
and full lips didn't make her a pretty woman, but they
surely made her appear to be one that could hold her own
in any dispute. He had no trouble believing Granger

Huddleston's remark that his wife kept her own counsel whenever the whim struck her.

Maud Huddleston's smile was so incredibly warm Judah thought she became a different person the minute she engaged people socially. "And how may I help you two young people?"

"I'm Judah Bell, and this is Ben Hardin. Your mister said you have a room available and Ben needs a place to stay. He took a Yankee's bullet in the arm two days ago. I'd like to give his wound a chance to heal where he can get plenty of rest and eat well. Cold ground and meager rations don't have much appeal when you're hurting."

Maud laid her rolling pin aside and wiped her hands on her apron. "I trust Mr. Huddleston told you I require payment in advance."

"Yes, ma'am, he did. I'm prepared to pay you for a full month for starters . . . in gold coin."

Apparently satisfied with his proposal, Maud Huddleston smiled brightly and nodded at the ageless black lady waiting patiently at the door of the kitchen. "Amanda here will show your Mr. Hardin the room I have available. I don't accept payment until the boarder says he's satisfied with his room. Go along with Amanda, Mr. Hardin. I have a few questions for Mr. Bell while we're waiting. Please close the door after you, Amanda."

Judah swore Maud Huddleston's hasty retrieval of the rolling pin matched the click of the latch on the door. He could also testify that the sudden fire smoldering in her tawny eyes was as foreboding as the muzzle of Dayton Ferrell's shotgun. Maud Huddleston tapped the palm of her free hand with the wooden rolling pin, an instrument looking sturdier to Judah with each passing second, and said, "I don't have much use for a man that lies, young or old, Mr. Bell. What do you mean bringing a girl dressed like a boy into a boardinghouse with a sign at the door that reads 'Only Male Boarders Taken'?"

Judah was taken aback by how quickly Maud had seen through their ruse. At the same time, he was disgusted with himself. Hadn't watching his Ohio sisters and his female cousins in Kentucky taught him that disguises never fool a woman? One female always recognized another female no matter the circumstances. It was like they were born with an extra sense denied men on purpose.

He stood staring stupidly at his accuser while searching for the right thing to say so as not to further muddy the water. He cleared his throat, swallowed hard, and said, "I apologize for trying to deceive you, Mrs. Huddleston. I'm desperate for a place where Brianna will be safe while I seek out Captain Morgan and his men at Three Forks. Her parents are both dead and she has no living kin that can be trusted to care for her. She showed up at our camp one night and has been in the company of a Cherokee half-breed named Asa Barefoot and me ever since. Believe you me, ma'am, finding a proper home for a wayward girl is quite a challenge for a single man headed off to fight in a war."

The fire in Maud Huddleston's green eyes banked a little. "Regardless of your intentions toward Brianna, and I'm not questioning them, her traveling with you and a half-breed isn't proper and fitting for a young, upstanding girl. She's already suffered a gunshot wound. The girl is trustworthy and decent in her behavior and manners, is she not? I won't have her under my roof unless you can honestly vouch for her. Well, can you?"

Thankful for that small concession, Judah said, "I can vouch for her."

"Will she work for part of her keep?"

"Yes, and she's quite resourceful," Judah assured Maud Huddleston.

"I'm happy to hear that. Amanda and I are at the age where an extra set of hands and a backside that doesn't hurt would be most welcome. In return for her help, I'll halve her room and board, if that's agreeable to her."

Judah relaxed a tad more after Granger Huddleston's missus laid the rolling pin on the table. "There will be rules she must follow, Mr. Bell, and you will explain them to her so we have no misunderstandings. I'll not have my name besmirched and the excellent reputation of my boardinghouse tarnished by inappropriate conduct. First of all, she will wear a dress. She may keep her revolver if she wishes. But we'll store it in my safe. Any monies you provide her will be locked away with the revolver. She may have access to the revolver and her money at anytime. I will clear a room on the first floor next to my quarters for her. If she can do sums, she can assist Tillie Jean in the millinery shop on Saturdays. She's not to be in the boarding rooms to clean or change bedding unless accompanied by Amanda or myself. She will dine with the boarders and me each evening. I assure you I will not work her to death and she will be treated well."

Hearing footfalls on the hallway steps, Maud Huddleston asked, "Is there anything else I should know about her for now?"

"Your husband is boarding the bay gelding I bought her and storing his saddle. Once Brianna's arm heals, I would like for her to ride him occasionally. Your husband suggested she might ride with you when that's possible."

Maud Huddleston chuckled deep in her throat. "Yes, and I bet my dear Granger liked the idea of her toting that revolver along seeing as how I can't abide firearms."

Brianna appeared in the kitchen doorway. "Miss Brianna Hardin, your Mr. Bell and I have been discussing an arrangement that would benefit the both of us. If you'll accompany him to the parlor, he will explain everything to you, and you can say yes or no. Go along the both of you," Maud Huddleston said, making a shooing motion with her hand. "My noodles are calling me."

Judah hadn't missed the fleeting expression of terror that widened Brianna's eyes when Maud Huddleston spoke her true name, for she, too, had seen the ONLY MALE BOARDERS TAKEN sign beside the front door of the boardinghouse. He walked her quickly down the hallway to Maud Huddleston's formal parlor with its overstuffed horsehair furniture, knitted doilies, lamps with globes made of blue-green glass, and corner shelves displaying ceramic oriental figurines with slanted eyes wearing brocaded robes.

They took seats on a four-person sofa with a polished oak frame and curved armrests. He repeated the financial terms and what would be demanded of her if she opted to work for Maud Huddleston. As he spelled everything out, her interest mounted steadily and full-fledged excitement livened her face. She had no objection to the rules governing her behavior. Instead, she surprised him by saying, "For once, I'd have a chance to dress and act like a real lady. I'd love that. Maybe I could make Mama proud of me, and Mr. Bell, I'd finally have my own room."

A delighted Judah made a mental pledge to Grandmother Nadine Bell that so long as his heart was beating, he would never again neglect his nightly prayers. There had to be a God watching out for him from somewhere for them to stumble upon the likes of Granger and Maud Huddleston on the same day. Good old plain luck had most certainly finished a distant second this turn of the wheel.

Trepidation creeping into her voice, Brianna asked,

"But can you afford all of this, including my new clothes? That's an awful lot of money."

Judah pulled his leather wallet from his coat pocket. "I've got two hundred dollars' worth of twenty-dollar gold pieces here. That will last you a year, if necessary. Store the money in Maud Huddleston's safe. You can trust her. She won't steal from you. Don't tell anyone how much you have and only take out the coins you need whenever you want to shop for yourself or pay room and board for you and that bay horse."

Brianna was flabbergasted. The wallet contained more hard money than she had ever seen with her own eyes in her whole life. "You know I'll never be able to pay you back, not even if you gave me a hundred years."

"You don't owe me a thin dime. If you hadn't yelled at your father, he would've killed me in Dayton Farrell's barn. And besides, I'd rather you have Uncle's money than have some stinking Yankee steal it off my body."

The joy drained from Brianna's face. In her excitement over a future with people she could trust who would treat her with respect and reward her efforts with something other than a blow or a kick, she'd momentarily forgotten that he was bound for places where men murdered the enemy every day with the fervor of maddened dogs. She bowed her head and pinched the bridge of her nose, not wanting to cry in front of him. Fessing up the necessary courage to keep her eyes dry, she lifted her chin and said, "I'll miss you."

With that simple admission, she rose from the couch. She feared her emotions could still betray her if they lingered any longer. She wanted him to remember her as a strong young woman in control of herself, not a tearful female afraid of going it alone. And she didn't want any sentimental gibberish from him offered up out of sympathy for her that he didn't truly mean. Much as it tore at her very being, any future relationship they might enjoy together had to wait until the war ran its course. Even that remote possibility depended upon his surviving the fight.

"You must be going. Mr. Barefoot is waiting for you and I need to let Mrs. Huddleston know I'm staying. There's nothing more you can do for me. I can never thank you enough for what you've already done."

Judah realized she was giving him an easy, non-committal way out of the parlor and the rest of her life if that's what he wanted. He wasn't sure if he could find the right words to express how he felt about her. He knew he had to see her again. Whatever they felt for each other must not end here.

Lacking words, he stood, pulled her to him, tilted her head, and kissed her hard on the mouth. She made no attempt to resist him. She seemed to melt against him, her good arm encircling his neck. The sweet taste of her was a lure that roused every part of him. She held secrets he could spend a lifetime uncovering and always be left wondering how the magic of her charm never flagged.

Dangerously close to ripping off her clothes, he broke off the kiss, gently removed her arm from about his neck, and said, "Don't worry. I'll be back for more."

Promise made, he turned and walked from the parlor.

CHAPTER 11

Judah and Barefoot trotted north through the Barrens, rolling brown grassland dotted with small copses of oak, hickory, walnut, ash, and sugar maple. While the tobacco fields of small farms now covered the open ground sweeping away to the horizon, Judah could imagine the herds of buffalo that grazed there in Kentucky's earliest years when red men had resisted white intruders. Tales of the frontier Indian wars had ignited Judah's imagination, and the excitement of them was renewed and magnified by the knowledge that he faced the same dangers the white settlers had. It made no difference that the gun bearer possibly waiting to ambush him around the next bend in the trail was white-skinned instead of red.

In the absence of significant rainfall in recent weeks, the wagon road provided solid footing for their horses. By mid-afternoon, Judah figured they had covered approximately twelve of the fifteen miles to Bell's Tavern. The closer they drew to their destination the greater the chance they would encounter Captain Morgan's sentries.

Despite his watchfulness, he was taken by surprise by the shout from trees bordering the roadbed just beyond the creek where they'd dismounted on the near bank to water their horses. "Hands up or you're dead men."

Another voice off to their right said, "Audie don't tell lies, friends."

Judah had expected a more formal military greeting from Captain Morgan's sentries on the order of "Halt and be recognized," but the makeshift challenge had captured his complete attention.

Two bewhiskered, armed, fully grown young white men slid from the thick woods. They wore red-sleeved jackets, faded cotton shirts, blue denim trousers, boots with naked spurs, and nondescript slouch hats. Judging by their clothing, they could have been State Guards, Home Guards, Morgan cavalrymen, or Yankee irregulars. What set them apart were their weapons. Though he had inspected but one or two of them at a Lexington gun shop, Judah pegged them to be Enfield percussion rifles with a feature new to him, sawed-off barrels, an adjustment to the original weapon that created makeshift shotguns deadly at close range for himself and Barefoot.

"Son, me and Audie got the edge on you. We'll have that pistol of yours and your horses. You don't mind, do you?"

Judah assumed both men were sentries given the proximity of Captain Morgan's camp. Standing on Jasper's left flank, he was fully exposed to the sentry who had spoken first. Barefoot was between the red stallion and his mare, partially shielding him from the view of both sentries. Judah thought, *They should have challenged us before we stepped down.*

The gazes of both sentries were locked on him, a second mistake. They had dismissed Barefoot as a harmless old half-breed traveling with his white master, leaving Judah with an ace up his sleeve if things started tasting too sour. Hands raised level with his shoulders, Judah said, "Gentlemen, I'm seeking Captain Morgan. I'm planning to join his forces. I have a letter of recommendation from an associate of his in Glasgow."

Both sentries froze like statues, considering this new wrinkle, their hesitation confirming their identity to Judah. If Judah were telling the truth, they couldn't risk riling Captain Morgan, but neither could they fail to do their duty. "We'll take you to Peterson," the sentry on the left said. "He can read your letter, if he wants to. Now, lift your pistol free with three fingers and hand it over butt first. I'll keep him covered, Wade."

The sentry on the right waded the shin-deep stream and Judah relinquished his Navy Colt. The sentries did not ask if Barefoot was armed and made no attempt to search him, which made Judah more inclined to follow their orders. Barefoot and he weren't defenseless yet.

While Audie kept his Enfield shotgun centered on Judah's belly hole, Wade fetched the sentries' horses, two geldings drawn up from much hard use—evidence Captain Morgan's men were in the field harassing the Yankees as much as available riding stock and ammunition allowed. Judah stayed alert and poised for action during their ride to Bell's Tavern, fully aware their well-bred and relatively fresh horses, particularly Jasper, could be tempting to Audie and Wade if they had nothing against murder and thievery. Who would find fault with two sentries for having killed strange riders defying their challenge?

Except for Bell's Tavern, Three Forks was a crossroads hamlet composed of a few clapboard houses and their out-door privies, a general store, a blacksmith shop, and a single, slat-sided tobacco barn. Bell's was a rambling, ram-shackle one-story log and wood structure that had been expanded five times with the addition of various-size rooms until it covered an exceptionally large area beside the turnpike. Half a dozen horses were tied in front of the

Tavern's westernmost section. The sentry on duty there toted an Enfield shotgun matching those of Audie and Wade.

Audie led Judah and Barefoot the length of the tavern into an adjoining field where unfinished stonewalls rose higher than Jasper's ears. Four rectangular wings branched from the square core of whatever was under construction. The tents of Captain Morgan's three hundred cavalrymen surrounded the unfinished building. Smoke rising from within the interior of the walls told Judah that Morgan's men were occupying those spaces.

Audie stepped down before a blank hole in the wall of the east wing. "Stay mounted. I'll fetch Peterson. Wade, you keep an eye on our guests."

Though Judah hadn't been trained regarding proper protocol and military discipline, he had read enough of Temple Bell's library on the subject to be intrigued by the casual manner of the two sentries. They hadn't addressed each other by rank. They had not asked for either his name or that of Barefoot. They had shown no concern about being relieved on the turnpike before abandoning their post, and, unless the so-called Peterson was in charge of the daily guard detail, they hadn't reported their situation to the officer of the day upon their arrival in camp.

What had happened to the strict discipline the Lexington Rifles had exhibited during their smartly executed public drill at the Scott County Fair just three short years ago on the afternoon John Hunt Morgan's celebrated private militia company had spawned a military zeal in Judah that burned like a raging flame for weeks? The bright tip of that fiery heat Jacob felt had been handsome Morgan himself, resplendent in the Rifles' brilliant green uniform, tail coat, trousers braided with gold lace, white cross belts, and a fancy blue cap. Had that organizational and personal discipline vanished with the advent of a shooting war when it was needed the most?

The trooper that emerged behind Audie had salt-and-pepper hair straight as stretched string. He also had the mournful eyes of the hunting hound, clean-shaven upper lip and jowls, an X-shaped scar on his right cheek, a slashing scar above his Adam's apple, a small-chested, lean-hipped body, and the bow legs of the veteran horseman. When he spoke, the hoarseness in his voice made Judah suspect the acquisition of the scar on his throat had somehow damaged his vocal chords.

"Sergeant Field Peterson, Company A, Morgan's Squadron here, and who are you?"

"I'm Judah Bell from Scott County. I've come all this way to meet Captain Morgan."

"And why would he want to fuss with you? He's a mighty busy fellow."

"I plan to enlist in his command. I have a letter of introduction to Captain Morgan from Mr. Granger Huddleston of Glasgow."

The mournful hound dog eyes looked Judah over a second time, and a wistful expression resulted. "Let me have it."

Judah pulled the folded letter from his jacket pocket and handed it down to Sergeant Field Peterson, who opened the single-page document and read it with more care than he anticipated. The doubtful expression faded. Peterson nodded and said, "Okay, I'll take you to headquarters. But I ain't making no promises about—"

Wade, his horse standing directly behind Jasper, interrupted the officer in charge. "Hold on a minute. There's something we need to check out first."

Not pleased with Wade's interference, Peterson snapped, "And what would that be?"

Jumping from his saddle, Wade came up beside Judah and untied his bedroll. Judah was as puzzled as Field Peterson until he saw the sleeve of the Yankee overcoat protruding from his rolled blanket. He mouthed a silent curse. How much trouble might this trick of fate cause him?

Wade unrolled the blanket on the ground, grabbed hold of the long blue coat, and held it up for Peterson's inspection. "Look beneath the rear of the collar," Peterson ordered. "If that's what I think it is, there'll be a label there that reads, 'PROPERTY OF THE U.S. ARMY.'"

"You're right. That's what it reads big as horse apples stink."

When Judah turned back to Field Peterson a familiar sight greeted him—the gaping muzzle of a gun. Peterson cocked his revolver and said, "You've some tall explaining to do, Mr. Judah Bell. If you're so hell bent on riding with us, why do you have a brand-new Yankee overcoat hidden in your bedroll? You spying for those damn blue-bellies? Find out if the black Injun has one, too, Private Caldwell."

Wade untied and shook Barefoot's blanket out next to Judah's, revealing Asa's matching blue overcoat. Bending at the waist, Audie then plucked two objects from the blanket, straightened, and said, "And he's toting a powder flask and bag of lead balls, too."

A scowling Field Peterson said, "Did you find a weapon on the half-breed?"

"He didn't have a holster like Bell to carry one."

A red splotch bloomed on Peterson's scarred cheek. "You didn't search him?"

"No, sir, Sergeant Peterson, we didn't," a suddenly formal Audie admitted reluctantly.

Judah suppressed a grin and thought, *Audie might be in more trouble than me.*

"Search the half-breed, Private Caldwell."

Wade circled Jasper. Barefoot made it easy for him by opening his coat. He offered no resistance as Wade clutched the butt of his Navy Colt and yanked it from behind his waist belt.

"Same brand of pistol as Bell's," Wade announced.

"Is it loaded?"

Breaking open the Navy, Wade spun the cylinder. "Yes, sir, Sergeant Peterson."

Field Peterson stared first at Wade, and then Audie had his opportunity to blink, drop his head, and make a concerted study of his boot toes.

There was an edge sharper than a freshly honed knife blade in Peterson's hoarse voice when he said, "And one of you did ride to camp and arrange to be relieved before bringing in your prisoners?"

Audie was the one who said, "No, sir, Sergeant Peterson."

Stepping to the blank hole from which he'd emerged, Peterson yelled, "Corporal Grubb, front and center."

An apple-cheeked, blond-haired trooper with a pencil-thin wisp of upper lip hair barely qualifying as a worthwhile mustache hustled into view, stumbled to a halt, and saluted Peterson. "Yes, sir."

"Corporal Grubb, Privates Caldwell and Jefferson are under arrest. Collect their weapons and those of their prisoners. Hand the revolvers to me."

Judah noticed that Peterson's cocked revolver was covering his fellow troopers as well as him and Barefoot. Grubb secured the two shotguns first, leaned one of them against the wall beside the blank doorway, and armed himself with the other. He then passed the revolvers to Peterson.

Peterson stashed the revolvers in the pockets of his frocked coat and said, "Good work, Corporal. Now, escort them to B Company headquarters and turn then over to

Lieutenant Bowles. Inform him I will be along shortly to press charges. Make sure you let him know that the Glasgow Road is unguarded. Carry on, Corporal."

Judah's low opinion of the discipline within Morgan's command was changing for the better rapidly. The laxness he'd observed was perhaps an isolated incident, for Field Peterson was clearly a no-nonsense, no-excuse, by-the-book officer, and Judah was anxious to learn what he had in store for him and Asa.

The departing corporal and his newly arrested prisoners marched off in quick time. Field Peterson watched them until they were out of sight among the growing number of troopers drawn to the scene by the lightning-fast rumor racing through the camp that the sentries had captured a civilian riding a magnificent red stallion traveling in the company of a mounted half-black Indian, a rare enough phenomena in itself to warrant a gander. The discovery of the Yankee overcoats had caused a stir among the onlookers and the arrest of two of their own and not the strangers added to the growing uncertainty and confusion. Judah hadn't noticed the crowd forming behind them, but the increasing volume of its mutterings corrected that oversight.

Still covering Judah and Barefoot with his revolver, Field Peterson, voice loud enough to carry to the back of the listening troopers, said, "Now, Mr. Judah Bell, we'll proceed to Captain Morgan's headquarters with your letter. You can explain the Yankee overcoats there. I'm sure you'll have a story worth hearing. I'll let Captain Morgan and his staff decide the fate of you and your half-breed."

Singling out two troopers with blunt jabs of a finger, Peterson continued, "Privates Starr and Goodman, take charge of these horses and the half-breed. Keep a close eye on him and see that the animals are fed and watered. I'll hold you responsible for their well-being in the meantime. Understand me, the half-breed is to be guarded and not harmed. The rest of you men return to your tents or your regular duties. Step down, Mr. Bell."

The privates led off Jasper, the sentries' horses, and Barefoot's mare with Asa still atop her. The half-breed gave Judah the slightest nod to indicate he had no qualms about being held somewhere else until Judah made other arrangements. Field Peterson waited for the troopers to disperse, holstered his revolver, motioned for Judah to follow him, and quipped, "No man's ever outrun a bullet."

The sentry in front of the westernmost section of Bell's Tavern came to attention with their approach. Field Peterson returned the sentry's salute, waited for Judah, and let him enter the building first. Trained to respect his elders, Judah removed his hat as he stepped through the door.

The anteroom of Captain John Hunt Morgan's headquarters had been a parlor before the war. The one remaining piece of parlor furniture, a cloth-covered couch, sat along the east wall of the room. A fireplace occupied the opposite wall. The balance of the space had been given over to two desks manned by a master sergeant and a corporal. A hallway flanked by four rooms on each side extended to the rear of the building. The door at the very end of the hallway facing Judah was open and he saw the corner of an iron stove and smelled bread baking. His empty stomach growled of its own accord.

The master sergeant rose to his feet. "Please state your business, Sergeant Peterson."

"This man says his name is Judah Bell and he claims he's from Scott County. The sentries captured him and a half-breed and brought them into camp. You should know, sir, we found U.S. Military overcoats hidden in their bedrolls. Bell desires to meet Captain Morgan. He has a letter of introduction from a Mr. Granger Huddleston of Glasgow."

"I was watching from the window, Sergeant. That's a

fine stud horse you're riding, Mr. Bell. Mind telling me
how he came into your possession?"

"He was a gift from Temple Bell, my uncle. Uncle won
him in a winner-take-all race."

A lopsided grin creased the taciturn features of the
master sergeant. "Match race at the Fayette County fair-
grounds, 12 October 1858. I was there. The stallion lost by
a half yard to your uncle's Denmark Thoroughbred. If
they'd run another tenth of a mile it would have been a different story."

The master sergeant's smile lingered and he stepped
from behind his desk. "Sergeant Peterson, Captain Morgan
is available. I believe we can take a chance on this young
chap and his letter. I'm certain Mr. Bell can explain the
Yankee overcoats, and being the horse lover he is, Captain Morgan will want to hear about Mr. Bell's stallion. You
need to be careful, though, Mr. Bell. The captain may want
that stud for his own use, and he's mighty persuasive when
he wants to be. Come along, gentlemen."

Parting with Jasper for any reason had never occurred
to Judah. He might consider letting Captain Morgan ride
the stallion, but a transferring of ownership, even if it hurt
his chances of joining Morgan's command, was not on the
table.

The master sergeant knocked on the last door on the
right at the end of the hallway. Before a voice gave permission to enter that room, Judah's quick glance into the
kitchen caught an aproned, young, handsome black woman
lifting a large baking pan from the oven he'd spotted earlier.
The smell emanating from the pan was divine, and the
insane thought crossed his mind that he might consider
trading Jasper for a mouthful of warm bread lathered with
butter if he didn't eat soon. If, as he had read, and as he was
coming to believe, hunger was the soldier's truest friend,

than he vowed to wear himself out praying for a quick end to the fighting. Glory, he found, held no attraction for the famished.

Sergeant Peterson opened the door for Judah and the master sergeant. Captain John Hunt Morgan was reclining in an oversized leather chair with a cup of coffee within reach on the top of his desk. Upon sighting Judah's strange face, Morgan straightened in the chair, ran fingers through his dark auburn hair, stroked his precisely trimmed imperial beard, and helped himself to a swallow of coffee.

Judah remembered Morgan's fair skin, small white hands, and keen gray-blue eyes from the public militia drill at the Scott County Fair. His welcoming smile displayed the same perfect white teeth. When he hurriedly came to his feet, Judah judged Morgan to be six feet tall and weighing one hundred eighty-five pounds. He was an imposing figure enhanced by a gray frock coat with heavy gold braid, knee-high riding boats polished to a rich, glossy blackness, and the black hat on his desk with its right side pinned up by a golden wreath-around-a-tree embroidery.

"And who do we have here, Master Sergeant Hooper?" Morgan inquired.

"Captain, meet Judah Bell from Scott County. He wants to enlist. Sergeant Peterson has a letter of introduction for him. The letter, if you please, Sergeant."

Captain Morgan read the proffered letter in short order. "Granger Huddleston is a good friend and his word is solid. Gentlemen, is there any reason why we shouldn't enroll Mr. Bell?"

Sergeant Peterson cleared his throat. "Sir, we did find a brand-new Yankee overcoat in Mr. Bell's bedroll, and that holds true for the armed half-breed traveling with him."

"An armed half-breed, you say. Who would that be, Mr. Bell?"

Shaky nerves disarmed by Morgan's infectious smile,

Judah answered, "That would be Asa Barefoot, sir. He's actually half-Cherokee and half-African blood. He served my uncle, Temple Bell, until his death. He's armed by my choice. Barefoot scouted for General Taylor during the Seminole Indian Wars. He's a first-rate soldier in his own right. He's saved my life twice."

"Mean as that Florida action was, your Barefoot is undoubtedly a valuable man in a fire fight. We'll find a place for him, too, if he so desires. Now, before Peterson here has a caterwauling fit and shames the lot of us, explain those Yankee overcoats. How *did* you come by them?"

Judah wasn't a braggart, but he realized he had a chance to advance his military career with the tale-spinning talents he'd inherited from his father and his uncle, and he pounced on it. "Me and Barefoot stole them from a detail of blue-bellies in the middle of the night outside Campbellsville. They weren't exactly pleased about being awakened by gunshots."

Judah paused.

Had Captain Morgan swallowed his hook?

Dropping into his chair again, Morgan said, "Sergeant Peterson, ask Miss Loomis in the kitchen for a fresh pot of coffee and mugs for everybody. This is a story we want to hear."

The pot was procured, the mugs were distributed, the coffee was poured, and Judah began, "There were eight Yankees all together, seven of them asleep and one standing guard. We . . ."

Captain Morgan and the two sergeants were an attentive audience, hanging on Judah's every word until he finished his recounting with, "And once we were away at a gallop, we rode hard until dawn."

An amused John Morgan sipped coffee and stroked his beard. "Mr. Bell, any other commanding officer would probably dismiss as youthful exaggeration your claiming a young girl you picked up along the way ran off the Yankee horses while you and your Barefoot held them at gunpoint. But I've led enough attacks on superior numbers to know anything is possible so long as you maintain a clear head and utilize every man, or in your case, every woman, available. Next time we're in Glasgow, I must meet this Brianna Hardin."

Pouring the last of the coffee into his mug, Morgan said, "Maud Huddleston will look after that young lady. She always wanted a girl child. Mr. Bell, I admire your zeal and your courage. I commend your thinking and planning. I don't believe I and my men could have done better in that instance."

The closely knit relationship Morgan shared with his men allowed Master Sergeant Hooper to correct his superior officer without fear of censure. "Sir, we would have thrown the Yankee rifles on the big fire he built and eliminated any possible chance of armed pursuit."

Judah had, of course, realized his oversight as they fled the Yankee campsite, but he made no mention of that now. He had made his good impression on John Hunt Morgan and nothing was to be gained by offering excuses for a tactical error that had not affected the outcome of his night attack. "Master Sergeant Hooper is correct, sir, and I can assure you that I won't make that mistake again."

The future "Thunderbolt of the Confederacy" treated his guests to another dazzling, white-toothed smile. "Gentlemen, I believe Mr. Bell has passed muster. The question now is what to do with our new recruit and his black Indian scout? And don't be timid with me."

Sergeant Field Peterson, who hadn't experienced a timid moment since whipping the school bully in the second year of grammar school, spoke first. "Sir, the loss of Private Reynolds of my scout company left an empty bedroll in my tent. I suggest Mr. Bell take his place."

"And his Indian scout?"

Given the disdain borne by most Kentuckians for those of Indian and black blood, Judah had assumed from the beginning that Barefoot's heritage would preclude his serving in Morgan's Confederate command. But Captain Morgan had stated otherwise straight out of the chute. Judah was confident Peterson and Hooper would follow his wishes.

"We can provide Private Barefoot his own tent so we don't trample on any tender toes and cause a ruckus, if that's what you want, Captain," Master Sergeant Hooper suggested. "He can ride with the scouts if Field has no objection."

"I'll accept any man that can stay on a horse and handle a firearm regardless of his color," Field Peterson said. "His scouting for General Taylor in Seminole country will set well with some of our boys. I can temper things with the rest."

Captain Morgan said, "Then that's how it will be, gentlemen," and rose to his feet. "Do we have further business to conduct?"

"Yes, sir, you being such a great admirer of quality horseflesh, we need to make you aware of Private Bell's personal mount, a handsome red stallion."

Curiosity aroused to a fever pitch, Captain Morgan's face was beaming when he said excitedly, "Tell me about your stallion, Private."

"Jasper is from Arabian and Bluegrass American Standard Bred stock. He's nine years old. My uncle, Temple Bell, gave him to me just before he was killed a few weeks ago."

John Hunt Morgan frowned. "Temple Bell, do you mean Temple Bell the Denmark breeder from near Buffalo Stamp?"

"Yes, sir."

"I raced against your uncle's Denmarks. I read in the *Lexington* paper one of the troopers found in the L and N depot at Munfordville of his murder by renegade Union cavalry and the confiscation of his entire stable. His death was a great loss to the Confederacy."

Captain Morgan's gray-blue eyes narrowed. "Is his murder what brought you to my camp, Private?"

"Yes, sir."

"Then you're doubly welcome, and I believe we can help you avenge his untimely death quite nicely in the coming months."

Knuckles rapped on the door behind Judah. The bare head of the anteroom corporal popped into sight. "Lieutenant Basil Duke to see you, sir. He says it's urgent."

"Send him to me, Corporal," Captain Morgan said with a chuckle.

The bare head disappeared.

"Gentlemen, not even your leader dares to keep his brother-in-law and second in command dangling for long. Private Bell, perhaps you could bring your Jasper around after supper and introduce him. I'm sure Sergeant Peterson wouldn't miss you for an hour. Would you, Field?"

The impromptu coming together ended with that arrangement, and Captain Morgan's sergeants and his new recruit took their leave. In the hallway they passed the arriving Lieutenant Duke. The physical differences between the two brothers-in-law wrung a stare from Judah.

Basil Duke was of slight build and weighed one hundred and thirty pounds sopping wet. He features were angular, his hair dark, and his eyes darker yet. What held the observer's gaze was Duke's massive, jutting jaw and wedge-shaped beard. Despite his gray frock uniform coat with its lieutenant's bars, Duke looked to Judah more like an engineer, banker, or court judge than he did a military officer.

Little did Judah know that he had met that afternoon the two officers—Sergeant Field Peterson and Lieutenant Basil Duke—who were to play vital roles in defining his service with Morgan's raiders, and, more important, whose decisions would either enhance or diminish the odds in favor of his surviving the conflict between Union and Confederacy.

What Judah Bell did know with rock-solid certainty that same afternoon was that he faced a chancy future in which nothing was guaranteed, not even from one day to the next day.

CHAPTER 12

Colonel O. P. Ransom read the regimental order, "March to the Front," to his officers of the First Ohio Volunteer Cavalry on the morning of 8 December 1861. Excitement rippled through his headquarters' tent in a palpable wave. The weeks of what had become mainly a monotonous training regimen had been terminated. The prospect of travel, new faces, new challenges, a different campsite, and, more important, the possibility of finally meeting and engaging the enemy sparked an enthusiasm akin to young boys visiting the woods for the first time with their own gun.

"There is much to be done," Colonel Ransom concluded. "We have rations to prepare. We have weapons and gear to inspect, pack, and stow. Personal items are limited to what can be rolled into your blanket and gum poncho or carried on your person. Bear in mind that the bulk of the regiment's horses have never traveled by train or boat, and extra vigilance will be required on your part to keep them under control. Lastly, it is our responsibility to rid the tents and grounds of debris and burn it. With the demands this order places on each and every one of us, normal Sunday personal activities, including the receiving of visitors, are suspended. Be prepared to begin the entraining when 'Boots and Saddles' sounds tomorrow morning."

Jacob Bell shared the full-fledged excitement of his fellow officers. His sole misgiving stemmed from his failure to gain an audience with Felicia Denning since their spirited introduction. Regimental practice marches over the National Road leading out of Columbus to the west and large-scale training on site involving the First Ohio's entire complement of one thousand plus troopers had intensified in the past two weeks. Both exercises had drawn large crowds along Broad Street and on the far fringes of the parade ground.

Troopers to the man had quickly surmised that nothing attracted the attention and adoration of the fair maiden like the drawn sabers, holstered revolvers, new uniforms, well-groomed horses, and clanking spurs of a cavalry regiment on the march. The charge of the regiment across an open field during drill elicited cheers and delighted squeals from watching male and female adults, future recruits, and young boys and girls, and dampened the cheeks of Mexican War veterans with straggling tears. For Jacob, every fair maiden they passed on the march and the ones who crept to the perimeter of the parade ground brought Felicia Denning to mind in a heated surge. But the rigorous pursuit of the daily schedule from darkness to darkness excluded the possibility of making arrangements to entertain guests personally. His frustration mounted with each passing day.

Jacob exited Colonel Ransom's headquarters with Major Dance Walker. Walker's teasing statement to the effect that it was a total shame Felicia Denning hasn't been spotted lately made Jacob aware more than chance had put them side by side. "I sort of sensed you and the Denning gal had a hankering for each other in a finger snap. She struck me as a determined young lady accustomed to having things pretty much as she wants. Has she been in touch by mail or sent a message or anything?"

"No, sir, I haven't heard from her."

"Have you written to her?"

"No, sir, I was expecting her to return for a Sunday tour."

"Damn it, boy, you got to grab the bit away from her. You truly want her, write to her tonight without fail. A soldier can't be around every sweep of the clock like those jaspers that never don a uniform. Hesitate and your single chance may go a-wanting. I lost the finest gal to ever grace my blanket by being God-awful backward and not staying in touch, and I'll regret it in the grave. You got pen and paper in your tent?"

"Yes, sir. I write home and maintain a journal."

Major Walker's head cocked. "You jot down anything about me, I'd appreciate it if you'd try to be fair with me. If you want to be a successful officer that makes troopers out of green recruits, you must accept the fact that many subordinates won't like you. Some will hate you, but you can win their respect, and that's what counts the most in this blood-and-guts game we insist on pursuing to the death of too many young men. Now, get along and make time for that letter. Have Corporal Howard bring it here to Colonel Ransom's tent and I'll make certain it's posted."

Dance Walker chuckled. "I take the trouble to play Cupid, I don't want my arrow to miss."

With a scheme to make contact with Felicia Denning in place that had every chance of succeeding thanks to the intervention of Major Dance Walker, the daytime hours sped by for Jacob. At one p.m., the customary Sunday inspection was initiated. On Captain Cam Logan's orders, tents were emptied for his personal look-see to insure all debris and nonmilitary personal items acquired from the sutlers and families, too cumbersome to pack, had been removed and discarded. An inspection of each individual trooper from head to heel along with his weapons followed with deficiencies recorded in writing. The final leg of the inspection occurred at the stables. Each horse was checked from nose to tail. Saddles, saddle blankets, curb bits and bridles, and every tool required to tend and sustain the trooper's mount from surcingle, curry comb and brush, nose bag, lariat, halter, watering bridle, and picket pin were confirmed present and in proper working order. The top-to-bottom inspection lasted almost three hours, and the collective sigh of the Company M troopers when Captain Logan declared them fit for travel was equivalent to a minor hurricane wind. Watching the backsides of Captain Cam Logan and Lieutenant Tor Shavers disappear up the company street was a joy to behold.

With their Sunday duties satisfied, Jacob's mess undertook the stocking of rations and packing of their gear. The Bainbridge boys—Nate Bush, Frank McCarran, and Luke Purcell—were always starving and took first turn at frying meat over the cooking fire till it was devoid of moisture, part of the mess's plan to subsist on fried meat and worm-castle hardtack for the duration of their travel time. After packing their gear, Tom South and Fritz Howard seated themselves at the checkerboard. Lyle Tomlinson buried his nose up to his ears in his Bible. The pasteboard covers of the book Sam Kite was reading were so worn and tattered that he had to hold it together with both hands. Isaac Wood told hunting stories to anybody who would listen, tales tall enough they made bears sound as common on Chillicothe streets as stray dogs. Homesick Lawton Anderson penned his latest letter to the sweetheart he'd left behind to help save his beloved Union. The Spencer twins, more addicted to sleep than a barroom drunk was to cheap liquor, sawed logs loud enough to fell a forest in a mere day.

In late afternoon, a hullabaloo at the head of the company

street caught Jacob with his pen poised over his journal, fishing for the proper salutation to open his letter to Felicia Denning. Cheers and whistling swelled to a crescendo. Jacob's entire mess rose to their feet and stared. What they saw sprung every jaw open. The source of the commotion was a woman with her gloved hand resting on the arm of Lieutenant Tor Shavers.

The skirt, blouse, shawl, and gloves adorning her shapely body and her parasol were the brightest of whites and emphasized her caramel-colored hair, blue eyes, and red lips. She dabbed at her nostrils occasionally with a folded white handkerchief when the dust stirred by her passage tickled them. The only thing not perfectly feminine about her were the toes of the black boots sticking from beneath her skirt.

"Who the hell is she?" Nate Bush blurted.

"Her name is Miss Felicia Denning," Jacob answered.

Feet covered with spilled checkers, Tom South asked, "Wonder what officer she's coming to visit?"

"I'm proud to admit, gentlemen, that she's seeking me," Jacob said, admiring the gentle sway of her hips.

Walking mince-footed, face ashen and sober, Lieutenant Tor Shavers guided Felicia Denning straight to Jacob, relief flooding his heavy features. "Here you are, ma'am. Here's the man you asked for."

The pure deviltry in Felicia's eyes intrigued Jacob. She patted Tor Shavers's arm and said, "Thank you, Lieutenant. You've been most kind and I will mention your gentlemanly manners to Colonel Ransom. I'm certain Sergeant Bell is capable of escorting me to Colonel Ransom's tent after I visit with him. Please, don't let me keep you unnecessarily."

Lieutenant Tor Shavers nodded and scurried for the safe haven of the street behind him, a street packed curb to curb now with troopers. Shavers's hasty departure made Jacob aware that the whole company was trying to discern what would happen next. The sight of a beautiful woman being delivered to a mere sergeant, one of the rank and file like themselves, was as rare as a spotted elephant that could fly, and they couldn't avert their gazes.

"Seems you brought a crowd with you," Jacob said to Felicia.

"I feared this might happen when I told the colonel I wanted to meet you at your tent to learn what camp life is about. He relented after I told him I would proceed on my own without his permission."

Jacob couldn't resist asking, "And where does that leave your unintended spectators?"

"Why, in the palm of my hand, of course," Felicia Denning responded.

She advanced twenty paces toward the watching troopers and motioned for them to gather around her. After they settled and stopped jostling each other, Felicia raised her hand for silence and said, "I regret that I can spend time with but one of you today. But I know that back home there are mothers, wives, and sweethearts that long for your safe return. Do not 'disappoint them. Write to them often. Do not leave them wondering if you are safe. Never deny that love is a virtue we can both give and receive. May I be excused, Company M, to pursue my chosen man?"

The resulting cheers had to carry to downtown Columbus. With much back-slapping and verbal acknowledgments as to how they'd at last met a fine woman they could dream about, the crowd, considering itself lucky to have seen her at all, broke up and returned to their tents and other pursuits.

"Can we meet her?" Sam Kite asked.

Anxious as Jacob was to talk with Felicia Denning alone, he didn't forget his manners. "Most certainly. Let me retrieve her."

The mess did Jacob proud. They each shook Felicia's gloved hand as he introduced them. Their fascination with her was such not a one of them said more than "Hello" or "Pleased to meet you, Miss." Nor did they shy away from the kiss Felicia gently planted on their unshaven cheeks. The swooning looks they gave her as she moved to the next messmate indicated they'd gladly die rather than disappoint her.

Introductions completed, Jacob led her into the open ground past the end of the company street. They halted in the shade of a tall white oak tree and Jacob said, "I wasn't expecting you this afternoon."

"That's not what the messenger said," Felicia quipped with a wide smile.

Puzzled, Jacob asked, "What messenger?"

"The young private sent by Major Walker. He said you wished to meet with me this afternoon since your train is leaving in the morning."

Jacob laughed aloud. Apparently, the major had decided not to trust Cupid's arrow.

Felicia frowned and said, "What's so funny?"

"Major Walker sent the messenger, not me. But I'm glad you came. I was starting to write you a letter and the next minute you're here in the flesh."

Felicia's smile returned. "I was so hoping to hear from you. It seems we both owe Major Walker our thanks."

Remembering Colonel Ransom's orders that public visitations were canceled for the day, Jacob asked, "Colonel Ransom voiced no objection to your request to see me?"

"No, by his boyish grin, I believe he knew about the messenger in advance and played along with Major Walker. Those two men seem to have quite an interest in furthering your love life."

Jacob felt heat on his cheek and said, "And in a hurry, too."

Felicia's laugh held the charm of melodic piano notes. "I think they believe you have the makings of a commissioned officer. I have an inkling they'll be pushing on that front soon."

"You're right. The colonel, the major, and I have discussed detached duty on the colonel's staff with the rank of acting lieutenant."

"Is that what you want or are you content with the rank of sergeant?"

Jacob snorted and said, "Actually, I made sergeant by a vote that was taken without my knowledge before I left home. I couldn't bring myself to disappoint the Ross County lads who voted for me, and I must admit serving in the ranks has been an invaluable teacher. I have acquired an understanding of how non-commissioned officers should exercise their authority, how privates view the cavalry, what they expect from their superiors, and what they will and won't stand for from anyone. I'm convinced that what I've learned training, eating, and sharing a tent with the rank and file will make me a better officer, if and when I'm promoted. My sole regret is that the higher your rank, the harder it is personally to associate with those beneath your command. Those Ross County boys are an ornery bunch, but they love their families, take training seriously, and once you win their loyalty, they'll take a bullet for you in a heartbeat."

A mistiness dampened Felicia Denning's eyes, and for a few seconds, Jacob thought she might cry. "Damn this war anyway. You meet a man worth getting to know and he disappears like a puff of wind."

With obvious effort, Felicia Denning straightened her shoulders, toyed with her dust-stained handkerchief, and forced a smile. "Sergeant Jacob Bell, if it isn't too great a bother, will you write to me? I've spent but twenty minutes with you at the most, yet you've somehow become very important to me. I promise I won't bore you with those long, overwrought, gushing letters my female acquaintances insist on writing to anything wearing trousers that will read them. I'm not a silly girl or a tease. I'm a grown woman who would like the privilege of loving a man that I can trust and whose feelings and wants ring true and will love me in return."

Felicia Denning's head lowered. "I'm sorry if my being so forward embarrasses you, but there isn't much time and I don't know when, or if, I'll see you again."

Jacob reached out his hand, cupped Felicia's chin, and, not sure how she would react given the public setting and the fact some of his messmates had to be watching, kissed her softly on the mouth. Her reaction jarred Jacob to his very soul, creating the sensation he was being sucked into the center of an emotional whirlwind. Her arms swept about his neck, and with a deep moan, she pulled herself tightly against him and refused to end the kiss.

When they were both out of breath, Felicia relented and placed her forehead on Jacob's shoulder while he held her in his arms. "I don't care if I've shamed myself and tarnished my reputation as a lady," she whispered. "Some things are meant to happen."

Jacob cleared his throat. "Your reputation will suffer irreparable harm if I throw you down on the grass and have my way with you. We best start back to Colonel Ransom's headquarters."

With another melodic laugh, Felicia pulled free and presented her arm to Jacob. "Well, it's interesting to learn you don't keep your intentions a secret, Sergeant Bell. That I can deal with. Please escort this fallen woman to her buggy before I have *my way* with you."

During her return trip up the company street, polite nods of the head and infrequent waves replaced the momentous cheers and whistles that had greeted Felicia upon her arrival. "You're right," Felicia said. "They are superb men prepared to die for their country. I would take any of them for the brother I didn't have."

The sun was sinking and lanterns were burning in Colonel Ransom's tent. Felicia insisted they avoid making themselves known and proceed to her waiting buggy. "The colonel has much to do. He has given me as much of his time as I dare take."

Her hatless driver was a shriveled toad of a man with scarred brows, cabbages for ears, an oft-broken nose, a lopsided jaw, and permanently swollen knuckles. "Paige Dolan was a prizefighter in his younger years. He is quite dependable. At Father's request, he carries a revolver under his coat whenever we're out and about. Father doesn't trust the public temper no matter how far we are from the battlefield."

Jacob respected James Henry Denning's intelligence in providing for his daughter's safety. It also relieved any concerns he might develop about her well-being in his absence. He could hardly believe that he was starting to feel responsible for a woman he'd seen twice and kissed once, but he was.

At the buggy, without so much as a "Good-bye," Felicia grasped Jacob's elbows and hurriedly kissed his cheek. She released him, lifted her skirt, stepped up, and seated herself next to Paige Dolan before Jacob could catch hold of her. She nudged Dolan, and the buggy shot off for the Broad Street gate, the crack of the Irishman's whip echoing behind it.

Jacob was never dead certain, but he thought he heard a muffled sob before the racing buggy blended with the growing darkness.

CHAPTER 13

Her alabaster skin is unblemished. Her breasts thrust against her sleeping gown. She moves toward him devoid of shyness. Her smile is inviting, bold, and wanton. She has longed for this moment with the man of her choice. The promise of what is to come is bound only by her imagination. She kneels beside his bed ripe with anticipation and reaches to awaken him, to ignite the passion she craves . . .

A rough hand shook Jacob Bell from a deep, warm sleep. He came half-awake, sullen and resentful of being robbed of his imaginary pleasures.

"Wake up, Sergeant Bell, wake up."

Who was it that dared roust him at this ungodly hour?

"Wake up, Sergeant Bell. We need you."

Jacob recognized Tom South's voice and swore. If you asked him, and nobody would, a pig farmer was a mighty lame substitute for Felicia Denning and her unquestioned beauty.

"Sergeant, some of our men are missing."

All thoughts not connected with Jacob's duties vanished. He jumped to his feet and grabbed Tom South's arm. "What do you mean missing?"

"Corporal Howard says they're not in their tents. He's looking for them at the stables, sir."

"Why there, Private?"

"He suspects they stole their horses so they could raise hob in Columbus tonight."

The first order of business was to learn who was absent from the mess without permission. Tom South replied to Jacob's query without hesitation. "Bush, McCarran, Purcell, and Aaron Spencer, sir."

The names matched Jacob's familiarity with his messmates. The three boys from Bainbridge equated the bare ankle of a female with the bloodlines of a prize bull and talked incessantly about the varying virtues of girls from their hometown and their purported availability. Aaron Spencer, who had probably never kissed a female other than his mother and a sister and a puppy, had hung on every carnal word spoken by the Bainbridge trio for weeks on end.

Jacob pulled on boots and belted his revolver around his waist. "After you, Private. We've no time to waste."

Jacob ran for the stables behind Tom South, cussing under his breath. He had overheard snatches of conversation the past week alluding to how the enlisted men were planning a clandestine visit to the taverns and houses of joy on the east side of the capital city the night they were ordered south, and he'd foolishly ignored them, believing *his* men were too disciplined for such shenanigans.

How could he have been so outrageously stupid? He was commanding flesh-and-blood men, not toy wooden soldiers. They shared his desires and wants. They dreamed of warm bare-skinned female bodies the same as he did. It didn't matter where they found them. And who knew, this might be their last chance to howl before they were killed in battle.

A surprise awaited Jacob when he reached the entrance

to the regiment's open-air stables that consisted of a roof and rear wall. In the weak glow of lanterns held by two privates, a third trooper was saddling the most recognizable mount of the First Ohio, the buckskin with black mane and tail belonging to Major Dance Walker.

"By my calculations, Sergeant Bell, we have twenty empty stalls," Major Walker said, stepping from behind the buckskin. "Any of them your men?"

Corporal Fritz Howard, holding the reins of Jacob's saddled chestnut, halted next to him and said, "Yes, sir, four of them belong to Company M."

With a cunning smile, Dance Walker said, "Corporal, report what's happened directly to Colonel Ransom personally. Ask him to hold the provost guard in camp. We'll bring them home."

"You know where to look?" Fritz Howard asked cautiously.

"Hell, son, I've been there myself more than once," Dance Walker said with an exaggerated wink. "You were wise to bring your sidearm, Bell. We'll be dealing with rough folks who will most likely take offense at our curtailing of their services. Acting Lieutenant Bell, please mount. Your detached service has commenced."

Once Jacob was in the saddle, Major Walker said, "Swing up behind him, Corporal. We'll drop you at the colonel's tent."

At the Broad Street gate, the infantry sentries challenged the two trotting riders until Dance Walker moved into the halo of their lanterns on his buckskin. "How many men on horseback ignored your challenge and headed for the city?"

"Just four here at the gate, Major Walker. At least a dozen, maybe more, jumped the railing at the far end of the parade ground. Everyone of them whipped past at a gallop, hunched down in the saddle with their hats over their faces."

"Well, the numbers add up. It was best you didn't shoot them, Corporal. We'll let the Johnny Rebs have a go at that later. If you'll allow us to pass, we'll retrieve our misguided puppies before they get into more trouble."

Dance Walker held their horses' gait to a trot. Houses rose on both berms after they passed the Four Mile House and Tavern four miles from downtown Columbus. The city rose ahead of them, a dark bulk on the far bank of the Scioto River. They rattled across the wooden planks of the Broad Street bridge into downtown Columbus with the poles of its unlit streetlamps resembling knobby spears. At Broad and High, the Ohio Statehouse was a ghostly apparition of glistening gray limestone bisected by tall black windows in the shine of the post-midnight moon. Streets were deserted in all directions.

They continued due east on Broad Street. A block from Capital Square, they encountered a police station fronted by a paddy wagon with empty shafts and weak light leaking around the frame of its front door. "Good break for us," Dance Walker shouted over the pound of hoofs. "Coppers aren't on the alert yet."

Railroad terminals, stockyards, warehouses, and neighborhoods prone to crime, alcoholic consumption, and prostitution dominated the southeastern portion of Columbus. Judah had claimed a man who ventured there should be able to shave with a blunt-edged piece of stone or risk losing his manly parts as well as his money.

A turn south on Clifton Avenue and within four blocks candlelight showed at every high and low window, horses were tied at hitching posts, hansom cabs filled alleys, and humans, in all manner of dress or undress and in various states of inebriation, roamed the cobblestones. Immaculately uniformed Dance Walker appeared as out of place as a cock rooster in the muddy corner of a pigsty. He looked neither left nor right and seemed indifferent to the bodies ducking and scrambling to avoid the hoofs of his trotting buckskin.

When Dance Walker eased his mount into a walk, Jacob straightened in the chestnut's saddle. Their destination was a wide, three-story brick structure with a banner above double front doors that read SEVEN PRINCES. Two sizable, mustachioed gentlemen, wearing tunics and turbans, braced the twin, eight-foot entryways. Scabbards holding big-handled swords hung from the men's wide leather belts, the most outlandish garb Jacob had ever witnessed.

The door guards came to attention when Dance Walker lifted his leg and stepped down. At his signal, Jacob followed suit. "Lieutenant, there's a corral out back and I suspect that's where our boys' horses are. When we leave, we'll take the rear door. Stay behind me and follow my lead."

A toothless old-timer dressed in baggy pants, plaid shirt, and straw hat shuffled around the corner of the building. "Here's Danni O'Brien, the hostler," Dance Walker said.

The old fellow recognized Dance Walker, and his smile exposed barren gums. "What's your pleasure, Major?"

Dance Walker placed a gold coin in the hostler's cupped palm and said, "Danni, I want you to hold these two horses outside the corral with the gate open. If you aren't there when I come out the back door with the lieutenant and my boys, you better have a relative in St. Louis or some point farther west that will provide for you. Do we understand each other?"

"Yes, sir, I don't want any trouble with the likes of you and that fancy revolver of yours."

Danni O'Brien led their horses off, and Dance Walker and Jacob presented themselves at the front door. The gaze of the two hulking guards never left the major. "Good evening, Paul, Robert. I need to forewarn you that I'm here on official military business."

Jacob suppressed a chuckle. Paul? Robert? He'd expected names like Otto and Turk, not Paul and Robert.

"What official soldier business would that be?" the dour guard on the left inquired.

"The First Ohio is departing Columbus this morning. About twenty of our boys are inside. I intend to round them up and herd them back to camp. I'm on a short rein and short on time. Once we step inside, if either of you follow us, I'll shoot him dead. Understood?"

The two guards' necks stiffened. A man seeming half their size sporting a gimpy leg had threatened to shoot them if they didn't follow his orders, and they resented it. Paul and Robert tried. They stared with all their scowling might, weighing the odds of their smearing the cobblestones with this bold whippet before he could get his revolver into play.

But Dance Walker's no-nonsense, buckshot eyes, the iron set of his jaw, and his deep thrumming voice that hardened with each word won out as they did whether he was drilling a thousand men or preparing to take a life. Convinced Dance Walker's pearl-handled revolver would clear its holster while they were still drawing their swords, and that he would indeed shoot the both of them, Paul and Robert hustled to open the doors behind them, treating the newest guests of the Seven Princes to welcoming bows.

The main room on the first floor of the Seven Princes was spacious enough to house twenty tables for drinking and dining and a stand-up bar thirty feet in length. A door opposite the main entryway led to a kitchen attached to the rear of the building. Oil-fueled lamps on each table and two wheel-shaped ceiling chandeliers with similar lamps secured by chains provided light dimmed by a swirling cloud of tobacco smoke. The smell of cooked beef, boiled cabbage, raw whiskey, stale clothing, and rancid sweat assailed Jacob's nostrils. The conversation was loud and boisterous, and heated exchanges could be heard here and there. Jacob was accustomed to those smells and the commotion, but he didn't find them as consistently thrilling as brother Judah had.

"Food and liquor here, gambling on the second floor," Major Walker said, "with the girls on the third. An outside stairwell facing the corral connects all three floors, but it's for departures only. Shotgun guards at the stairwell doors can be quite discouraging to anyone climbing the outside steps. We'll ask for Sheldon Pierce, the owner, at the bar. Keep a lookout for any of our boys."

Dance Walker surveyed every inch of the room making a path to the bar. "There are three troopers in the corner by the fireplace. Tell them I'm ordering them to wait for us in the corral. Come straight to me afterward. I'll need you upstairs."

Sighting Major Walker and Jacob, the three troopers accepted Walker's orders without protest and bolted for the front door. Jacob rejoined Dance Walker and overheard him ask, "Mr. Pierce, what's the situation with the ladies?"

The proprietor of the Seven Princes equaled the size of a Spencer twin and was dressed in a gray cotton suit with wide lapels and ivory buttons. His attire also included a linen shirt, gold cravat, and a brocaded vest of the same color that featured hand-sewn Arabic symbols and letters Jacob thought elegant in design, but which would forever remain a mystery to him. Smallpox scars had decimated Sheldon Pierce's cheeks and forehead, and his frank purple eyes were bright jewels floating between those hideous swatches of skin.

"Henri La Beau rules the third floor and the ladies. He is his own master. If your men are up there, you'll have to pry them loose. I will send word to the second floor that you are here and have ordered any government chaps to proceed to the corral. If any refuse, my employees will escort them for you."

"And if La Beau resists?" Dance Walker asked.

"He answers for himself, not me, and the consequences are his to endure. He makes me money, but the suffering of errant fools exceeds my patience. I have others waiting in line if they can match the quality of his girls."

"Thank you, Mr. Pierce, and I bid you good night," Dance Walker said. "I doubt we'll meet again, but it was entertaining watching you conduct your business. You'd make a fine cavalry officer."

"I was that in the long-ago past, Major Walker, with the Ottoman sultan. We would have complemented each other to the delight of his highness. Good night to you. I pray you survive the secesh."

The exchange captivated Jacob. Two men who had fought on faraway continents had met each other not on foreign soil, but in a Columbus, Ohio, house of ill repute. The odds against that were greater than a brown horse turning blue. In his reading of history, the fate of men had commanded Jacob's interest the most. The origins of great men were often rooted in obscurity and chance, and their success fed the daydreams of young boys. Boys like a Chillicothe lawyer's son reading by candlelight under his blankets on school nights to hide from the waspish tongues of a mother and grandmother not easily deceived.

The steps to the third floor were steep and challenged Dance Walker's gimpy leg. He paused at the top of them and rubbed his thigh. Doors dotted both sides of a building-long hallway. Giggles, lewd comments, squeals of excite-ment, and grunts of sudden satisfaction drifted from the private rooms. Jacob pondered how Dance Walker would proceed. It would take forever to knock door by door and locate the missing troopers.

With the self-assurance he evinced in front of a regiment, Dance Walker drew his pearl-handled revolver and fired three shots into the hallway ceiling. The discharges echoed throughout the entire building. A wet-blanket silence settled over the third floor. When you could have heard the chirp of a bird in full throat, the man in charge spoke. "This is Major Walker. I want every trooper, pants or no pants, out here where I can see him damn quick . . . or I'll put a bullet in the ass of the man I spot last."

A tousled mass of red hair surrounding a painted female countenance poked from a door past the mid-point of the hallway. Eyes widened and their owner screeched, "That crazy soldier with the limp is back, the one who—"

Arms yanked the screeching lady of the night back into her room and troopers in various states of undress tried to exit her door at the same time. Much tugging and pulling ensued, and then four bodies cleared the doorway and tumbled into a pile, blocking the hallway. Doors popped open beyond the stacked bodies and more men in blue emerged, tightening belts and buttoning their blouses on the move.

A sharp yelp of pain in the room to Dance Walker's immediate left swung his head that direction. Walker tried the room's door and discovered it was locked. Motioning for Jacob to join him, Walker stepped aside and said, "Kick it in."

From the experience of escaping a burning barn at the age of ten, Jacob knew to kick the door a few inches from the handle. Wood splintered and the flimsy door flew open. Jacob followed after Dance Walker. They plunged into a lamp-lit room with a four-poster bed, small fireplace, clothes closet, and a marble-topped dresser.

A slim female with her breasts exposed and holding fingers to bleeding lips was crouched on the floor at the bottom of the bed. A male bigger yet than the door guards,

Paul and Robert, had Aaron Spencer pinned to the wall beside the fireplace with a forearm locked under his chin. The giant's off hand, drawn back for a blow, held a fifteen-inch police Billy club.

Oblivious to what was occurring elsewhere, the giant applied more pressure to Aaron Spencer's throat and growled, "Where's the money you owe me, Yankee?"

Dance Walker gave no warning. Reversing his grip, he clutched his pistol by the barrel, walked calmly up behind the giant, and whacked him behind the ear. The rap of the revolver's butt made Jacob wince.

The giant stood shock still. Jacob gulped. Nobody could withstand such a blow. Then the huge man's legs quivered and he released his hold on the Billy club. Switching his pistol to his left hand, Dance Walker caught the Billy in mid-air and struck two rapid blows, one to the giant's kidney and the other on the outside of his right knee. Jacob heard a bone snap. The giant moaned, collapsed in the middle, and thudded to the floor beside the bed.

A shoulder bumped Jacob's arm. He saw a curved knife slide past, and a voice blurted, "I'll kill you for that, you bastard."

There was no time to warn Dancer, whose back was to Jacob. Jacob stuck his foot out and tripped the attacker. The knife-wielder stumbled but didn't lose his feet, and fought to regain his balance. Before the assailant could steady himself and resume his assault, Jacob planted his boot on the seat of the man's striped trousers, put all his weight behind a sudden shove, and sent Major Walker's would-be killer careening nose-first into the cold fireplace.

"Thanks for covering my backside," an admiring Dance Walker said, chuckling. "I believe that's fancy pants Henri

La Beau's first taste of ashes. Better grab his knife. We don't want him making a fool of himself again."

A sputtering Henri La Beau rolled over and sat up. He spat twice, coughed, and clawed ashes and pieces of unburned coal from his precisely trimmed mustache and spade beard. His owl eyes filled with equal portions of disgust and hate. Jacob swallowed to stifle a guffaw. The streaks of gray ashes on La Beau's black coat matched the color of sun-dried bird droppings. The reigning whoremaster of the Seven Princes had suffered for him the ultimate indignity short of castration.

Dance Walker holstered his pistol, tossed the giant's Billy club atop the marble-topped dresser, covered the half-naked harlot with a blanket from the bed, and knelt in front of the outraged Henri La Beau. "I figure our boys might have run short of cash. I'll leave a sum with Danni O'Brien to cover any shortage and the cost of a doctor for Moab and your girl. I won't have you and Moab badmouthing the First Ohio or any other Yankee regiment. Agreed?"

The unanticipated offer to make things right was quite generous. A mollified and appeased Henri La Beau nodded and said, "That's how it will be."

Dance Walker rose to his feet. "Return Mr. La Beau's blade, lieutenant, and come along. We have bigger troubles pending elsewhere."

A stark testament to the respect and fear Dance Walker had embedded in the ranks of the First Ohio awaited them in the hallway. The absent-without-permission troopers were standing in line at attention, presenting expressions as innocent as those of newly born children. Jacob knew it was a facade. They had to be quacking with fear and speculating about what punishment would be brought to bear by their superiors.

Major Dance Walker walked the length of the troopers' line, inspecting them individually. "If we weren't entraining in a few hours, I'd have each and every one of you bucking the wooden horse or ball and chained at sunrise. But we've got a war to fight, so here's how it's going to play out. We will return to camp a disciplined, trained cavalry unit, not a bunch of fence-jumping, pussy-chasing hellbenders. Once we clear the corral and the alley down below, we will form columns of four. When we reach the Broad Street gate, I will call a halt and answer the sentry's challenge. We will remain in columns of four to the stables, where you will dismount, groom and feed your mounts, and retire."

Dance Walker paused and scanned the entire line. "Mark my word, this night will not be forgotten. A suitable punishment will be rendered after our arrival in Kentucky. You may follow me or return to Camp Chase alone and risk arrest by the provost police. The punishment will be more severe and of greater duration, if you are arrested. It's your choice. If you want to risk it alone, step out of line."

Not a single pair of boots moved. A fleeting smile tugged at the corners of Dance Walker's mouth. "Gentlemen, left face, march."

The shotgun guard normally stationed at the rear door on the third floor was not in sight. Neither was the guard on the second floor. Danni O'Brien and the three troopers Dance Walker had flushed from the first floor earlier manned the corral gate. While the troopers sorted out their mounts, Dance Walker talked briefly to O'Brien and filled the hostler's palm with gold coins.

"Make La Beau sweat for a while, Danni," Dance Walker said. "It will prepare him to greet his maker humble to the core."

The streets were empty until the column approached the

police station on Broad Street. There a row of blue-uniformed Columbus policemen formed a human barricade from curb to curb. Jacob counted fifteen helmets in all. Twenty yards short of the barricade, Major Dance Walked halted the column. "Ride forward with me, Lieutenant Bell."

Jacob's nerves were bouncing on pins and needles. Physical force and military authority wouldn't work in this situation. He was about to learn how much diplomatic skill Major Dance Walker possessed. The Columbus Police Department had a reputation for strict law enforcement and no tolerance for Camp Chase soldiers disturbing the peace, harassing public citizens, or interfering with local business operations. And bribes were scorned, an admirable attitude for a big city force.

An officer with a glorious walrus mustache that buried his upper lip stepped out ahead of his fellow policemen. His eyes were lost in deep shadow beneath the bill of his helmet. He let Jacob and Dance Walker advance within a dozen feet and said, "Far enough. Identify yourselves."

"Major Dance Walker, First Ohio Volunteer Cavalry, and Lieutenant Jacob Bell, sir."

"Major Walker, a departmental runner reported gunshots at the Seven Princes. He also reported cavalry from Camp Chase were present and involved. Would that have been your men, Major?"

The problem confronting Dance Walker was how to tell the truth so as to negate the need for police involvement after the fact—a feat, given the circumstances, Jacob considered about as likely to happen as his licking the behind of a woods panther without being clawed and eaten.

"Yes, sir, a few of our boys were seeking a little excitement before departing Camp Chase later this morning for Kentucky. I fired the shots in question to inform them it was time to call it a night. Before we left, all financial obligations for services provided our boys were paid for and gold money was left to cover any additional, extraordinary expenses incurred by Mr. Pierce and Mr. La Beau. If you like, we will hold tight while you have your runner check with those two august gentlemen and substantiate what I'm telling you."

Jesus jump, Jacob thought, *the man should have been a lawyer.*

"Major, I will take you at your word that you left the Seven Princes in the good graces of Mr. Pierce and Mr. La Beau," the senior officer said. "You wouldn't be upright in the saddle otherwise. You have my permission to proceed to Camp Chase with no stops in between whatsoever. Cross me and I'll have you jailed. Officers, clear the street."

Declawing and defanging of the Columbus Police Department now past history, Major Dance's impromptu column trotted westward past the statehouse, crossed the Scioto, and bore down on Camp Chase's westernmost Broad Street gate. Fully alert and threatened with punishment for earlier deficiencies, the sentries were at wit's end. They felt like nurses without tourniquets. The mandatory "Who goes there?" was a high-pitched shriek followed by the ominous rolling snick of cocking weapons.

"Major Dance Walker here. Take your fingers off those triggers, lads. We mean you no harm."

A relieved corporal of the guard had the sanity and self-control to order, "Stand down. Stand down. Stand down."

Rifle butts struck the ground and Dance Walker led his wayward troopers to the regiment's stables. Captain Cam Logan; Major Ambrose Hodges, regimental provost; and three of his guardsmen were gathered at the gate accessing the yard fronting the long rows of stalls. Jacob had no difficulty catching the stern expressions of

Major Hodges and Cam Logan in the light of the lanterns borne by two jittery privates who looked like they wanted to be elsewhere.

Dance Walker raised his arm and the order to halt was passed down the column. "Major, I was not happy with your circumventing my office," Major Hodges said. "These men should be under arrest."

Jacob squirmed in his saddle. Dance Walker had told the troopers he'd corralled that if they accompanied him, they wouldn't be subject to arrest by the provost guard, and not a trooper in the First Ohio would stand behind any officer who lied to them. Dance Walker, the diplomat, was needed front and center one last time.

"With all due respect, Major Hodges, if you and your detail had tried to arrest these men at the Seven Princes, I guarantee you there would have been shooting and blood spilled. I used my acquaintance with the proprietor to our advantage. They are back in camp unharmed and remorseful."

"Being remorseful is not punishment enough," Major Hodges said. "They belong in the guard house with the twelve troopers we arrested at the Four Mile House until we can convene a court-martial."

"Again, with all due respect, Major, we're entraining this very morning. If you will record the names of the deserters, I guarantee you that once we reach Kentucky every trooper will regret having done so. They will consider a fight under fire with the Rebels light duty when I finish with them. We can always press charges later, if that becomes necessary. Right now, these men need to fall out and turn in."

Jacob admired Dance Walker's ability to keep the welfare of the First Ohio's troopers and the prosecution of the war first and foremost in his thinking. Walker's prescribed course of action would preserve the fighting integrity of the regiment while having the least impact on availability of the rank-and-file troopers. Every cavalryman languishing in the guardhouse worked to the advantage of the enemy. Dance Walker, Jacob realized, thought like the great generals in Jacob's books on military history.

Major Ambrose Hodges thought for a long silent minute before saying, "I will accept your proposal subject to Colonel Ransom's approval in the morning. If he rejects it, these men will be arrested for desertion."

"We have one more order of business, Major Hodges. Captain Logan, I encountered Sergeant Bell in the stables and commandeered him to cover my backside. I felt it necessary to reach the city as quickly as possible and had your Corporal Howard inform the colonel of my intentions. I hope Corporal Howard then reported the sergeant's absence to you."

A bland-faced Cam Logan said, "He did, sir."

Jacob sensed Cam Logan's resentment that his assigned duties as captain of Company M had been conveniently circumvented. Cam Logan should have delivered the update to Colonel Ransom, not a non-commissioned subordinate officer that mocked him and Tor Shavers behind their backs.

If Jacob had learned nothing else in his weeks at Camp Chase, it was that the success of any officer depended on his ability to lock away his self-interests and his ego and lose the key. Petty jealousies and fits of anger and resentment demeaned an officer and stole his ability to lead. If you lost the respect of your men, you were equally lost, and Cam Logan was well down that perilous road.

Cam Logan confirmed Jacob's conviction as Jacob finished grooming and feeding his buckskin. Making certain they were out of the hearing of those close by, Logan said, "I received written orders from Colonel Ransom that you will be subject to detached duty at his whim with the rank of acting lieutenant. Just remember this, a lot can befall a trooper between Camp Chase and Kentucky. You'll be a hero over my dead body, and I'll make sure that Denning gal has the opportunity to cry over your grave. Good night, Sergeant–Acting Lieutenant Bell."

CHAPTER 14

Jacob Bell was thankful the sky was clear at first light on 9 December 1861. The weather had been remarkably dry and unseasonably warm throughout the three months the First Regiment Ohio Volunteer Cavalry had resided at Camp Chase, and the continuation of such weather would greatly enhance the regiment's chances of meeting its most demanding challenge to date: the transporting of one thousand troopers and their horses, equipment, and rations by rail and boat to a new campsite in Kentucky.

The "General" call sounded, tents were struck, and the straw and debris that had accumulated over the ninety-day encampment were put on fire. The ensuing black, suffocating smoke that swirled through company streets burned eyes and provoked coughing spells in the ranks. Bugles blew "Boots and Saddles," and relieved troopers hustled to the stable toting their personal belongings in wrapped blankets and pants pockets.

Horses were fed and then allowed to drink freely for the upcoming train ride. For the first time, Jacob saw cavalry saddles with double blanket, rubber poncho, overcoat, shirt, extra suit of underwear, socks, nose bag, lariat rope, the sundry items required to care for the trooper's horse, and a large comforter tied at pommel and cantle. Fully packed and ready for the horse's back, each saddle seemed to rival the size of a Pennsylvania freight wagon. By Jacob's calculation, each trooper had baggage enough for three men. Two troopers were required to lift a saddle up on a horse's back. After an intolerable nerve-stretching wait of two hours, the order to mount was finally given and troopers swore later their mounts groaned as they swung into the saddle and fell into line.

The rally of a thousand cavalrymen—armed and equipped, with heavy marching orders—marching by fours along the old National Road, through the streets of Columbus to the rail yards and depot in the city's eastern quarter, was an exhilarating, never-to-be-forgotten experience. The First Ohio was at last off to the war and the real fighting. No more of the same old routine day after day after day. The crowds awaiting them heightened their excitement and enthusiasm to the point where it was hard to maintain discipline and sit still and erect in the saddle.

Word had gone out the day before by telegraph, and scores of relatives from Franklin, Madison, Union, Licking, Fairfield, Ross, and other adjoining counties had lined the First Ohio's route to bid their fathers, brothers and sons, cousins and sweethearts good-bye. Jacob spied many tearful souls and heard numerous shouts from folks begging the Lord to protect their loved ones.

Excitement of a different stripe arose in the stretch from Four Mile House to the Broad Street bridge. A number of the cumbersome loads burdening the horses shifted, causing the frightened animals bearing them to break and run, with their riders valiantly trying to regain control. In some instances, after troopers had been thrown or had dismounted, their mounts kicked the well-packed saddles to pieces. As a result, the big comforters provided each trooper by the Franklin County Sanitary Commission took a frightful pounding, and hoof-torn puffs of cotton stuffing filled the air so thickly they reminded Tom South of winter snowball fights with his many sisters. The laughter subsided with their crossing of the Broad Street bridge.

With Troop M positioned near the rear of the column, Jacob observed that the crowd was filling the street behind the column and intending to follow them as long as they could. At the intersection of Broad and High streets on the northwest corner of Ohio's Capital Square, a pining trooper launched into "The Girl I Left Behind Me." The entire column quickly joined him *en mass*, and the image of Felicia Denning popped into Jacob's head.

She'd been lurking in the back of his mind since they parted company the previous evening. He could still feel the hungry press of her lips on his mouth and the swell of her ample breasts against his chest. She was a sensitive, charming, intelligent, lush-bodied beauty that could haunt a man till he could think of nothing else. He somehow had to keep his craving for her at arm's length and pay attention to his duty. He vowed that, as much as it could be done, he'd confine his throbbing memories of her to nightly dreams and letter writing.

They drew abreast of the statehouse. Initially, Jacob thought he was hearing things. Then he was not so certain. Somehow the calling of his name drifted to him above the din of the cheering crowd, the clopping of hoofs, and a thousand singing troopers. He peered in the direction of the calling voice and located a pair of frantically waving arms holding a forage cap and a small flag among a group of somber, dark-suited men in the center of the statehouse steps. The mop of black hair was a dead giveaway. Jacob hadn't noticed before that Jarrod Bell's height matched that of their senator father standing next to him. His youngest brother jumped up and down when Jacob waved back, bumping against those on either side of him.

While Jacob was pleased Jarrod had come to see him off to war, the sight of his youngest brother saddened him and he had to fight back tears. The thought that this might be the last occasion on which he saw any member of his immediate family brought home with a vengeance a stark reality: The relatively safe environment of a training camp was a vastly distant world from the persistent danger of a shooting war where men were often killed by enemy fire as callously as a reaper cut down hay. He suddenly felt small and ineffectual, as if his life was no more important than that of a fly, that he could very well die in some far-off field in a battle whose outcome he would never know, just another corpse to be covered with the fresh dirt of a hasty burial.

He shook himself violently and cursed aloud, drawing curious looks from those around him when they discovered nothing amiss. He would not die needlessly. He would find a means to contribute to a Union victory that honored himself, his family, and his heritage. He would be borne to the grave surrounded by those who loved and respected him, knowing his country had called upon him in a time of great peril and Jacob Franklin Bell had given his best serving her flag.

The final memorable event of the march to the Columbus railroad yards for Jacob occurred a few blocks past the Ohio statehouse. The senior Columbus police officer—the same one with the glorious walrus mustache they'd encountered a few hours ago—was conversing with Major Dance Walker from his perch atop the precinct paddy wagon parked in front of his jail. From the bounce of the officer's helmeted head and his uproarious fits of laughter, Jacob surmised Dance Walker would receive red carpet treatment from the Columbus Police Department should he have occasion to visit Camp Chase in the future. Jacob admired Walker's habit of never burning a bridge behind him, physically or personally, if wisdom spared the timbers.

Miles of cheering and singing gradually lost their luster, and the rail yards were a welcome sight. The regimental sergeants had reviewed the entraining procedure with their charges at supper the night before and issued two leather cards bearing the troopers' names to each of them; the first card was to be affixed to his horse's mane and the second to his packed saddle to avoid confusion and disputes later during loading and unloading. To start the loading, each troop walked down the rail line and located its designated freight and stock cars. Sergeants then assigned a corporal and two enlisted men to each freight car to take receipt of the marked saddles and gear as troopers handed them up. As the unsaddling continued, horses ready for loading were led to slat-sided stock cars accessible by wooden ramps. The ramps were four feet wide and twelve feet long with three-foot-high side rails; wooden cross-cleats had been nailed a foot apart to the wooden floors to keep the horses from slipping.

To prevent slippage of horses within the stock cars, civilians had shoveled sand four to five inches deep onto their floors. Horses were led quietly up the ramp one at a time with the next animal waiting at the near end of the ramp until its predecessor was wholly within the car and away from the doorway. Inside, halters were removed after each horse was placed across the car, alternating head to tail and close enough together to prevent any horse from turning around. Each car was loaded at both ends with each end working toward the middle. When the last horse was led into place, thus "wedging" the load, the doors on both sides of the car were rolled shut and locked.

The entraining of the regiment's horses, saddles, and

gear required the balance of the daylight hours. It was almost dark when the troopers—toting their arms, haversacks, and canteens—massed at the depot and sought seats in their assigned passenger cars.

An awestruck Sam Kite took the seat next to Jacob and said, "Sergeant Bell, I've never seen anything like it."

"What's that?"

"I kept a count, sir. Sixty cars for the horses, twelve for baggage, and forty for troopers made up into three separate trains. It's like a whole town is moving."

Realizing Sam Kite had never in his life been more than five miles from Chillicothe in any direction prior to his enlistment, Jacob sipped water from his canteen and said, "Sam, we're bound to witness a whole host of things fighting this war, some enjoyable, some terribly painful, that neither of us has seen before. If we're lucky, we'll live to tell our grandchildren about them."

Couplings clanged, the car jerked, jerked again, and then they were under way. From his travels settling legal disputes, Jacob knew they were riding the rails of the Columbus and Xenia Railroad and would switch to those of the Little Miami Railroad at Xenia for the final leg into Cincinnati. He was bone tired and sound asleep not far beyond the outskirts of Columbus despite the wooden benches with their straight backs and lack of padding. Even the coal smoke and cinder ash whipping through the cracked window at his ear couldn't keep sleep at bay.

An hour short of dawn, the air blowing in the window cleared briefly and Jacob heard engine whistles echo in the hills flanking the train. They were on the bridge in the valley of the Little Miami River at the start of their descent into the Queen City. Jacob came upright and fought through the cobwebs of deep sleep slowing his thinking. He needed to be on his toes for the major chore of the new day: the transfer of the regiment from rail to boat.

The horses and saddles were removed from the cars in reverse sequence of their loading. After each trooper negotiated the off ramp with his mount, he led him to open ground adjacent to the rail yard supplied with feed bins and watering troughs by the local quartermaster corps. He then proceeded with his horse to the appropriate freight car and secured his saddle. The unloading, completed in an orderly fashion without accident or injury, consumed the greater part of the forenoon.

Once lined out, the regiment rode through the streets of Cincinnati to its levee where boats with steam up awaited them. With the Queen City being accustomed to the presence of large numbers of Union military units and their comings and goings, the reception given the First Ohio was lukewarm and nearly cheerless compared to the rousing send-off they had received in Columbus. Jacob's single distinct memory of their ride to the Ohio River waterfront stemmed from the antics of the troopers when they spied carts of fresh vegetables and fruit lining the curbs in the city's open market area. Sabers rattled free of metal scabbards, and troopers on the outside edge of the column were soon spearing delicacies right and left and sharing them with those who couldn't reach the carts. Jacob was unable to interpret the vitriolic curses the vendors used to scream their outrage, but they were most certainly the best the German language had to offer.

The customary noise and bustle of the crowded levee were strange to the horses, and a number of them shied and tried to turn away the closer they drew to the narrow, high-sided loading chutes of the steamboats. Designated corporals and privates manned large wooden boxes at the foot of the chutes into which the regiment's numbered saddles were deposited for hoisting to the upper deck by crane. Once horses were in the chute and pressured by the animals behind them, they kept moving forward. Many hesitated at the top end of the chute, however, unsettled by the slight sway and bob of the waiting deck that resulted from the river's current lapping against the hulls of the steamboats. Occasionally, the shoulders of two troopers shoving against hindquarters provided the final impetus for the truly recalcitrant animal.

At three p.m. gangplanks for foot traffic and regular freight were hauled aboard, and the steamboats backed away from the dock and the loading chutes, turned to port, and set sail downriver for Louisville, Kentucky, the First Ohio's port of call. Jacob had to laugh when the boys cheered their own departure. First Sergeant Dan Clutter sidled up to Jacob as the steamboat assigned to Companies M and N, the *Tennessee Belle*, neared mid-stream. "We need to mount a round-the-clock stable guard for the horses. Per Captain Logan and Captain Whittier of Company N, your mess will cover the midnight-to-four-a.m. watch."

The hurricane deck of the *Tennessee Belle* was jammed with troopers, and Jacob doubted there was enough room to bed down all the men come nightfall. Some grumbling arose about the empty cabins beneath the pilothouse on the Texas deck above that their officers weren't using, but petered out for lack of any real interest on the part of tired troopers. Card playing, checkers, letter writing, shooting the bull, munching on meager rations, and sleeping consumed the idle hours for the enlisted troopers once their interest in watching the progress of the *Tennessee Belle* waned.

In the early evening, clouds scudded in from the west, threatening a storm. Soft rain began falling as Jacob's mess relieved the stable guard on the main deck at midnight. Jacob considered the lack of thunder and lightning a godsend after listening to Dan Clutter's report on the temperament of the crowded horses.

From the outset, the hiss of steam, the noise of the machinery, and the dashing of waves against the hull had frightened certain horses, which kept the whole herd agitated. The problem worsened when the boat swayed, causing a horse to slip and fall in the horse urine and manure slowly coating the bare wooden planks of the main deck. "Man could get trampled in there among them," Clutter warned Jacob. "Lest it's absolutely necessary, we best stand clear."

The initial two hours of the watch passed without incident. Unable to locate Sam Kite during his obligatory circling of the main deck at mid-watch, Jacob confronted Corporal Fritz Howard at his post in the bow of the *Belle*. "Where's Private Kite?"

"I wasn't aware he was missing until now, sir. I stationed him in the stern outside the engine room. I do remember him telling me on my first round that one of the ship's crew had seen him leaning over the rail watching the paddlewheel and offered to give him a tour of the engine room and let him watch the paddlewheel at arm's length. Sam was pretty excited about doing that. But I know Sam like he's my brother, sir; he wouldn't desert his post."

Remembering Sam Kite's fascination with the trains that had transported the regiment to Cincinnati, Jacob wasn't so certain he couldn't be lured away from his post for a few minutes to witness what perhaps for him was an even more enthralling sight. Hadn't Jacob himself spent a sunset hour at the stern of the hurricane deck studying the paddlewheels? Hadn't he woven a path through a maze of reluctant-to-move troopers to do so?

Wasn't curiosity history's acknowledged troublemaker?

Corporal Howard suggested, "Should we start a search, sir?"

"No, I'll check the engine room. If he's not there, we'll

take other measures. He's probably gawking at something, somewhere."

Jacob coursed along the rim of the horse pen, maintaining a firm grip on the rail of the main deck. The rain had ceased and the night was quiet except for the stomping of a horse and the distant threshing of the paddlewheel.

He was hoping Sam Kite had returned to his post and that a stern private lecture would put the fear of Colonel Ransom's wrath in the wandering private and resolve the matter to Sam's betterment without the invoking of punishment. But a simple reckoning was not to be. No one was manning the post in front of the engine room.

Jacob eased past the corner of the engine room, again clinging tightly to the railing. At that juncture, he refused to dwell on the possibility that Sam Kite had fallen overboard. If he had, with the *Tennessee Belle* last in line, there was a chance no one would have heard his yell for help over the sound of the paddlewheel, and it was a considerable distance to the bank of the Ohio in either direction if one were swimming in a soggy cavalry uniform and riding boots.

More disappointment greeted Jacob at the door of the engine room. Peering through the door's glass porthole, he had a clear view of the engine room and the two bare-chested, sweating firemen feeding the yawning mouths of the *Tennessee Belle*'s boilers. They were alone in that overheated, nightmarish space.

That left the open area before the paddlewheel itself if Sam Kite was still on the main deck of the ship. Easing his way along the starboard side of the engine room, Jacob leaned forward, snuck a peak at the paddlewheel, and was lured closer by its noise and sheer power.

He stepped around the corner of the engine room and stumbled over a pair of blue-clad legs with yellow stripes lying parallel with the rear wall of the engine room. The owner of the legs was resting facedown on the vibrating deck. Jacob hastily knelt beside what he believed was Sam Kite's chest and pressed his fingers against the side of his neck and felt for a pulse. He found one. It was weak but it was there.

Later, he could never pinpoint precisely what warned him. He thought maybe it was the sudden appearance on the engine room wall of a shadow, belonging to a shape forging itself between him and the moonlight slanting over his shoulder. Or it could have been the sixth sense he'd possessed from early childhood that told him he wasn't by himself, that some unknown person was drawing down on him. As he had in the past when that alarm had rung in his head, he assumed something bad was about to befall him.

Thrusting his hands behind his head in hopes of warding off any blow that would render him unconscious, he sprawled on his chest and rolled toward the paddlewheel, the direction from which an assault had to be coming, if one was.

His shoulder encountered a hard object. He heard a loud grunt, and a club of some sort struck the deck behind him with a hearty rap. Jacob rolled again and came upon his hands and knees, desperate to get his bearings and locate his assailant.

The attacker was squarely in front of Jacob, rising from one knee and drawing back his club for another blow. He was a big fellow, stocky and wide at the chest, but with legs like sticks that made him appear top heavy. There wasn't enough room for Jacob to slide by him without moving into the range of the club. Jacob jumped to his feet with his hands raised in front of face, and, feigning fear, retreated until spray whipped by the spinning blades of the paddlewheel dampened and chilled the back of his neck.

Being the initiator and using his quickness in a fight

had always served the unarmed Jacob well, and his charge
caught the bearded mate by surprise. He raised his free
arm to hold Jacob at bay and strike a crippling blow with
his cub. Jacob ignored the club, ducked under the raised
arm, grabbed the mate's belt with both hands, and reared
backward, dragging the man after him. Jacob planted his
feet, jerked with all his might, and, turning his shoulders
as he did so, flung the mate into the blades of the paddlewheel.

The churning blades never slowed. Jacob heard two
crunching sounds. There was no scream of pain. A leg
severed at the knee arched into the moonlight on the far
side of the paddlewheel a few seconds later. He saw no
more of the mate but suspected that the dark blob surfac-
ing briefly in the steamboat's wake was the rest of his body.

Jacob went to Sam Kite and gently turned him over,
cradling his head in the crook of his arm. The groan and
cough that movement wrought from Sam Kite was music
to Jacob's ears. He waited, and shortly, the downed
trooper's eyes opened. "How are we feeling, Private?"

Sam Kite blinked and said, "Head hurts something
awful."

"Exactly what happened, Private? Why did you desert
your post?"

"Red Baker, the mate, saw me trying to watch the
paddlewheel over the side and offered to show me the
engine room and the rudders in front of the blades that
steer the ship. I refused him the first time, but he came
around again and said it would only take a few minutes and
nobody would miss me for that long, dark as it is."

"Why did you trust him? Didn't it seem odd that he
wanted you to leave your post? He had to know you would
be charged with desertion if you were caught."

"Sir, it's not an excuse for what I did, but I saw Captain Logan talking to Red Baker on the main deck while

we were loading the ship in Cincinnati. I guess that made me think Baker was trustworthy."

That statement answered a multitude of questions for Jacob. The attempt on his life had been planned in advance with Sam Kite serving as bait. Cam Logan had known which ship Company M would board and made sure Jacob's mess was assigned to the midnight stable watch. That would bring Jacob around on a mid-watch inspection at a set hour; then it was merely a matter of finding a man willing to kill for money and working out a nifty scheme for committing murder. Two murders, in fact, for once Red Baker discovered Sam Kite had survived the first strike of his club, Jacob was certain the private would have followed him over the side. And had Sam not fallen for Red Baker's ruse, it would have been just as easy to club him senseless on an otherwise deserted deck and drag him to the back of the engine room.

Jacob helped a wobbly Sam Kite to his feet. "Private, did the firemen see you?"

"No, sir, we just looked in the porthole. One peek was enough of that operation for me. I could feel the heat through the door."

"Did anyone see you with Red Baker the second time he approached you?"

"No, sir, and I looked around real sharp, too."

"Private, I don't want to see you hung or cashiered out of this army. Here's the story we're going to tell, and, with a little luck, we'll get away with lying. You thought you saw somebody lurking by the door of the engine room. You went to investigate, stepped in a puddle of water, fell and hit your head, and I found you during my mid-watch inspection. Can you stick to that story no matter what?"

"Yes, sir, I surely can. I want to put this whole thing behind me something fierce."

"Then come along before Corporal Howard mounts a

full-scale search for the both of us. And remember, Private, one word of what really happened tonight to *anyone* and you *will* have your chance to stretch a rope."

Sam Kite stepped aside and said, "After you, sir. I can walk on my own now."

Returning to the horse pen, Jacob took a perverse delight in imagining Cam Logan's confusion upon discovering his paid executioner was no longer aboard the ship and the man he wanted dead was still very much alive.

Jacob remembered Logan's contention that night in the Camp Chase stables that anything could transpire during the regiment's journey from Columbus to Kentucky. Well, it had, but not according to Logan's designs.

Jacob nodded at Sam Kite's backside.

Yes, sir, being alive and able to savor the thought of Cam Logan's money filling Red Baker's pockets on the bottom of the Ohio River was worth a brush with death.

CHAPTER 15

Sergeant Field Peterson sought out Judah Bell on 28 January 1862. "Corporal Bell, Captain Morgan has asked for nine men mounted on the best horses to accompany him on a special raid. That red stallion and fine mare of yours made it easy for Lieutenant Duke to include you. We depart at dusk."

Field Peterson's message came as no surprise to Judah. Captain Morgan had been much impressed the evening Judah introduced him to Jasper. What had stuck in Judah's mind was Morgan's sentiment that "Before it's over, this war is going to wear out a lot of animals, excellent, good, and poor. You need to preserve this Jasper of yours the best you can. If you can acquire a second mount to spare him on occasion, do so. I follow that practice with my filly, Black Bess. Never forget my main objective is to harass the enemy at every opportunity and then elude his pursuit, and the condition of the horse under you is almost always more important than that of your weapon."

Judah had subsequently acquired a second mount by default. Captain Morgan, Master Sergeant Hooper, and Peterson had been presumptive regarding the reaction of the Southern-bred rank and file to the idea of Barefoot riding with Peterson's scout company. Snide, insulting remarks, and hard stares made it apparent straightaway that the half-breed's service in the Seminole War counted for naught with those in Morgan's command who would fight to their dying breath to uphold slavery. To them, black blood was black, no matter that an equal amount of red flowed through Barefoot's veins. The disgruntlement about the prospect of having to side with a black Cherokee swelled despite every attempt by their officers to quell it. Judah grew fearful the racial hostility would lead to a violent confrontation endangering Barefoot's life, if the stubborn Hooper and Peterson didn't cease and desist.

Resolution came from the object of the slander. Having endured the perfidies of white masters for years, Asa Barefoot had no intention of letting the situation reach a point where he, and perhaps his master, was no longer welcome in camp. The half-breed insisted Judah and he call on Sergeant Peterson.

The meeting took place as Barefoot desired in front of Captain Morgan's headquarters with half the camp pretending they weren't watching. "Sergeant Peterson," Barefoot said, "my legs are too old and my back too stiff for long rides day after day. I wish to cook for your mess and help care for your horses. I will do the same for others at your bidding. My only request is that I be allowed to stay with Master Judah."

Before Peterson could respond, Barefoot opened his coat and slowly passed the revolver that had been returned to him by a direct order from the sergeant in full view of every watching trooper. "Many will feel safer if I'm not armed. My horse, of course, belongs to Master Judah, also."

Recognizing when a squabble was lost, Field Peterson handed Barefoot's revolver to Judah. "Private Barefoot, I would have enjoyed serving with a veteran scout like you, but I will abide by your wishes and make them known to Captain Morgan and my fellow officers. Gentlemen, you're dismissed."

The matter was never again mentioned in Judah's presence, and the objecting members of the squadron, willing now to openly recognize Asa's exemplary skill with skillet, pan, reflector oven, and horseshoe hammer, began calling the half-breed Mr. Barefoot. Barefoot's hot meals at the completion of his mess's patrols were soon envied by the whole camp. On occasion, Barefoot assisted handsome Miss Loomis in Captain Morgan's kitchen, much to the delight of that particular female and the captain. One evening Judah thought he detected a sly, lecherous grin on Barefoot's craggy face as Barefoot returned from his culinary duties at headquarters. Apparently, the half-breed's stamina wasn't lacking in the right circumstances.

Under the tutelage of Field Peterson, Judah had quickly adopted the habits of the veteran cavalryman, and that overcast afternoon, after choosing the well-rested Jasper for Captain Morgan's special raid, he checked the stallion's legs, hoofs, and shoes, and fed and watered him. He then reloaded both Navy Colts, filled his cartridge and cap boxes, topped off his powder flask, stuffed his saddlebags with cold salt pork and bread from Barefoot's larder, filled his canteen at the well, and tried to nap until "Boots and Saddles" sounded. Sleep was scarcer than a five-legged dog once John Hunt Morgan had the bit in his mouth.

Sleep eluded him, and the now Corporal Judah Bell laid in his tent and took stock of all that had happened to him since his arrival at Bell's Tavern eight weeks ago. From the start, he had been assigned to A Company commanded by Lieutenant Basil Duke, and made a member of Sergeant Field Peterson's mess. The action in the field that Judah craved had commenced shortly thereafter with the burning of the Bacon Creek bridge on the Louisville and Nashville

Railroad, a scant two miles from the Union lines. One hundred and five of Morgan's men mounted on the Squadron's best horses, including Judah and Jasper, departed Three Corners at dusk, rode through the night for fifty miles, and cold-camped the next morning behind a wide peninsula of trees that shielded them from the workers rebuilding the bridge the Confederates had burned during their retreat south of the Green River the previous month.

At nine o'clock that evening, Captain Morgan led the advance and discovered the workers and their military escort had chugged north on the construction train after finishing the relaying of one of the rails, leaving the site unguarded. Field Peterson had bragged as they dismounted that Captain Morgan had the Union's civilian contractors so terrorized they didn't feel safe unless they were behind Yankee lines come nightfall.

Judah's first bridge burning excited him to the core. He gleefully helped his fellow troopers heap stubble and loose wood on the cross beams of the bridge. At Morgan's signal, Judah applied the torch handed him by Field Peterson to the woodpile on the north end of the bridge. Judah and Peterson then trotted toward the south end of the bridge as other troopers lighted additional fires and followed them.

The dry wood caught immediately and a roaring conflagration was soon backlighting the surrounding hills, but Captain Morgan was in no particular hurry despite the nearness of superior Union forces and allowed the squadron to stand and watch the fruits of their labor. Beams popped, cracked, and crumbled. One end of the bridge fell, then the other. The hungry flames consumed four of the bridge's thirty-foot uprights, and the fifth lay smoldering in the middle of the creek when Captain Morgan called, "To Horse."

"The blue-bellies will rebuild it again within the week," Field Peterson predicted, "but it pleases me they'll worry that we'll show another night or maybe catch them working some morning."

They rode all night again, and a mile from Bell's Tavern Judah was introduced to a spirit-rousing custom of Morgan's men that rivaled the excitement of bridge burning. At a shout from within the squadron, the returning troopers stood in their stirrups in unison and started singing at the top of their voices. A regular member of the Buffalo Stamp Baptist Church choir, Judah joined them in singing the Southern songs he'd learned outside the pews from his female Kentucky cousins.

A few nights later, Judah was part of a detail that burned a ferryboat at Munfordville on the Green River. The next week, he and Field Anderson were two of the five men picked by Captain Morgan for a sneak attack on the Woodsonville L & N Railroad depot not two hundred yards from the Union's picket fires. They had crept in afoot after tying their horses in a clump of trees along the right-of-way. Near the depot, Captain Morgan pointed at Field Peterson and Judah. Judah drew his Navy Colt and backed Peterson's rushing of the front door. Judah saw heads through the depot's tall lobby windows. Then they were inside and chair legs were scraping and squealing as five blue-belly stragglers caught playing cards by lantern-light at a corner table sought a direction in which to flee the muzzles of the revolvers suddenly aimed at them.

Field Peterson's raspy voice barking, "You can't outrun a bullet, boys," quelled the Yankees' desire for a hasty exit. Hands shot for the ceiling, and five frightened souls impersonated statues without orders to do so.

A laughing Captain Morgan sized up the scene and said, "One of you Yankees gather up the cards and the loose money on the table. John Hunt Morgan's not known for petty thievery; good playing cards are scarce, and I won't burn any soldier's winnings."

Five pairs of blue-belly eyes widened and Judah spied a quaking lip here and there. The Confederate instigator of haunted Yankee nightmares stood before them, though they couldn't discern the devil's horns, flaming tongue, and alligator skin and tail so many attributed to him. He was dressed instead in a civilian, black broadcloth suit, vest of the same color, snow-white shirt, and a string tie. Standing casually with his hat under one arm, he appeared less threatening than a charming schoolmaster. But hadn't the poker players' preachers and mothers warned them the devil had many guises at his disposal?

"We best step outside, gentlemen," Captain Morgan said. "My boys are dousing the outside of the depot with coal oil courtesy of the L and N, and they get a little anxious on me every once and a while."

The chubby Yankee swept the cards and loose money from the poker table, and the room emptied in a hurry. At Morgan's nod, three torch-bearing Rebel privates set fire to all four sides of the depot. In the light of the leaping flames, Captain Morgan made prisoners of four of the Yankees, beckoned to the Yankee he was releasing, and said, "Tell your commanding officer next time I'll burn the entire village."

In the distance, bugles were blowing and drums were beating a disciplined rat-a-tat, rat-a-tat, rat-a-tat in the Union camp. Spying the strengthening depot fire, the Union officers in Woodsonville were taking no risks and forming lines of battle. Field Peterson sniggered and said, "They won't catch a wink the whole night."

As December surrendered to colder January weather along the Green River, Federal forces stayed tight to their camps, and to avoid patrols that did little other than reconfirm Yankee positions and their lack of activity, Captain

Morgan and Lieutenant Duke targeted Union pickets. One night an attack taught Judah the essentials of the only aspect of guerrilla warfare he came to detest. Armed with sawed-off Enfield shotguns, squadron members padded silently through the brush in the middle of the night to within mere yards of a Yankee outpost, close enough they could hear the pickets talking and laughing. Then they waited patiently until the moon disappeared behind a cloud or went down for the night.

At Captain Morgan's signal, they rose to their knees and aimed their shotguns low for maximum effect. The surprised Yankee privates never forgot the sudden flash and roar of the Rebel shotguns, and neither did Judah. Screams and groans seemed to follow every shotgun blast, and the worst of it for Judah was sighting enemy soldiers writhing on the ground in the deadly illumination provided by exploding powder charges. Eventually, his conscience won out and he aimed high enough to avoid being part of the carnage, but not so high any officer or fellow trooper would notice.

When the Yankees attempted to spare themselves by withdrawing from advanced outposts at sundown, Captain Morgan changed his tactics accordingly. Possessing intelligence from his scouts that pinpointed the location of the house where the members of a Yankee cavalry outpost camped each night, he had his men fake charges on the outpost during the daylight hours, and that evening, when the twenty-five Union horsemen withdrew, he was waiting in ambush at their temporary residence. At Morgan's discretion, Judah and Field Peterson and two other troopers, armed with shotguns loaded with buckshot, were hidden with their commander behind a low fence in the house's front yard. Other squadron troopers had formed a hidden picket line in the dark woods along the road accessing the house.

The lead Yankee officer, exercising appropriate caution, halted his troopers thirty feet from the house and sent two of them to reconnoiter on foot. Cold of the winter ground seeping through his jacket, shotgun firmly in his grasp, Judah heard the nervous stamp of the Yankee horses and the rustle of dry grass disturbed by the boots of the troopers checking each side of the road. The two troopers yelled there was nothing to be found, but their officer, still leery, ordered the entire company to dismount and form a skirmish line in the yard.

The Yankees began their advance upon the house and Judah prayed his nerves wouldn't fray. Five Rebels were about to be exposed to the fire of twenty-five blue-bellies, and the odds didn't bode well for their survival. He was certain of one thing in those few tense, uncertain minutes. He wouldn't be firing high this go-round.

The instant one of the Yankees sighted John Hunt Morgan—whom Judah never found wanting when it came to steely resolve, outright courage, and total control in the bleakest of situations—he jumped to his feet and screamed, "Now!"

Judah and his saddle mates jumped upright with Morgan, and their simultaneous volley ripped into their startled foe. The Yankee officer and several of his troopers, blinded and shredded by lethal buckshot fired into their faces at close range, crumpled to the ground like discarded rag dolls.

The brutal, blood-spewing devastation of their comrades sapped every ounce of courage from the remaining Yankees, and they rushed to their horses without firing a single shot. Scrambling into the saddle, they galloped northward toward the main Union encampment past the picket line of Rebels awaiting them in their hiding places in the dark woods. The sequential blast of shotguns continued until the last panic-stricken Yankee still alive was clear of the woods and madly spurring for the safety of his own lines to sound the alarm, spreading the fear and panic John Hunt Morgan so dearly loved to inflict on his enemies.

The frequency of the squadron's night patrols turned Judah's days around and he became accustomed to treating breakfast as his evening meal. His messmates were a hodgepodge of characters from different points on the compass with a common zeal for taking the fight to the blue-bellies, and Judah found them excellent company during their idle hours when he missed Brianna Hardin the most. He eventually stopped trying to dismiss the one-armed parlor kiss and the clinging softness of her body, and struggled to keep his longing for her at arm's length and concentrate on the business at hand: killing Yankees before they killed him.

In quiet moments, he thought of his Ohio family. He dreamed of his mother and grandmother, father, his sisters, and his brothers—Jacob and Jarrod—and his years with them growing up. He marveled in those dreams how nighttime gunfire in a Kentucky barnyard had converted a horse-loving young man with a penchant for mischief into a young man capable of killing without warning from the dark of night. Judah acknowledged in those moments how he had turned his back on every principle his father supported and joined with those Senator Clay Bell deemed his ardent enemies, the misguided Confederates who would destroy his beloved country for their own gain.

Judah expected he might live to regret the snap decision fostered by his uncle's unwarranted death to ride south instead of north, but it was too late to change his mind. He was committed to a cause, and he prayed his allegiance to that cause, God forbid, didn't somehow bring him to grief with his brothers. He couldn't imagine Jacob and Jarrod wearing anything but Union blue.

The nub of it all was that no soldier in a war of divided

loyalties could fathom how the conflict would unfold once hostilities began. A soldier did his duty and hoped no off chance brought him muzzle to muzzle with his blood kin supporting the other side. In that regard, Judah took considerable comfort in the knowledge that the "War of the Rebellion" would be fought over a vast landscape by thousands of combatants, greatly enhancing the odds against such an encounter.

He refused to dwell on the possibility he might be reunited with his Ohio family at some point in time. The uncertainty of his future made such speculation a foolish game of random guessing that unsettled and frustrated him. As Grandmother Nadine Bell preached, "A man has his choices, and he must endure the good and the bad that flow from them."

Amen, I say to you, Grandmother, amen.

January 1862 had blustered forth with cold rain and icy sleet storms, and camp life for Morgan's Squadron morphed into a dreary, miserable existence. The routine chores of cooking over an open fire; gathering firewood; procuring horse fodder; watering, grooming, and shoeing horses; sink digging; and carting off trash and manure seemed doubly difficult for men constantly burdened with wet clothing in the absence of gum ponchos. Keeping riding gear, saddle blankets, weapons, powder, and rations dry shrank tent space and had men sleeping spoon fashion like old-time surveyors lacking shelter.

In the persistent, penetrating cold, a dozen diseases struck at once. Measles, typhoid, pneumonia, and dysentery spread through the camp at Bell's Tavern with alarming speed. One morning, the camp runner for Field Peterson's mess, Corporal Grubb, he of the pencil-thin yellow mustache, awakened with a rash on his face and chest. With a quick look inside Grubb's mouth, Peterson detected the red spots associated with measles. The sergeant had lost three of his siblings to the disease, and aware of its rapid contagion and after a consultation with Captain Morgan, he provided Grubb with rations and a sound mount and sent him home to Glasgow to recover. With Grubb's departure, Peterson called the mess together and informed them that Captain Morgan, upon Peterson's recommendation, had promoted Judah Bell to the rank of corporal. Though it was a roundabout path to promotion in Judah's mind, the cheers and back slapping following Peterson's announcement eclipsed any feelings he was taking advantage of Grubb's illness.

"Lord almighty," Judah said when asked to say a few words by the mess, "I hope Corporal Grubb has more success overcoming the measles than he did growing a mustache." The resulting laughter brightened what promised to be an otherwise drab morning.

January's bad news continued in a steady stream. Morgan's Squadron learned on 28 January of the defeat of General Zollicoffer's Confederate forces by George H. Thomas's Union Army at Mills Springs in eastern Kentucky, a defeat costing Zollicoffer his life and imperiling the thin Southern line of defense stretching westward from Cumberland Gap through Three Corners to Bowling Green. Gloom spread throughout Bell's Tavern and poisoned the atmosphere among troopers for a solid week. Judah and Field Peterson were caught in those same doldrums, and the invitation to accompany Captain Morgan on a special raid was the perfect balm for disheartened troopers anxious for action no matter how dangerous; so anxious both officers ignored the damp smell of rain in the late evening air.

The nine troopers picked from Company A by Lieutenant Basil Duke to accompany Captain Morgan met in his headquarters office at seven o'clock. Morgan was dressed in the civilian clothing he had donned for the attack on the Woodsonville depot. The garb of his small command was so nondescript it was difficult to deem them regular Confederate soldiers. The designation as "Home Guards" was more fitting.

"The Yankees have established a base camp in a log church south of Lebanon. I suspect they're planning to string telegraph lines from there eastward to connect with their new headquarters near Cumberland Gap. I intend to destroy the telegraphic equipment and take prisoner anyone at the site. Any questions?"

The detail set out in a driving rainstorm. Fortunately, the enterprising Basil Duke had acquired gum ponchos for Morgan and each trooper. The rain was so heavy for brief spurts that it was hard for Judah to make out Jasper's ears. Captain Morgan trusted the local guide he'd engaged, and they slogged nonstop until a blurry glimmer of dawn light peaked through the bare tops of the rain-shrouded trees ahead of them.

A large farmhouse and barn swelled in the mist on the north edge of the road, and their guide led them to it without hesitating. Nodding to Captain Morgan, the guide dismounted in front of the house, scampered across the porch, knocked hard four times on the solid wooden door, waited a good five seconds, and then knocked four times again. The door swung inward and the white adult male holding the handle filled the entire doorway from top to bottom and to both sides.

He was the biggest human being Judah had ever laid eyes on and was larger by far than the supposed world-famous giant he'd paid to see at a traveling circus in Louisville. For all his mature size, the giant before him had the clear-skinned, hairless, robust face, and bright demeanor of a child. He smiled hugely, stepped out onto the porch bareheaded, wearing a thin, sleeveless shirt that emphasized the huge muscles of his chest, and said in a small voice barely audible over the hiss of the rain, "Captain Morgan, welcome to my humble home. Here you and your men are always welcome. Jeffrey, my son, will help your men stable your horses out of sight in the barn. Then they will join us inside. My family are prepared for your visit."

Jeffrey led Judah and his fellow troopers into the bowel of the large barn and pitched hay down from the loft. Judah and his fellow troopers then unsaddled their horses and rubbed them down with empty feed sacks from a bin Jeffrey pointed out. Judah hustled and saw to the care of Captain Morgan's filly, Black Bess, as well as Jasper. Field Peterson did the same with their guide's horse. Judah had come to respect Peterson's devotion to accomplishing what needed to be done with the minimum amount of hassle, and emulated him whenever he could.

The giant master of the house hadn't lied. His family surely had prepared for their visit. When the boots of the detail thudded on the hallway floor inside the front door, they smelled kettles of cornmeal mush and ham with diced potatoes and onions steaming on the burners of an iron stove. Loaves of bread were baking in the stove's ovens, the kettles and ovens capable of feeding a small army.

"Just like coming home to a full table after making hay and swatting at yellow jackets all day," blurted Private Jack Holland.

The exhausted detail ate their fill and retired immediately. The Hanson family had shoved the furniture in the formal and sitting parlors against the wall and covered the floors with blankets. To escape the snoring that would soon fill those spaces, Judah moved his blanket to the pantry with the permission of plain-faced, kindly Mrs. Hanson.

The rain continued to pour down. The Hanson family

abandoned the lower level of the house and went off to their quarters on the second floor for the day. Judah could hear the rain drumming on the tin roof of the rear porch, and the rhythmic sound lulled him into a sleep too deep for dreams. It took some vigorous shaking by Field Peterson to awaken him late that afternoon.

The rain ceased while the detail was enjoying another sumptuous meal. They saddled up and set off again at dusk. The road was a virtual quagmire now and the creeks were threatening their banks. At a substantial stream their guide called Conner's Creek, Jack Holland came close to drowning when his horse slipped while scaling the far bank. Quick rope work by Lew James, the detail's sole Texan, saved both rider and horse; the roping caused hair-lipped Jack Holland to quip later, not in James's presence, of course, "Guess that jug-eared, Lone Star Ranger wasn't lying about roping a live buzzard out of the air, after all."

Captain Morgan's hand-picked guide circled the detail around the fires of two Union encampments. They found shelter at dawn in the barn of another loyal Southerner half the size of Doyle Hanson. Their new host offered them his barn, but not his home. The farmer gave them hay for the horses, but with eight children to feed in the family, there was little food to spare those with two legs. The detail munched on cold rations from their saddlebags and took turns sleeping in the haymow.

That Thursday night they resumed their march. As they exited the barnyard, Jack Holland leaned in his saddle and whispered to Judah, "I'm beginning to believe Captain Morgan's log church is on the back side of the moon." Judah was beginning to consider Jack's comment gospel truth by midnight, but the horses withstood the physical toll of hock-deep mud and swam four cold, swollen creeks without protest. Sixty grueling miles later, the log church, a squat structure beneath its white steeple in the pale light of dawn, popped into view.

With a quick gander roundabout, Captain Morgan led them into the churchyard at a gallop while signaling the detail by hand to surround the church and the three Union supply wagons drawn up beside it. Field Peterson and Judah dropped from the saddle at a run and charged inside, surprising nine Union soldiers who were trying to shake free of sleep, pull on their pants, and learn what the hoof-pounding commotion outside their quarters was all about. None of the Yankees had a weapon in their possession. Nine rifles were neatly lined up in front of the altar, and Peterson motioned for Judah to step between the rifles and their owners.

"Hold it right there, boys," Field Peterson yelled, his rasping shout and wagging revolver capturing the Yankees' attention. "Put on your pants, shirts, and shoes, and then form a single file. Do anything else, or make a wrong move, and we'll treat you to a bullet. Understood?"

Nine heads nodded vigorously. In three short minutes the march to the churchyard commenced. Captain Morgan greeted them from the saddle of Black Bess. "Well done, gentlemen. Why don't you Union boys have a seat on the ground up against the wall of the church and Private James will watch after you. Sergeant Peterson, let's check the contents of those wagons."

An inventory of the three wagons uncovered telegraphic instruments, Union Army overcoats, pork, beans, hardtack, and other stores. The detail passed the day guarding the road in the event they might have Yankee visitors, cleaning and reloading their weapons, feasting on pork and beans, swilling the good blue-belly coffee, and feeding, watering, and grooming their horses. Aware their commander intended to take the Yankee prisoners with them, Field Peterson and

Judah guarded the Yankees while two of them at a time performed the same chores for their mounts.

At five o'clock sharp, Captain Morgan met with Peterson, Judah, and Henry Martin, their middle-aged, gimlet-eyed, pipe-smoking guide whose hacking cough heralded an early grave. "Most likely somebody along the way has reported seeing us to the blue-bellies," John Morgan said, "so we'll follow a different route returning to camp. We'll swing around to the south and follow the southwestern road through Glasgow, and then take the northern road from there to Bell's Tavern."

Judah's ears perked at the mention of Glasgow. Might he be able to arrange a brief visit with Brianna Hardin? Hadn't Captain Morgan said he wanted to meet her?

"Fine by me, sir," Field Peterson said. "How do you want to handle the prisoners?"

Morgan's impish smile hinted at how much he enjoyed playing cat and mouse with his opponent. "We and our prisoners will wear Union overcoats, except Henry here. We'll place a Yankee between each of us with an unloaded rifle. With any luck, we should pass for a squad of enemy cavalry. Once we're across the Green River, it's an easy ride to Glasgow. Tell the men to fill their saddlebags with all the food they can carry. We'll burn everything along with that pile of telegraph poles over yonder. Let's have at it."

They lit fires at dusk inside the church and wagons and under stores piled in the churchyard, and heaped telegraph poles on the blaze. The detail departed in Yankee overcoats with their similarly clad prisoners toting unloaded rifles, Jack Holland flying a large United States flag on a staff near the head of the column, Lone Star Ranger Lew James with his twin revolvers belted around his waist bringing up the rear. That same Lew James had explained in detail the fate he would administer to any Yankee that decided to flee, and by the peaked cast of their faces, Judah determined they had hung on his every word. Without a doubt, if the situation were reversed, Judah would have. The Lone Star Ranger had described the tortures employed by Comanche warriors in such exquisite detail he had Judah's skin crawling.

Morgan's Squadron adhered to their usual habit of riding all night. The next morning they cold-camped deep in a large ravine containing enough of a stream to water the horses. Captain Morgan posted guards on each point of high ground and at the ravine's mouth. Twice during the day, small Yankee patrols stopped and watered their horses where the road crossed the stream and then proceeded on their way, never suspecting enemy rifles covered them the whole while.

They pushed hard the following night and at dawn were within reach of the Green River. Captain Morgan passed word summoning Field Peterson and Judah to the head of the column. "Gentlemen, I've an uneasy feeling the Yankees are pursuing us in significant numbers. I believe it's time we make straight for the Green River ferry. We get across the Green, we can cut the ferry loose, and Glasgow is ours for certain."

As this was the first sign of concern about Yankee pursuit on the part of their unflappable leader, neither subordinate officer, though dog tired, found fault with his thinking. After all, any sizable Yankee force could overwhelm nine Confederate raiders in short order. "We're with you, Captain. I'll have Private James keep a sharp lookout to our rear."

They rode at a constant trot with two brief halts to water and blow the horses, and they reached the Green River ferry in early afternoon. The muddy, swiftly flowing Green was flooded over the top of its banks. The ferry operator was not interested in taking them aboard. The four trips required to ferry the entire detail was simply not possible in those extreme conditions. That was when Judah witnessed at close range John Hunt Morgan's unique talent for deceiving his fellow beings.

From intelligence reported to him at Bell's Tavern, Morgan was aware of the ferryman's liking for Abraham Lincoln, so he started his spiel by claiming, "I'm Captain John McDonald of the Fourth Indiana Cavalry. My men and I are on special assignment for General Don Carlos Buell, commanding the Union Army. Per General Buell's orders, we are bound for Glasgow to arrest fifteen members of John Hunt Morgan's raiders camped outside the city. Morgan himself may well be there. I would suggest it is not in the best interest of your ferry and future business to hinder the completion of a mission so vitally important to the most powerful Union general west of the Appalachian Mountains."

The ferryman pondered Morgan's veiled threat for Judah's quick count to three, then yelled at the top of his lungs, "Hump your butts, ropers. These soldiers can't wait for calmer waters." Despite his Northern political persuasion, the ferryman had no problem owning three black slaves with ox-yoke shoulders to man the pull ropes of the ferry.

Out in the main current, the ferry lurched and heaved, and Judah clung to Jasper's saddle horn with both hands, praying the stallion didn't lose his footing on the boat's urine- and manure-slick floor. He was firmly convinced the side rails of the ferry couldn't withstand the weight of a horse and its terrified rider. Dry land became a scared quest fulfilled only when Jasper lunged down the ferry's gangplank on the far bank. A relieved Judah didn't mind the laughter spawned by his losing the contents of his stomach in a foul retching that wet his boots.

Trouble erupted on the ferry's final leg with Lew James,

Private Joe Fellows, and the last two Union prisoners aboard. As the craft drew down on the bank, the ferryman started screaming at Lew James and threw the steering oar to starboard. He turned the ferry downstream, heading it under low-hanging willow trees in an obvious attempt to rake the horses' passengers into the water. But the ferryman lost control of his craft in the powerful current, and it ran aground under the willows.

In a sequence of moves that defied logic, Ranger Lew James, caring nothing about the fate of the Yankee prisoners and the ferry crew, grabbed Joe Fellows by the seat of his pants, boosted him into the saddle of a tall roan, grabbed one of the roan's stirrups, drew his revolver, and fired two shots into the air. Already unnerved by the trauma of its ferry ride, the roan bolted for the same terra firma that had rescued Judah.

Ranger James's heels were higher than the roan's rump when it sailed skyward over the ferry's starboard side. The roan landed on the bank with a jarring thud. James jackknifed his body upright at the exact same moment, let hold of the roan's stirrup, and somehow landed on his feet with revolver still in hand. It was a feat of horsemanship so unbelievable in execution, those who witnessed it would pinch themselves afterward to make sure they hadn't imagined it.

In response to Captain Morgan's query as to what had gone haywire, a deadpan Lew James answered, "The ferryman was friends with one of the prisoners and the Yankee squealed on us."

Seldom remiss in performing his duties, Field Peterson noticed movement across the Green and shouted, "Better have a gander at this, Captain Morgan."

A curious Judah vaulted into the saddle and kneed Jasper atop a spot of higher ground to the left of the ferry where he had a clear line of sight to the far bank. By his hurried count, he was watching two full companies of Union cavalry, which were the most of the enemy he'd ever seen at once.

A Union officer in the van of the blue-uniformed horsemen scanned his Confederate enemy with field glasses. The glasses panned left and right, and then scanned right again, lifted upward, and Judah swore they focused squarely on him. The blue-belly officer handed the field glasses to a much smaller individual and pointed in Judah's direction. The smaller trooper stared at Judah through the lens of the binoculars, and then he handed them back to the inquisitive Yankee officer.

At that juncture, Field Peterson hailed Judah. "Lest you want to be the last man to spy Glasgow, you best come along jack quick."

The main street of Glasgow was nearly deserted on a late Sunday afternoon, but the sighting of a Union cavalry detail flying a large United States flag spread the alarm like wildfire in the Southern-oriented city. Noses kissed window glass, doors creaked open, and curious souls—some armed and some not—slipped into the dusty thoroughfare behind the Northern enemy while clinging to the shadowy overhangs of buildings in case trouble erupted.

Right off, an alerted Granger Huddleston saw through the ruse of his friend John Hunt Morgan. He walked from his wife's boardinghouse with a napkin draped over his left arm, a coffee mug in one hand, a pistol in the other, and blocked the path of Black Bess. "Union soldiers are not welcome here, sir."

"Well, sir, owing to such a cold welcome, you'll be the first man we jail."

"You best secure my woman's permission first."

Unable to maintain a poker face for another second, Morgan laughed and proclaimed, "Well, then, sir, you'll be a free man forever."

With a sweep of his coffee cup that embraced everybody lurking in the shadows of buildings, Granger Huddleston said, "Citizens of Glasgow, meet Captain John Hunt Morgan, the most wanted Confederate officer in the entire state."

Morgan's convincing impersonation of a blue-belly officer wrung cheers and whistles of admiration from the onlookers, and the seven Yankee prisoners were suddenly squirming in their saddles, undoubtedly concerned they might be identified as the real thing in the middle of a potentially hostile crowd.

Fortunately for the Yankees, Captain Morgan alleviated their fears. He waited until Glasgow's citizens quieted, and then with a sweep of the arm that matched Huddleston's, he said, "And what about these loyal young men riding with me?" The second round of cheers was equally loud, but not as sustained.

A woven shawl wrapping her substantial shoulders, Maud Huddleston called to her husband from the porch of her boardinghouse. "Mr. Huddleston, I'd like Captain Morgan to dine with us. He can surely forgo toying with the Yankees for a single evening. I'd like to extend the invitation to young Mr. Bell on the red stallion, also," Maud said, nodding at Judah in the middle of the disguised column.

Judah had been listening to Morgan and Granger Huddleston have their fun, wildly speculating how he might somehow contrive to meet with Brianna Hardin, with Morgan's permission, of course. And Maud Huddleston,

God love her, had for whatever reason done him a favor of the highest order. Had she been within reach he would have jumped off Jasper and kissed her cheeks.

"But both men will pay a visit to the Smythe establishment first," Maud Huddleston stipulated. "I'll send Willie to tell Dade to get everything ready."

Without waiting for a yea or nay from Captain Morgan or her husband, Maud Huddleston spun and disappeared into her own establishment. Granger Huddleston snorted and said, "Well, John Morgan, seems as though our dinner plans have been made. What say you?"

"Great a table as Maud sets, you don't dare refuse her. Granger, I'd appreciate the loan of your barn, haymow, and pasture for the night. I'd like to give the men and the horses a proper rest. We've been on the move for six nights. If you have any corn liquor handy, two or three jugs would wet their dry throats quite nicely. They can cook their Yankee plunder in front of your wood lot, if you don't mind."

Granger Huddleston nodded. "Stay as long as you like. Let me grab a coat, and we'll make the arrangements with my night man. I've had a cousin standing watch since the kettle boiled over last year."

An hour later, with Sergeant Field Peterson in charge at the detail's new campsite under the proviso that none of the Yankee prisoners were to have a drop of the corn liquor so graciously provided by their host, Granger Huddleston parted company with Captain Morgan and Judah in front of a one-story building bearing a sign reading BARBERSHOP & PUBLIC BATH. "Corporal Bell, I believe Maud Huddleston is expecting two gentlemen at her table, not two ragamuffin scalawags frightened of soap and water, and we best do her proud."

Judah said, "That we will, sir."

The barbershop was deserted when Morgan and Judah stepped inside. A barber chair fronted a tall mirror. A wall shelf beneath the mirror held scissors, combs, straight razors, and mugs for mixing shaving lather. A leather strop hung next to the mirror. A sink and hand pump filled the corner behind the barber chair. Two plain wooden guest chairs and a table sporting a pile of old newspapers filled the vacant wall to Judah's right.

A blunt voice drifted through the open doorway leading to the bathhouse at the rear of the building. "Yes, sir, Maud Huddleston snaps her fingers and every male in this burg in the middle of nowhere jumps like a knife's about to remove his private parts. It's unseemly, I tell you, Willie, for a female to be the most powerful being within ten miles, hell, maybe fifty miles. And that husband of hers is useless as teats on a boar hog when it comes to grabbing her halter for even half a second. I tell you—"

Captain Morgan shouted, "Anybody here?" and the rambling diatribe ceased. A finger-thin fellow with a seamed countenance the color of mahogany wood, mischievous hazel eyes, bent nose, and ginger beard bolted from the bathhouse, and was not the least bit concerned he might have been overheard. Dade Smythe said, "If I kept you gents waiting, remember, water boils at its own pace. Willie said two gentlemen needed spiffing up for dining at Maud Huddleston's table. Well, rest assured, you've been sent to the best. I've shaved and bathed governors, generals, and men rich ten times over without a single nick of the razor or a drowning, lest they did something foolish, of course. So, let's not delay the inevitable. Quite frankly, filthy dirty and as long in the tooth as you two are, Maud will think you're the cat's meow when I show you the door. Senior officers bathe first. Willie has hot water in abundance waiting, Captain. Move along now. It ain't wise to keep Maud Huddleston on the hook overly long."

Within his tonsorial kingdom, Dade Smythe ruled supreme, and John Hunt Morgan made a beeline for the bathhouse. Judah quickly acknowledged Dade Smythe was no braggart. He told him to leave the mustache and take the rest and Smythe did just that with nick-free precision. Facing the mirror, Judah watched an almost strange face emerge as Dade scraped the whiskers from his bearded cheeks and neck. He'd been grubbier looking than he'd realized, but with no women around to deal with, he'd given it no thought.

Willie had partially drained the bathing tub and added boiling hot water, achieving a temperature a few degrees short of scalding. Judah slowly lowered himself into the tub, glad he didn't smell burning flesh. While he scrubbed with brush and bar soap, Willie beat dust out of his trousers and jacket, removed food stains from his shirt with a wet cloth, and cleaned and polished his boots. Skin red from the rough bristles of the scrubbing brush, Judah stood in the tub and let Willie wash the soap residue from him with buckets of cold water, his teeth chattering and goose bumps blanketing his skin.

Judah dried off with a thick towel. Willie's finishing touch was to splash Florida Water cologne on his cheeks, neck, and chest, a smell not unlike that of his father's favorite. Thankfully, the cologne was stronger than the dried sweat populating his clothing that nothing short of a washboard would eliminate.

John Hunt Morgan greeted Judah with a huge smile when he stepped back into the barbershop. Judah noted that except for a trimming of his beard, Morgan's facial hair was still intact. Reaching for his wallet, Morgan said, "Mr. Smythe, I believe you've made us presentable enough for a wartime meal at Maud Huddleston's table. Trust me, I will compliment you quite generously in her presence."

They left a grinning Dade Smythe shaking a pair of gold coins in his hand. Outside in the street, Captain

Morgan said, "He'd sell his own hair for mine if it were the same color."

They walked two blocks to Maud Huddleston's establishment. Black Amanda answered the door and led them to the dining room across the hall from the parlor. Maud's regular boarders had eaten and dispersed for the evening. The ten-person dining table had been reset with plates, saucers, and cups made of kiln-fired china featuring painted apple blossoms, silverware with scrolled apples on the handles, and white napkins. Beeswax candles in a trio of silver candelabra were spaced along the middle of the table, and a fire in a grated fireplace lit the room. A silver tea service and a tray of the same metal containing a spouted glass pitcher filled with an amber-colored liquid and five brandy snifters rested on a sidebar table. Judah barely kept from whistling aloud. Maud Huddleston had laid out her "Sunday finest" for Captain John Hunt Morgan.

Carrying a brandy snifter in one hand and an unlit cigar in the other, Granger Huddleston crossed the hall from the parlor and joined them. "Would you gentlemen care for a little libation before we dine?"

The kitchen door opened and Maud Huddleston, dressed in a blue gingham dress with swirls of white lace on the bodice and at the wrists, hair swept back sleekly in a "waterfall" secured with a net behind her neck, made her appearance and seized control of her dining room. "Brandy and cigars in the parlor afterward, if you please. Dinner is ready. Let's be seated."

Granger Huddleston pulled out a chair near the kitchen door for his wife and seated himself at the head of the table. Maud placed Morgan and Judah directly across from her. Judah was beginning to wonder where Brianna Hardin was. He could only assume she had been assigned to help serve the meal since she hadn't been offered a chair at the table.

Maud Huddleston's eyes lifted and she glanced in the direction of the parlor. "Please stand, gentlemen, a special guest is about to join us."

There had been but few occasions in Judah's life when he was confronted with a scene so rare and so unexpected he could have been bowled over by the tap of a baby's finger. The baby's breath would have sufficed now. Brianna—he was almost certain it was she—stood in the doorway of the dining room. Her four-button coat, loose cotton shirt, and baggy pants were gone, replaced by a green silk dress tight at the waist, curved at the bosom, and open at the throat. Her auburn hair had grown long enough to be held in place by a jeweled headband. Her blue eyes were just as lively as Judah remembered, perhaps more so, and her chin was still delicate. But her skin had lost some of its deep tan. A light powdering he had seen his sisters apply hid the freckles that usually dusted her cheekbones, the faintest of rouges gave her cheeks a rosy glow, and her lips had a slight gloss to them. Maud Huddleston had transformed a road tramp of a girl into a stunningly attractive young woman who had Judah speechless and transfixed.

The always-mannerly John Hunt Morgan laid his napkin on the table and walked to the newly arrived female guest. "I'm Captain Morgan. You must be Miss Brianna Hardin. I've heard a lot about you. May I escort you to your seat?"

Morgan offered Brianna his arm, and Maud Huddleston's beckoning hand drew the two around the table to a chair next to her. Once Morgan had regained his place, without further ado, Maud Huddleston rang a small silver bell sitting on the table. "You men must be starving."

Amanda and a purple-coated Willie proceeded to load the table with bowls of Hopping John, a stew made from black-eyed peas, crumbled bacon, chopped onions cooked in bacon fat until yellow, long-grain rice, Tabasco sauce, and red pepper. Added to this were a large platter of fried country ham with red-eye gravy made by mixing the drippings from the ham with black coffee, wire baskets of hot cornbread muffins, dishes of fresh butter, and pots of hot tea and coffee. It was simple, delicious fare known to every native child of the South regardless of color. *Some eats*, Judah thought, *satisfy your innards forever.*

To keep from staring at Brianna, Judah kept his gaze anywhere but on her for the duration of the meal with very little conversation, and plotting, probably futilely, how he could break her free at some point. He had enjoyed the shave and bath, the unveiling of the new Brianna, and Maud Huddleston's superb dinner, but none of that would amount to squat if he departed without exchanging a single word with her in private. That was suddenly the most important thing in the universe to him.

Dining completed, host, hostess, and guests moved to the parlor for post-meal conversation replete with brandy and cigars for the men and tea and sugar sweets for the ladies, just as it was done in Judah's Chillicothe home when Senator Clay Bell's legislative duties didn't draw him elsewhere. Granger Huddleston was disappointed to learn neither Morgan nor Judah cared for a cigar, but their interest in enjoying a snifter of brandy with him restored his high spirits.

A loud knocking at the front door drew Amanda past the parlor door. She returned shortly with a solemn man of medium size wearing a ministerial collar. Amanda waited for the parlor to quiet. "Reverend Dickerson to see you, Mrs. Huddleston."

"Thank you, Amanda, we can now proceed with the main event of the evening."

Totally perplexed, Granger Huddleston frowned mightily and inquired, "And what would that be, my dear?"

"Why, the wedding, of course, my dear husband," Maud Huddleston answered with a sweet, disarming smile.

The import of Maud's lightning-bolt, out-of-the-blue announcement wasn't lost on Judah. It was aimed straight at him. What other eligible bachelor Brianna's age was present in the room?

The boardinghouse owner confirmed his instinctive reaction by curling a protective arm around Brianna Hardin and saying, "Mr. Bell, I perchance witnessed the kiss you gave this young lady in my parlor that afternoon and overheard your departing promise to return for more. I knew the moment you saw her this evening, you would want to fulfill that promise at the first opportunity, and I can't risk having this girl hurt in any manner. She's become much too dear to me. Even if I forbid it, the two of you will somehow meet somewhere, and since we older ladies aren't fresh from the turnip patch, I know that would be anywhere other than a chaperoned parlor."

Cocking her head, Maud Huddleston paused to enhance the drama of what was unfolding in Judah's mind. "Mr. Bell, I'm proposing you do the honorable thing and marry this girl here and now. I'm sure Captain Morgan will agree to at least a day of honeymoon leave, and I have prepared a bridal suite in secret for you and your new bride."

Judah glanced quickly at his commanding officer. The benign expression of pure amusement on John Hunt Morgan's features told Judah there was no concern there that he was perhaps being railroaded into marriage—albeit without a shotgun—though Maud Huddleston's concoction of a compelling reason for a public marital commitment was potentially as lethal as a bullet. He didn't bother looking in Granger Huddleston's direction. No happy husband risked sticking his foot into a steel trap with open jaws unless it was to save his own union.

Judah had matured bearing arms and understood a long

war awaited him, a war that he might not survive. He put everything else out of his mind and studied Brianna Hardin. Maud Huddleston's admission she had created a honeymoon room in secret meant that, most likely, Briana hadn't been informed of what awaited the both of them whenever he returned to Glasgow, either.

He relived in rapid order their chance meeting on the Nicholasville Road, her yelling out in Dayton Farrell's barn and saving his life, her not holding a grudge against him for killing her father, and her savage attack on his assailant with a wooden plank in Elam Huddleston's livery barn. His mind's eye saw once again her monumental, skin-flaying anger when he tried to foist her off on her deranged uncle and addle-brained cousin, and her near miss with the coffeepot after being caught bathing naked in a creek by two Yankee farm boys. He remembered in amazement her taking a bullet during the night raid on the Yankee supply wagon to secure a mere overcoat for each of them and Barefoot, and not complaining when he treated her wound, and then her acquiescing and agreeing to Maud Huddleston's offer of board and employment while he rode off to find Captain Morgan and his squadron.

The blunt truth was she had more intestinal fortitude and sheer grit than all the truly voluptuous girls with doe eyes, sweet-smelling perfume, and witty asides he'd romanced from Cincinnati to Columbus with their mothers draped over him like wet clothes and their fathers wringing their greedy financial paws behind his back. Unlike those fortune-seeking young ladies, Brianna's beauty was unique and without contrivance, flowing from an innocence and natural feeling of love for others that all the family hardship and degradation she'd endured had failed to diminish in the slightest. Judah saw in an instant of stark clarity that he either took his chances with this girl, or wondered the balance of his days what had happened to her. That, he decided, was a fate worse than death.

"Mrs. Huddleston, I'll marry her if she'll have me."

The joy suffusing Brianna Hardin's face matched a bright burst of sunlight.

"I will."

She was deeply passionate, demanding, and giving, everything he'd dreamed and prayed she would be. There was a depth to her love physically and emotionally that awed and inspired him at the same time. Nothing was ever halfhearted with her.

Judah spent two wondrous days with Brianna Hardin Bell. When they lay spent and exhausted, they talked of their feelings for each other, family, the present, and the future. After knowing only upset and grief in her own household, the love and mutual respect that prevailed in the Bell family fascinated Brianna. She insisted he tell her about growing up with his father and his brothers. She was thrilled by his tales of racing horses with Jarrod and Fritz Howard, and laughed uproariously when he described the pranks the three had pulled on their classmates and other unsuspecting souls, youthful fun she'd never experienced. She was saddened that Judah had lost contact with those close to him, and she insisted he write home soon, aware his news might not please everyone, particularly his siding with the Confederacy.

The killing of his uncle and the stealing of his horses by renegade Union cavalry had outraged her initially. Speaking of it again led them to address their situation in earnest during their last night together in light of the growing conflict that threatened to overrun all of Kentucky for months to come. She, of course, would stay with the Huddlestons until the war wound down and he could come for her. Any decision regarding their future after that had to wait.

He made her promise that *she* would write to his father if anything happened to him. No Bell in the history of the family had been disinherited because of his personal decisions and political beliefs, and she, as his wife, was entitled to what was rightfully his. He made her repeat that promise on the front porch of the Huddleston boardinghouse as he prepared to leave.

Granger and Maud Huddleston, Amanda, Willie, even Dade Smythe, were present to see him off. Not the least bit shy in their presence, Judah pulled Brianna to him, kissed her long and deep, stepped from the porch into Jasper's saddle, and looked his bride straight in the eye.

"Never fear, my darling, I'll be back for more."

CHAPTER 16

"That's Judah for certain," Corporal Fritz Howard exclaimed.

"Just as I thought," Captain Cam Logan agreed.

Turning in the saddle, Logan smiled wickedly and held out his field glasses. "Lieutenant Bell, you might want a gander at your traitor of a brother. Damned if he ain't riding with that miserable bushwhacker, John Morgan."

Jacob Bell had no choice. He saw the raised eyebrows of Tor Shavers and the other riders near him and couldn't risk any sign of indifference. The identity of the Confederate trooper Logan and Fritz Howard had sighted, given the long chance it was Judah, would be a subject of discussion around mess fires for days whether or not he looked for himself.

Mind racing, Jacob kneed his chestnut to the head of the column. What if it was Judah? How in the name of the Lord had he spurned his whole upbringing and joined the hated enemy? How could he bring himself to kill his fellow countrymen? How could he fight with the rabble that favored slavery? But then maybe it wasn't Judah. Wasn't he judging his own flesh and blood too quickly? It couldn't be Judah. Maybe it was someone who resembled Judah, but not the Judah Bell he knew and loved.

Jacob took the field glasses from Cam Logan and trained them on the spot of high ground to the right of the Green River ferry landing. He was too late. What filled the lens was the backside of a blue-clad Rebel trooper, the flat brim of a planter's hat, and the rear haunches and swishing tail of a red horse.

Jacob settled in the saddle and returned the field glasses to their owner. "Captain, I didn't catch his face. Are you certain that was my brother?"

Fritz Howard blurted, "Oh, that was Judah, all right. I recognized him right off. He wrote to me about a red stallion his uncle Temple had given him."

The words were hardly out of Fritz Howard's mouth when a stricken look contorted his features. Judah Bell's best friend realized too late that he shouldn't have confirmed Judah's identity for Cam Logan. He'd been so excited to learn his childhood idol was alive and well that he'd done Jacob a disservice that embarrassed and disgusted him. Cam Logan and Tor Shavers would never let Jacob forget his brother was a traitor. Would he ever just once keep his big trap shut and think before he opened it?

While Jacob's thinking paralleled Fritz Howard's, and while he was overjoyed to know Judah was alive, he was more concerned with the future well-being of his middle brother. Jacob had agreed with his father from the beginning. The war would be bloody and costly to both sides, but to a rational, forward-thinking man like Senator Clay Bell, so long as the North didn't lose its will to fight, the Yankees' superior manpower, abundant weapons and ammunition, iron works, and vast financial resources would eventually win out. If he survived, the reckoning for Judah for straying from his roots would come at the end, and who knew what price the triumphant North would extract from the perpetrators of the secession that had torn the country in two.

With the Green River ferry out of commission and its waters too deep and swift for swimming horses, Captain Cam Logan, in charge of the two companies of Union cavalry at the moment, decided further pursuit of Morgan was too risky for tired men and exhausted animals, and the column was left nothing but the promise of a long, low-spirited ride back to their camp outside Lebanon, Kentucky.

The failure to engage the infamous Morgan capped two weeks of frustration and disappointment for the First Ohio. It had started on 28 January with their orders to join General Thomas at Mill Springs where a battle with General Zollicoffer's forces was imminent. They had marched seven miles that first afternoon and twenty-five miles the next day in a driving rainstorm, and camped for the night on the banks of the Salt River in a cornfield boot-deep with mud. The rain drenched them for twenty-five more bone-chilling miles the following day, and their camp the second night was worse yet.

The site chosen by Regimental Quartermaster John Frankenberger was a steep hillside beside Rolling Fork Creek. The hillside was too steep for the mule teams and it was all troopers could do to climb it dismounted, leading their horses. The supply wagons didn't arrive until after dark, and with no cooking utensils to make coffee, supper consisted of a cracker and cold slice of pork. The ground was too stony to hammer home tent pins in most places. The majority of the regiment stood around fires all night, sat on saddles, or leaned against tree trunks.

Inviting disaster, Company K pitched their tents on a narrow piece of ground flanking the creek's bank. Sure enough, the Rolling Rock rose without warning in the middle of the night. A torrent of madly swirling water swept through the valley. Only the divine hand of Providence kept every single trooper from drowning. The washed-away tents, saddles, and equipment were never recovered.

The subsequent failure of the First Ohio Cavalry to reach the battlefield in time to play a role in the resounding Union victory at Mills Springs further depressed the regiment's mood. Would they ever fight the big fight? The upshot was a cold weather march back through Lebanon out Somerset Pike to Camp McCook and the resumption of their daily drills, a sequence by now duller than the copulation of ants.

Then had come fresh intelligence regarding the current location of John Hunt Morgan, the skulking free-booter the Northern newspapers wanted executed for his random sojourns within Union lines to murder, loot, pillage, and burn without restraint in defiance of the laws of civilized warfare. With the bulk of the First Ohio dispersed on daily patrols, Colonel Minor Millikin, the regiment's commander since the resignation of Colonel Ransom in early January 1862, for reasons of poor health, assigned Cam Logan, the senior captain on duty, to lead two available companies totaling 134 men in pursuit of the North's most wanted enemy. He dispatched his personal liaison, newly promoted Lieutenant Jacob Bell, to accompany Captain Logan as his personal eyes and ears.

The two companies rode out from Lebanon and had no doubt their intelligence regarding Morgan's location was accurate when they reached the burned-out log church ten miles to the south. The blackened shell of the church, the charred beds of the supply wagons, and the ashes of separate fires whose remains revealed supplies, telegraphic equipment, and telegraph poles had been burned, garnered the ire of every trooper. First Sergeant Dan Clutter poked at the ash heaps with a stick, uncovered a few live coals, and surmised the fires had burned at least twelve hours.

Captain Cam Logan had resented Jacob's promotion to lieutenant and his assignment to Colonel Millikin's staff. He seized every opportunity afforded him to put Jacob on the spot publicly and find fault with him wherever he could. "Given what's transpired here, and the fact the soldiers guarding the line crew are missing, how would you assess the situation, Lieutenant Bell?"

Jacob had been following John Morgan's exploits via the eastern newspapers delivered by the mail courier to the headquarters of Colonel Millikin, official reports he was privy to, and comments by senior officers. "If Morgan followed his usual strategy, he took our soldiers prisoner, set these fires at dusk last night, and traveled nonstop until dawn. He'll rest during the day today and then ride all night again."

A rider approached from south of the church and halted in front of Cam Logan and Jacob. Logan asked the rider, "Captain Dingus, what did your scouts find?"

"A curious farmer a half mile down the road with a loose tongue. He says the fires started just about dark yesterday and an hour later nineteen Union horsemen went past the end of his lane."

"He said 'Union' soldiers?" Cam Logan said. "What made him think they were Yankees?"

"They were wearing blue overcoats and flying a large Unites States flag."

"It was Morgan nonetheless," Jacob put in. "I'm betting he disguised his men with overcoats he stole from the supply wagons he burned. He's done it before. He's passed through our lines countless times without our knowing it."

Cam Logan's eyes narrowed and he stroked his chin whiskers. "We missed the big fight at Mills Springs, but bagging Morgan would wash the bad taste out of our mouths. We'd be by God heroes to every Union picket alive if we were to take him prisoner. He's got a twelve-hour lead on us. We'll ride until late afternoon, find a place to water and feed the horses, and then light out again and ride all night just like him. If anything slows him down, we should overtake him late in the morning day after tomorrow. Even if we ride a few horses to death, we'll still outnumber him."

Logan stared at Jacob and then at Captain Dingus. "We can take a try at Morgan or go home to more drill and picket duty. Are you with me, Dingus?"

As the most senior officer present, Logan could simply order Dingus to follow his company with his own, but Jacob suspected Logan wanted Dingus to agree voluntarily in case things went haywire and their mad dash did nothing but wear out a host of good horses—what with horses being harder to replace than men.

Dingus's yellow-toothed smile was as crooked as the hind leg of a hound. "Let's go tree the bastard."

Undisturbed by rain, the hoofprints left by Morgan's disguised troopers were easy to track and the column alternated between a gallop and a trot. From experience, they forded streams in fours, and kept the fours intact with tight reining, allowing the horses to support each other and reduce the strain on their legs. If they encountered hills of any size, they trotted up them afoot leading their mounts and trotted down the far side in the saddle. Halts were infrequent and confined to exactly twenty minutes.

Late that afternoon, they chanced upon a large stack of hay in an outlying lot near a red-painted barn and small farmhouse. The column unsaddled their horses and cooled their backs while a detail wrestled wet hay from the stack by hand until they reached its dry core. Hay was quickly scattered in piles for the hungry horses while pickets stood guard between haystack and barn with the weapons at parade rest. No owner appeared to dispute the confiscating of his hay. An hour and ten minutes later by Jacob's watch, the column was under way again, following a road that slanted to the southwest.

Cam Logan beckoned Jacob to the off side of his horse and slowed the column to a walk. "You've studied maps at Millikin's headquarters. Any clue where Morgan is headed?"

"I think so. This road leads to a ferry on Green River."

"What's on beyond the river?"

"Glasgow, a town with strong Southern ties. It would be a fine spot for Morgan to rest his men and their horses. If the sightings of him reported to us are correct, he's been on the fly for nearly a week. His main camp is reputed to be within a few miles of the Confederate stronghold at Bowling Green, Kentucky."

A glimmer of anticipation brightened Cam Logan's eyes. "And I'll bet with the rain we've had, the Green River is flooded out of its banks. Maybe flooded to where the ferry can't operate. That just might be the break that will enable us to catch up with him."

With the prospect of success goading him now, Cam Logan pushed the column even harder through the night. Curses and complaints about tiring horses drifted to the head of the column, none of which were repeated when Cam Logan deigned to glance rearward. As it was, Logan's entire attention was glued to the road ahead of them.

The shocking cold of the streams the column forded became mere nuisances once the troopers accepted the inevitable slosh of freezing water in the bottom of their boots. Many troopers consumed their rations and relieved a ravenous hunger by chewing on twigs and daydreaming of the homemade pies, cakes, and custards they'd taken for granted at their home dining tables before enlisting. If the water in their canteens had a muddy taste, they were thankful they'd had time to fill them while the horses drank and weren't dying of thirst. What they vowed they'd do to that murderous rascal John Hunt Morgan when they had him in chains would have made angels of mercy flee.

Dawn was something witnessed but not appreciated. The new day brought no relief to tired backs, aching joints, and numb posteriors. Unlike Morgan's hardened troopers, few in the Union column had undertaken a ride of twenty-four continuous hours in the saddle. They began to flag with their animals. Cam Logan called a halt long enough to cull forty plus horses from the two companies that couldn't continue without rest and forage. Leaving a corporal from Walt Dingus's company in charge of the dropouts, Cam Logan forged ahead, the increasing fresh-ness of Morgan's trail revealing how close they were drawing to him.

The column's hopes soared when the advanced elements passed back news that the Green River was flooded out of its banks. The dullest witted among the Union troopers realized their quarry might be snagged on the near bank with no clear-cut escape route. The collective groan that followed was loud and profane, for with it came word the ferry was operating and Morgan and his entire band of marauders along with their Union prisoners had been spied on the far bank. The chase was over. Their Confederate renegade had miraculously escaped their clutches and would soon be harassing their pickets again at his whim sure as horses dropped dung.

The column camped for the night in a meadow abutting the eastern landing of the ferry with a treed hill close by. The first order of business was to water the horses and gather firewood. Though Jacob had been promoted and assigned to Colonel Minor Millikin's staff, he still ate and slept with his original mess from Camp Chase. After unsaddling and tying his chestnut gelding to the mess's picket rope, he wasn't surprised to find Private Sam Kite plopped on his gum poncho with his bare feet mere inches from warming heat. Jacob's replacement, now Sergeant Tom South, and the other regular members of the mess, horses unsaddled, groomed, and fed with what little forage the meadow offered in January, were standing around the fire, sharing with each other their remaining rations, which didn't appear sufficient for a small family of mice.

Little wonder that the mess to a man was staring at the coffeepot Lyle Tomlinson lugged everywhere after the fiasco at Rolling Rock Creek. They might have to share just two cups, but a few sips of hot coffee made a tired, weary trooper feel his world would eventually right itself.

"Was that really your brother Fritz saw?" Sam Kite inquired.

Jacob had anticipated Sam Kite's question. While leading his chestnut gelding through the freshly established campsite in search of his messmates, pointing fingers, angry glares, and shouted as well as muttered curses were aimed in his direction. The reception told him how fast rumors of his turncoat brother had spread through the column and how easy it was for troopers frustrated by a long, arduous ride for nothing to latch on to the first available scapegoat to blame for their failure.

"It was Judah," Fritz Howard said, stepping around Jacob with an armload of firewood. "I just wish I'd been smart enough to let well enough alone. I feel like I turned my back on the best friend I'll ever have. Sir, it was a real shock to see him with the Rebels."

Jacob had been thinking of nothing else. "It was for me, too. My guess is Judah's joining Morgan's crowd has to do with the death of our Kentucky uncle. We're not entirely certain what happened the night Uncle Temple was shot, but it appears he was killed by a cavalry detail of ours determined to confiscate his Thoroughbred horses. As you well know, Fritz, Judah's not one to debate what's right and what's wrong once he makes a decision."

Fritz Howard added his armload of firewood to the kindling pile. "Yes, sir, I'm aware of that. If you win Judah's respect and anybody wrongs you, he'll risk his life to make things right for you."

Sam Kite massaged his bare feet and said, "Sir, unlike some others in this regiment, I don't think our mess is put off by you having a brother fighting with the graybacks. It surely sounds to me like he had a good enough reason for joining them. Right, men?"

Heads nodded around the fire, every trooper joining in, which pleased Jacob. There were only eight of his ten original messmates remaining. Isaac Wood's leg had been shattered when his horse fell while charging a Rebel outpost. He was transported to a Union hospital in Cincinnati with little chance of returning to duty. Luke Purcell had succumbed to measles after disease ran rampant in Union camps with the advent of winter. With no new recruits available, the two troopers lost by the mess had not been replaced. Jacob realized his mess was no exception. In less than eight weeks of service within the state of Kentucky, the First Ohio Volunteer Cavalry had lost ten percent of its troopers to disease, accidents, disciplinary actions, and desertions. In the absence of a major battle, the First Ohio's losses in skirmishes with the enemy could be counted on the fingers of a single hand.

After the sun had set, just Jacob and Tom South remained by the fire. The pig farmer had been promoted to sergeant over Corporal Fritz Howard—with Fritz's blessing—after earning the respect of every trooper he commanded with his steadfastness, attention to detail, and sincere interest in their well-being so long as they did their duty and obeyed his orders. Sergeant South spat into the fire and spoke in a low voice. "Lieutenant, what I know about the politics of this gosh-darned war is from the gossip I hear and old newspapers. It's none of my business, but it seems to me if word of your brother's situation reaches the folks back home, it could cause your father great harm. I'd be sorry if that happened, sir. Senator Bell loaned my father money for new breeder pigs after a nasty winter and saved our farm when I was waist high. My pa served a term in the Ohio House and he believes your father is one of the few truly honest men in the Senate."

"I appreciate your sentiment, Sergeant, and you're right, word will get back to Ohio, that I will guarantee you. This is a war that rubs civilian nerves raw far from the battle-field, and your enemies love new ammunition wherever they happen to be."

A hungry and worried Jacob retired. Wrapped in a blanket atop his gum poncho, he tossed and turned on the cold ground, aware Cam Logan would write to his father, Brice Logan, Senator Clay Bell's political nemesis, the minute they returned to Camp McCook.

And then there was young, impetuous Jarrod Bell.

How would Jarrod react to his beloved brother Judah being branded a traitor to both family and country?

CHAPTER 17

Jarrod Bell was livid. The heat of his anger popped sweat on his forehead and a red film clouded his vision. But he could still make out the shape of Snot Wilcox's big bony head and wide shoulders. "Say that again and I'll beat you to within an inch of your life, you big sack of nothing."

Snot Wilcox swiped at his perpetually runny nose with the back of his hand and leaned forward at the waist in a confident, taunting pose. "Your brother Judah is a traitor, and a lousy piece of secesh trash. He deserves to be hung."

That was all Jarrod could stand. He lunged at Snot and lashed out with his right fist. The off-balance punch glanced harmlessly off Snot's shoulder. Snot's countering blow caught Jarrod high on the forehead and every church bell in Chillicothe rang in his skull.

Jarrod staggered backward, shaking his head in an attempt to clear his mind and his eyesight. He had the sense to cover his face with his arms, and Snot's next two punches sent lightning bolts of pain lancing through his shoulder and arm. He managed to stay on his feet, and the exasperated Snot, accustomed to finishing a fight with one or two powerful blows with his oversized fists, lowered his big bony head and charged.

Jarrod's crashing body snapped the bar of the hitching rail behind him in half, and then Snot had his arms locked around him, driving hard with his legs. They bounced off a porch post and toppled sideways, landing on the plank floor of the porch inches short of the plate glass window of Gamble's Mercantile with Jarrod mostly on top of Snot.

The impact stunned Snot enough to cost him his grip on Jarrod. Jarrod got his feet under him and rested his back against the wall by the door of the mercantile. Fighting to regain his breath, he desperately searched for a means to avoid a battering by the enraged Snot as his bigger foe rolled over and rose from the porch floor with a primeval growl that honestly scared the bejesus out of Jarrod.

The door beside Jarrod swung open, and a slender arm grasping the handle of a long-handled shovel appeared. A feminine voice said, "Don't let him get close to you again."

Thank the Lord for Lorena Gamble. Thank the Lord Jarrod's original destination had been Gamble's Mercantile. And thank the Lord a third time that Lorena was present and willing to come to the rescue of a young man who had not been overly responsive to her desire for him to court her.

Any thanks due anybody can wait until later, Jarrod decided, grabbing the handle of the shovel. He jumped from the porch and moved out into the street where he had room to maneuver and keep Snot at bay. Nose running profusely, Snot trailed after him, circling warily to his left, his gaze glued to the pointed blade of the shovel.

Jarrod was glad Snot was unarmed. Perhaps he could end the fight with no further physical harm to either of them. Jarrod regretted losing his temper in the middle of Water Street on a busy Saturday morning before a crowd quite content to enjoy a good fight when in no danger personally. He was making an unnecessary spectacle of himself, and his father, already out of sorts over the political and personal lambasting he was receiving from the *Chillicothe Gazette* for the supposed sins of his Confederate-loving Kentucky brother and turncoat middle son, would find any excuse from Jarrod short on merit and intelligence.

"Lane," Jarrod said, addressing Snot Wilcox by his true first name, "I don't want to hurt you, and I won't take a beating over a few harsh words. You're bigger and stronger than I am and I was a damn fool to cuss at you. It's up to you now—"

"No, it's not up to either of you," a calm, smoothly modulated male voice said from the edge of the crowd. The shotgun slanted across the chest of Chillicothe police chief, Emil Millwright, quickly negated any concern about his thin physique and reinforced his considerable authority under the law more forcefully than a blow from a Billy club.

"Lane Wilcox, Jarrod Bell, the fight is over. Wherever you were bound is unimportant to me, but I want you out of my sight in one short minute, or you'll eat dinner in my jail. Move!"

With a slow nod and withering glance in Jarrod's direction that told him the fight would continue at another time in a place where the police chief couldn't intervene, Lane Wilcox shrugged his shoulders and walked off. Jarrod, happy he was without the great pain he'd so recently envisioned, thanked Emil Millwright, wished him a pleasant day, and walked into Gamble's Mercantile to return Lorena's shovel.

From a position behind the front window with her father, Lorena Gamble skirted a flour barrel and met Jarrod with a relieved smile. Lorena's black hair was pulled back into a bun that lent emphasis to a face dominated by prominent brows and cheekbones, dark almond-shaped eyes, deep dimples, and full lips. Lorena Gamble was a strikingly handsome girl with a buxom, high-hipped body not even a loose-fitting cotton dress could hide. At eighteen, she was a full year older than Jarrod and not the least bothered by the disparity in their ages. She had set her hat for him years before and brazenly told him in grammar school that no one else would suit her.

To Jarrod's amazement, she always managed to cross his path on a regular basis. Their senior year at the Chillicothe Academy, she had learned he served as a runner delivering documents for the Bell family legal office in the late afternoon and on weekends. He would return after stabling his horse at Howard's Livery and there she would be, waiting in the outer office with hot coffee and sweets. Jarrod was certain his amused oldest brother was leaking his schedule to her, but he found her company too delightful to end the charade.

Then in the autumn of 1861, Jacob, Fritz Howard, and Sam Kite had enlisted in the First Regiment Ohio Volunteer Cavalry. Shortly thereafter, Jarrod found living at the Bell family residence with his mother, Grandmother Nadine, his three natural sisters, and his four female cousins from Kentucky intolerable without Jacob's stabilizing influence. The prolonged absences of a senator father tending to his wartime legislative duties in the state's capital compounded the situation. In return for Jarrod personally caring for the Bell family horses stabled at Howard's Livery with no decrease in financial remuneration to the owner, Fritz's father and mother allowed him to move into the carefully appointed space off the tack room they had provided orphan Sam Kite when they took him in after the death of his parents. The fastidious Mrs. Howard washed and ironed Jarrod's clothes, provided him clean sheets weekly, and fed him if untoward circumstances caused him to miss regularly scheduled meals at the Bell household.

In the absence of Jacob, Jarrod had assumed the daily

oversight of the family legal office. This was essentially a chore of forwarding documents to his father for review and concluding opinion, along with the same old clerk duties, and paperwork he found duller than studying the skin on an elephant's behind. It helped Lorena's cause that Gamble's Mercantile was four doors east of the Bell law office. She knew of his comings and goings day and night because her family lived above the father's business.

Lorena also knew more about Jarrod personally than any other being. She was intelligent, a good listener, and very adept at coaxing information from him. When she saw him buy a revolver and a supply of paper cartridges from her father, and then started riding past the mercantile early in the morning, she later asked him, "How's your target practice coming along?" Unwilling to lie to her, he had answered, "Quite well, thank you," and changed the subject, which she never mentioned again.

Jarrod suspected Lorena sensed the public hassle and ridicule he was enduring over Judah was beginning to eat a huge hole in his patience. What she didn't yet know was that the tussle with Snot Wilcox was the final straw. He'd had enough. It was time to move forward with the plan he'd devised to escape the whole scene regardless of what others thought was best for him.

Jarrod passed the long-handled shovel to Lorena. "Thank you, you've saved me a beating. Snot was leery of your shovel just long enough for Chief Millwright to make an appearance, and no one argues with a shotgun."

Jarrod followed Lorena to the rear room of the mercantile where she placed the shovel with other hand tools. "Must have been quite a run to the front door for you?"

Lorena laughed. "Yes, Father was waiting on Miss Goudy, the old maid. They had no idea what was happening out in the street. Her eyes got big as saucers when I whipped past them with the shovel. Her indignant snort was louder than a farting horse."

Jarrod laughed uproariously, but was saddened by the prospect of leaving Lorena Gamble behind. He would miss her down-to-earth wisecracks, her penchant for finding humor in the worst of situations, and her knack for surprising him to no end. He recalled the afternoon she asked if she could borrow a volume of *Blackstone's Commentaries* from his father's Water Street office and declared she intended to read for the law by the time she was twenty. And true to her word, she became a serious student of the law and asked Jarrod pointed questions that often forced him to read the same passages in *Blackstone* so as to provide her accurate answers. She forced Jarrod to learn more about the law than Senator Clay Bell in all his years of futile pleadings. Jarrod even chuckled over Fritz Howard's comment in a letter that "He'd been done in by a pretty face."

Jarrod took a deep breath to steady his nerves. "Lorena, I'm glad we're alone. I would never intentionally hurt you, but there's something I must tell you."

Dark almond-shaped eyes virtually pinned Jarrod to the wall. "You're leaving, aren't you?"

Thankfully, he saw no sign of tears and plunged ahead. "Yes, I must find Judah. He went to Kentucky as a favor to Father to help our uncle, and now every Federal soldier would gladly shoot him dead. Judah always stood by this family no matter what was asked of him. He needs to know what's being said about him and that we haven't deserted him."

"Can't you try writing to him first?" a desperate Lorena inquired.

"It might take forever for a letter to reach him, and besides, would the enemy deliver it? General Grant took Fort

Henry and Fort Donelson in early February. It's late March now, and a big battle, maybe the biggest of the war to date, is shaping up in the western theater. According to War Department dispatches printed in the *Cincinnati Times-Ledger*, General Grant is amassing a huge army to match that of General Johnston on the Confederate side. They'll probably engage each other in northern Tennessee. I intend to locate Judah before that happens."

"I read the papers, too, Jarrod, and that's hundreds of miles from here. How will you get through the Union checkpoints between here and there?"

"With the cooperation of J. Rodgers Black, publisher of the *Cincinnati Times-Ledger*. His paper competes with the *Times* and *Gazette*. Mr. Black loves a sensational story and I have one for him. A personal interview with Judah Bell, the son of the Ohio senator whose Chillicothe-raised middle son joined the Rebels to avenge his Confederate uncle's murder by Union cavalrymen, an interview conducted by the senator's youngest son, yours truly, to boot."

"Have you ever met Mr. Black?"

"No, but Mr. Black wants Father to run for governor, so he'll see me when I call on him. If I can convince him I might be able to restore Father's reputation among skeptical Republican voters statewide, he has everything to gain and nothing to lose. Besides, the *Times* skewered Father badly after some rascal leaked Judah's story to them, and that had to irk Mr. Black something fierce."

"But, Jarrod, why would General Grant's army let you breech Union lines to search for Judah?"

"I haven't thought that part through yet. I'm counting on Mr. Black's press credentials to let me travel unimpeded until I figure out how to hook up with Judah."

Lorena Gamble sighed. "I know there's nothing I can say that will keep you from seeking out your brother.

Aren't you concerned about what your father will say about all of this?"

Jarrod's expression hardened. "Father would jail me to keep me from risking my life. The truth is he would do the same thing were he me. He saved Uncle Temple's life in the Mexican War when the rest of his squadron crapped their drawers and turned to jelly. You turn your back on your own blood and you're nobody of any account. He can forgive me later."

The dark almond-shaped eyes assumed a somber cast and Lorena repeated her earlier question, "When are you leaving?"

"In the morning. I'll ride to Xenia and catch the train to Cincinnati there."

"I'll miss you terribly," Lorena blurted.

"And I'll miss you," Jarrod croaked, his throat tight and hot, aware with their last minute together how much he truly cared for Lorena Gamble.

Jarrod seldom showed his feelings in public. He detested people who lived their lives on their sleeves, and good-byes had always been difficult for him. He had wept in private after Judah left for Kentucky and barely avoided tears when Jacob departed for Camp Chase to begin his service with the First Ohio. And he had enough of a stubborn streak in him and too much foolish male pride to linger and risk breaking down in front of Lorena.

So, he fled. His good-bye a quick kiss on the forehead and a promise he would write to her when he could. The shock on her face was a dismaying, wounding sight that hurt a heap as he turned and walked away from her.

He expected her to call after him.

She didn't.

* * *

Jarrod spent the balance of the morning preparing for his journey. In his room at Howard's Livery, Jarrod placed in a leather carpetbag that had belonged to Jacob an extra shirt, a pair of socks, straight razor, bar soap, small cotton towel, leather-bound writing tablet, pens, ink bottle, revolver, holster, cartridge box, and a powder flask. The loose pistol, capped and loaded, lay on top of the bag's contents within easy reach. He was concerned wearing the revolver on his hip would attract attention that he didn't want. His target shooting and practice loading gave him confidence that he could defend himself should that occasion arise.

For clothing he laid aside a brown corduroy suit, a starched white linen shirt with black buttons, a string tie, half boots, a light wool overcoat, and a flat-crowned planter's hat. Grandmother Nadine claimed Clay Bell's sons shaved early and appeared five years older than they were. Jarrod was hoping J. Rodgers Black saw him in that same light and took him for a mature young man by age and dress, and not a young lad still wet behind the ears and unworthy of his trust.

Keeping one eye peeled for Lorena, he returned to the family law office building by the alley door and devoted the afternoon to processing court documents, answering correspondence, and filling a mail pouch for forwarding to his father on the daily stagecoach to Columbus. The work of the office would fall under the prevue of Ramey Knowlton and his father's senatorial staff with little interruption.

He then undertook the hardest task of the day besides saying good-bye to Lorena: how to inform his father of his intentions. After debating for a while, he settled on a simple, straightforward note he would add to the Columbus mail pouch:

Dear Father:

I'm leaving tomorrow morning to seek out Judah and learn the truth of his situation. I have ample savings and the necessities to undertake such a journey, including a revolver for defending myself, if necessary. I have no plans to join the Confederate Army. I will write to you regarding Judah when that becomes practicable. I trust you will understand my imperative need to let Judah know he still has our love and support, war or no war. Please forgive my abrupt departure, failure to say good-bye to the ladies of our home, and any inconvenience my absence might cause you,

  You loving son,
  Jarrod.

He read the note when he finished writing, the import of what he was planning fostering last-second doubts. He could tear up the note, take Lorena's advice, and send Judah a letter, and then pray it would somehow be delivered. But, once again, he decided there was too much at stake to leave anything to chance. If Judah perished on the battlefield, he must at least die knowing his family had not forsaken him and still loved him. Jarrod believed he owed that much and more to a brother who had always protected him against the likes of Snot Wilcox. That same brother had taught Jarrod to ride, shoot, fish, hunt, swim, stay upright on a bicycle, fly kites, shoot marbles, play chess, enjoy teasing his sisters, get a bellyache from eating green apples, and laugh until he shed tears. More than anything else, he wanted to thank Judah in person for the sheer joy he had brought to growing up in the busy and crowded Bell household.

The streets were dark when he eased open the alley door of the building with his mail pouch in hand. He would trust Fritz Howard's father to include it with other baggage and mail in outfitting the morning stagecoach at his livery. No lights were showing on either floor of Gamble's Mercantile. He kept watch all around for Snot Wilcox and any of his pesky crowd and reached the livery stable and his living quarters unmolested.

He had informed the Howards of his plans the previous day and was pleased to find a towel-covered plate of cold roasted beef, bread, and a jar of blackberry jam on the small table where he dined and wrote. The night air was cold and he stoked the stove with fresh kindling. Once he had a good fire going, he dumped a handful of coffee in an enamelware pot, added water, and set the pot on top of the stove.

By the time he finished eating, the room was downright toasty. He undressed, donned a flannel nightshirt hand-sewn by Annette Howard, blew out the candle, and climbed into bed. The long day had tired him and he dozed off in the wink of an eye. Later, he was vaguely aware of a disturbance of some sort that caused a horse in the livery to whinny and stomp his foot. Whatever was bothering the horse apparently went away, and he rolled over and let sleep embrace him again.

He didn't know what awakened him, but the room felt different. He was facing the wall behind his bunk. His straining ear detected a soft thump, followed by rustling sounds. Jesus Jump, did Snot Wilcox have the unmitigated gall to come after him in the middle of the night in his own bed?

Warm fingers touched his shoulder. He tensed from head to toe. But why would Snot give him any warning whatsoever?

"It's not who you think it is," said a voice he swore was purring like a cat.

His coverlet lifted and he was no longer in bed by

himself. A body pressed against his backside and warm lips touched his ear. "I thought I'd give you the opportunity to say good-bye properly, you darling man."

He lifted the coverlet, rolled over, and beheld in the faint light of the dying stove fire the pale white skin of a nude Lorena Gamble.

Lorena reached for the hem of his nightshirt. "Can't run out on me now, can you?"

She kissed him flush on the mouth before he could answer.

CHAPTER 18

"Mr. Black's office is at the end of the hallway, back there," the scribbling reporter said, pointing over his shoulder. "Best of luck whatever your business might be. He's in one of his foul moods and mean enough to bite the head off a live snake was somebody to hold it for him."

Jarrod stepped around the reporter's desk and walked past other desks manned with what he assumed were more reporters. At the back of the newsroom, two bespectacled young men wearing sleeve garters and visors sat atop tall stools at a high slanted desk with finished copy spread before them, too engrossed in their proofreading to notice Jarrod.

The painted letters on the frosted glass of the door at the end of the short hallway read: J. RODGERS BLACK, OWNER & PUBLISHER. Jarrod took a deep breath and let it out slowly. He then sipped water from a pint glass bottle to keep his mouth from drying out, capped the bottle and dropped it into his carpetbag, took a firm grip on the bag's handles, and, with no further attempt to delay the inevitable, he removed his hat and rapped sharply on the wooden frame of the door.

"Come in," a rough voice shouted. "Must be a damn stranger if you bothered to knock."

Somehow Jarrod kept his jaw from dropping and his eyes from bugging when he removed his hat, opened the door, and stepped into the domain of J. Rodgers Black. A diminutive man, assuredly the smallest human Jarrod had ever encountered, was seated in a leather-armed chair behind a massive mahogany desk. Publisher Black's forehead was as wide as it was tall; hooded eyelids did their best to hide bulging eyes. His nose resembled a lean red pepper, and the width of his mouth with its overly generous lips equaled the distance between his knob-shaped ears. His fingers were toying with an unlighted cigar that appeared like he was holding a baseball bat in his small hand.

"Unless you want to buy advertising space," Mr. Black barked, "you'd best skedaddle. I've got no time for anything else."

"I do that and you'll miss out on one of the most fascinating stories of the war, a headline-grabbing yarn people will be dying to read."

Jarrod had deliberately rehearsed how he wanted to begin his conversation with J. Rodgers Black and went for the jugular right out of the chute by appealing to his need to sell newspapers, the thing dearest to his ink-loving heart. "And it's a story only I can bring to you."

Publisher Black snorted and leaned back in his chair. "Either you've got more gall than a dozen bank robbers or you really do have a story that might interest me. I'll probably regret this, I have before, but I'll hear you out. Maybe you can brighten what's been a snooze of a day newspaper wise. Have a chair."

Jarrod seated himself in a plain wooden chair in front of Publisher Black's desk, wondering if his reluctant host didn't want to keep visitors from becoming too comfortable, a likely scenario given the lush furnishings of the balance of his office. "Let's start off with your name, shall we?"

"My name is Jarrod Bell."

"Where are you from?"

"Chillicothe, Ohio, sir."

J. Rodgers Black straightened in his chair. "Any relation to Senator Clay Bell?"

"Yes, sir, I'm his youngest son."

"Thought so, you're a dead ringer for him thirty years ago. Does your great story concern your brother Judah?"

"Yes, sir, it does."

His nose for news on the scent, J. Rodgers Black said, "What else can be said about the wayward son of the state's most influential Republican senator that hasn't been printed in a dozen papers already?"

Jarrod knew this was his one opportunity to win Publisher Black's endorsement and support. He either sold him whole hog, or the set of press credentials he needed to safely travel behind Union lines beyond Cincinnati would never see the light of day. "Mr. Black, nobody wrote the story from my brother's perspective. The sighting of Judah riding with Morgan's raiders swung the pro-Union crowd against him and my father without any real consideration of why Judah joined the Confederacy in the first place. Rumors abound about what really happened the night my uncle Temple was killed by a detail of Union cavalry, if he was. Even my father can't pry a straight answer from Union military authorities. Nobody but Judah knows the truth of his dilemma about having to choose between Yankee and Rebel camps due to events beyond his control, how that decision changed his life for better or worse, and how it impacted his family. It's the kind of story *Harper's Weekly* thrives upon. It cuts to the bone and exposes how the political differences between the South and the North splinter families the same as it has an entire country. That's the story I want to tell your readers."

Publisher Black struck a sulfur match on his pants leg, lit his cigar, and blew smoke rings that grew larger as they drifted toward the tin ceiling of the office. His bulging eyes closed while he concentrated on whatever he was considering, and then popped open. "You reason better than the nimrods I have chasing the news. They walk past the personal stories that sell papers following what's exciting the crowd at the moment. If you write as well as you express yourself in person, you have possibilities. Possibilities, mind you, for like my editor father, the Lord rest his soul, preached. Any cub reporter can cast a line, but can he hook and net the fish?"

J. Rodgers Black blew his biggest smoke ring yet and pinched out the cigar with his bare fingers. "What exactly is it that you want from me?"

Jarrod's heart raced. "A formal letter on *Times-Ledger* stationery signed by you introducing me as a reporter for your paper. I understand I need such a document to obtain a pass from the Union high command."

"Yes, you will. How did you learn about press passes?"

"I read how Timothy Bullard of the *Columbus Dispatch* obtained a Union military pass last year and observed the Battle of Bull Run firsthand."

"I'll address my letter to Major Yule Autry of General Buell's staff. We can present it to Major Autry at Federal Army headquarters here in Cincinnati. General Buell and his Army of the Ohio are occupying Nashville at the moment, but I know Major Autry quite well, and I'm certain he will wire General Buell and obtain permission to grant you the pass in the general's name. I will state that your assignment is to report on the campaigns of the homegrown soldiers making up General Buell's Army of the Ohio. That should gain you enough latitude to move about freely, and I have a feeling General Buell wouldn't mind creating some goodwill back home. After all, he was born in Lowell, Ohio, to the north of Marietta. What else will you need?"

"Just the pass is all."

"No job? No salary?"

"No sir, I have funds to support myself in the field."

J. Rodgers Black sucked wetly on his now cold cigar. "Just how old are you, Jarrod?"

Not knowing how much of his family history his father had shared with one of his biggest political boosters and donors, and allowing for his father's penchant for bragging on his sons, Jarrod opted for the truth. "I'll be eighteen this summer, sir."

"That's about what I calculated. Your father was fascinated that Jacob took to the law like a duck to water while you and Judah devoured as much history, philosophy, government, and mathematics as he could shove at you, but found the law dry reading. I've often wondered what it was like growing up under your father's tutelage. He's a very demanding individual."

"Regular school work was the easiest part of our education," Jarrod admitted. "It was the extra reading Father assigned, and the summary essays we had to write when we finished them, that devoured the evenings except for Sundays. Let me tell you, we burned coal oil in bedroom lanterns year-round."

"Yes, but he gave you the equivalent of a college education at home. No mean feat if you ask me." J. Rodgers Black pursed his lips thoughtfully. "I'd venture to say the senator is not privy to your current travels?"

"I left him a note, but made no mention of you."

Publisher Black grinned. "That was clever of you, lad. I'll follow suit. Jarrod, in light of your father's notoriety, I believe there will be widespread interest in Judah's story that will attract readers, but there is one caveat. We don't print a word of it without your father's consent. I won't be a party to anything that might further besmirch his reputation or impugn his integrity. He is a fine man in a tough spot. I won't throw garbage when a man's hanging fire in the public eye, not even if it costs me those same readers."

"I have no problem agreeing to that, sir. It's my hope I can rectify some of the stain on his character Father didn't deserve."

"Then we have an accord that suits both of us just dandy. I do have one serious concern, though, and that's your personal safety, or the lack thereof, in the coming weeks."

"I have a loaded revolver in my carpetbag, Mr. Black, and I won't be hesitant about using it."

"All well and good, just remember we're after a story here, not to see you killed. Don't put yourself at risk unnecessarily. A good reporter's first objective should always be to live to write his story. Understood?"

"Yes, sir."

J. Rodgers Black glanced at a grandfather clock in the corner of the office. "It's nigh onto five o'clock. What are your plans for dinner?"

"Nothing as yet, sir."

"Then you will dine with me at the Claymont. You might want to book a room there for the night. I'll dictate your letter to Stacey beforehand. He can typeset it, and the boys out back can print it while we dine. One of them can run it over to the hotel for you to review after dinner. How does that sound to you?"

Buoyed by the complete success of his meeting with the notoriously difficult J. Rodgers Black, Jarrod came to his feet, leaned forward, and thrust his hand across Black's massive desk.

"Great, sir, just great."

A calloused hand shook Jarrod's shoulder. "Wake up, Mr. Bell."

Jarrod had dozed off after finally adjusting to the constant clackety-clack of train wheels and the squeal of couplings. He was riding in the caboose of a Union Army supply train on the L&N main track bound for General Don Carlos Buell's headquarters in Nashville. He had entrained in Louisville, Kentucky, after journeying on a Federal mail packet down the Ohio from Cincinnati.

Gray-haired conductor Henry Jeffers, blunt nose and firm jaw flanking an ornery grin, feisty blue eyes peering at Jarrod over the frame of his wire-rimmed spectacles, chuckled and said, "Didn't shake you too hard, did I?"

"Naw, but I hope you have a good reason for bringing me around shy of Nashville."

Henry Jeffers poured coffee in a tin cup, returned the coffeepot to the top plate of the caboose's small stove, and plopped onto the wooden bench across the narrow aisle from Jarrod.

"You claim you're a reporter. Well, I have a firsthand story your readers will enjoy. I'm talking about John Hunt Morgan's raid on Gallatin just over a month ago. We'll be stopping there in twenty minutes—thirty miles from Nashville—to take on coal. The story of Morgan's Gallatin doings was in the papers, but there was a few interesting twists to the tale that got left out, maybe because them Union soldier boys in Nashville was as embarrassed as a lad caught screwing a pony over his striking so near their big camp. And what I'll tell you, if you're interested, is the gospel truth. My brother owns the livery barn in Gallatin near the train station, and he saw the whole of the raid unfold right before his eyes. You want to hear me out, or not?"

Fully awake now, Jarrod nodded with vigor, opened his carpetbag, and dug out his stiff-backed writing pad, ink bottle, and metal pen. He didn't have to be taught that a reporter never passed on a chance to acquire a story about a man that loomed large in the public eye. It seemed John Hunt Morgan was on every mind and wagging every tongue.

Henry Jeffers swallowed coffee and said, "Let's move up front. You can sit at my desk. This is rather a long story."

Once Jarrod had lowered the folding wall desk and pulled its chair beneath him, Jeffers waited until his freshly inked pen was poised and then began, "Morgan had to know there was no Union garrison at Gallatin. He appeared with one of his men, both disguised in Federal clothing, about four o'clock on Sunday afternoon, 15 March. They went straight to the telegraph office, and according to Aden Evans, the operator, they stole his codebooks and secret military dispatches. Aden was scared nigh unto death and couldn't do nothing except drop his pistol and watch them walk off.

"About that time, the rest of Morgan's men, forty of them more or less, rode into town. You should have heard the hullabaloo when Morgan announced they were spending the night. Every man, woman, and child couldn't do enough for them, whether it was food, a place to sleep, or anything else they desired. The women surrounded Black Bess, Morgan's mount, and started clipping locks of hair from her mane and tail. That's what got my brother, DeWitt, involved. A lieutenant fetched him from his livery and turned Morgan's mare and a couple of other fine horses over to him for their protection.

"Just before dark, a construction crew came through and Morgan's guards captured the engine, the tender, and put the crew in the town jail. Then the singing, dancing, sipping, and making merry started for everyone and lasted well past midnight. In the morning, it was like the town's men had joined Morgan's raiders. DeWitt watched what they did from the front door of his livery. The locals helped Morgan's guards chop down the L and N water tank and set fire to nine boxcars. They weren't finished. They filled the boiler of the construction crew's locomotive engine with turpentine, shut the valves of the engine, gave it a full head of steam, and started it for Nashville. A half mile along the track, the engine exploded. DeWitt said chunks of metal from the engine looked like black rain. After that, Morgan and his men headed out. Believe it or not, a crowd of females followed Morgan for three miles before turning back."

Jarrod stopped taking notes and said, "I remember that the report carried by the *Chillicothe Gazette* didn't mention how much assistance the entire town provided Morgan."

"They didn't make much mention either of the Union code books and secret dispatches Morgan stole. Aden told DeWitt that a smart soldier like Morgan could read those dispatches and figure out General Buell's army had begun a major move south out of Nashville. If the Rebels weren't aware of that, seems to me that would have been important for them to know."

"Yes, it was. Today is March twenty-seventh, and it's common knowledge that the Union is amassing troops to oppose the Confederate forces General Johnston has brought together at Corinth, Mississippi. The Rebels knew about General Grant's forces in southern Tennessee twelve days ago, but they probably didn't know for certain about

Buell moving south to reinforce him until Morgan's Gallatin raid confirmed it for them. Little Gallatin might well prove to be an important footnote in the history of this war."

Jarrod added that premise to his notes and asked, "Did your brother tell you anything else that might interest our readers?"

"DeWitt did mention he didn't really understand all the fuss over the Black Bess horse. But then he was thinking like a horseman instead of a woman mooning over a dashing Rebel officer."

"How's that?"

"The corporal that fetched him to watch over Morgan's black mare was riding an even better horse, a tall red stallion he called Jasper."

Jarrod's pen skidded to an abrupt halt, ripping a hole in his writing pad. Seeing that, Henry Jeffers hesitated before asking, "Anything wrong, Mr. Bell?"

"DeWitt said he was riding a tall red stallion?"

"Yes, sir, that's what DeWitt said," Conductor Jeffers assured Jarrod.

Jarrod sat quietly, his hand shaking. Mere word of Judah's whereabouts sent his blood racing wild yet again. He reminded himself how many miles Morgan and his men traveled in a single day, let alone twelve, which meant they could be anywhere at that moment like the newspapers trumpeted nearly every edition. His best possibility, then, was to keep tempering his excitement, be patient, and follow General Buell's path south from Nashville as he'd originally planned, for Henry Jeffers's story, while enlightening and informative, didn't alter what Jarrod was counting on the most: that Morgan's men would be present the day General Johnston's forces came to grips with

Grant's army, and there was where he was most likely to find his brother in the shortest amount of time.

The three long blasts of an engine's whistle echoed the length of the train. Henry Jeffers put his tin coffee cup aside, jumped to his feet, plucked a red-globed lantern from a wall hook, paused at the caboose's rear door, and said, "Gallatin, Mr. Bell. You rest easy. I'll bring you some eats. Help yourself to coffee from the stove. Nothing's too good for a reporter toting a personal pass signed by General Buell himself."

A hungry Jarrod, delighted he didn't have to worry about filling his belly, filled a coffee cup at the stove and began fleshing out Henry Jeffers's recounting of the Gallatin raid. As he worked, he wondered if he would receive the same cordial reception at General Buell's Nashville headquarters as the L&N had extended him.

The three-story, gabled, turreted mansion with a Federal-style brick and arched window exterior was elevated six steps above the cobbled surface of Eighth Avenue. Jarrod paused at the bottom of the steps, taking in the carefully spaced trees and numerous plantings of the front yard. He was sorry he wouldn't be present when the buds they bore were in full bloom. Corporal Wayne, the escort who'd guided Jarrod from the temporary L&N depot to the Cumberland River ferry, a water crossing necessitated by the Rebels having burned the city's bridges when they'd withdrawn the prior month, and then to the mansion, saw Jarrod glancing about and said, "Seems a strange place for General Buell's headquarters, doesn't it?

"He moved here from the St. Cloud Hotel after the Rebel owner decided his family would be safer well away from the fighting. I heard the general thought he could hold off big city reporters better in tighter, less crowded quarters."

Corporal Wayne, not much older than Jarrod, blushed and said, "No offense intended, sir."

"And none taken, Corporal. What say we go find General Dumont?"

Inside the converted mansion, desks lined a parlor, a library, and a dining room devoid of other furniture. Jarrod could hear the clicking of a telegraph key over the subdued hustling of the headquarters staff. With permission from the officer of the day, Corporal Wayne led Jarrod to the second floor and to General Ebenezer Dumont's private office, a former bedroom. Metal filing cabinets lined two walls, and maps of Tennessee and Mississippi adorned the other two. The remains of a meal littered a wooden tray on one corner of Dumont's rectangular desk. An abundance of coal oil lamps indicated the office's occupant put in abundant hours commanding the diminished Union garrison left behind to fortify Nashville and maintain public order, which was no small task in a Southern city whose population made no attempt to hide their resentment for the Northerners presuming to control their lives and destiny.

Corporal Wayne saluted and announced Jarrod. Indiana-born Brigadier General Ebenezer Dumont wore his brown hair combed straight across a high forehead with locks of it curling over the top of his ears. His soulful eyes were penetrating, his mustache and beard had been recently trimmed, and his cheeks were shrunken and spotted with minute red veins. Maintaining his seat at his desk, General Dumont waved off Wayne's salute, and with his voice sounding tired and impatient, he said, "I trust you have papers stating who you are and what you're about, Mr. Bell?"

Treading carefully, a cautious Jarrod said, "I have a

pass approved by General Buell granting me permission to report on how the Army of the Ohio fares in the coming campaign against the Rebels, be that good, poor, or indifferent."

"Well, by damned, have I at last met a reporter that can record the honest truth without embellishment or denigration and give credit where credit is due? Are you that scribe?"

Jarrod stood mute, searching for a response neither too bold nor too meek. General Ebenezer Dumont enjoyed Jarrod's discomfort for a few seconds, then spared him a tactical error with a sudden smile and hearty chuckle so out of character with what Jarrod supposed was the general's normally dour demeanor he had to swallow to keep from laughing aloud.

"Please forgive the teasing of an old soldier having a bad afternoon, Mr. Bell. I mean you no disrespect. Were I in your shoes, I would want to know what's happening with General Buell and how soon I could catch up to him, seeing as how the coming battle will take place far from the confines of Nashville. Am I right?"

"Yes, sir. I don't want to miss out on anything that impacts the Army of the Ohio. Mr. J. Rodgers Black, my publisher, is counting on me to provide a fresh perspective and I dare not disappoint him."

General Dumont dismissed Corporal Wayne with instructions to wait in the hallway outside his office. He then came to his feet, fisted a wooden pointer, walked around his desk, and went to the wall map of Tennessee. "Mr. Bell, step over here, please. A bird's eye view eliminates a lot of questions."

Tapping a point near the top of the Tennessee map, Dumont said, "This is Nashville. General Buell's immediate objective is the village of Savannah on the Tennessee River, one hundred and twenty miles south of us where he will rendezvous with General Grant. Right now, the Army of the Ohio, having covered forty-two of those miles, is hung up on the near bank of the Duck River attempting to reach Columbia on the far bank. The Confederate Army destroyed the Duck River bridge during their retreat to Corinth, Mississippi. With the heavy spring rains we've experienced, the Duck River is flowing forty feet deep and two hundred yards wide. Not trusting a pontoon bridge in those conditions, General Buell has crews rebuilding the frame trestle the Confederates burned. General Buell has restrung the telegraph line between Nashville and Columbia, and the latest wires from him say the new frame bridge won't be completed for a few days yet."

Tapping his palm with the pointer, Dumont continued, "So, with the loan of a good horse, a hard ride would easily put you at the Duck River by late tomorrow afternoon, if that suits you."

Nothing would have pleased Jarrod more. "Yes, sir, it's more than I have a right to ask, and I thank you."

General Dumont extended his hand and said, "Glad I could be of some assistance. We can spare Corporal Wayne from his escort duties for a few days. He'll help you pick a mount from the headquarters stable and ride along with you."

Jarrod shook the general's hand and picked up his carpetbag. He had turned to leave when General Dumont said, "May I offer you a piece of advice that might prove helpful?"

An intrigued Jarrod turned to face Dumont once more. "Absolutely, sir."

"Were I a reporter and could choose to be in the middle of the vital moves of General Buell's column where I could hear the opinions and strategy of its officers in the most colorful language, I'd keep an eye and an ear peeled for General Bull Nelson, the commander of the Fourth

RIDING FOR THE FLAG

Division. If he's not at the head of the column when you arrive in Columbia, he will be before you reach Savannah. Some in the corps can't stand him, but Bull Nelson has a knack for being first on the scene, and I believe that's a priority for you news hawks, is it not?"

Jarrod smiled and nodded. "Mr. Black would agree with that in a heartbeat, sir, and I thank you again. I'll surely seek out General Nelson."

"I'll have written orders prepared for Corporal Wayne while the two of you secure horses from the stable out back. Good day, Mr. Bell."

Jarrod fairly skipped from General Dumont's office. There had been no doubt expressed about his military pass and no questions about his age. Furthermore, his potential problem regarding fast transportation beyond Nashville had been resolved, and General Dumont had suggested an approach that might allow him to gain the van of the column, the ideal position from which to steal away and locate Morgan's men and Judah once they neared Savannah.

Corporal Wayne was ecstatic when Jarrod passed the word they would be traveling to Columbia together. "Thank you, sir. I'm tired of the ferry rides and escort duty. I've felt more like a hotel doorman than a soldier for weeks, and I'm a farm boy who loves to ride horses."

At the stable, Corporal Wayne showed some knowledge of horses by choosing two animals over five years in age. The animals had small heads and long necks, moderately high withers and sloping shoulders, straight backs with good conformation at the hip, straight limbs, and strong cannon bones, the characteristics Judah had trained Jarrod to watch for in judging a horse for endurance and stamina. As they were saddling and bridling the matching brown geldings, Corporal Wayne informed Jarrod that a veteran soldier had pointed out that too colorful a horse attracted a lot of bullets on the battlefield and had been directly responsible for the death of many fine officers, an insight that made Jarrod wonder if Judah has ever considered that where his red stallion was concerned.

Jarrod waited outside the Eighth Avenue mansion while Corporal Wayne obtained his written orders. When Wayne emerged, Jarrod saw he had strapped a cartridge box around his waist and was armed with an Enfield rifle. His off hand held a cotton bag Jarrod was certain contained food of some kind and a canteen.

At Jarrod's request, they mounted and rode to a saddle and harness maker's shop known to Wayne on Third Avenue. Jarrod went inside, sold his leather carpetbag, and paid the difference for a set of saddlebags. He had no intention of riding into General Buell's camp with a carpetbag bouncing on his thigh. He was a legitimate, albeit unpublished, reporter, and not a cheap drummer selling his wares.

After transferring his personal possessions to the saddlebags, he paused, and mind made up, retrieved his revolver, holster, and cartridge box and belted them around his waist. He didn't know if it was customary for reporters to arm themselves, but citizen Jarrod Bell wanted the means to defend himself readily available. Outside, Corporal Wayne made no mention of the revolver he'd donned.

Jarrod had completed his account of Morgan's Gallatin Raid during the time it took for his train to take on coal and water there, which was a lengthy process since the water had to be hand-fed into the locomotive's boiler from water wagons in the absence of a water tower, and the train's last miles before it reached Nashville. Jarrod and Corporal

Wayne's last stop was the local telegraph office where a Yankee private sitting in for the civilian operator per General Buell's orders inspected Jarrod's credentials and military pass and wired his first story to the *Cincinnati Times-Ledger.*

As pronounced on Jarrod's pocket watch, they were under way on horseback by four o'clock that afternoon.

CHAPTER 19

Five miles from Nashville, it was evident Jarrod and the corporal would hardly ever be out of the Army of Ohio's sight, or some element thereof. Separate infantry divisions, complete with their own cannon and quartermaster wagons, had marched from Nashville on successive days and, without a hint of mercy, ground the rain-soaked Franklin-Columbia Turnpike alongside the tracks of the Central Alabama Railroad. They had turned the road into a wheel-clogging, hoof-sucking, fetlock-and-shin-deep quagmire that wore out men, riding animals, and harness horses. The air was rendered blue by a nonstop torrent of curses and rants about the injustices and burdens foisted on the unwary webfoot soldier by the military brass in Washington City, their counterparts in the field, and the lousy secesh responsible for bringing those same military tyrants into power. Though they were used to such abusive language, Jarrod swore he spotted blushing mules as he and Wayne pushed past with profane insults from the foot-slogging infantrymen centered on those lucky enough to travel on horseback trailing after them.

Accustomed to the tree-dotted plains south of Chillicothe and the open expanse of the Kentucky Bluegrass,

Jarrod was captivated by the dense growth of Central Tennessee timber that bordered the turnpike for miles. The vast cedar glades were frequently penetrated in every direction by roads. Watercourses were commonplace, and, here and there, trees loomed over a spring. It was an awesome country with a singular beauty. A more learned Jarrod would later relate in his two-volume history, *The War of the Rebellion Beyond the Appalachian Mountains*, how much the terrain was ideally suited for partisan cavalry given their constant need of water, hidden campsites, and multiple routes for attacking and fleeing, a key factor in the tactical successes of mobile forces such as Morgan's raiders.

The pine forest fell away periodically and exposed acres of fertile, cultivated ground divided into plantations with magnificent brick homes. Most of the homes had been abandoned by the their slave-holding owners out of fear of the advancing Union forces, a sign of how effectively war displaced those immune to outside influence in peaceful circumstances. The abandoned homes reminded Jarrod of his uncle's death and the loss of his Denmark Thoroughbreds.

Jarrod and Corporal Wayne rode until dark, rested, waited for the moon to rise, and then rode again until the moon set. Corporal Wayne's supply of cornbread biscuits and slices of smoked ham exhausted, they awakened at dawn hungry and shivering in their overcoats after three hours of sleep propped backside first against scaly-barked trees. Stranded on an open stretch of road between infantry regiments with no breakfast fires in sight, they tucked in their empty bellies, watered and saddled their horses, and resumed their journey, thankful no rain was falling from an overcast sky—the morning's first blessing.

A mile down the road they encountered a generous company mess with a pot of broiled beef, potatoes, carrots, white beans, onion, and flour seasoned with salt ready for serving. The accompanying biscuits were piping hot to the touch, the coffee even hotter. The second blessing after a man's rising was always better than the first, was it not?

Pulling Corporal Wayne's rank, they acquired forage for their horses from a quartermaster wagon and fed them while they savored a final cup of coffee. The mess cook appreciated their hearty thanks, and they were in the saddle again within an hour only to find the turnpike more and more congested the closer they drew to the Duck River.

A sea of tents blanketed both berms of the turnpike and idle soldiers lounged about. Manure and trash piles on the fringes of the temporary camps lent a sour smell to the slight breeze bumbling between the tent rows. Wagons stalled for days had by necessity been left in the middle of the turnpike and their teamsters had camped beside them, leaving but a narrow open track on either side for travelers' horses. In some places, Jarrod and Corporal Wayne had to leave the turnpike, circle through tented ground, and then regain the narrow open track along the berm to continue on their way.

The sun was sliding toward the horizon when the two riders reached the field headquarters of General Don Carlos Buell on the west side of the turnpike a mile from the Duck River. Jarrod and Corporal Wayne dismounted and approached the sentry standing before General Buell's Sibley tent. Jarrod had made Wayne aware his first order of business would be to seek an audience with the column's commander so as to present his credentials.

Corporal Wayne answered the sentry's "who goes there" challenge. "Corporal Sean Wayne and Mr. Jarrod Bell. Mr. Bell would like to speak with General Buell."

The sentry nodded and said, "Wait here." He opened the canvas door of General Buell's tent and disappeared. He reappeared in short order with a soldier with the single bars of the Union lieutenant on his sleeves.

Corporal Wayne came to attention and saluted. The burly lieutenant, pale-eyed with hair and a precise mustache the color of freshly washed carrots, returned Wayne's salute with what Jarrod deemed the welcoming smile of a friend. "Sean, who is it you have in tow?"

"Lieutenant Gray, this is Mr. Jarrod Bell. He's a reporter with the *Cincinnati Times-Ledger*. General Buell approved his press pass by telegraph some days ago. He would like to introduce himself and make the general aware of his presence in camp."

"Lieutenant Lowell Gray," the burly soldier said, offering Jarrod his hand. "I'm attached to the general's staff. I wired Major Autry in Cincinnati on the general's behalf. We've been expecting you, and I must say, you need to be thankful Major Autry enjoys the trust of General Buell. Otherwise, it's not likely you'd be here at all."

Jarrod shook Lieutenant Lowell Gray's hand and said, "Major Autry was most helpful, and I intend to honor my promise to him to be fair, precise, and truthful in whatever I write. If the general prefers, I will share my submissions with him before I file them with the *Times-Ledger*."

"We'll let General Buell decide that," Lieutenant Gray responded. "He's meeting with his staff at the moment." The lieutenant's chin lifted and he glanced over Jarrod's shoulder. "And here comes General Nelson, the subject of the meeting."

Jarrod turned his head and nearly swore aloud. Someone on high was watching over him, for upon his arrival in General Buell's camp who was falling smack into his lap without any effort on his part whatsoever but the very officer General Dumont had advised him to seek out.

Towering four inches over six feet and weighing close to three hundred pounds, General William "Bull" Nelson had a barrel chest that threatened to explode the brass buttons off his uniform coat. He was hefty at the waistline. From there he tapered off in size, and his feet seemed small for a man of his bulk. Nelson's eyes were deep set and the expression on his face was intense and determined. His appearance and what little Jarrod had heard of him guaranteed Bull Nelson would be a difficult person to argue with and win. Everything about him—physique, stubbornness, and fiery temperament—justified his nickname.

General Nelson charged past the sentry, Lieutenant Gray, Corporal Wayne, and Jarrod without so much as a nod of recognition for the soldiers present and swept into General Buell's tent. "He's in a whopping big hurry, huh, Lieutenant?" Sean Wayne offered.

"Yes, and I best be joining him. Come along, Mr. Bell. You'll enjoy the latest act of the Bull Nelson traveling theater. We can introduce you to General Buell after the final curtain. Corporal Wayne can care for your horses in the meantime."

Ten officers stood in a half circle in front of General Don Carlos Buell's desk. Lowell Gray put a finger to his mouth, tugged on the sleeve of Jarrod's coat, and positioned him at one end of the half circle where he could have a clear view of the standing officers and the seated Buell. One look at the commanding general and his subordinates and the tense feeling pervading the atmosphere within the tent was as obvious to Jarrod as the pain of a crisp slap on the cheek.

Bull Nelson had naturally taken the middle spot in the half circle, directly before his commanding officer. "Sir, what I'm requesting is permission to ford the Duck River in the morning and push ahead. My men are tired of waiting for the new bridge to open. Couriers have confirmed that General Grant is no longer safely camped on the east bank of the Tennessee River at Savannah. He's camped on the west bank seven miles below Savannah at Pittsburgh Landing. I feel we must reinforce him as quickly as possible with however many soldiers we can provide him. We don't know the exact strength of General Johnston's Confederates, but he at least matches General Grant's numbers. He may exceed them. Any more delay on our part may invite disaster for General Grant, sir."

"Captain Glover assures me the frame bridge will be complete with its wood beamed floor in place by late tomorrow. The pontoon bridge I ordered will also be finished by then. General, I'm not inclined to take unnecessary risks with men, wagons, and cannons with the river still so high."

"Sir, I beg to differ about the state of the river. I checked the situation myself late this afternoon and the water was barely brushing the beds of fully loaded wagons returning from Columbia. The river is fast reaching its ordinary stage, sir, and I'm certain my whole division can be across in six hours."

Nelson's bold assertion garnered sly, disdainful smiles from the members of General Buell's staff except for Lowell Gray and a captain with mild features and a luxuriant, forehead-covering head of hair that made him appear to be peering from under a hedgerow when he spoke. Making no attempt to his hide his irritation with his fellow staff officers, the captain said, "General Buell, I have found General Nelson always comes up to his talk. I, for one, have no trouble taking him at his word in this instance."

The dark complexioned General Buell was half the physical size of Bull Nelson, but equally decisive. With an agreeing nod, he vented some of his frustration with the Duck River. "General Nelson, if you can get your men safely across the river with all your artillery and baggage, I'll go you one better. Your Fourth Division can keep the lead until the Army of the Ohio reaches Savannah."

Lowell Gray explained to Jarrod later that evening how important "having the lead" was to divisional commanders. "To them, it's a matter of seniority, recognition, and pride. They goad their companies, and then brag when they gain that coveted position out front and fight to keep it. Frankly, I've never been able to nurture the desire to die first."

General Buell's decision in favor of Bull Nelson terminated the staff meeting. The bit in his teeth at last, Bull Nelson barged from the tent. J. Rodgers Black had made Jarrod aware reporters from both eastern and western newspapers would be hounding Buell's column for the latest news, and he couldn't squander a golden opportunity. "Lieutenant Gray, I need a word with General Nelson."

A wise Lowell Gray said, "Don't trip over your pen. Hurry back if you still want to meet General Buell tonight."

Bull Nelson had a lengthy stride, and once free of the tent, Jarrod had to break into a run to pull within shouting distance of him. Throwing caution to the winds, Jarrod called out, "General Nelson, might I have half a minute of your time?"

To Jarrod's surprise, Bull Nelson slowed, turned, and motioned for him to come forward. "And just who are you? I haven't seen you before, have I?"

"No, sir, you haven't. My name is Jarrod Bell. I'm a reporter for the *Cincinnati Times-Ledger*. General Dumont told me in Nashville to seek you out if I wanted stories that would sell papers. I'd like to ford the Duck River with you in the morning, sir, and accompany you to Savannah."

Bull Nelson's frank eyes assessed Jarrod. "Well, by damned, I like your spunk, young feller. I'm sick and tired of snobby ink men. The same goes for the meek ones who try to sway me with meaningless flattery and pettifogging ideals a hungry dog wouldn't swallow."

Bull Nelson's impish grin had to belong to someone

else. "And if you know how to shoot that revolver, you might be capable of defending yourself if need be instead of hiding behind my coattails. The van of my division will reach the river at approximately six a.m. If you don't have a horse, acquire one. The eighty miles to Savannah won't be child's play. Good evening, Mr. Bell."

Jarrod wasn't insulted when found himself saying "good evening, sir" to Bull Nelson's broad backside.

Jarrod slept fitfully that night, if at all. He did satisfy two major concerns before retiring. After his brief talk with Bull Nelson, Lowell Gray had slipped an equally brief introduction to General Buell into the late-evening staff schedule, and the obviously tiring Buell had voiced no objection to Jarrod traveling with Bull Nelson's Fourth Division on the morrow since he had Nelson's permission to do so. Jarrod's second concern was the status of the seal-brown gelding provided him by General Dumont at Nashville. He had proposed to Gray that he purchase the gelding from the army. Gray had proposed a viable, less expensive alternative. Since General Dumont had been able to spare the animal for Jarrod's travel to Columbia, Gray saw no reason why Jarrod couldn't ride the gelding to Savannah. If any questions arose, Gray would simply reply that he thought that was the arrangement from the start. The lieutenant had then offered Jarrod blankets, a gum poncho, and sleeping space in his tent.

A far off bugle sounded in the pitch-blackness of the cloud-covered night. "That would be Nelson's four a.m. 'First Call,'" an awakened Lieutenant Gray surmised. "He needs an early start to slide past the Second Division and come up to the river by dawn."

Rolling out of his blankets, Gray sniffed loudly. "Mr.

Reporter, I smell rain. I'll have Haney stoke the fire. A quick early breakfast may be wise."

A sleepy Private Haney dug live embers from the previous evening's ashes and soon had a nice blaze burning. His breakfast fare was a new taste for Jarrod. Haney had soaked squares of hardtack in water until the cracker had soaked completely through. In a skillet, he first heated salt pork grease he'd saved in tin cans, and then browned the sodden squares of hardtack on both sides. After seasoning the fried squares with salt, he served them with mugs of hot tea from the personal stash of Lowell Gray.

Munching carefully to avoid burning his tongue, Gray said, "The boys call this skillygallee. It goes down easier when you're hungry. Some prefer to eat it cold. Either way, the best I can say about it is it beats starvation."

The skillygallee had hardly warmed Jarrod's stomach when a cold rain began to fall. He was thankful the hustling Haney was there in a whipstitch with gum ponchos from Lowell Gray's tent. Slipping a poncho over his head and shoulders, Gray said, "My assignment is to observe the fording for General Buell and report any difficulties that might imperil its success. You may want to watch with me. The logistics required to successfully move an entire regiment and its equipment and wheeled weapons across a fast flowing river might entertain and enlighten your readers. You can catch General Nelson later in the day."

Jarrod's initial determination to stick with the van of the Fourth Division like glue gave way to his constant need to always appear a working reporter committed to Buell's campaign for the duration to allay any suspicion to the contrary. He had filed his Morgan story in Nashville, but a legitimate reporter was always hungry for fresh copy, and Gray was right in saying he knew where he could find Bull Nelson at any hour. He had no legitimate reason to hurry off and stand in the rain elsewhere.

"Sounds promising, Lieutenant, and you'll be available to answer my questions."

As was his wont now during idle moments, Jarrod's thoughts drifted to Lorena Gamble as he sipped a second mug of hot tea. Lord, what a supple, warm, joyfully entangling lass she'd been in his bed. The naturalness of the whole thing for two people new to the act still mystified him. Was it like that for everyone?

Afterward, Lorena had nestled quietly in his arms without speaking before departing his bed with a deep kiss, dressing, and saying sweetly at the door, "I don't believe you'll forget me during your travels, Mr. Jarrod Franklin Bell."

His last memory of her unexpected visit was how fast the bed had turned cold without her. And how much he wished she had lingered for more.

He didn't have a clue about any possible future relationship with her, or when he would be with her again, but he would be, for the feelings she'd unleashed in him hadn't cooled since the closing of that bedroom door and ran hot in his veins whenever he dwelled upon her.

Suddenly, a person was shaking him. "Mr. Bell, are you all right?"

A totally embarrassed Jarrod snapped out of what he jokingly called in private his "female funk."

"Yes, I'm fine, thank you."

Corporal Sean Wayne's request to travel on to Savannah had been denied, and leading Jarrod's saddled gelding, he had come to bid him farewell. "He's been watered, fed, and groomed, Mr. Bell. I wish you the best in your journalistic pursuits. Unfortunately, my orders send me in the opposite direction. It's the Cumberland River ferry again for me."

"Corporal, I appreciate your thoughtfulness," Jarrod said, "and I enjoyed your company immensely. I wouldn't worry needlessly about your current duty being dull. I'm sure Lieutenant Gray can agree that this will be a long war, and you'll most assuredly be under fire before the peace, maybe more than you want."

Jarrod and Lowell watched Sean Wayne depart with his head held a tad low. "Never pays to become friends with the military and vice versa, Mr. Bell," observed Gray. "We're here today and gone tomorrow, either to a new duty or the grave."

At six a.m., true to General Bull Nelson's word, the Twenty-fourth and Sixth Regiments, Ohio Volunteer Infantry, and the Thirty-sixth Regiment, Indiana Volunteer Infantry, marched through the tents of the Thirty-fourth Regiment, Illinois Regiment, generating a plethora of derisive yells and astonished shouts. "Now, the fun begins, Lowell Gray said as he was slurping down the last of his tea. "The other generals aren't aware of what's transpiring. Mr. Bell, the curtain will soon rise on the stage of the Bull Nelson theater on the bank of the Duck River. Shall we proceed to our seats?"

The astonishment of the Thirty-fourth Illinois turned to ugly curses and threats of retaliation and outright resentment when they realized in the growing daylight that the Fourth Division was preparing to ford the river and "steal" the lead from the Second. Bull Nelson's name was soon leaping in full volume from every Second Division tongue in the most blatantly damning forms imaginable. Jarrod was sorry he didn't have writing pad and pen in hand. The creativity of the damnation of Bull Nelson was truly historic and epic.

At eight a.m., Jarrod and Lowell Gray were in position downstream of the ford. Upstream, the replacement wooden frame bridge spanned one hundred eighty feet of open water. The bottoms of the floating sections of the pontoon bridge, which were lashed in place by ropes at either end to trees on the banks of the river, were visible beneath the floor of its rigidly anchored counterpart. The brown current of the Duck River curling around bridge supports and sweeping by from under both structures appeared swift-flowing and strong, causing Jarrod to shudder. He'd be in that current himself before the day was out.

Lieutenant Lowell Gray pointed at the far bank. "Seems as if some local fans bought tickets to Bull's carefully scripted drama and are claiming their seats."

Sure enough, a crowd of men, women, and children from Columbia had gathered over yonder. Lowell Gray chuckled and said, "What they're about to witness may offend any tender eyes among them."

At the appropriate commands, the eager infantrymen of the Fourth Division stacked arms, shed pants and blouses, rolled them up, and attached their clothes to their bayonets. The soiled state of the underwear exposed by this maneuver wrought gasps, giggles, and guffaws from the local crowd. "They ain't got no soap, Maw," one young voice yelled, producing a round of sidesplitting laughter.

But the real show had yet to unfold. With cartridge boxes tied around their necks, the infantrymen eased down the slippery riverbank behind a local guide. Instead of a direct crossing, the column followed a tortuous S-shaped ford one hundred and seventy five-feet wide. It seemed a perilous route. Yet a Thirty-sixth Indiana footslogger Jarrod interviewed the next day stated, "The water was about waist deep and very swift and most awful cold, and still it was sport for us." Another soldier claimed it was the rock-hard bottom that made for the easy going.

The climax of the first act of the Bull Nelson drama occurred once the footsloggers clawed their way to the top of the far bank. There they stripped off their underwear to a chorus of jeers from the locals, wrung it dry, and redressed in full uniform while offering some spirited, sincere invitations to the younger ladies in the crowd to become camp followers.

The infantry of the Fourth Division was across the Duck River in four hours. Next came the supply wagons and artillery. Each regiment supplied a company of strong men to assist with the loading and movement of horses, vehicles, supplies, ammunition, and wheeled limbers and cannons. In response to a question from Jarrod, Lowell Gray explained that the scows made by turning one wagon bed over and placing it on top of another stemmed from the Polish military experience of Lieutenant Joseph Pietzuch. After tents were packed in the top part of each scow, the artillery ammunition was removed from the limbers of the cannons and aligned on the tents, the safest means of dry passage for an essential staple of war.

Jarrod sat atop his gelding in the steady rain and composed in his head how he would describe the Fourth Division's fording of the Duck River. The story of Morgan's Gallatin Raid had captivated him and he had loved piecing it together. But writing the history of a past event, based on secondhand accounts, was a simple task compared to observing the event in person and re-creating the scene in a style and manner that made the reader feel he'd been there, standing beside you all the while.

Jarrod was a devoted fan of the gripping war stories and illustrations that appeared in *Harper's Weekly*. To snag the attention of the *Times-Ledger*'s audience as *Harper's* did theirs, he had to portray in precise and colorful verbiage the danger of the Duck River current and its S-shaped ford. He had to describe in meticulous detail the infantry's tactics in getting across the river safely with dry clothes, the weapons, and ammunition. Furthermore, Jarrod could not leave out the humor the local citizens saw in soldiers clad in the less-than-tidy underwear marching into the water from one bank and then stripping to bare skin in front of them on the opposite bank to wring that same underwear dry. Nor could he fail to mention the use of strongman companies and scows, the pivotal role of General Bull Nelson, and how today's fording unplugged the river that had frustrated the forward advance of General Buell's column for ten days and delayed the reinforcement of General Grant at Pittsburgh Landing.

The challenge of doing justice to what he deemed an important event that might impact the outcome of the big battle—soon to be fought—didn't frighten Jarrod. He wasn't a total neophyte when it came to storytelling. He had compiled his father's Mexican War reminiscences with his uncle Temple at two family reunions and his own law office conversations with visiting Chillicothe veterans of the same war. That project had tugged at his curiosity and, much to his father's satisfaction, he'd read histories of wars and battles from the Roman Empire through the America Revolution and the Mexican War and recorded the details of each battle, skirmish, and siege, the names and ranks of the officers involved, the types of weapons employed, and the strategy and tactics of both armies. Nothing else had enthralled and entertained him like the stories of soldiers and their victories and defeats.

A tingling sensation ran through him. Now he had been given a chance to write about the soldiers of his time, their trials and tribulations, their successes and failures. The appeal of such an undertaking was a virtual magnet for him because he fumed and worried incessantly if he'd ever find a profession he honestly and truly wanted to pursue.

Was the chronicling of the war his destiny?

At the age of fifteen, he'd told Grandmother Nadine Bell on New Year's Eve he didn't want to read for the law. His father's surprise Christmas gift of McFadden's *Legal*

Treatises had done nothing to alter his decision. He didn't know how to confront a father who equated the intricacies and logic of jurisprudence with the finding of the Holy Grail.

"You're too impatient, Jarrod. Your good fortune is that you will have choices. You are a member of a family with means. You're blessed with a father that has your best interest at heart. Granted, he will be bitterly disappointed if any of his male offspring reject the law as their chosen profession. However, he will not reject or disown any of you if you choose to do that.

"Bide your time and obey your father. What you choose to do with your life will pop up like a jack-in-the-box and everything will be clear to you. Don't discount what I'm telling you, dear boy. I've watched this awakening occur in many people's lives. It's a wondrous event that you don't try to explain. You just accept what has been made known to you."

Grandmother Nadine had paused and patted his arm before sending him off to bed with a final nugget of advice. "And always bear in mind, a little prayer now and then might speed things along more than you think."

"Mr. Bell, the sun's sinking," Lowell Gray said, interrupting Jarrod's circumspection of his life's future. "I would recommend you ford the river before the water gets cold enough to freeze your vitals."

Only the cannon of the Fourth Division remained on the north bank. "I better hustle along and catch up with General Nelson," Jarrod agreed.

"Here," Gray said, passing a cloth bag to Jarrod. "Take the rest of Haney's biscuits to nibble on until you find a supper fire."

Though it was not likely if his plans came to fruition,

Jarrod said, "Thank you, I'm sure we'll meet again in Savannah, sir."

Jarrod halted his gelding well clear of the limbers and their cannon, dismounted, estimated the water was no deeper than his horse's belly, removed his boots, pants, and half drawers, tied them in a bundle, looped the belt holding his holstered revolver and cartridge box around his neck, and draped his saddlebags over his shoulder. He swung into the saddle with reins and biscuit bag in one hand, clothing bundle in the other, and, at a signal from an alert sergeant of artillery, kneed the gelding into the river between two of the cannon horse teams.

The blood-numbing river came to the top of his knees. The seal-brown gelding had no fear of water. He answered the pressure of Jarrod's knees and followed the cannon in front of him like a foxhound on the scent. Emerging from the river after an uneventful crossing, Jarrod trusted his mount to find solid footing in the churned mud of the upward slope of the bank, and the gelding did so with minimal difficulty.

Jarrod resolved as he donned his drawers, pants, and boots without spectators, the local crowd having returned to their homes for supper, that he must somehow gain title to the gelding. If he was to venture far and wide in the coming weeks, or perhaps months, searching for newsworthy stories, he wanted a solid and reliable mount between his knees.

Except for a few cannons, the Fourth Division was across the Duck River, suffering only minor mishaps not worth mentioning in print. Jarrod threw back his head and laughed. As Lieutenant Lowell Gray would say, the final curtain was near to falling on a dramatic and comedic performance by the cast of the General Bull Nelson theater. He'd miss Lowell Gray and his sense of humor.

He set off to find General Nelson and some hot food. He would begin his accounting of the successful fording of Duck River this evening, knowing Bull Nelson would string telegraph wire as he raced for Savannah, which would enable him to forward the story to J. Rodgers Black before he abandoned Nelson's division and went searching on his own for Judah.

CHAPTER 20

The rain petered out and Jarrod located the Tenth Brigade of the Fourth Division and Bull Nelson two and a half miles south of Columbia. The sentries had spotted Jarrod and Lieutenant Gray observing from beside the ford earlier, and one of the pickets—with permission of the detail's sergeant—escorted him to a fire on the lawn in front of a plantation home. The home belonged—reporter Jarrod was to learn—to the father-in-law of Confederate General Gideon J. Pillow, the richest and most powerful of the local pre-war landowners.

Nelson and his staff were dining on hominy, ham, and tin cups of black coffee, as well as crumbled hardtack, while passing a flask of brandy in celebration of the day's success. The general himself spied Jarrod and his greeting was loud and boisterous, peals of thunder notwithstanding. "Come join us, Mr. Bell. I do hope all that watching of yours has made you hungry as well as thirsty. We are across the infernal Duck River with the lead and there will be no end to the glory that awaits us and the ink of your pen at Pittsburgh Landing, or Corinth, or wherever the shooting begins."

Swallowing a swig of brandy from the revolving flask,

Nelson said, "Eat and drink your fill, Mr. Bell. The owner of the fine dwelling behind me is nowhere to be found. He, therefore, can't object if you'd care to commence writing the story of the bravery and zeal my men displayed today in his library, can he?"

Jarrod couldn't believe his good fortune. Apparently, he was the only reporter that had made the crossing in harmony with the Fourth Division. But, while he had not yet seen them personally, the relentless reporters of other newspapers were present somewhere in General Buell's column, and they would come sniffing out what was happening at the column's head once they were across the river.

An hour later, Jarrod was bent over his tablet at a desk in the library of the William P. Martin home, totally engrossed in his writing and unaware he had company until a throat cleared behind him. He spun about in his chair and discovered his surprise visitor was none other than Lieutenant Lowell Gray.

Gray's sleek carrot hair and mustache glowed like a banked fire in the light of Jarrod's coal oil lamp. His tone blunt and impersonal, Gray wasted no time on social amenities. "Sorry to barge in on you, but we need to have a serious chat, young man."

Jarrod was more surprised by Lowell Gray's apparent hostility than his sudden appearance. For the life of him, he couldn't think of a solitary thing he'd done to offend Gray personally, and he certainly hadn't done anything contrary to his wishes. He laid his pen aside and asked, "What is it you want to talk about, Lieutenant Gray?"

"Mr. Bell, I'm General Buell's intelligence officer. I gather information I believe is of importance to him from all points of the compass. I separate the wheat from the chaff whether the information comes from our scouting reports, our own ranks, captured Rebels, or local citizens.

I couldn't quite put my finger on it at first, but I knew something was amiss where you're concerned. I was born and raised in Cincinnati. My father is a press operator at the *Times-Ledger*, and growing up I hawked papers on street corners for your Mr. J. Rodgers Black. Mr. Black has a citywide reputation for pinching a coin until it screamed for mercy. I've never seen your name in print in any edition of the *Times-Ledger*, and what I couldn't fathom is why he would spend money he holds dear to send an inexperienced reporter to cover General Buell's campaign when he had a cadre of experienced scribes to choose from. Can you explain that?"

"What if I told you I'm covering my expenses out of my own pocket?"

Gray's carrot-haired head shook. "Naw, there's more to your being here than that. Black called in a favor by asking Major Autry to vouch for you and request a press pass from General Buell. Why pick this particular campaign? Why not Grant's or Sherman's?"

Jarrod's gut tightened. Lowell Gray was smart and perceptive, and he had General Buell's ear. One disapproving word from Gray and he might find himself traveling north instead of south. "We thought copy about General Buell's Army of the Ohio would be more interesting to Ohio readers than accounts of Grant's and Sherman's forces."

"Yes, that's what the request for your military pass said, but I then remembered Major Autry's telegram also said that you're from Chillicothe. The name Bell rang in my head, and I had no trouble pegging you for a son of Senator Clay Bell. You are the senator's son, are you not?"

Jarrod stifled a groan. If Gray had perused the Cincinnati papers he'd spotted in General Dumont's headquarters before departing Nashville with General Buell, there was a strong possibility he was privy to public information that would sink Jarrod's boat with a single shot broadside. "Yes, sir, I am."

"Then that makes you Judah Bell's brother, doesn't it?"

Jarrod's boat was sinking fast. Was Lowell Gray going to unravel his whole scheme for finding Judah?

"Yes, sir, it does."

"Mr. Bell, I was a police detective before the war, and I have a knack for connecting pieces of information together where others see no relationship. I read the newspapers' wild carrying-on when they learned your brother had joined John Morgan's raiders. It made quite a splash among Ohio political circles. Both the Republicans and Democrats lambasted your father up one side and down the other. Have I said anything you don't agree with yet?"

"No, sir."

"That's good. So, I got to thinking about your father's dilemma and Mr. Black, your father's biggest supporter in southwestern Ohio, and wondered if there was anything he could do to at least partially restore your father's reputation. And you know what I came up with, Mr. Bell? It dawned on me that the only avenue open to Mr. Black, if he wanted to be of help to your father, was to interview the person who instigated the whole mess, your brother, and pray he lucked into an explanation that would arouse a modicum of sympathy for the man he wants to be the next governor of Ohio. Does that make sense to you like it did to me, Mr. Bell?"

Jarrod was on the verge of drowning in the truth of Gray's words. He started to intercede on his own behalf, but decided to keep quiet. Maybe there was wriggle room he couldn't foresee. But he doubted any existed.

"Yes, sir."

"I debated for a while about whether you contacted Black or he approached you. But it was most likely you, what with you being in Chillicothe and he in Cincinnati.

He might have never met you before. The point is the both of you agreed that after you caught up with General Buell's Army of the Ohio, you'd slip through our lines when the right opportunity arose, hopefully find your brother, and latch on to the confession that might save your father's political career. Am I ringing the correct church bell for you, Mr. Bell?"

Jarrod was what Grandmother Bell called a cooked goose—a man adrift in swift water without a boat or a prayer. "Yes, sir, I asked Mr. Black to obtain the military pass for me. I wasn't so much concerned with saving Father's political future initially as I was letting Judah know his family loved him no matter what had befallen him. I swear that's still the most important thing with me, Lieutenant Gray."

Lowell Gray plucked a cigar from the inside pocket of his uniform coat, stuck it in the corner of his mouth without lighting it, and paced back and forth. The longer Gray paced, the better Jarrod began to feel. He'd admitted duping Major Autry and Generals Dumont, Buell, and Nelson, sufficient grounds for Lieutenant Gray to send him packing with an armed escort. Then what was the holdup? Was there hope for him yet?

Lowell Gray stopped his pacing and stuck his unfired cigar back in his coat pocket. "Mr. Bell, my game is intelligence, no matter the source. I've taken risks with spies that would make the Holy Mother blanch. I could send you packing with no questions asked, which gains me nothing. I don't know of another soul more anxious to infiltrate the lines of our enemies than you, Mr. Bell, and I'm inclined to help you fulfill that desire, so long as I get something in return."

In his elation, Jarrod fought off the urge to jump out of his chair and kiss Lowell Gray on both cheeks as he had Grandmother Bell. He'd been thrown a saving rope and he meant to catch it no matter how high the price. "What would you want in return, Lieutenant?"

"Knowing the numerical strength of the enemy is as critical as knowing his location when you're devising a strategy that best fits your army. A feel for the state of the enemy—his weapons, ammunition, food, and fighting spirit—often foretells how well he will fight when the hat drops. That's the kind of information I want you to ferret out for me, Mr. Bell. Can you do it?"

"Yes, sir, I believe I can."

"I think there's a solid chance the graybacks will take you to your brother. You won't be in a uniform of any kind, and seeking out blood kin in wartime is a plausible excuse for asking to cross an enemy picket line. If you're successful, but it's too dangerous to try sneaking away and reporting back to me, stay with Morgan's men. An idea of the state of an army after it wins or has been defeated is equally important. Sooner or later, providing we both survive, we'll find each other."

Lowell Gray's expression grew deadly serious. "You are fully aware, are you not, Mr. Bell, that I'm asking you to become a Union spy? Spying is a dangerous business. Not being in uniform helps you gain access to the Confederate camp, but it can cost you your life if the gray legs get even a hint you're gathering information for their blue-belly enemy. Are you willing to take that risk to meet with your brother and interview him for J. Rodgers Black?"

Jarrod nodded. "Lieutenant, my brother went to Kentucky to help my uncle after he hurt his leg. Judah wrote to me and another close friend every month for two years, and then his letters stopped. The next thing we hear back home in Chillicothe is that Uncle Temple is dead, his house and barn burned to the ground, Judah is who knows where, and Uncle's Thoroughbred horses are missing. The newspapers made vague references holding renegade

Union cavalry responsible. I'd like to hear the real truth from Judah. I'm sure our father would, too."

Lowell Gray cocked his head sideways and said, "Your father wasn't involved in the scheme you and Black cooked up, was he?"

"No, sir, he wasn't. He would have tried to discourage me."

"Then there's one condition involved in my sending you behind Rebel lines. After you're out of my purview, I telegraph your father via J. Rodgers Black and let him know about our arrangement. He deserves to know your whereabouts, whether he's pleased with the news or not. So does the rest of your family."

Gray's proposal relieved Jarrod of a heavy burden. He had felt badly about his sudden departure from Chillicothe with no more warning for his family than a handwritten note mailed to his father. He had no regrets about what he'd done, but he had no desire to worry his father and his family unnecessarily. Gray's telegram would at least inform them that he was alive and coming closer to Judah each day. Beyond that, there was nothing else he could do except pray they would forgive him for acting out of brotherly love.

"I have no problem with your proposed telegram, Lieutenant."

Lowell Gray nodded. "We'll talk more between here and Savannah. You best start that pen working. You'll have more company in a few minutes. George Villard of the *New York Tribune* is filling his belly at General Nelson's fire as we speak. Villard's been chasing after Nelson for weeks, and the General can't afford to offend a veteran reporter by not offering him the same accommodations he provided you, especially if you love publicity and fanfare like Bull Nelson does. I'll see that your story is on the wire as soon as the telegraph line is strung. Good night, Mr. Bell."

Jarrod leaned back in his chair, awed by the phenomenal string of good luck he'd enjoyed since leaving Chillicothe. First J. Rodgers Black, then General Dumont, followed by General Nelson, and now Lieutenant Lowell Gray had each and everyone acted positively on his behalf, sweeping aside obstacles that threatened to squelch his quest to find Judah.

The good luck string would eventually snap.

It always did.

In the meantime, he'd pray this particular string stretched far enough he'd get to hug his brother and tell him how much he loved him.

The marching order of the Fourth Division the next morning clarified Jarrod's true standing in General Bull Nelson's ranking of individual reporters trailing after him. Veteran New York reporter George Villard rode at the side of the general dressed like a military officer on a big black charger that matched the size and color of Nelson's own seventeen-hand stallion. Instead of feeling disappointed or insulted, Jarrod was relieved. He didn't have to converse with Nelson and risk saying something he would regret later, and, most important, he was moving in the direction he wanted to travel.

Riding beside Jarrod, Lieutenant Lowell Gray informed him that George Villard was a recent German emigrant determined to be a successful English-writing reporter. The dispatches of Villard's that Gray had read eliminated rumor, wild speculation, strident politicizing in favor of either North or South, and favoritism in favor of the truth of events, the same philosophy pursued by penny-pinching

J. Rodgers Black. Gray couldn't say the same for the other eastern news hawks he'd met and read. That testimony made a wet-eared amateur like Jarrod feel privileged to have spent an evening sharing a library with such august company.

The next evening Bull Nelson's staff occupied Clifton Pace, the seven-hundred-acre estate of Confederate Brigadier General Gideon J. Pillow. To Jarrod, the Pillow plantation was a small city with its own blacksmith, carpenter, brick-layer, horse handler, gardener, housemaid, cook, mid-wife, schoolmaster, and black field hands.

The next day they entered a landscape so radically different Jarrod likened it to journeying from the earth to the sun. The fertile ground of the baronial slave plantation country gave way beyond Mount Pleasant to worthless yellow clay tilled by poor whites that thronged their farm lanes and gateways with streaming eyes, eager to salute and cheer the Yankee invaders. The change in soil quality was a death knell for the railroad, telegraph, and hard-sur-faced roads. The final seventy-two miles to Savannah would be over a rough track in ill repair, a farm-to-market road built by Gideon Pillow some twenty years past. When Bull Nelson saw the rail fences bordering the narrow, deeply rutted pathway, he had them torn down and ordered the commanders of the companies assigned that task to provide the telegraph workers all the assistance they re-quired.

On Thursday, 3 April, a fifteen-mile march brought Nelson's advance party to Waynesboro, where homes dis-played small United States flags in their windows. Jarrod was fascinated watching an artillery battery sign up new recruits while a regimental band played "Yankee Doodle" at the request of several local women. He had a hunch

Southern forces collected fresh soldiers drawn to the fight by patriotic fever in the same manner.

They dined that evening in the home of a local magistrate. After a meal of pork belly and beans, boiled vegetables, knobby bread laced with honey, and dandelion root coffee, Jarrod found Lowell Gray on the porch of the house smoking instead of sucking on his ever-present cigar. Jarrod had sensed Gray's growing impatience with the progress of Nelson's column. Waynesboro was only thirty-two miles from Savannah, but the lighted cigar hinted at Gray's mood.

"Forty miles in four days is a snail's pace. We're riding forward with the scouts in the morning. I want to be in Savannah tomorrow evening. We can't afford to tarry much longer. I want you behind Confederate lines before we engage them. The scouting detail moves out at five a.m. Private Haney will have our horses watered, fed, and saddled beforehand. Be ready."

Jarrod and Gray bunked on the floor of the magistrate's porch wrapped in blankets supplied by the dependable Private Haney. Jarrod had hoped to finish polishing his Duck River story and add copy about the column's march in the meantime. He lacked sufficient light for writing, and General Nelson's staff, including George Villard, had occupied the balance of the magistrate's home. He dozed off with little difficulty and spent the night dreaming of what he would say when he caught up with Judah, and the beauty and warmth of Lorena Gamble's body, an odd combination that reflected the uncertainties of his life at the moment.

Lowell Gray, having obtained permission to accompany the scout detail the previous evening before retiring, had ordered Private Haney to fetch their horses to the magistrate's home on schedule before daylight. Haney had tied canteens filled with fresh well water and cloth bags of flour biscuits he'd baked in the magistrate's oven during the night to the saddle horns of both animals. Jarrod and Gray donned gum ponchos before mounting, and were prepared when a steady, pelting spring rain began to fall as they exited Waynesboro behind the scouting detail.

Jarrod and Lieutenant Gray traveled all day in the steady rain, alternating their pace between a trot and a fast walk. The scouting detail fell away after ten miles, their destination an intact bridge over a sizable creek, which they would guard until Nelson's Fourth Division hove into sight. With two halts to water and rest their mounts and nibble on biscuits and sip well water from their canteens, Jarrod and Gray reached Vansant's, the first plantation they'd seen after a score of subsistence farms since departing Waynesboro, at eleven o'clock. They were ten miles from Savannah and pushed ahead. At mid-afternoon, the eastern edge of Savannah was a mighty welcome sight to riders and horses alike.

A massive expanse of mud compared to the pittance of a narrow road they'd traveled awaited them at the site of the Union camp once the home of General Grant's whole army, now a camp occupied by a single infantry company pending the arrival of General Buell's Army of the Ohio. The infantry company's ten Sibley tents looked lonely and forlorn in the big open area to Jarrod, as if they'd been accidentally left behind.

They circled the Union campsite and proceeded into Savannah. They found what Lieutenant Gray sought—a livery and small inn—on Savannah's main thoroughfare, stabled and unsaddled their horses, and enjoyed a hot meal of fried chicken, rice and beans, day-old bread, and real Yankee coffee at a table in a back corner of the inn.

Coffee mug in one hand, unlit cigar in the other, Lowell Gray put his forearms on the edge of table, leaned toward Jarrod, and spoke in a low voice though the inn wasn't particularly crowded. "It's time we part company, young man. You can't afford to waste a minute. Take the road south out of Savannah. According to the maps I've studied, the south road intersects the Tennessee River twelve miles from here. That puts you roughly between Pittsburgh Landing and Corinth. Find a way across the river. If you don't think your horse has enough strength left to swim you across, find a local farmer with a rowboat, and then hike southwest for Corinth, or buy or steal the first decent horse you see. My calculation is that once you reach the west bank of the Tennessee, you're only twenty odd miles from Corinth."

Lowell Gray sipped coffee and sucked on his cigar. "I have this gut feeling that you need to locate your brother by tomorrow evening. I don't believe General Johnston is planning to hunker down in Corinth and wait for us to besiege him. He has to have intelligence that General Buell's army is on the march to Savannah. Knowing that, he'll attack before Buell can reinforce General Grant at Pittsburgh Landing."

Lowell Gray summoned the inn's owner and sole waiter with a beckoning gesture. "We need a sack of this fine chicken and some bread to take with us. Can you arrange that?" Gray asked, laying three Federal one-dollar bills on the table.

The delighted owner hustled off to the inn's kitchen. Turning back to Jarrod, Gray said, "Remember, don't commit anything you observe to paper. Use your military press pass to identify yourself when it's to your advantage. Trust no one until you see nothing but blue uniforms around you again. That's about all I can teach you about gathering intelligence behind enemy lines. You'll have to depend on ingenuity most of the time and lie effectively when you must."

Lowell Gray pocketed his unlit cigar and studied Jarrod with his pale eyes. "You still sure you want to be a spy? It's not too late for you to continue reporting on the war and seek out your brother later."

Jarrod answered, "No, sir. I'll stick by you. From my history reading, I've come to understand countless men disappear in big battles such as the one we're facing, where more than eighty thousand soldiers will take part, and are never heard from again. They are among the dead hastily buried when the fighting is over and never identified. I can't let that happen to Judah."

"You are one stubborn young cuss. Are your father and brother as ardent about what's important to them as you are?"

"Yes, sir, including my oldest brother, Jacob. He's with the First Regiment Ohio Volunteer Cavalry. Not to brag, but there's no quit permitted in our household. You set your course and finish what you start."

Lowell Gray came to his feet. "I believe you've enough sand to make a spy, Mr. Bell. On second thought, more than enough. Let's collect that sack of chicken and bread and check on our horses, shall we?"

At the livery, they found the owner's son had earned his money. Both horses had been rubbed dry and groomed, and were munching hay. The strapping lad insisted on an inspection by Jarrod and Gray, lifting the two hooves on which he'd replaced shoes. He then insisted on saddling both animals for them.

Lieutenant Lowell Gray escorted Jarrod a half mile beyond Savannah on the south road.

Passing Jarrod the sack of food from the inn, Gray chuckled and said, "Hopefully, I'll be dining with General Grant's staff this evening on the lawn of the Cherry Mansion on a bluff overlooking the river. And don't worry, I won't forget to file your story with J. Rodgers Black."

Gray sighed, extended his hand, and said, "Mr. Jarrod Bell, take care with your life. Test-fire your pistol once you're farther down the road a ways to make certain your powder's dry. Do the same thing on the far bank of the river. Just give our cause your best."

With that handshake and farewell, Gray slapped the rump of Jarrod's seal-brown gelding with his horse's reins and wheeled his mount about, leaving Jarrod to fend for himself come what may.

The flatboat was anchored by hawsers tied to thick posts driven deep into the bank fifteen feet from water's edge in a cove that deflected the main thrust of the Tennessee River's bloated current. Cleated walkways for pole men ran along the port and starboard sides of the craft. A long steering oar atop the rear cabin was tied clear of the water. The vessel was a throwback to the days of yore before steamboats when farmers grouped together, packed a flatboat with saleable goods, floated downriver to New Orleans, sold flatboat and goods, and hiked home to Tennessee afoot.

What appealed to Jarrod was the flatboat's capacity to carry half a dozen men and horses. He would find no better means of crossing the flooded Tennessee short of a steamboat or a ferry, if he searched for a decade. The question facing him was how to best commandeer the vessel for his purposes.

He wasn't a thief, and he had a considerable sum of money in his saddlebags. He suspected his uncle's Denmark Thoroughbreds had been stolen under the guise of "spoils of war," and he couldn't countenance such an act. The flatboat had value to whoever owned it. He was splitting hairs in the middle of a war, but that was the curse of being Senator Clay Bell's son. You didn't take what didn't belong to you.

In the dim twilight, coal oil lamps lit the downstairs

windows of the two-story house across the road from the moored flatboat. The house rested on a small knoll, and was well above any danger the flooded river might serve up. The dark bulk of a large barn and the sweep of open ground south of the house suggested a river bottom farm that would require the labor of more than just the owner. Perhaps there was a crew handy for the flatboat.

Jarrod stepped down, tied his gelding to one of the flat-boat's mooring posts, fisted his saddlebags, and walked across the muddy road. It was the supper hour for farm country and no one was out and about. Thankfully, there was no watchdog for him to deal with.

Once on the porch of the house, Jarrod was determined to gain the upper hand straight off. He decided against knocking, threw his saddlebags over his shoulder, and drew his revolver. The knob of the front door turned freely. He eased the door open, stepped boldly inside the house, and found himself alone in a center hallway running the length of the house.

The lighted parlor to his left was empty. He heard laughter toward the rear of the house. The rest of the house was devoid of noise. Fearing a creaking floorboard, he walked slowly forward. Six people were seated around a dining room table. The mature man at the head of the table was of medium build and bearded, with bangs cut level in the middle of his forehead. His merry brown eyes were fixed on his tablemates.

Jarrod was in full view of everybody at the table. The family, immersed in eating and what the bearded man was saying, took no notice of him. A full minute passed before an attractive young female seated across the table from Jarrod spotted him and his leveled revolver.

She was approximately Jarrod's age. Her frank face showed no sign of alarm. She raised her hand and her father, not the least perturbed about being interrupted, said, "Yes, Cassie, my dear. What concerns you?"

With a nod in Jarrod's direction, Cassie said in the same lighthearted tone she would use when introducing a new friend to her family, "Father, we have company."

The father's head turned and the merry brown eyes came to rest on Jarrod. "Well, brother, thee are the first person that believes he must bargain for a seat at our table with a weapon. I can assure you we have enough food prepared to include you. What say thee?"

One young male family member was seated next to Cassie. Two older appearing males sat opposite them, peering at Jarrod over their shoulders. The female head of the family occupied the far end of the table. Taking their cue from the male head of the house, the entire family was watching Jarrod with keen interest, unruffled by the sight of an armed stranger who had yet to utter a sound.

Jarrod thought better of lowering his revolver until he saw how the father and the two older sons reacted to his wants. "My name is Jarrod Bell. I don't mean to be rude and unmannerly, but I'm in a hurry. I'll pay handsomely if you'll ferry me and my horse across the river on your flatboat yet today."

The bearded father did not respond at first. Dabbing at his mouth with a cloth napkin, he pursed his lips, and then, his expression eager and curious, said point blank, "How handsomely?"

Jarrod patted his saddlebags. "One hundred dollars in gold coin, sir."

The father's eyes bugged just enough to suggest that sum of money in gold coin had genuinely surprised him. It was two years of Jarrod's personal savings and enough money to replace the flatboat with funds to spare. Jarrod was figuring the patriarch might risk his flatboat on a flooded river for sure money, for there was a real possibility one of the opposing armies or renegades in the area might confiscate the flatboat for transportation purposes and pay the owner nothing. Stranger things had happened in wartime, and the newspapers he'd spied in the parlor indicated the family patriarch had some grasp of what had transpired thus far in the conflict.

The patriarch's beaming smile lifted Jarrod's spirits. Nodding at his two older sons, he said, "Boys, thou heard Mr. Bell, he's in a hurry. Jump into your rain gear. There's enough light left for us to make Hanson's Landing before full dark is upon us."

A firm female voice interceded from the far end of the table. "Enoch, my dear, the river is awfully high. Are thee sure the reward is worthy of the risk?"

"Mary, the weather wasn't always fair during my three trips down the Ohio to New Orleans. Hanson's is but a mile-and-a-half voyage and downriver to boot."

The male family members rose from the table together. "Mary, we'll need grub sacks for a week as we'll wait for lower water at Hanson's. Cassie, help your mother, please."

Nearly dancing with joy, Jarrod holstered his revolver, opened his saddlebag, untied the strings of a leather pouch, and counted out the money. He laid the amount due the patriarch on the dining room table. His head almost shook by its self. How astronomical were the odds against his meeting the Quaker owner of a flatboat in need of ready cash in the middle of nowhere? He judged them to be higher than the odds against his visiting the moon.

Outside the house, the rain had tapered off. Approaching the flatboat, Jarrod realized enough daylight remained to make out the dark line of the far bank through the mist hovering over the river. The older brothers were built like their father yet blessed with steely muscles that rivaled the strength of much bigger men. After snubbing the flatboat tight against its mooring posts, the brothers with hardly a grunt manhandled a loading platform that extended from the bank to the rail of the vessel's hull, aligned a second platform from rail to deck, positioned themselves on either side of Jarrod's gelding, and had no difficulty leading him aboard.

The patriarch banished Jarrod and his gelding to the flatboat's open-faced cabin, climbed atop that same cabin, freed the steering oar, and signaled for his sons to cast off the dock-loading platform and the anchoring hawsers. The brothers then poled the flatboat past the protecting arm of the sheltering cove. It was a short voyage, as the patriarch had predicted, once the flatboat was fully exposed to the river's main current. The brothers manned poles on the starboard catwalk. With the patriarch steering and his sons fighting the onrushing drag of the current, Jarrod watched the far bank draw ever closer at what seemed a yard at a time.

Jarrod was questioning how they would escape the power of the current and land without the flatboat smashing into the bank when a yell rang out above him and the brothers doubled their efforts. It was touch and go, but of a sudden the flatboat rounded a point of land protruding into the river. To Jarrod's astonishment the flatboat slid by the outermost rocks of the point within the length of a human spit without suffering any damage. Crossing the last span of open water protected from the river's current and tying off the flatboat at Hanson's sturdy wooden dock was the easiest leg of the voyage.

The Quaker brothers moored the flatboat, took the gelding's reins from Jarrod, and led him up the dock-loading platform to the top rail of the hull. With some gentle coaxing, the gelding jumped the narrow gap between the flatboat and the dock.

The Quaker father sought out Jarrod at the rail. "Mr.

Bell, though it is none of my business, where are thee bound?"

"Corinth, Mississippi, sir. My brother is with the Confederate Army."

"Have you traveled this country before?"

"No, sir, I'm in need of accurate directions."

"Hamburg is a half mile downriver. Follow the road west from there to Monterey. The road running north from Corinth passes through Monterey to Pittsburgh Landing. If local rumor is correct and General Johnston plans to engage General Grant, the Confederate Army will be at Monterey or farther south on the Corinth Road. Thee can ask Granny Hansford to confirm what I'm telling you if thou wishes."

"That won't be necessary, sir. I have no cause to distrust a faithful man. I need mention that I'm a reporter with the *Cincinnati Times-Ledger* and I'd appreciate knowing your name. With your permission, I'd like to mention the help you've given me in my reports."

The Quaker patriarch raised a demurring hand. "Mr. Bell, notoriety would be of no benefit to me and my family. If my Rebel neighbors learn of what I've done, they might despair of my helping a Yankee, even a reporter."

Jarrod promised, "I will respect your privacy, sir," and stepped off the flatboat. He accepted the reins of the gelding from the patriarch's sons, led him to solid ground, mounted, waved good-bye, and rode into the rapidly darkening evening whistling "Dixie."

CHAPTER 21

"Are you ever afraid, Corporal Bell?"

Judah Bell's gaze remained on the clear-skied red sunset behind the tasseling oaks that surrounded the bivouac assigned Morgan's Squadron. He squirmed to make himself more comfortable atop his blanket and poncho on the uneven ground. How did an officer reassure a subordinate before the big battle without adding to his fright?

"Darnell, only a fool will say he isn't scared when the order to charge comes in the morning. If you're not afraid, you'll soon be dead. Take your time reloading and pick a target. Always remember, you won't be alone once the shooting starts."

"Thank you, sir, I just needed to know it's all right to be afraid of seeing the elephant for the first time."

Tomorrow, Sunday, 6 April 1862, that elephant would fill every soldier's whole world whether he wore blue or butternut gray. The engagement couldn't come too soon for Morgan's Squadron. It had taken two and a half days to march the forty-two thousand men comprising the four corps of General Johnston's Confederate Army the fifteen

miles from Corinth, Mississippi, to Mickey's, a farmhouse
at the intersection of the road from Monterey to Savannah.
Torrential spring rains had beset the Confederate column
throughout the second day of the march, interrupting the
flow of the four corps from head to rear. Men stood for
long periods in the steady downpour, then had to trot to
keep up when the column lurched forward.

Marching with Breckinridge's corps at the tail end of
the column, Morgan's Squadron traveled a roadway littered
with discarded equipment, bowie knives, playing cards,
overcoats, Bibles, and other sundry items suddenly too
heavy to tote or fuss with. The one welcome delay was
the rest given each regiment while its colonel read the commanding general's address, written by General Johnston
before their departure from Corinth. What had stuck in
Judah's mind most vividly from the address was General
Johnston's assertion that the hopes of eight million people
rested on this army, and they were expected to show themselves worthy of their race and lineage. The address had
elicited wild cheering and renewed the debate among the
rank and file whether or not the upcoming battle, the
largest ever to be fought on American soil and a battle not
a single man wanted to miss, would decide the outcome of
the war once and for all.

At daybreak, bright sunshine reflecting from flooded
fields was a welcome sight the last day of the march. With
the advent of drier weather, many footsloggers were
concerned that dampness had fouled the powder in their
weapons. Instead of drawing the charges and reloading,
they tested them by the simple expedient of pulling the
trigger. Weapons were soon banging off up and down the
column, sounding every bit like a sizable clash of pickets,
a racket well within earshot of Federal outposts. Soldiers
practicing their marksmanship on birds and rabbits and

fine-tuning their Rebel yell was the tipping point for
General Johnston, and a direct order from their commanding officer wrought a hurried change in individual behavior.

Deployment around Mickey's completed, the Confederate Army retired for the night to sleep on their arms in
line of battle. Final orders assigned Morgan's Squadron to
Colonel Robert Trabue's First Kentucky Brigade with instructions to be prepared to go into battle at daybreak.
The evening air had grown cool and after the squadron
finished nibbling on their cold rations, the bivouac quieted.
Judah heard strains of band music in the far distance that
Sergeant Field Peterson identified as Saturday night marches
being played in the Federal camps.

The jingle of approaching spurs warned Judah that
Texan Lew James was on the prowl, which from prior
experience meant something extraordinary was looming,
for Lew James attracted trouble and danger in equal
doses. "You have a visitor, Corporal Bell. Seems he's related
to you."

Thinking Lew James was playing the prankster again,
Judah stayed put in his blankets. "Contrary to the rumor
floating about, the devil is not my cousin, Lew, and I'm not
interested in meeting him."

"Might need to change your mind, Corporal. The young
man behind me claims he's your brother."

"Brother?"

Judah threw off his blanket and jumped to his feet. Lew
James stepped aside with a sweeping bow of introduction,
and there in the dimming twilight stood a smiling Jarrod.
The moon catching fire wouldn't have been any bigger
surprise to Judah Bell. The next thing he knew he was in a
bear hug tight enough to crack ribs.

"Great to see you, brother," Jarrod said. "It took me a
while to find you. A lot of people helped me along the way
and here I am."

Judah returned Jarrod's hug and then stepped back to get his breath, startled that his little brother had matched his physical size and strength before reaching his eighteenth birthday. During Judah's two Kentucky years with Uncle Temple, Jarrod had grown three inches and gained at least thirty pounds.

"Aren't you glad to see me, brother?" a frowning Jarrod asked.

After a deep gulp of lung-reviving air, Judah said, "Yes, I am. I just didn't expect you to show up in a Confederate Army camp the night before a major battle. This won't be a safe place for even noncombatants come morning. How did you get through our lines and locate me?"

"General Johnston ordered that all persons, black and white, encountered on the march were to be seized and sent to the rear to eliminate any chance they'd inform the Yankees he was preparing to attack them. I was passed along to General Breckinridge's adjutant. I told the adjutant I was seeking a brother serving with Captain John Morgan's cavalry and he, in turn, passed me along to Lieutenant Basil Duke. There was a caveat. If you didn't identify me, I was to be put in irons for the duration of General Johnston's campaign."

Lew James interrupted the two brothers at that point and passed Jarrod his holstered revolver. "Corporal, Sergeant Peterson said to return your brother's sidearm once you identified him. Good night, sir."

"Good night, Lew," Judah said, turning to face Jarrod. "I am happy to see you, but just what the hell are you doing here? Are you that anxious to get yourself killed?"

Jarrod raised a placating hand. "Now, calm down, Judah. I have to talk with you. Word leaked to the Ohio newspapers that you were spotted riding with Morgan and his men. The papers scalded Father with a venomous attack for days and his reputation is in tatters."

Judah dropped down on his blanket. Jarrod took a seat beside him, cradling his revolver in his lap. Judah sighed and asked, "How did the newspapers learn of my serving under Captain Morgan?"

"You probably don't know that Jacob is an officer with the First Regiment Ohio Volunteer Cavalry. You were identified riding with Morgan's raiders at a ferry crossing on the Green River. Cam Logan was commanding the Union detail pursuing you that day. He saw you through his binoculars. He pointed you out to our boyhood friend, Fritz Howard. Fritz, God love him, had a look with Logan's binoculars and blurted out that it was you. Seems you'd written him about the red stallion you were riding. Jacob was there, of course, but there was nothing he could do to keep Cam Logan quiet. I bet Cam wrote his father that night and I'm certain Brice Logan took great delight in giving the damning news to the *Chillicothe Gazette* and the Cincinnati papers."

"Did Father have any warning?"

"Yes, Jacob wrote to him. He received Jacob's letter in Columbus the day after the story broke in the Chillicothe and Cincinnati papers. Not knowing how you came to associate with Confederate raiders, there wasn't any way he could justify what you'd done and deflect the lambasting the papers gave of the both of you."

"I'm sorry for the stink I stirred up. I never intended to hurt Father. I was furious about Uncle Temple being killed and decided I could never fight beside the Union trash that murdered him."

"What really happened that night, Judah? I obtained a position with the *Cincinnati Times-Ledger* so I could find you and tell your side of the story. Mr. Black and I are hoping that his readers might at least view Father in a more favorable light once they learn the whole story."

"Hunt Baldwin was a horse trader and breeder in Scott

County," Judah began. "He's a staunch Unionist and resented Uncle Temple's Southern sympathies. Baldwin wanted to start his own Denmark stable, but Uncle refused his generous offers for a mare and a stallion, guaranteeing Baldwin couldn't buy or trade for what he wanted. Then came secession and Baldwin recruited his own Union volunteer cavalry company in Scott County lightning-quick. He immediately went after property held by an ardent secesh in a neighborhood that favored the Union and President Lincoln."

Judah stared into the growing darkness, remembering. "They came solely to kill that night and steal the Denmarks. I escaped because of Uncle Temple's foresight. While Asa Barefoot and I couldn't do anything to save him, he'd seen that we had horses and enough money and food hidden nearby to elude any pursuit by Baldwin and his supposed Union cavalry. I doubt Baldwin had orders from any legitimate Union officer to do what he did. I don't believe he had the military authority to act on his own, either. None of that mattered. No local official was going to risk incurring the wrath of his Unionist neighbors to right a wrong. That's when I made the decision to ride south instead of north. I've never been one to abide unfair treatment of others, particularly those that share my blood. Before the war ends, I'll meet up with Hunt Baldwin in his blue uniform and have my chance to avenge Uncle Temple, the burning of his home, and the theft of his Denmarks."

Jarrod sat quietly, thinking through what he'd been told. "Judah, there are still a number of fair-minded people that can ignore the greed, the hate, the wrongheadedness, and the chest pounding that ignited the war and discern the reality of events. To them, murder is murder regardless of the color of a soldier's uniform. They are the readers who will see Hunt Baldwin not as a soldier prosecuting the war, but a common murderer and thief hiding behind a uniform to take unfair advantage of civilians. If I can expose Baldwin publicly, we will have taken the first step toward bringing him to justice. Who knows, he might prove an embarrassment to his fellow Yankee officers. Whether it helps Father or not, that's why I must write your story and file it with the *Times-Ledger*."

"Jarrod, do as you wish with my blessing. Nothing you do will make the situation any worse for Father and me. I just hope Father isn't too angry with me. I have no desire to be the family outcast."

"Not a single member of our family holds you at fault. They all send their love. Every one of us prays the whole family can be together again once the war is over."

"That's important for me to know, what with my being a married man now."

The sudden slackening of Jarrod's jaw tickled Judah. "What? What did you say?"

"I took a wife a month ago."

"What's her name?" a fascinated Jarrod demanded.

"Brianna Hardin Bell," Judah said with considerable pride.

Painfully aware of how Judah loved to tease him, Jarrod reined in his rampant curiosity before he started firing off questions like an overly anxious schoolboy. "Tell me about her."

"She's about your age, feisty, and independent."

"She sounds a little young and high spirited for an old war horse like you."

Judah chuckled and said, "She can be quite a challenge at that. She can be a tomcat or a lady, whatever the occasion demands. She saved my life twice."

"I can't wait to meet her. Where are you hiding her?" Jarrod asked, swiveling his head left and right as if he were searching for the missing bride.

"Let's be serious for a minute," Judah said, pausing to insure he had Jarrod's complete attention. "If anything untoward happens to me, Asa Barefoot can take you to Brianna. She's staying at Maud Huddleston's boardinghouse in Glasgow, Kentucky. Brianna's parents are dead and she has no relatives that she can rely upon. She helps Maud Huddleston with boardinghouse chores for part of her keep, and I left her with enough money to sustain her otherwise for a considerable period of time. That money, of course, won't last forever. I know I'm asking a lot of you, but you're the answer to a problem that's been keeping me awake at night. I married this woman with honest intentions and I won't have her left at loose ends if anything happens to me. Jarrod, I want you to promise me you will look after her if need be, and see that she receives whatever inheritance I'm rightfully due. Will you promise me that?"

A sober Jarrod nodded. "I promise you I'll do whatever I can for her."

"I appreciate that, little brother. It settles my mind a heap. Brianna deserves the best I can provide her."

With that, Judah loosed another big sigh. "Our family in Ohio is out of harm's way. We can't be certain any of us of fighting age will survive. You may be able to continue your newspaper reporting unless the war drags on and the Federal government starts drafting men, then you'll have to bear arms. Many Confederates think the outcome of the battle tomorrow will lead to a peace accord of sorts. I don't. Both sides are afflicted by a fierce stubbornness that refuses to countenance not winning the war."

Jarrod said, "A rumor is floating in the Confederate ranks saying General Johnston's fellow generals made him aware the Yankees have been alerted an attack is imminent and he won't catch them by surprise as he intended. Johnston said he would still fight them if there were a million of them. That's the kind of zeal for battle you're talking about, isn't it?"

"Yes, and it may lead to a slaughter of epic proportions. Basil Duke claims Johnston and Grant have more than eighty thousand men at their disposal, and that estimate doesn't include the twenty thousand men under General Buell marching to reinforce Grant."

Jarrod said, "Basil Duke's intelligence is correct. I heard those same numbers traveling with General Nelson's Fourth Division from Nashville to Savannah. Johnston's forces have tomorrow to pin Grant's present army against the river and destroy it or face certain defeat the next day at the hands of a reinforced Grant once Buell is across the river."

Judah uncorked his canteen, sipped a few swallows of water, and passed the canteen to Jarrod. "I want one other promise from you."

"What would that be?"

"A promise you will hang back with Asa Barefoot come morning," Judah said.

Jarrod weighed Judah's request. Judah had described the half-breed and his background in his letters to Jarrod, and Jarrod realized Barefoot could be quite helpful if he found himself in a threatening situation. "I'll do as you ask, so long as you realize that I can't write about what happens from miles away. I want to talk to soldiers while what they felt and saw is still fresh in their minds. That's what distinguishes the reporting in *Harper's Weekly* and the *New York Herald* from the dry copy of the daily rag sheets filled with which flank was turned at what hour and the estimated number of dead and wounded."

Judah laughed. "You always did hog the firsthand accounts of past wars in Father's library. The point I'm making is don't expose yourself to direct fire. I'll provide you troopers from Basil Duke's Company A to interview at the first opportunity. If we're overrun at any time, use your Union military pass to identity yourself as a Yankee reporter. Don't let them take you prisoner. If you see me in circumstances with the blue-bellies not beneficial to you, ignore me. Do we have an understanding, little brother?"

"We do," Jarrod conceded.

A kneeling shadow fell across Judah and Jarrod. "If I may interrupt you two fine gentlemen, Corporal Bell, I'd like a quick word with you and the rest of the mess."

While the tone was civil, the ring of authority in the speaker's hoarse voice was unmistakable. "I want to review one last time what's in store for us in the morning," Field Peterson said, rising to his feet. "Men, gather 'round for a little palaver."

With no comment and quick movement, ten troopers gathered around Judah, Jarrod, and Peterson. Peterson removed his hat, and his string-taut salt-and-pepper hair resembled streaks of white and black in the faint light of a sickle moon. His large, mournful hunting-hound eyes were dark blobs above the skin of his cheekbones. "General Hardee's corps will initiate the attack in the morning. General Bragg's corps will follow behind him. General Polk's and General Breckenridge's corps are to mass to the left and right a half mile behind Bragg. When Bragg goes forward, Polk will spread out wide and support him, leaving Breckinridge in column as a general reserve. We're part of Breckinridge's corps, so it may be some time before we see any action tomorrow. Don't lollygag on me. Be ready to move out on short notice."

Peterson looked at each of his listeners in turn. "No fires tonight. No test-firing of weapons. If you're concerned about your powder, draw the charge and reload. There will be no bugle 'Calls' or drum signals in the morning. General Johnston wants to maintain whatever element of surprise we still possess. Remember what General Johnston said about making eight million people proud of you. Let that sentiment and that necessity guide your actions on the morrow. You're dismissed."

Kneeling beside Jarrod and Judah again, Peterson said, "Corporal Bell, we will escort Lieutenant Duke in the eventuality such a service is required tomorrow. One last thing, just where will this sudden-to-the-scene brother of yours be located after sunrise? He is a noncombatant, is he not?"

"Yes, sir, he is, and he will be in the rear of us with Asa Barefoot. I have his word on that."

Peterson patted Judah's knee. "Good, that will satisfy Lieutenant Duke. Jarrod Bell, I admire your spunk. Takes a lot of nerve to travel all these many miles on family business no matter how important it might be."

"Thank you, sir," Jarrod said. "I appreciate that."

Field Peterson rose to his feet. "Corporal Bell, when will Barefoot arrive with the breakfast fixings?"

Asa Barefoot was well down the Corinth Road between Mickey's farmhouse and Monterey where a fire couldn't be seen from the Confederate rear, frying bacon and baking flour and salt biscuits to provide Peterson's mess a cold breakfast. "He'll be here at four thirty a.m. sharp, sir."

"Your half-breed's sense of time fascinates me," Peterson said. "He has no watch but he's never late. Good evening, gentlemen."

Jarrod watched Field Peterson cross to his blankets at the edge of the trees circling Morgan's bivouac. "He has command of his men, the situation, and he doesn't waste words."

"Yes, and he holds fast under fire. He deserves a higher rank, but prefers the company of the rank and file. He's a model soldier for privates."

Jarrod decided a portrait of Sergeant Field Peterson would enhance the credence of his story. Besides his rather unique physical appearance and unnaturally hoarse voice,

Peterson's short speech to his charges the night before combat had created an image of duty and sincerity that he was positive he could convey in printed words.

"Jarrod, Barefoot will deliver his breakfast rations awfully early. I suggest we try to sleep a few hours. Who knows how much rest anyone will get tomorrow night. We may be watering our horses in the Tennessee River or riding hell bent in the opposite direction for Corinth."

Judah lay awake studying the pale stars and the sickle moon. Every solitary soldier in the Confederate Army was sick to death of rain and mud. To sleep dry for one night was a gift from on high. A chance to fight just the enemy and not the enemy and the weather for a whole day was a most heartening prospect and boosted morale proportionately.

He wasn't scared of engaging the enemy. He'd survived numerous armed skirmishes with blue-belly cavalry and infantry during his four months with Morgan's Squadron. If asked, though, he would admit he was apprehensive about how much the elephant had increased in size. The manpower and arms of the two opposing forces was the equal to those of the Napoleonic Wars and unrivaled in American history. To help win such an epic battle, individual soldiers had to ignore the massive noise and confusion of two giant armies coming together, obey their officers, and fight until the last enemy had been driven from the field. A soldier couldn't allow anything he saw, heard, or felt on the battlefield to dampen his fighting ardor and lust for victory. Those were the virtues of the great armies of history, and Judah would hold himself to those high standards until his dying breath out of fear of shaming his bride and his family.

Tiredness won out over apprehension. He dozed off and dreamed, oddly, of the small rose-shaped birthmark on Brianna Hardin's right hip.

CHAPTER 22

Fading stars were minute blips of white when Asa Barefoot's rough hand shook Judah's shoulder. Soft gray light outlined tree trunks and crowned the brush growing at the edge of the woods. Judah shook dew from his rubber poncho, showering the sleeping Jarrod's face with wet droplets. His not-so-little-brother-anymore came awake with a start, uttered a string of curses befitting a maturing young male, and jumped to his feet to confront his tormentor.

"You better mind that temper," Judah warned. "It might sink your reportorial ship before it sails."

Though he had yet to meet Judah's brother in person, a bemused Asa Barefoot said, "Are you two going to fight or eat?"

A smile burst on Jarrod's face and he lowered his cocked fists. "Might as well eat. He'd whip me like usual anyway."

"Looks like you're evenly matched," Barefoot teased, holding forth cloth bags filled with cold bacon and biscuits.

"May look like that, but Judah's meaner than I am. Always has been."

Troopers were stirring and climbing from their blankets.

Word spread that Barefoot was present, and he was suddenly the most popular soul in sight. Every Rebel bearing arms in General Johnston's Army had departed Corinth with three days' rations. The upshot was they were mostly gone within the first day, reinforcing the old saw that, "for the defenders of the Confederacy, rations were always lighter to carry in their bellies than on their backs."

Sergeant Field Peterson drew his share of breakfast from Barefoot's food bags, did some serious chewing, and sipped water from his canteen. "It will be a lean day on an empty belly for many of our men. Might be a problem if the battle rages overly long."

Cornering Judah off to the side of the others, Peterson said, "It would be wise to provide Barefoot a revolver. Despite the abolitionist posturing of Northern folk, a lot of those blue-bellies over yonder don't have much use for blacks or half-breeds carrying black blood. Clever as Barefoot is, he'd do well to keep a gun out of sight until he needs it."

Judah complied, drawing a rare grin from the craggy-faced half-breed. "Keep a sharp eye on Jarrod for me."

With the silencing of bugles and drums, officers issued the morning "Calls" in softened voices. Judah was positioning Jasper's saddle blanket when Barefoot stepped alongside him. "The stallion will draw much enemy fire. Seeing you on a fine red stud like him, the blue-bellies will take you for an officer, and they're trained to kill officers first. Take the mare instead. She is nimble on her feet and trustworthy. You trained her to take the stallion's place should anything happen to him."

Judah had no difficulty calling to mind the widespread attention the red stallion had drawn wherever he had taken him. Jasper would stand out in a crowded paddock filled with nothing but stallions, and the battlefield would be no different. Besides, he had grown quite fond of the big red horse and hoped to stand him to stud after the end of hostilities.

"I'll take the mare," Judah decided, removing Jasper's saddle blanket.

Barefoot bridled the mare and cinched Judah's saddle on her. The order to "Mount" was passed down the line. As Judah put his foot in the stirrup, he heard the rattling fire of musketry to the north.

A hush gripped the bivouac. Judah settled into the saddle and sat shock still. The small arms fire intensified, each short volley a rippling string of sharp *pops*.

Field Anderson shouted, "She's started, boys."

Judah yanked his watch from his jacket pocket and mentally marked the time: five fourteen a.m.

Jarrod appeared at Judah's off stirrup. "I'll pray for you, brother."

Judah nodded, "You do that, little brother. A lot of men will die today. I don't intend to be among them."

Morgan's Squadron advanced from the tree-surrounded bivouac onto more open ground and dismounted. They held their horses and tried to follow the progress of the battle by ear. During a short lull in the fighting, muted Federal bugle calls and long drum rolls flowed from the forest facing the Confederate Army. More and more surprised Yankees were on their feet and readying to join the fray.

Wild cheers drifted to Morgan's Squadron, and Hardee's corps, its colors a white medallion on a blue field, went forward *en masse*. To the squadron's left and ahead of them, sporadic rifle fire evolved into sustained volleys and the boom of artillery added to the clamor. Though it seemed impossible, the bang of small arms and roar of large bore weapons away on their right dwarfed the rest put together, and Judah wondered how any man could survive in that theater for more than scant minutes.

The rising sun burned away the mist lingering in the forest and the crisp morning air matched the bright shine of a newly minted penny. General Hardee's advance faltered. At seventy thirty, according to Judah's watch, General Bragg's corps launched a second assault on the Federals at a dead run. The screeching Rebel yell that arose from hundreds of throats and lungs in concert gave Judah and his fellow raiders goose bumps. Judah could only liken the ever-increasing volume of the screeches emitted by Bragg's lines to that of a charging barbarian horde under Genghis Khan or the blood-curdling screams of Scottish Highlanders.

At ten thirty, a high-borne flag with a blue cross on a red field was detected moving toward the forest, and a sigh of relief swept through Morgan's Squadron. They had spent five full hours watching and listening, and some troopers were beginning to worry that the battle would be over before the cavalry could join in. Polk's corps was now spreading out behind Bragg's regiments, and Morgan's Squadron knew they would soon be offering Union rifles and cannons fresh targets, namely, themselves.

Once sufficient space opened between Polk's corps and Breckinridge's reserves, the cavalry moved out platoon front, working to stay abreast as best they could through the trees. In four short minutes, they came upon the dead and wounded of both armies. Bodies were scattered hither and yon, in short rows and in small heaps on blood-splattered brown leaves.

Judah kept his eyes front and center, refusing to look at the corpses. He shut his ears to the wounded men's cries for help. There was nothing he could do for them. The stunning scene confirmed for Judah a raw truth that military glory and victory were achieved at a horrendous human price and were enjoyed only by the survivors with the dead soon forgotten.

The squadron emerged from the woods into a small valley. The deafening roar of cannons at close range assailed their senses, and artillery shells burst in puffs of white powder in the sky above them. Newly promoted Colonel John Hunt Morgan calmly formed his squadron into battle lines across a fallow field. An infantry regiment filed across in front of the squadron in precise measured steps. A lieutenant in Morgan's C Company recognized friends from home among the Fourth Kentucky Infantry and began singing "Cheer, Boys, Cheer, We'll March Away to Battle." In a whipstitch, Kentucky infantry and cavalry were singing together, fostering an interlude of unplanned levity in the teeth of cannon fire that temporarily eased the strain the lads of the Bluegrass were feeling.

Right about noon, Colonel Trabue's brigade, including Morgan's Squadron, was ordered to swing around to the left and join General Hardee's corps. A new terror awaited the squadron as it approached the front lines.

Pish! Pish! Pish! Pish!

The air was suddenly filled with flesh-seeking Minié balls. Judah cringed at first, and then bucked up his courage and straightened in the saddle. He'd been shot at before and this was no different. Though more men were shooting in his direction at once, he still couldn't duck a bullet he couldn't see. Like the dead and wounded, enemy fire had to be ignored in the heat of battle.

While the Confederate right and left were advancing, the left center of their line was being repulsed with Federal artillery atop an eminence ringed at the bottom with thickets and underbrush. The Yankee artillery was firing with such precision the entire eminence was sheathed in blooming flame and drifting clouds of smoke. The return fire of General Hardee's battery wasn't having any success in diminishing the rain of grape and shell pouring from the hill. Hardee's forces had completely flanked the position, but every attempt to storm it was met by a hail of bullets. To Judah frontal attacks on the eminence afoot was the same as trying to batter down the impregnable gates of the devil's lair with a stick of wood.

A mounted messenger approached Lieutenant Basil Duke at the head of the column. Words were exchanged and Duke beckoned to Field Peterson and Judah. They rode forward and braced Duke's mount. "General Hardee wants to palaver."

Lieutenant Duke, Peterson, and Judah followed Hardee's messenger across the rear of the Confederate lines through clouds of smoke so thick at times Judah's eyes kept watering. Barefoot's mare ignored the commotion about her and trotted head up and alert. Nothing seemed to perturb her and she answered Judah's knee and rein instantly. She was proving as stoic as her normal half-breed rider in nerve-testing situations.

General Hardee's orders were terse and succinct. "You boys have been dying to rape the elephant and here's your chance. Tell Colonel Morgan to form his squadron and charge the enemy battery on the hill to our right."

Riding back to join Morgan's Squadron, Judah's gaze was glued to the hilltop battery. He judged the angle of the slope leading up to the rapidly firing cannons as best he could. He reckoned a horse could climb it, but the danger was extreme. His rider would be in point blank range of blue-belly rifles all the while. The concerned look on Lieutenant Duke's features told Judah that Colonel Morgan's second in command shared his doubts about whether a mounted charge into the teeth of a well-defended gun emplacement with several pieces of artillery could succeed. But General Hardee wanted those guns taken and orders were orders.

They were nearing their own squadron when Field Peterson passed Judah an envelope. "Note inside has my wife's address written on it. If I don't make it, write to her for me."

The squadron began forming for the charge. Field Peterson pointed suddenly at the hill and yelled, "Lieutenant Duke, I believe the Yankee fire is slackening."

Much to the delight of even the hard-shell, glory-at-any-price men in Morgan's ranks, the smoke obscuring the Federal battery slowly cleared and blue uniforms were seen scurrying for the top of the hill to escape being surrounded with the black muzzles of their abandoned cannons jutting from the underbrush behind them. A wave of gray-clad infantry sprang from concealment in the brush at the bottom of the hill and swarmed the abandoned position.

"Damn glad we missed out on that action," Field Peterson muttered to no one in particular.

Judah's involuntary, "Me too," drew a barking laugh from the relieved Peterson.

A lieutenant from General Hardee's staff delivered fresh orders to Colonel Morgan. The squadron commander turned in his saddle and addressed Basil Duke. "We're to move to the extreme left and charge the first enemy we see."

Wheeling off the left in twos, the squadron galloped along a narrow bridle path until they came to a marsh, which was the first open space fronting toward the battle line. As Morgan's troopers moved onto the grass of the bog, they spied a blue uniformed regiment performing evolutions strange to them. The squadron came to a rein-jerking "Halt!" as the sergeants passed Colonel Morgan's command the length of the column.

The mystery regiment's dress was like that of the Yankees, but other Confederate troops were nearby and paying them no mind. A puzzled Colonel Morgan sent the First Section of Company A under Sergeant Peterson to investigate. The accent of the stump-high, stocky colonel shouting commands and flourishing a wickedly curved saber was like a soft staccato drumbeat on Judah's ear.

A frowning Field Peterson leaned from the saddle and listened intently to what the fast-talking colonel was spouting. The colonel's face assumed the perfect red of a beet. With a nod, Peterson shook his head, reined his horse around to face Section A, and announced, "It's Colonel Mouton and the Eighteenth Louisiana Infantry. They're tired of being fired upon by our men. I told him sky-blue wasn't exactly the best choice for their uniforms. I think he was kindly and cussed me out in French."

Mouton's Eighteenth Louisiana was preparing to charge a Federal camp in a field to their left. When apprised of their plan, Colonel Morgan decided to join the assault. To get into position to charge, the squadron had to circle a deep ravine, the curse of the terrain within a dozen miles of the Tennessee River in every direction. In the middle of the circling maneuver, a company of Texas Rangers drew down upon Morgan's troopers from the rear.

The Rangers' flamboyant red shirts, broad-brimmed hats, quality horses, weaponry, double-cinched saddles, and the gigantic rowels of their spurs thrilled Judah. Each rider seemed to be carrying two pistols or a revolver and a rifle. They were spoiling for a fight and had no worry whether the odds favored them or not.

A strong contingent of Federal infantry was ensconced in the middle of the field containing their camp, and the Eighteenth Louisiana rushed upon them with such a fury Judah swore the bayonet would carry the day. The exchange of musket fire between Rebel and blue-belly infantry drowned out the crash of artillery. The strictly disciplined Federals withdrew in classic fashion, pausing frequently to pour a fresh volley into their pursuers and taking heavy losses in return, but never allowing their lines to fall into disarray. The enemy contingent disappeared into the woods in perfect order.

As Morgan's Squadron and the Ranger company pressed across the field behind the Eighteenth Louisiana, Federal skirmishers emerged as if from a magic hat at the edge of the woods upon their far left, not more than eighty yards away, and began peppering a Confederate battery caught in the open. The Rebel artillerymen were pinned down and unable to unlimber their guns.

The lead Texas Ranger stood in his stirrups. "Hey, Kentucky, what're you going to do?"

Half of Morgan's Squadron, their frustration at being deprived a role in deciding the outcome of the war's greatest contest to date mounting by the minute, yelled spontaneously, "Go in!"

Back came in greater volume, "Then we'll go in, too!"

And with that, Morgan's Kentucky Squadron and the Eighth Texas Rangers swung into a full gallop charge; a dream come true for every last ounce of adventure in every single rider. The Federal skirmishers quickly withdrew into the trees, but there was no hesitation and no dismounting to fight on foot. This was a dream that would not die short of fruition, not if every mounted cavalryman died in the trying.

Judah felt silly brandishing a saber still feeling strange to his hand after days of drill in an open field. He was glad when a tree limb ripped the blade from his fingers at the fringe of the woods and made him resort to his revolver. The headlong dash of the Kentuckians into the trees crowded them together, and any semblance of straight lines of attack vanished. But the massive thrust of their horseback charge in crowded quarters ripped asunder the enemy formations they encountered and sent them scrambling for dear life beneath the hoofs of Rebel horses after firing one quick volley.

Urged on by a joint Rebel yell so powerfully wrought it hurt his lungs when he joined in, Judah rode down the enemy, dispatching them at close range with his revolver until the hammer fell on empty chambers. His was enraptured with a powerful urge to kill and regretted loaning Barefoot his second revolver. It was as if, for a short while, he were an assassin given the dispensation of the Almighty without accountability and free of regret for his deeds.

"Duke's down! Duke's down!"

The portent of that cry shook Judah from his killing craze. He holstered his empty revolver, looked behind him, and spied Field Peterson kneeling beside a prone body with Basil Duke's orderly hovering over the both of them. Before turning his back on the enemy, Judah surveyed the woods. The squadron had ridden clean through the Federals to their front as the only blue uniforms in sight among the surrounding tress were on the ground like Basil Duke and not one of them was moving.

A protracted volley of small arms fire wafted from the woods off to the right of Judah. A pounding of hoofs coming from that direction was followed by the rapid appearance of horses with empty saddles. One terrified blue-haired horse with a white splotch on his shoulder bolted past Judah. It was the mount of one of the Texas Rangers. Judah knew beyond a shadow of a doubt that the charge of the Eighth Texas had struck the main body of the Federal brigade and suffered severe casualties.

Judah rode to Field Peterson and dismounted. "Is he alive, Sergeant?"

Peterson pressed his fingers against the arteries beneath Basil Duke's jaw. "There's a pulse. The Yankee that shot him was toting an old-fashioned Brown Bess musket. I can't see he's lost a lot of blood. Why don't you and Private Winslow lift him up in front of me and we'll move him to that Yankee camp Colonel Mouton's Louisiana boys overran before we made our charge? Bound to be blankets and a fire there."

At Colonel Morgan's command, buglers in the clearing vacated by his squadron blew "Recall" and Judah and his fellow troopers fell back, aiding the wounded where possible. Basil Duke moaned a lot while riding double in front of Field Peterson. Otherwise, his condition was the same once he was gently placed on a cot in a Yankee tent.

A cursory examination revealed an entry wound in Duke's left shoulder and a second wound behind the right shoulder blade. Peterson surmised the shooter had loaded his old musket with a single ball and three buck shot. Colonel Morgan had to be satisfied with an amateur prognosis that the odds favored his brother-in-law surviving both wounds. When a doctor might be available was unknown given the circumstances.

To guard against a surprise attack by the blue-bellies, Morgan dismounted his troops, sent skirmishers well forward of the clearing, and explored the fringes of the Owl Creek thickets on the left. The Federals, however, had apparently vanished for now into the marshy brakes of the creek.

Idle troopers began searching the abandoned tents of the Yankee camp. From Federal prisoners they learned the squadron had routed Colonel John A. McDowell's Sixth Iowa Infantry of General Sherman's Fifth Division. The pride and satisfaction the squadron was enjoying as a result of their successful charge evaporated an hour later when the first rumors of General Albert S. Johnston's death washed over the Confederate Army like a tidal wave. They could hear the battle raging full tilt to the north of them, but the thought of engaging the enemy without their leader dashing about the Army of the Mississippi on his bay Thoroughbred, Fire Eater, ignoring zipping Minié balls and exploding shells, urging them on to the victory that could be had with just one more attack, tore at their will to fight and diminished it markedly.

The mood of the captured Federal camp turned sour. Men stood or sat staring into the distance or at the ground, pondering how General Johnston's death might alter the outcome of the battle and wondering how soon they would see action again. The troopers having reloaded their weapons, officers busied the bulk of them with the chore of watering and seeking forage for their horses while the balance guarded the camp and tended their wounded comrades.

Master Sergeant Elias Hooper located Judah and Field Peterson sneaking quick cups of Yankee coffee brewed by an orderly over a fire before the tent housing the wounded Lieutenant Basil Duke. "Gentlemen, the day is lengthening rapidly."

Field Peterson handed Hooper a tin cup and pointed at the coffeepot. "Help yourself, Elias. Any orders from the colonel yet?"

Colonel John Hunt Morgan could be seen pacing back and forth along the edge of Owl Creek while he conferred with his two remaining lieutenants. "Colonel Morgan's in a quandary," Hooper said. "He has an aversion to putting his entire command at risk. He prefers to pick his fights where he has the advantage. Throwing away the lives of your men in frontal assaults against equal or superior numbers is repugnant to him. He's hoping the Yankee lines will collapse before that happens. If he receives contrary orders, he'll naturally obey them."

"And in the meantime?"

"We hold fast and wait until we're told where we're needed next," Hooper said. "General Breckinridge knows our position."

No messenger appeared with fresh orders, and the balance of the afternoon seemed to drag on forever. In the distance, savage bursts of gunfire separated brigade and regimental assaults from the routine, sequenced popping of holding actions when both armies caught their breath. The battle was drawing farther and farther away, which gradually lifted the spirits of Morgan's Squadron and the Eighth Texas. Hemmed in by Owl Creek on one flank and Lick Creek on the other, the Yankees were slowly being pushed back against the Tennessee River in accordance with General Johnston's original plan. Was a total Confederate victory over General Grant before he could be reinforced about to bring joy to General Johnston's "eight millions of people"?

Compared to the slow passage of the daylight hours, dusk descended with surprising speed. The distant guns went silent almost simultaneously as if both sides had reached a mutual agreement to end hostilities for the day. The resulting silence created an eerie atmosphere after the violent clamor of arms that had made bells ring in heads for hours, and made troopers keep sneaking glances at the forest and the brakes along Owl Creek in case the quiet was some clever trick the Yankees were playing on them.

Sergeants passed the order to stand down. Horses were unsaddled, buglers blew the "Supper" call, and Kentuckians and Texans alike delved into abandoned Yankee stores and enjoyed a bountiful meal of unspoiled salt pork, hardtack, desecrated vegetables, dried fruit, and a variety of hard candy and canned delicacies foreign to the Confederate stomach, but damn tasty nevertheless.

One unspoken, sobering question lingered in the minds of the commissioned and non-commissioned officers of Morgan's Squadron as they dined that early evening: What was the condition of Grant's army, for no wild cheering celebrating his surrender had been heard? And where, precisely, was General Buell with his blue-belly reinforcements?

Judah swore under his breath.

An entire day of mass slaughter by two armies and the wasting of vast quantities of munitions had decided absolutely nothing of lasting importance.

CHAPTER 23

By mid-morning, Jarrod was dancing from foot to foot, barely able to restrain himself. History was being made smack in front of him and he was witnessing none of it, relegated to the backwater like an overly protected child.

At the outset, Asa Barefoot managed to keep him occupied and the situation was tolerable as long as he could at least listen and guess what was happening beyond the bivouac. The half-breed insisted they take gum ponchos left behind by Morgan's men and rig a shelter by tying them to trees at waist level in the fringe of the woods. When Jarrod asked why that was necessary on a bright clear morning, Barefoot's response was, "It will rain this evening."

"How do you know that for certain?"

"My bones ache."

"How do you know we will still be here come dark?"

"Neither army will win today. Two dogs will just tear at the same leg of the bear."

Judah's Kentucky letters had recounted Barefoot's uncanny weather predictions and his knack for sensing what was most likely to happen around him beforehand, and

Jarrod wasn't about to argue with either assertion. "What next?"

Barefoot pointed at Jarrod's revolver. "Reload your pistol with fresh powder. You will need to fire it before nightfall."

That prospect intrigued Jarrod and under the half-breed's scrutiny he reloaded his revolver. But too soon, he was left with nothing to do except wait. He spun about and faced a reclining Barefoot. The half-breed was seated on a blanket with his backside leaning against a tree and his hat shading his eyes.

"I'm going forward."

"Wait until sun is straight above us."

"Why not now?" Jarrod demanded.

Barefoot ignored Jarrod's impatience. "The fight will be beyond musket range by noon. Many muskets are being fired, many more than rifles."

To Jarrod, enduring the eternity between mid-morning and noon matched the excitement of watching a weed grow. He managed to keep a tight rein on his frustration and did not move from his perch on a deadfall tree or utter a word until Barefoot sat up on his blanket and donned his hat. Judging by its sweat-stains and torn brim, Jarrod calculated the half-breed's headgear was older than creation.

Rising to his feet in sections, the elder Barefoot made certain his coat was hiding the revolver stuck behind his belt and said, "Bring your rubber poncho and an extra canteen. Water will be scarce before we return."

Barefoot paused beside the last sheltering tree of the bivouac. "I lead. You follow and listen to what I say, or I'll hogtie you and drag you back to your blanket. Never fear. I'll fill your belly with war, maybe more than you can stand."

Jarrod thought he had a strong stomach. He began to doubt that when they crossed the open meadow bordering the bivouac, slipped into the woods beyond, and encountered the first dead bodies. Blue- and gray-clad casualties lay everywhere in every manner of repose. The serene calm on the faces of many that had perished surprised Jarrod. They looked as if they had simply fallen asleep in their beds at home. How could any soldier struck down on the battle-field die with such effortless grace?

The moaning and cries of the wounded were a differ-ent story and hit a raw nerve with Jarrod. Canteens were scattered about, and men too hurt and too weak to move begged for water in plaintive tones that made Jarrod's heart bleed for them. Fisting his canteen, he started toward one of those yelling for water.

Barefoot's arm shot out and his fingers locked on the sleeve of Jarrod's coat. "Stay with me. Others will come with water."

Jarrod wanted to protest that these men had suffered their wounds six hours ago. Had he done so, he would have been wasting his breath. Barefoot's grip was stronger than a tightening vise, and he had no choice but to move along or be dragged from the scene.

They eased into an unfenced field. The farther across the stubbles of last year's crop they walked, the deeper the dead piled up until it was impossible to avoid stepping on a prone body. Jarrod fought back the queasiness of a riled stomach and kept pace with Barefoot. The dead were equally numerous at the edge of the tree line and then tapered off as the Federals retreated. "In the trees after the line breaks, they fight like my people. Every warrior for himself."

They came to a succession of deep gullies that funneled them to the left. "Bad fighting country," Barefoot judged. "It's hard to flank the enemy here. Only place to attack is straight down his throat. He has cover while you must stand in the open and reload between charges."

Judah had mentioned Barefoot's scouting in the Seminole Wars. From the astute observations he was providing, the half-breed had garnered much practical knowledge of how terrain determined tactics that Jarrod knew only from reading selected works in his father's library. The respect for Barefoot that surfaced in Judah's letters had been genuine, and Jarrod was beginning to understand how the half-breed could twice save his brother's life.

When they came to where the blue-belly line had broken the second time, the ugliness of the results was magnified tenfold. Here Confederate artillery had played a key role, and the injuries wrought by solid ball and exploding shell had torn bodies in two, twisted arms off, impaled men on their own bayonets, made bits of firewood out of legs, sliced heads open like melons, and crunched skulls into globs of pudding. Here and there a severed head sat upright, seeming to search for its missing owner.

Though his breakfast was lodged in the back of his throat, Jarrod refused to turn away. What bothered him most was that the mass of bodies had become a pile of gore from which all semblance of humanity had been ripped with the callousness of an iron claw. It was as if it made no difference that what was lost were sons born to caring mothers who didn't deserve such an ignominious shortening of their time on God's earth. He regretted that he had seen so much of it that the blood splotched hither and yon bothered him no more than the spilling of buckets of scarlet paint.

Up ahead, out of their sight, the increasing *rap-rattle* of musket volleys and the heightened *poum* of artillery fire indicated the killing was for far from over. The next area of open ground they reached contained an abandoned Federal camp. Jarrod was amazed at the plunder in the form of personal belongings, including letters and diaries, that trailed out of the Yankee tents, strewn by Rebels grabbing what they could as they swept by. Overturned cooking pots and pans and chunks of teeth-marked bread and spilled plates atop trestle tables told the story of how short on rations the graybacks had been at the start of the day. Barefoot echoed Jarrod's thinking. "They are a rich man's army."

The half-breed's crawling pace slowed even more as they closed on a section of the front lines. Their course veered to the right. They ascended a treed hillside and eventually reached the edge of a shallow overlook that provided a point of observation allowing them to view the attacking Rebel army with a degree of safety that satisfied Barefoot.

Across the valley before them, a battery of Federal artillery ensconced in the trees of a blossoming peach orchard was blasting away with great effect. The Confederate advance had stalled. Their return fire was disjointed, and Jarrod noticed several men prone on the ground were not dead or incapacitated. They were trying to reload their weapons, using those out of the fight for cover. Officers were scurrying here and there among the grayback regiment, waving swords and brandishing revolvers, desperately trying to mount a charge.

A rider on a bay Thoroughbred left a cluster of his mounted counterparts and fast-walked his mount from the rear to the very front of the Rebel line. Barefoot pointed a finger and identified the daring rider. "General Johnston, the top dog, in the flesh."

Ignoring the enemy, Johnston weaved through the Confederate's shattered lines, tapping the points of soldiers' bayonets with what Jarrod finally determined was, of all things imaginable, a tin cup. When the grayback lines had again formed under Johnston's prodding, some were still reluctant to charge into the smoking death awaiting them. Not the least discouraged, Johnston stood in his stirrups, removed his hat, and called to them over his shoulder.

The memory of the following sequence of events froze in Jarrod's memory in precise detail. As Johnston touched the flanks of the bay Thoroughbred with his spurs, the entire Confederate line moved with him and ran straight into a blazing sheet of flame without missing a stride. Bright pink blossoms shaken from the peach trees showered down on the screeching Rebels as they overran the Federal battery and routed the blue-bellies defending it.

Jarrod couldn't take his eyes off the jubilant Johnston. He knew he'd witnessed a rallying of soldiers in desperate straits by the sheer will of a consummate military leader that would inhabit the pages of every history written of the War of the Rebellion, no matter who emerged the victor.

General Johnston's fellow officers scattered to carry out various assignments while their commander lingered to watch his charges celebrate the taking of the orchard and the Federal batteries. Without any warning, Johnston reeled in his saddle. Jarrod had heard no shot fired, but something had clearly gone wrong. The lone rider with Johnston, a civilian by his dress, clasped the General about the shoulders to keep him from falling and guided the bay Thoroughbred into a nearby ravine.

"Bad sign," Barefoot judged. "His would be a great loss."

A newly arrived rider entered the ravine. He exited quickly. Soon more riders rode up, dismounted, and hustled out of sight. The hanging heads of the officers that popped from the ravine a few minutes later told the story. General Albert Sidney Johnston had taken his last breath.

Barefoot tapped Jarrod's shoulder. "Bigger battle coming yonder," the half-breed said, pointing to the left beyond the peach orchard.

In the short lull that followed the Confederate triumph,

the jingle of harness, the squealing of wheels bearing great weight, the neighing and snorting of horses, and the blowing of bugle commands drifted to Barefoot and Jarrod on the overlook.

"Many Rebel cannon being moved," Barefoot concluded. "We stay here a while."

The Confederate cannonade opened with a series of individual blasts and grew into a sustained roar of such fury it pounded on Jarrod's ears like a thousand trip hammers. Whoever was on the receiving end of that concentrated fire had to believe he was in the depths of an exploding hell filled with eye-burning smoke, flying chunks of sod, brush torn out by the roots, splinters of wood, and sizzling hot shrapnel that gouged, ripped, and tore flesh with impunity. For two solid hours the cannons raked their targets with a suffocating hail of grape and canister. Jarrod suspected that he was listening to the largest artillery assault in American history. There had been nothing to match it during his country's previous wars or at the 1861 Battle of Bull Run.

The cannonade petered out. A massive outpouring of Rebel yells jarred the very air. The Yankees had either broken off the fight or surrendered.

The ever-impatient Jarrod pulled his feet under him.

"Stay there," Barefoot ordered. "Bloodied ground is safer to cross in the dark. Sleep a little, if you can."

"Can't we at least scout around for Judah behind the Rebel lines?"

"He could be anywhere. If he's alive, he will return to our camp of last night. We will wait there."

The idea Judah might be dead jolted Jarrod. Despite the lifeless bodies he'd observed, he had naively assumed his brother would survive while countless others lay staring blankly at the sky or sat the earth beneath their noses. And what about Jacob? He hadn't given a moment's thought to the possibility the Ohio First Cavalry might be attached to the Federal forces. What if he were to lose both brothers?

He couldn't fathom that outcome. The odds against it were too great, and the Lord surely wouldn't make his family suffer a calamity of that magnitude.

But then, wasn't that asking an awful lot? Why should the Lord protect the Bell brothers in particular and allow them to fight the war with none of the three paying the ultimate price?

The true terror of the war, Jarrod realized with a start, was the uncertainty it imposed on the soldier and those close to him each waking hour, and sitting there with Barefoot waiting for nightfall, he could but pray for the survival of his brothers and himself.

The pitch-black darkness was a surprise. He didn't remember falling asleep and wasn't sure what had awakened him. Since he could hardly make out his own boots, he listened to what was happening around him and decided it was the sound of the cold wind coupled with its chill brushing of his cheek that had roused him.

"Rain coming," Barefoot announced softly. "Chew a little bacon and drink some water, and we'll mosey along."

Barefoot pressed the canteen against Jarrod's chest and put a cloth bag in his hand like a mother directing her child. Not the least insulted, Jarrod drank and chewed as ordered, feeling refreshed when he finished.

"Did the Federals surrender? Or will there be more fighting tomorrow?"

"There will be more fighting. I didn't hear any big hulla-baloo on either side when both armies' cannons finally stopped firing."

A bolt of lightning wove a tall spiderweb of jagged light

on the western horizon and thunder rolled ominously. "Big storm will be here double quick," Barefoot said.

Jarrod got his legs under him and slipped his gum poncho over his head. Barefoot produced a length of rope from a coat pocket and handed one end to Jarrod. "Hold tight to your end. If you lose your grip, I'll know. Just stand still until I pass it back to you. It will be easy for us to lose track of each other once the storm comes."

Jarrod had never developed any skill at night hiking. His perpetual clumsiness and loud tumbles on midnight hunts for small game had angered Judah and earned him cussing outs that would offend the ears of the devil's mule. Needless to say, he was filled with considerable trepidation as Barefoot led him from the hillside overlook.

No campfires were visible in any direction. Small lights bobbed along at ground level in several places. Jarrod determined they were the lanterns of soldiers confirming the death of comrades and friends and searching for wounded soldiers of both sides desperate for medical assistance. The plaintive cries and pleadings of the wounded Jarrod had heard earlier against the noisy background of a raging battle paled in comparison to what he was hearing in quieter surroundings. "My leg is gone. Where's my leg . . . Water, just one drop of water, please, I beg you . . . Oh. Mother, tell me I'm not dying . . . Father, forgive me my sins . . . I'm hurting bad, will someone please shoot me? . . . Oh, my Lord, bring me home to you now . . ."

Jarrod's first clue they weren't following the same path they had followed during the day was brought home with a vengeance when a bolt of lightning revealed a grayback infantryman with his arms draped over a low tree branch and thick wet strands of yellow dangling between his legs. A second flash of lightning revealed the strands were the Rebel's intestines and Jarrod nearly vomited up the bacon he'd eaten. He would not have forgotten such a horrific sight in a million years.

A wild neighing and thrashing and fresh screams of anguish erupted to Jarrod's right. Barefoot angled toward the commotion. Lightning flashed and Jarrod caught the image of a crazed and bleeding artillery horse with long reins dragging behind him. The reins had caught fast to something on the ground and halted the animal's trampling of wounded soldiers. Without any hesitation Barefoot walked over to the crazed horse, drew his revolver, and shot it in the head.

By then, an emotionally spent Jarrod was beginning to believe the nightmarish hike had exhausted the surprises it could lavish on him. With the first splash of fat raindrops on his hat, a red dot streaked across the sky from the north, arched downward at a steep angle, and blew apart with a *BOOM* heard for miles. A second dot traced the trajectory of the first and equaled the explosive power of the first. Jarrod was astonished at how long he could hear the projectile tearing across the underbelly of the rain clouds before it made its descent. He had a hunch the next half hour proved correct. The Yankee gunboats on the Tennessee, the only possible source of shells that large, were intending to fire them at regular intervals all night long to ensure not a single weary Rebel slept a wink. It was a cruel but effective strategy.

Within fifty yards the rain was a torrential downpour, and Jarrod was clinging to Barefoot's lead rope with an iron grip. The half-breed changed their course. Trees loomed ahead and Jarrod sensed they were climbing to higher ground. A deeper darkness on his left side told Jarrod they were walking along the edge of a gully of some sorts.

He didn't spot the tree root that tripped him. He was off balance in a heartbeat. He was going over the edge and nothing could be done to save him. Fearing he would drag Barefoot after him, he opened his hand and grabbed the butt of his revolver. He might break a bone or two, but he wasn't losing his weapon.

Luckily, he landed on the bare earth of a cut bank and slid down into the gully on his backside. He came to rest minus his breath with his boots lodged in rising water. Lightning flashed and he saw scary, chalk-white faces. They were smeared with black powder between their noses and chins from biting open paper cartridges; the faces were aligned in a neat row on the opposite side of the gully. Jarrod came shakily to his feet, and, drawn by morbid curiosity, he waded toward the bodies belonging to those haunting faces.

He hovered until the next flash of lightning. With that illumination, he saw that the left hands of the dead gray-backs were clutching the barrels of their rifles, their pants were unbuttoned, and their right hands held their male members. Even more bewildered, Jarrod stood in the knee-deep water, unable to move, thoroughly puzzled. For sake of all that was holy, what had happened here?

Fingers gripped Jarrod's shoulder and Barefoot inched alongside him. "They ran out of water this afternoon and hid in here pissing in the barrels of their muskets to rid them of fouled powder. The blue-bellies must have spied them from up above. Must have been like shooting boys playing jacks."

Jarrod shook his head. The night had to finally be out of surprises. There was a limit to the leeway God granted his underlings to unnerve each other, was there not?

"We're a quarter mile from our camp," Barefoot said.

Boots filled with water and his sodden hat brim drooping over his ears, Jarrod latched on to Barefoot's lead rope and let the aging half-breed guide him out of the gully in measured tugs. He wished he had Barefoot's stamina and endurance. He was near to collapsing but determined to reach their shelter upright on his own feet.

One final surprise awaited him, the most shocking of all. He was dragging his feet forward a stride at a time as they wove a path through the bodies dotting the site of the first battle of the day. Suddenly, fingers possessing enormous strength wrapped snakelike around his ankle. Frightened, he balanced on one foot and tried to jerk his leg free, but to no avail.

He stopped trying to escape and gathered his wits about him. Then a croaking voice said, "Help me, Charlie."

A shadow knelt in front of Jarrod, and Barefoot said in a kindly voice, "Let go, son. You're not alone."

The trapping fingers slowly relaxed. Jarrod stepped back. Barefoot seemed to be ministering to the fallen soldier. Though he couldn't make out the words, Jarrod heard whispers. A rustling ensued, followed by a sharp grunt of pain.

Barefoot came upright. "Shot twice in the belly. He wanted his bayonet. He didn't want to die alone in the dark."

A dazed Jarrod trudged along behind the half-breed. The wounded soldier had wanted help taking his own life. Jarrod tried to fathom the kind of courage it required to make that decision and carry it out. He didn't know his name or the color of his uniform, but he'd been privileged to meet one of the bravest men on the entire battlefield.

In the driving rainstorm, the bivouac was to the exhausted Jarrod the equivalent of a desert oasis. He ducked under the shelter he'd built with Barefoot that morning, shed his poncho, removed his boots, and wrapped a gloriously dry blanket about his torso.

Barefoot had given him a bellyful of war as he'd promised, and it had been terribly hard to swallow. What fascinated Jarrod the most was the zeal with which armed men undertook the slaying of each other. How they could rush into the jaws of death with so little regard for their lives? Too wrought up to sleep, he sat in dry quarters thousands lacked, listening for the next round of shells from the Yankee gunboats, mentally pouring over all he had learned about war from his prior reading and what he'd observed personally, searching for an answer to that nagging question.

When the answer came to him, he marveled at its simplicity.

Regardless of his uniform, every young soldier who perished that day had died believing *his* was the *right* cause, a cause so paramount he would sacrifice what was most precious to him—his entire future—in hopes of defeating its enemies.

CHAPTER 24

From the outset, the second day of the battle of Pittsburgh Landing didn't bode well for Morgan's Squadron and the Army of the Mississippi. True, the rain had stopped. Good news beyond that improvement, however, was scarce as teeth on a butterfly. The Rebels had passed a miserable night trying to stay dry and ignore the Yankee bombardment, mostly failing at both. Their cartridge boxes were half-empty and the powder in their weapons damp and untrustworthy. No line officer dared hazard a guess as to when a new supply of ammunition might be obtainable. On top of that, the tired and sluggish graybacks had rolled out of their wet blankets just in time to hear the initial barrage of General Grant's counterattack, a clear sign General Buell's reinforcements had been ferried across the Tennessee River during the night.

Breakfast was whatever amount of hardtack and water a Morgan trooper could down in a hurry. Field Peterson ordered all weapons test-fired and reloaded. Buglers then blew "Boots and Saddles." Saddling his horse next to Judah's mare, Field Peterson commented wryly, "Don't believe any of our horses will taste the waters of the Tennessee during this campaign."

At seven o'clock by Judah's watch, the heavy-caliber Yankee bombardment ceased and the whole front line of the Union army extending from Owl Creek in the west to Lick Creek in the east began their advance. Peterson and Judah were dispatched by Colonel Morgan to secure a source for much needed ammunition from General Breckinridge's staff. Two troopers were sent by Morgan to enhance the odds that one would return.

Field Peterson opted to seek out the heaviest fighting, figuring that's where General Breckinridge would be most easily found. As Peterson and Judah rode through and skirted grayback units, the disarray of the Army of the Mississippi was painfully obvious. The Rebel infantry had scattered through the captured Yankee camps the previous evening in search of food and shelter, and their officers had been negligent in keeping track of them. Now a mad scramble was under way to get men into proper lines, restore order, and prepare to receive an attack.

Somehow the Rebel front formed in sufficient strength to avert disaster. Judah swore the world was awash with blue and the air abuzz with Minié balls, not to mention Yankee beards and facial features plain as the hairs on the back of his hands. But a massed grayback volley halted the Federal charge for a few vital minutes, allowing the Rebels to fall back under the control of their officers.

"Good shooting, Corporal Bell," Field Peterson shouted.

A disbelieving Judah discovered his hand held an empty revolver. For the life of him, he couldn't remember drawing, aiming, or pulling the trigger. He had heard of soldiers acting in "the heat of battle" and not really grasped what the term meant. He did now.

General Breckinridge's staff had no solid information regarding the quartermaster department and the availability of fresh ammunition. In an attempt to avoid returning to Colonel Morgan empty-handed, Field Peterson led

Judah on a quick ride to the Confederate rear. The road to the rough-hewn Shiloh Chapel where General Pierre Gustave Toutant Beauregard, the fallen Johnston's replacement, had established his headquarters was a muddy quagmire twenty inches deep and clogged with horse-drawn wagons carting Rebel wounded south to Corinth. Not a single supply wagon was moving the opposite direction toward the battlefield.

A frustrated Field Peterson swore a blue streak. "We fight with what ammunition we have and that will be our undoing. We've lost the edge we gained yesterday because of poor discipline and poor coordination. The blue-bellies have fresh reinforcements and plenty of ammunition. We'll be retreating by the noon hour, if not sooner."

Field Peterson's assessment of the Confederate's fragile situation was dead on target. Unable to hold out against the pressure of relentless Federal assaults, Morgan's Squadron, the Eighth Texans, and Colonel Mouton's fancy-uniformed Eighteenth Louisiana Infantry were already conceding yesterday's gains along Owl Creek at a rapid rate. Peterson and Judah had a much shorter ride to report their findings to Colonel Morgan than they anticipated.

The Confederate lines thinned and weakened as a Union Army superior in manpower and firepower gained momentum. The action was so intense at times Judah had trouble keeping his revolver loaded and regretted the loss of his sword. Though Minié balls nipped at the sleeve of his shirt, holed his hat, severed the shoulder strap of his canteen, gashed the top of his boot, and left a streak of blood on the mare's left front shoulder, Judah and his mount were spared a killing or crippling wound.

His mouth became so dry he couldn't lick his lips. With the arrival of each of the intermittent rain showers that occurred throughout the morning, he held out a cupped hand and then smeared the moisture on his face and mouth in preparation for the inevitable burst of steamy sunshine that followed each downpour.

With each backward shove the graybacks endured, Judah's admiration for their courage heightened. Yesterday had seen them the victor on the verge of annihilating the hated blue-bellies. Today, instead of completing a monumental victory, they had lost the advantage and were losing in every quarter of the field. The change in fortune was a devastating blow that brought many Rebels to tears, and, though the outcome was inevitable, they fought tooth and nail while their comrades melted away, defiant to the last. Judah witnessed Rebels still trying to load their weapons as Yankee boots, hoofs, and caisson wheels ground them to pulp in the mud, leaving nothing to mark their shallow grave but a protruding hand or foot.

Just after two o'clock couriers appeared with orders from General Beauregard to initiate a full-scale retreat. Escorted by a detail from Morgan's Squadron commanded by Sergeant Field Peterson and Corporal Judah Bell, General Breckinridge's batteries hustled down the Corinth Road past Shiloh Chapel and took station on a ridge beyond that structure at the cost of much profanity from the teamsters the mounted escort forced to the berm, often at gun point. Breckinridge's cannons maintained a steady rate of fire as the other Confederate corps retired without incident, and brought with them captured goods by the wagonload. Judah saw wagons bearing Union regimental colors and numerous flags of the United States, coup booty of the highest order when it came to bragging rights.

By four o'clock the retrograde maneuver was complete with no indication Grant's army was seriously interested in trying to breech Breckinridge's line of defense. Judah watched at the side of the road with the rest of Peterson's escort while the corps commanded by generals Hardee, Bragg, and Polk marched a mile past Shiloh Chapel and

Breckinridge's batteries and went into camp where they had slept two nights before, aligned for Sunday's now ancient dawn assault.

The ever-vigilant Field Peterson caught Judah's attention with a pointing finger and said, "I believe that's fresh blood on your mare's hip, Corporal."

Judah dismounted. He hadn't noticed a change in the mare's gait. Upon close examination, he determined a bullet smaller than a Minié ball had passed through the fleshy part of her outer hip. While not life threatening or disabling, the damaged hip would stiffen overnight and make even walking painful for her come morning.

"Sergeant Peterson, what are our orders?"

"Breckinridge's corps, including our squadron, will provide the rear guard for Beauregard's army however many days it takes to march south and reach Corinth."

"Sir, I'd like to visit our original bivouac at Mickey's and fetch my stallion. I'd like a fresh horse under me as soon as possible. I won't be gone but an hour."

"Permission granted," Peterson said with a chuckle. "Maybe you ought to check on that brother of yours, too, and learn if he stayed put like he promised."

The Corinth Road was jammed with foot and wagon traffic. Judah angled across the ridge holding Breckinridge's batteries on a game path, walked the mare down the far slope, and approached the bivouac from the east through the woods, a route less challenging than the hunting hills surrounding Chillicothe and Paint Creek.

As he'd hoped, Jarrod was where he was supposed to be. His little brother was seated beneath a makeshift shelter of gum ponchos, writing table propped on his knee, scribbling furiously with his pen. Barefoot was nursing a pit fire inside a log lean-to roofed over with bound tree limbs. Neither his brother nor the half-breed seemed to notice Judah's arrival. After giving the stomping, head-tossing Jasper his customary pat on the neck, Judah unsaddled Barefoot's mare and walked to the lean-to.

Barefoot placed a skillet over his fire and said without so much as a glance at Judah, "I've been expecting you. The fight has changed directions and brought you with it."

The smell of frying meat had Judah salivating in a tick of the clock. He sniffed and said, "What is that?"

"Rabbit. I snared three of them during the night. They got hungry and left their nests to search for food. I saved them for our supper."

Judah had to smile. He couldn't remember all the occasions on which the half-breed had brought game to Temple Bell's table the local rifle-and-hound enthusiasts swore had been hunted to extinction. Barefoot merely assumed that wherever he was wild meat could be had whether he was in the wild swamps of his native Florida or the settled hills of Kentucky.

"Has Jarrod been a problem?"

"No, we followed the advance of your army in the afternoon yesterday. We returned here after dark."

"I thought we agreed he wouldn't leave the bivouac, and you would keep a tight rein of him."

"Your little brother is no less bullheaded than the rest of you Bells. He has decided to be a newspaperman. I am no fool. A horse you feed hay. A newspaperman you feed words. I fed him a bellyful, and he liked to choke on them. He has spent the whole day where you see him now."

Judah should have known Barefoot would appease Jarrod's thirst for being part of what was happening in a manner that satisfied the interest of all parties involved. "You are a wise warrior," Judah conceded. "I should tell you that more often."

"I would only tire of it," Barefoot said, spearing a rabbit leg with a sharpened stick and offering the hot morsel to Judah.

The fried rabbit was beyond delicious, and Judah didn't mind burning his tongue in his urge to taste it. He savored every bite. For a few moments, he was removed from the human carnage he abhorred. The peaceful interlude wouldn't last, but it relaxed and soothed nerves drawn tight as the wires on a violin by the constant threat of sudden death.

"Call the newspaperman to supper," Barefoot ordered, "before he starves on those words I gave him."

Once his concentration was broken, Jarrod sat aside his tablet, rushed from his makeshift shelter, and bear-hugged Judah. Judah was prepared this time and spared his ribs a second bruising. The reunited brothers ate on their feet with Judah answering Jarrod's many questions as to the course of the day's events on the battlefield.

Barefoot fried bread to augment the rabbit and surprised the brothers with a canteen of water cut with brandy. When Judah's brows knotted together with his first sip, Barefoot explained, "It belonged to a blue-belly officer. He's not missing it."

Knowing the hour and mindful of his duties, Judah asked, "What are your intentions, little brother? We secesh are headed for Corinth. Are you traveling with us?"

Jarrod answered, "No, I'm planning to show my press military pass and return to Cincinnati. I want to publish my account of the battle. It makes no difference to me who won. I want ordinary folks to be aware of how ruthlessly both sides sacrificed countless lives. How wounded soldiers, blue and gray, died in a cold rain without medical attention and nobody to hold their hand and pray for them or kiss them good-bye. How families were torn asunder, wives widowed, and fathers lost to their children. I want to make people understand how steep the price of political freedom is. Does that make sense to you, brother?"

Judah had a fleeting impression he was talking with a

stranger. It took him a bit to come to grips with how much Jarrod's thinking had matured during Judah's Kentucky hiatus. Jarrod Bell was a grown man in both mind as well as body; the little brother was but a pleasant memory.

"Yes, it makes perfect sense to me. I understand your calling, and I commend you for answering it."

"And there's still the truth about Hunt Baldwin for us to deal with," the wound-up Jarrod continued. "I haven't forgotten that scoundrel and never will."

Judah said, "Neither will I," and helped himself to a final swig of watered-down brandy.

"Field Peterson will be expecting me. Asa, your mare has a hip wound that needs doctoring. I'll be taking Jasper."

Jarrod followed Judah and Barefoot to the picket line. He watched Judah saddle the stallion while Barefoot attended to the mare's wound. Barefoot daubed black salve he scooped from a small round can extracted from a coat pocket, which set Mr. J. Rodger Black's reporter to guessing just what all the half-breed toted on his person. The supply of essential items that materialized from Barefoot's pockets at his whim seemed limitless.

Judah was afraid to linger. There was a profound possibility he would never see either of his brothers again. But shedding tears and exchanging maudlin good-byes merely delayed the inevitable partings war demanded. He gathered Jasper's reins, looped them over his head, and swung into the saddle. He nodded at Jarrod and said, "Brother, write your stories. Say hello to the family for me when you get home. And remember your promise regarding Brianna."

Judah's eyes misted as he reined Jasper about and rode into the woods, bound for the path he'd used earlier to cross the ridge. He didn't look back.

Jarrod watched his brother disappear into the trees. He felt like someone had poked a hole in his heart. He daubed at his eyes with the sleeve of his jacket and walked to his makeshift shelter, praying he could lose himself in his writing.

The twin blasts of rifles nearly startled Jarrod from his boots. He glanced at Barefoot and saw the half-breed was peering at the edge of the woods where Judah had disappeared. Jarrod hung fire, unsure how to proceed. Low branches at the edge of the bivouac parted and Jasper burst from the trees, his saddle empty and its stirrups flopping madly.

"Grab your revolver and follow me," Barefoot ordered in a low growl.

Jarrod snatched the pistol from atop his blankets and raced after the half-breed. He ignored the brush and limbs that clawed at his upraised arm, barged ahead, and nearly ran up Barefoot's backside. He regained his balance and peered over the half-breed's shoulder. Judah's body was lying chest down on the brown loam of a sizable clearing. He wasn't moving or making a sound.

Jarrod tried to squeeze by Barefoot and a steely-muscled arm pinned him against a tree. "Be still," Barefoot whispered.

Breathing shallowly to keep from making the slightest sound, Jarrod pretended he was night hunting with Judah and froze stiffer than a hide-stretching board. Their patience was rewarded when a hand shoved brush aside on the opposite perimeter of the clearing and a slovenly, drooling white male well along in years wearing clothes more dirt than cloth slid into the open. A younger version of the oldster followed on his heels. Both woodsers were armed with flintlock rifles.

Apparently satisfied they were alone and that their shots had not attracted anybody's attention, the two bushwhackers turned Judah's body over. The eldest helped himself to Judah's Navy Colt and stood watching his companion rifle through the fallen Judah's pockets. With a gleeful, black-toothed smile, the younger bushwhacker showed Judah's watch to his companion.

"Follow my lead," Barefoot whispered. "Take the pup. The old goat is mine."

The half-breed stepped between trees and gained an unobstructed view of the two gloating woodsers. Jarrod moved up beside him on the left. Barefoot raised his revolver to shoulder level and sighted on his target, and Jarrod, mystified by how calm he was, did likewise. Neither bushwhacker was aware of what was about to unfold till Barefoot spoke.

"You jackanapes killed the wrong white man. He has friends."

The oldster reacted faster than the pickpocket. He turned in one fluid motion and snapped his rifle to his shoulder. He was tugging the hammer home when Barefoot's bullet struck him square in the middle of the forehead. With a grunt, the elder bushwhacker fell across Judah's body.

The younger bushwhacker panicked, jumped to his feet, and nearly dropped his rifle. Jarrod had no mercy in him. Icier-veined than a judge delivering the death sentence, he relied on his Chillicothe target practice and put a bullet in the frantic bushwhacker's chest. When his target teetered on his toes, uncertain which direction to topple, Jarrod put a second bullet two inches from the first and made the decision for him. His black-toothed countenance came to rest at Judah's feet.

Jarrod holstered his revolver, ran to Judah, grabbed the old bushwhacker's body by coat collar and rope belt, and dragged him off his brother. Dropping to one knee, he unbuttoned Judah's jeans jacket, tore open his shirt, and pressed his ear against his brother's bloody chest. The heartbeat he detected was faint, but steady. "He's alive."

"Let's move him to your shelter before it rains again," an equally delighted Barefoot said. "Grab his other arm and help me stand him up."

Once the two of them had Judah upright, Barefoot draped Judah's body over his shoulder and said, "Bring your brother's gun and watch."

Barefoot was already out of sight by the time Jarrod had retrieved Judah's belongings. Thankfully, it was a fairly short hike to the bivouac. Barefoot laid the unconscious Judah on Jarrod's blankets, and, with Jarrod's help, removed his jacket and shirt.

A bloody hole just under Judah's left collarbone was seeping blood. Barefoot slipped his hand around behind Judah's back and his fingers came away bloody. "Bullet went all the way through him."

"He was lucky," a relieved Jarrod said. "No more blood than we're seeing, the bullet didn't hit an artery. There's no blood on his lips, so it likely missed his lung, too. The other shot we heard missed him all together."

Jarrod had no experience with gunshot wounds. He knew to keep a sickly person warm and dry. Beyond that, he was a medical neophyte. "What can we do for him?"

Barefoot said, "Fetch me the ramrod from the old goat's flintlock, and be quick about it."

Jarrod didn't ask time-wasting questions. He plunged into the woods and scurried to the final resting place of the two woodsers. Ignoring a gurgling in the throat of the youngest bushwhacker, he slid the metal ramrod from under the barrel of the oldster's rifle and beat a hasty retreat. An uncharitable thought matched his mood: *May the bastards rot in hell, by damned.*

Barefoot carried the ramrod to his lean-to, doused it with watered brandy from the Union officer's canteen, and stuck the top half of it directly into the flames of his fire. For his age, the half-breed was surprisingly fast in covering the ground between the lean-to and Jarrod's rubber-roofed shelter.

"Help me sit him up. I watched a doctor save a soldier in the swamps doing this."

Judah jerked when the hot metal touched his flesh. Jarrod kept a tight grip on his shoulder while Barefoot pushed the tip of the ramrod into the bullet wound and probed to find and follow the path the bullet had taken. Judah moaned and threw his head back.

Unfazed by Judah's obvious pain, Barefoot persisted, free hand fingering the hole in Judah's back. "Aw, there it is. I'm through. Don't lose your grip on him."

With a slow steady pressure, Barefoot pulled the ramrod from Judah's chest. Judah's head lolled and, for an instant, Jarrod was afraid they'd lost him. A healthy groan absolved his worry.

Barefoot completed his doctoring by smearing entry and exit holes with a hefty dollop of his black salve. Jarrod could only surmise the half-breed believed what was good for his horse was good for any human wound. Though he doubted any medical text specified Barefoot's healing technique, Jarrod had to admit there was an elemental logic in his thinking that was hard to refute.

They tore Judah's shirtsleeves into long strips and used them to bandage his wounds. Afterward, they wrapped him in blankets, carried him to the lean-to, and laid him on a gum poncho behind the pit fire. He was as warm and dry as they could make him.

Lightning flashed and thunder careened across the darkening sky. The rain that followed presaged a night of steadily worsening weather. The wind veered around the north, tormented tree branches, and gradually turned the rain into sleet. Jarrod sat beside the sleeping Judah and watched a layer of white ice coat his surroundings. Hailstones the size of the top knuckle of his thumb pounded the roof of the lean-to and threatened to collapse his makeshift shelter. His heart ached for the hundreds of wounded adorning the battlefield with no means of escaping the wet and cold that would be the death of them.

He did have the presence of mind to rescue his writing tablet, ink, and pens from the sagging shelter. There was nothing to be done for the horses except keep them secured to the picket line. Barefoot hung their saddle blankets from the ceiling of the lean-to and switched their saddles and bridles to the poncho shelter. It was tight quarters, but the half-breed's lean-to held the three of them, for which Jarrod was doubly grateful.

Jarrod was aware of what his brother needed to give him a fair chance to survive: a roof over his head and solid walls around him to protect him from foul weather, a warm fire around the clock, fresh bandages every other day, and nourishing food morning and night, more often as he grew stronger.

Union and Confederate field hospitals would be of no help. Most of the wounded he'd observed required immediate attention, and those that survived another raw night would overwhelm whatever battlefield accommodations both armies could drum up. If the Federals had hospital ships at Pittsburgh Landing, he doubted they'd agree to make room for a wounded Confederate soldier by displacing one of their own.

Jarrod knew with rock-hard certainty that the answer was Savannah. There he could rent the necessary accommodations for Judah and livery stables for their horses. The problem was how to transport Judah and the animals once the storm let up.

The rotten weather solved part of his dilemma. The rain since yesterday evening had surely kept the Tennessee River well flooded, stranding the Quaker patriarch and his sons at Hanson's Landing. Jarrod had an inkling a tidy sum of money could persuade the Quaker to sail the flat-boat an additional ten miles downriver to Savannah on the opposite bank.

That left the problem of how to safely cart the wounded Judah to the landing. Obtaining a wagon and team, or even a stretcher, whether Rebel or blue-belly, wasn't feasible as they were more precious than gold to both armies at the moment; and riding double that distance might kill Judah.

As had been Judah's habit, Jarrod leaned on Barefoot's wisdom and experience before frustration goosed his fickle temper. He explained the flatboat, what could be had for Judah in Savannah, and the necessity of moving him. The half-breed nodded that he understood the situation. "I'll make a travois with blankets and poles. How far must we carry Master Judah?"

"Not more than five miles at the most," Jarrod answered.

"You sleep. I make travois."

Jarrod felt a twinge of guilt and then realized he might be more of a hindrance than an asset where travois building was concerned. He swore he heard chopping noises as he drifted in and out of a sleepy haze, never really resting. Judah stirred twice during the night. He swallowed a few drops of water Jarrod dribbled on his lips from a canteen. His forehead was cool when Jarrod covered it with his palm. He seemed on the verge of regaining consciousness, but couldn't quite exert the effort required to open his eyes.

By first light, the rain was a drizzle of little consequence. Jarrod marveled at the ingenuity of Barefoot's travois. With two long poles, two blankets, and lashings cut from a gum poncho, he'd fashioned the equivalent of a canvas stretcher strong enough to bear Judah's weight. The inexhaustible half-breed waved off any compliments from Jarrod. "We go now, across country to your Hamburg Road, while the rain holds off."

"What about the horses?"

"We'll tie their reins to tails with the stallion at the head of the string. He will follow Master Judah without a fuss."

Jarrod saddled the horses while Barefoot packed his camping gear. The saddling done, Jarrod lined them up in the prescribed order and the half-breed tied them in a string with gum poncho lashings. Barefoot's cloth storage bags were assigned to Jarrod's bay to avoid burdening the wounded mare. Their hurried breakfast consisted of cold biscuits, a few bacon crumbs, and water.

The rising sun was an orange blur behind a screen of tattered clouds as they departed the empty bivouac toting Judah on the travois with Barefoot at the front end of its poles and Jarrod at the rear with the docile Jasper following at his heels like a trained soldier.

Savannah, here we come!

"That bay has a Federal brand on his hip and a U.S. Cavalry saddle on his back, and none of you is wearing a blue uniform. So how'd you lay hold of that horse, sonny?"

Jarrod fought the old fight with his quick-trigger temper. They had gained the Hamburg Road without encountering mounted troopers or foot soldiers from either army. They had negotiated the muddy road with only a minor stumble here and there, slipped through Hamburg without incident, reached Hanson's Landing, and found the Quaker flatboat snubbed tight to the dock. The Quaker patriarch had relented and agreed to chance transporting all three of the horses for yet another additional sum, of course. Fifteen minutes later, they set sail for Savannah.

The city's levee was crowded with Federal steamboats plying the Tennessee to Pittsburgh Landing and back at top speed. The Quaker wisely chose to make his landing short of that unholy congestion. Off-loading the horses was tricky because of the steepness of the bank. The Quaker's sons worked their magic with the flatboat's loading platforms and got them to dry land minus any injury to themselves and the animals. Through it all, the unconscious Judah's shallow breathing didn't weaken and he didn't show any hint of fever.

Savannah was more congested than its public levee. Stores cleared of merchandise and empty church pews had been converted into temporary hospitals. Federal wagons were busy hauling the wounded to the hospitals and carting off the unfortunate who died in them. There were blue uniforms everywhere. The frenetic activity kept blue-belly attention pretty much everywhere else except on Jarrod's party until they approached a tavern near Jarrod's destination: the livery stable and small inn on Savannah's main thoroughfare where he had dined with Lieutenant Lowell Gray four days ago.

The broad-hipped, wide-shouldered Yankee sergeant leaning against the wall of the tavern had snapped to attention upon sighting Jarrod, who was now carrying the front poles of the travois. Had there been a crowd around him, Jarrod would not have caught the sergeant's scowl and noticed how he leaned sideways and stared past him at Barefoot. Jarrod risked a backward glance and caught the sergeant within a pace of his bay Federal horse studying it closely.

Assuming the sergeant would follow them in lieu of writing the incident off as an overly curious bystander, Jarrod walked straight to the livery stable, called over his shoulder for Barefoot to leave the horses in the street, and marched into its dim, musty interior without breaking stride. If there was to be a confrontation, he didn't want it to occur in public and attract even more unwanted scrutiny.

They had no more than laid Judah's travois on the dusty floor of the livery when the sergeant entered the livery with his right hand clasping the butt of his revolver. His florid face made it difficult for Jarrod to tell whether he was angry or not. Lest you had backbone, the sergeant's no-nonsense gaze was downright withering.

"Well, I'm waiting, sonny," the sergeant barked. "How did you come by that bay horse?"

Jarrod raised his hands and said, "Sir, if I may reach inside my jacket, I can explain everything to your satisfaction."

The sergeant opened his mouth to speak, but a restrained voice at the door of the stable stilled his tongue. "Sergeant Longstreth, what's happening here?"

Lieutenant Lowell Gray had made a most opportune appearance. The sergeant clearly recognized Gray's voice. "Lieutenant, this man is not wearing our uniform and he has possession of one of our horses."

"Mr. Bell has use of the horse and saddle with my permission, Sergeant. He is in the employ of our government. You may go about your routine duties."

The matter concluded to his satisfaction, Sergeant Longstreth pivoted smartly, saluted his superior officer, and marched from the stable. "He's a right proper soldier, Mr. Bell. I would gladly command a thousand like him."

Lowell Gray removed his gloves and offered Jarrod his hand. "Mr. Bell, you've been quite the busy lad."

"Yes, sir, it's been somewhat hectic since we parted company," Jarrod said, shaking Gray's hand.

"And who is the chap on the stretcher? He isn't perchance the brother you went searching for?"

Jarrod dropped to a knee beside the travois. "Yes, sir, he is. Judah was shot in the chest late yesterday by a bushwhacker. He's alive thanks to Mr. Barefoot," Jarrod said, nodding at the half-breed. "He cauterized the wound with a heated ramrod. We hired a flatboat to bring us down the Tennessee to Savannah. Judah's swallowed a little water, but he hasn't fully regained his senses. I'm desperate for a place to house him while he recuperates. I was hoping to secure a room at the Brass Horn."

"There are no rooms available at the Brass Horn," Lowell Gray said. "Well, that is, except for mine. I'm attached to General Grant's staff at the moment. I can bunk with his other officers in the staff tent at the Cherry Mansion and make room for your brother."

"I can never thank you enough, Lieutenant," Jarrod said. "We'll bring him there straightaway."

Without orders, the listening Barefoot sought out the livery owner, and together they led the horses in from the street, the liveryman happy to have paying customers.

Jarrod checked Judah's pulse for the hundredth time. "A little weak, but steady."

Lieutenant Gray donned his gloves. "Perhaps it would be best if the two of us move your brother to my room at the Brass Horn. Your Mr. Barefoot can see that your horses are properly fed and watered and join us later."

Lieutenant Lowell Gray's quarters at the Brass Horn were a reflection of his background, training, and personal habits. The spacious room was spotless, the bed clothes freshly laundered, floor recently swept, and the papers on the top of the portable writing desk neatly and precisely stacked. Even the globe of the coal oil lamp had been wiped clean.

"The landlord may object to bloody sheets," Jarrod said.

"He won't if he's paid sufficiently," Lowell Gray said. "His wife changes the linens weekly. Sarah Allen reared six boys and seems to understand the male species in a bold sort of way."

Gray and Jarrod maneuvered the travois alongside the four-poster bed, uncovered Judah, and lifted him onto the feather-stuffed mattress. Jarrod assumed the task of undressing his brother. Other than a single gasp of pain, Judah remained in the dark world of unconsciousness, which was beginning to worry Jarrod. Thankfully, he found no fresh blood on Judah's chest or back when he removed his shirtsleeve bandages.

"Seems your half-breed did a pretty fair job doctoring your brother," the observant Lowell Gray said. "What did he treat his wounds with?"

"Black salve from a round tin he carries. I suspect it is part of his Cherokee heritage."

"Origin doesn't matter," Lowell Gray said. "The important thing is the salve stopped the bleeding and sealed the bullet holes. There's a spare bed sheet in the dresser you can use for fresh bandages. It's nearly suppertime. I'll have some broth made up for Judah and something more substantial for you. Mr. Barefoot can eat in the kitchen. I'll discuss our new arrangement with Sarah's husband so we don't have any misunderstandings. I'll return within the hour."

With Lowell Gray's departure, Jarrod tore the spare sheet into long strips, wrapped Judah's chest, and covered him with a blanket. Unable to get Judah to swallow water from the canteen he'd brought with him from the livery, he laid his revolver on the dresser and flopped into a large leather chair beside Lowell Gray's writing desk.

He was worn out physically and mentally, but much remained on his plate. He didn't dare rest for more than a few quiet minutes. Besides caring for Judah, he had stories to write for J. Rodgers Black, as well as letters that couldn't be postponed. He had to write Brianna Hardin Bell, his father, and Jacob. And he owed an overdue letter to a certain young lady he missed desperately the more he dwelled on her, especially when he remembered her unique way of saying good-bye.

He felt as if Lorena Gamble had crawled under his very skin, a sensation that filled him with a want for her that astounded him. He was thankful she'd come to him. Had she not been bold and forthright, he might never have known how deeply he was capable of loving a woman. How he longed to be with her.

He leaned back and closed his eyes. What he'd observed, endured, and survived in four days was equivalent to the arms-bearing soldier "seeing the elephant." He'd stood in the cauldron of smoke, fire, and quick death that left an indelible mark on the male soul. He would never again view life from the vantage point of the naïve and uninitiated. He was now a man in his own right. He had willingly paid the requisite price: every vestige of his boyhood.

Jarrod heard a rustling on the bed. He opened his eyes and Judah was awake and staring at him. "Where am I, little brother?"

Jarrod experienced an immense joy.

His world was whole again.

Two months later to the day, Jarrod descended the steps of a passenger coach at the L&N depot in Bowling Green, Kentucky. Judah's cane rapped hollowly on the metal edge of the top step, and Jarrod alertly extended an arm to safeguard against any mishap until Judah was safely on the ground. A fever had beset the recovering Judah upon their arrival in Nashville three weeks ago, and he still felt weak and shaky when exerting himself. Jarrod had wanted to extend their Nashville stay, but he finally succumbed to Judah's entreaties that he was well enough to travel by rail and agreed to their finishing their journey to Glasgow without further delay.

"A carriage will be waiting for us on the street side of the depot," Jarrod reminded Judah. "I talked to the conductor in Nashville and the train crew will help Barefoot unload the horses. I want you to wait off your feet in the depot until we're ready to start for Glasgow. Understood?"

"Yes, Jarrod, for the fifth time, I'll play the invalid and baby myself."

In traveling with Judah by wagon from Savannah to Nashville and by rail from Nashville to Bowling Green, Jarrod had grasped how much his brother resented having to rely on others. Judah Bell took great pride in doing for himself at his own accelerated pace and according to his calendar.

The train crew pleased Jarrod by off-loading their horses and piling their saddles, bridles, and newly purchased valises between the front and back seats of the four-passenger carriage—all within fifteen minutes. Jarrod held out Jasper's saddle. He would ride the stallion and lead the horses while Barefoot drove the carriage. The high sky and bright sun of a prime early summer day was more appealing and enjoyable from the saddle than under the roof of a carriage with a brother anxious to kiss a bride from whom he'd been absent too long by far.

Jarrod's Glasgow visit would be brief by necessity. Lieutenant Lowell Gray had obtained General Grant's permission to wire Jarrod's account of the Battle of Pittsburgh Landing to J. Rodgers Black. His emphasis on the horrors of the two-day engagement, its cost in wasted and crippled lives on the battlefield, and the pain and suffering it inflicted on thousands of families north and south struck an empathetic nerve in his Ohio readers. The *Cincinnati Times-Ledger* ran his story on the front page a chapter at a time for six consecutive days and generated an avalanche of letters from readers. Publisher Black printed the reader responses in a special edition that went to press three times before public interest waned. When *Harper's Weekly* paid the *Times-Ledger* for the right to carry Jarrod's story under his name, giving him instant national distribution, J. Rodgers Black, fearing the loss of his new star reporter, had offered Jarrod his own by-line, illustrator, and a handsome salary to boot.

Once Jarrod accepted Publisher Black's offer, J. Rodgers had started hounding him for fresh material by telegram. On top of that, he wanted Jarrod in his Cincinnati office as soon as possible to discuss future assignments. Jarrod's other key motivation for returning to Ohio quickly was, of course, Lorena Gamble. He was praying her father would allow her to meet him in Cincinnati, if not for a private talk, then a chaperoned dinner. He was reluctant to ask her to meet him without her father's consent. He had too much respect for her family to risk having them believe he was taking advantage of their daughter.

As they advanced up Glasgow's Main Street, Barefoot slowed the carriage team. "Ride ahead and warn her, Jarrod," Judah shouted. "I don't want to embarrass her."

Jarrod touched Jasper's flank with a boot toe and the stallion broke into a fast walk. The sign on Maud Huddleston's boardinghouse made it easy for Jarrod to locate. A willowy black female was sweeping the boardinghouse's wooden sidewalk. She spied Jarrod and Jasper, shrieked, cast the broom aside, and disappeared through Maud Huddleston's front door, slamming it shut behind her.

A bemused Jarrod lounged in the saddle, anxious to see what happened next. The front door swung open and a breathless female that fit Judah's description charged the sidewalk while shading her eyes with a hand against the bright glare of the sun. She recognized Jasper and a smile of excited anticipation livened her features. When she looked higher and saw Jarrod, her smile vanished. Amanda was mistaken. The man on the magnificent red stallion certainly resembled her husband, but he wasn't her Judah.

Jarrod laughed, said, "I'm Jarrod, Judah's brother," and turning in the saddle, pointed at a carriage approaching the boardinghouse.

"I believe that's the man you're looking for, the man who wants to finish his healing in your bed."

CHAPTER 25

After nine months of virtual nonstop campaigning on horseback, Lieutenant Jacob Bell was a seasoned cavalryman in mind, body, and heart. He had fought through the spring, summer, and fall into the winter of 1862 in minor skirmishes against the graybacks from northern Alabama to the outskirts of Louisville, Kentucky. On the evening of the day before New Year's Eve, he was hunkered over a fire three miles from Murfreesboro, Tennessee, part of Major General William Rosecrans's Army of the Cumberland totaling about forty-one thousand men. Between Jacob's mess fire and Murfreesboro stood General Braxton Bragg's Confederate Army of roughly thirty-five thousand Rebels. Tomorrow the two armies would clash to determine whether the Blue or the Gray controlled the city of Nashville thirty miles to the north and the geographic middle of the state of Tennessee. The First Regiment Ohio Volunteer Cavalry was about to participate in the first major engagement of its short history.

The nine months of campaigning that so sorely tested Jacob's intestinal fortitude, personal loyalties, and courage began in the aftermath of the battle Southerners called Pittsburgh Landing and northern newspapers called Shiloh.

The First Ohio Cavalry marched into Savannah, Tennessee, on 8 April and was greeted by the sight of wounded soldiers in numbers both startling and heartbreaking. The next day the regiment boarded transports that ferried them across the Tennessee River to Pittsburgh Landing and witnessed a slanting riverbank blanketed with dead and wounded to the very edge of the water. The wounded waited to be loaded on Union hospital boats, prompting Sergeant Tom South to remark, "Some of those boys died waiting for a stretcher, and it's likely more will."

Once on land, they found an overwhelming beehive of activity. Thousands of rations and tons of supplies were being lifted from the many transport ships lining the bank of the river and loaded into wagons from the front lines. Ambulances were continuing to bring in the wounded while still more wagons hauled in the dead to be piled like cordwood beside long burial trenches. Many corpses were slid into the freshly dug trenches absent a blanket to cover them, their burial attire reduced in the haste of necessity to their blue uniforms.

As the First Ohio advanced a hundred yards to the edge of the timber, the devastation wrought by the shells from the Union gunboats and land batteries was readily apparent. Tree limbs a foot in diameter had been severed like broken matchsticks, and additional limbs hung by slivers of wood, waiting to fall on the unwary. Whole tops were missing from some trees, and it was not uncommon for a solid shot to have completely pierced a trunk. Broken guns, carriages, caissons, and wheels, the flotsam of battle, littered the ground in all directions.

The regiment marched a mile and bivouacked without tents in a sea of mud. The bloating stinking carcasses of artillery horses baking in the hot sunlight brought former jockey Fritz Howard to tears and made the eating of rations a tasteless chore. The next day held new surprises. They

were seldom out of the sight of large numbers of dead
bodies. On the most hotly contested ground, bullets had
peeled away bark until trees turned into ragged white
poles. Aaron Spencer insisted Jacob view a five-inch-
diameter tree that wore a thick metallic coat of Minié balls.
The oddest discovery was a middling-size tree with five
Rebel bodies aligned directly behind it, a clear indication
the fighting had been so intense at some point all five had
tried to take cover behind the same tree.

The two-week battlefield bivouac proved a miserable
assignment. The water available for drinking and cooking
came from ravines, gullies, and rivulets swelled by rain
that had drained across ground covered by dead soldiers,
mules, and horses. No twenty-four hours passed without a
soaking rain; poor weather conditions delayed the arrival
of the regiment's tents. To compensate, troopers cut poles
ten to twelve feet long with their hatchets and put them
side by side with one end on a log and the other on the
ground. They then laid their saddle blankets on the poles
followed by their sleeping blankets, and if it wasn't too
cold on a particular night, their overcoats. Carbines,
sabers, revolvers, and ammunition were then laid cross-
wise at the head of the poles next to the log. The finishing
touch was to place their saddles atop their personal equipment for a pillow, an uncomfortable alternative to a downy
pillow since cavalry saddles were wooden trees covered
with rawhide. Sheltered beneath their gum ponchos, the
troopers could enjoy a reasonably dry night's sleep, except
for the Spencer brothers. Possessing extra long frames,
they had to decide whether their heads or their feet would
get wet before morning.

The march southward to Corinth in pursuit of General
Beauregard's retreating Confederate Army meant picket
duty for the First Ohio, and each day their front line saw

fresh evidence of the Rebels' hasty flight. Standing tents and hundreds of discarded small arms, bags of flour meal, and camp equipage characterized the typical abandoned enemy camp. Reports of two unusual discoveries galloped through the regimental gossip mill. The first occurred when the pickets stumbled on to half a wagonload of Bowie knives created from old files and butcher knives with leather scabbards and sheathes. The second involved the finding of twenty-four dead Rebels lying together in two rows with their feet toward each other, and a space of a yard or two between them. Jacob finally deduced they had originally been under a hospital tent, had subsequently died of their wounds, and the critically needed tent had then been removed. The troopers of Company M heaved a sigh of relief when an infantry detail was sent out to bury the swollen bodies with faces blackened beyond recognition.

General Buell's Union forces laid siege to Corinth, Mississippi, on 10 April. Heavy siege guns drawn by ten yoke of oxen per gun were deployed to blast away at the fortified and entrenched Rebels. For seven solid weeks, the First Ohio performed picket duty in front of the Federal infantry in such close proximity to the enemy the picket details could not be changed during the night without drawing fire, compelling them to stand on post from dark until daylight.

Scouting duties were equally dangerous. The country was thickly timbered with small, scrubby trees that impeded cavalry operations. Open ground consisted of a few cleared acres around rundown farmhouses. Streams were small, well water was bitter, and scummy ponds and swamps were often the only source of water.

Though the First Ohio was embroiled in many light skirmishes during the siege, losses in action were small;

however, the bad water took a fearful toll. Camp fever ran rampant. The death rate was not large within the regiment, but troopers became unfit for service and were hospitalized. Unable to overcome the disease, others chose to drift back home. By the time General Beauregard withdrew in the night and Buell's army entered Corinth on 1 June, the First Ohio had lost half of its troopers. Attrition by disease had firmly established itself as a major player in the war and posed an unrelenting threat to the well-being of both armies in camp and in the field no matter the locale.

With the fall of Corinth, Confederate and Union forces began a game of cat and mouse advance and retreat that eventually allowed Confederate General Braxton Bragg, who assumed command when General Beauregard fell ill, to launch one of the boldest schemes of the war. Union forces were dispersed in early June 1862 and Bragg took full advantage. General Grant was occupied in the west along the Mississippi where he would ultimately move against Vicksburg. General Buell's Army of the Cumberland was sent into middle Tennessee to begin a campaign long urged by President Lincoln.

General Bragg shifted his Army of the Tennessee to Chattanooga and combined it with General Kirby's Confederate army in East Tennessee. The prelude of Bragg's scheme was extensive raids by the cavalry of Nathan Bedford Forrest and John Hunt Morgan, which repeatedly cut Federal lines of communication, captured or destroyed huge stores of supplies, and overwhelmed several outposts. Early in August, columns of Confederate infantry and artillery began pouring through the passes of the Cumberland Mountains into the prized state of Kentucky.

Serving as an intelligence officer on the staff of Colonel Minor Millikin, commander of the First Ohio Cavalry since February, Jacob tracked the movement of Bragg's cavalry, infantry, and artillery via telegram and reports from the field. He helped orchestrate three sizable forays by the regiment to capture John Hunt Morgan and came away disgusted over the failure of other Federal units to coordinate their movements with him and put the "Thunderbolt of the Confederacy" in irons.

Colonel Millikin and Jacob discerned Bragg's intentions of invading Kentucky early on, but their warnings and projections went unheeded at General Buell's headquarters. On 23 August, Union General Bull Nelson and a small Union force were badly defeated by General E. Kirby Smith at Richmond, Kentucky, and the city of Louisville, practically defenseless, panicked. Within two days, northern newspapers were screaming that Confederate detachments had been spotted south of Covington within cannon shot of Cincinnati.

Still, the notoriously cautious General Buell required until 7 September to begin his pursuit of Braxton Bragg from Nashville and safeguard Louisville. The absence of a widespread engagement during the race for the Ohio River with the two armies but a few miles apart on occasion was credited later to the determination of both generals to spy Ohio waters first. On the other hand, an undermanned battalion detached from the First Regiment Ohio Volunteer Cavalry led by Colonel Minor Millikin, spearheading the northern march of Buell's forces, exchanged fire continuously with blue-belly battalions and scouting companies. The *pishing* whine of a speeding ball that missed was soon as familiar to Jacob as the buzzing of a wasp. The unexpected became the normal. A bullet tore the lieutenant's bar from his left shoulder with no enemy to be seen where a point-blank volley killed the two troopers beside him along with their horses and left him and his mount untouched. He sped away stunned and muttering a prayer of thanks.

Colonel Millikin's detached battalion reached Louisville with Bragg's forward elements on 1 October. The blue-bellies had won the race for the banks of the Ohio, stalling the major thrust of Bragg's scheme to retake Kentucky for the South.

Once Millikin's battalion companies were settled in at Camp Buell outside Louisville with their horses watered, fed, and groomed, Jacob, with Colonel Millikin's permission, sought out his original mess for his evening meal. Captain Cam Logan and Lieutenant Tor Shavers saw Jacob pass their mess fire but chose to ignore him, behavior to which Jacob had grown accustomed. Jacob's duty with Colonel Millikin's staff had kept him away from Company M for long stretches and negated any opportunity for Logan to confront him personally without witnesses. It was, Jacob knew, merely the postponing of the inevitable. Hatred was soul food for Cam Logan.

Jacob's mess was always glad to have him join them. Fritz Howard, the only member with a smidgen of taste regarding the proper seasoning of food, had evolved into his messmates' day-by-day chef. The vocal jabbering of the mess while they ate was as comforting to Jacob as an old shoe. He loved hearing each trooper spin yarns how pure chance had saved his bacon in a tight situation. The story repeated the most was Lyle Tomlinson's account of how his thick Bible, riding in his hip pocket, had spared him a bullet in a most embarrassing and tender spot. The most repeated retort to a supper-fire yarn was Nate Bush's comeback that, if Lyle were a better horseman, maybe his tender ass wouldn't have been so high in the air in the first place, meaning his shortcomings in the saddle and the Good Book had conspired to spare him. The veterans—

Tom South, the Spencer brothers, Sam Kite, Nate Bush, and Lawton Anderson—howled as uproariously tonight as they had when Jacob first heard the Tomlinson-Bush exchange. Those men new to the mess—Wesley Paine, Henry Stark, Winston Graham, Tim Bullard, and Tyron Clippinger—contributed their fair share of honking laughs and giggles.

The chatter lost its humorous bent over after-dinner coffee. Sam Kite asked, "Lieutenant Bell, it seems to us lowly privates that we Federals are not faring well. We lost at Bull Run in August, Stonewall Jackson captured Harper's Ferry the middle of September, and we fought the Rebels to a draw at Antietam two weeks ago. And now, here we are, driven back to our original Kentucky camp with our tail caught between our legs. It seems as if Shiloh didn't count for anything. Are we gonna lose this war?"

Aware most of these young Yankees read newspapers that circulated through camp or had them read to them, and soaked up rumors like a dry rag touching water, Jacob chose his words carefully. "Boys, I won't bore you with fancy hurrahs. I still believe we'll win the war. Be warned, though, the fight will become meaner and meaner the longer it lasts, and I don't know how many more lives, maybe including ours, it will take for us to prevail. The key question is which flag do we want flying when the victor writes the peace treaty? There are few things more precious to a man than his country, and to defend it is a man's highest calling. With our nation's whole future at stake, I don't think we're ready to concede we're whipped just yet, are we?"

The unanimous chorus of "No, sir" that answered Jacob's question was an affirmation that his mess, despite the recent setbacks the Federal army had suffered, hadn't yet lost their will to fight, and made Jacob proud to be one of them. He stood, drained his coffee cup, and said, "Corporal Howard, your beef and potato stew was delicious. Sergeant South, we haven't had a full night of sleep since the Lord's shepherd kissed his lamb good night. I'd surely hate to have anybody miss hearing 'Taps' after the roll is called."

The dog-tired mess was more than glad to retire to their blankets. Once he was bedded down in Fritz Howard's tent, Jacob's thoughts turned as they often did during his quiet times to Felicia Denning. He had written to Felicia upon his arrival in Louisville the previous December and initiated a correspondence with her. While her return letters to him were light and chatty with no hint of commitment beyond friendship, he enjoyed their exchanges and was happy with staying in touch and keeping his foot in the door with an eye on a deeper relationship in the future.

Then the belt had somehow slipped from the wheel. He could only attribute her change in attitude to what became his final letter. Stirred by what he'd observed upon the Shiloh battlefield, he had been quite explicit in describing to her the death and destruction he'd witnessed. Her letters had ceased like a well suddenly gone dry. He wrote to her twice more, received nothing in return, and, thereafter, confined his writing to his daily journal and a monthly update to his father.

If Felicia chose not to write to him, he could only hope and pray she stayed a single woman. If she did, he would call on her at the first opportunity and let nature take its course.

He drifted off and dreamed of the lingering kiss he had shared with her in front of his original messmates at Camp Chase, and the muffled sob he'd most certainly heard as she'd departed in Paige Dolan's buggy.

How could a woman capable of such passion dismiss him so callously?

* * *

Private LeVerne Wade, Colonel Millikin's personal messenger, interrupted Jacob's breakfast. "The colonel wishes to speak with you and Captain Logan without delay."

Jacob grabbed his holstered revolver from his tent and buckled it about his waist. Colonel Millikin was precise in his use of language when issuing orders and "without delay" meant with all possible speed. Captain Logan joined Jacob and the messenger as they rushed past his mess fire.

To Jacob, Colonel Minor Millikin—a graduate of Hanover College and Harvard Law School, former practicing attorney, former owner and editor of the Hamilton, Ohio, *Intelligencer* newspaper, successful farmer, and superb horseman—was the ideal cavalry officer: smart, opportunistic, resolute, devoted to his men and his country, and courageous under fire. Millikin's decisions in camp and in the field were based on honest assessments of the situation confronting his command, what action would best contribute to the success of his command, and his unerring instinct for choosing the officer best suited to carry out his orders. Jacob had been so impressed with Millikin's leadership in the intervening months since his promotion he would without hesitation follow him into the fiery hell of Dante's inferno.

Breakfast growing cold before him, Colonel Millikin stayed in his canvas chair, returned the salutes of Jacob and Cam Logan, and said, "Captain Logan, with Major Walker's concurrence, I'm dispatching Lieutenant Bell on a special mission to Ohio. Fifty head of horses are waiting to be claimed by our regiment at Camp Chase. Lieutenant Bell will be given orders under my name to travel to Columbus, claim our remounts, and oversee their shipment by rail to Cincinnati and boat to Louisville. If we depart Louisville before his return, we will leave a detail at Camp Buell to help him herd the remounts to wherever our camp might be located.

"Not knowing how much manpower will be made available to him during his short stay in Ohio, Lieutenant Bell will pick two troopers from his mess to accompany him. They will depart Louisville on the Federal packet boat at eight o'clock sharp this morning. Private Wade will deliver my written orders and military passes for boat and train travel to Lieutenant Bell's tent within the hour. He will escort the detail to the packet boat and return their horses to camp. Gentlemen, those remounts are critical to our future as a viable regiment. I won't have a single man of ours made a foot soldier for lack of a horse. Bear that in mind, Lieutenant Bell, and conduct yourself accordingly. Any questions, gentlemen?"

Millikin's explicit instructions had effectively mooted the need for questions. As he left Colonel Millikin's headquarters with Cam Logan, Jacob fought to keep his mind on the task at hand and failed miserably. Despite the urgency of his mission, there was no earthly reason why he couldn't steal a few minutes of Federal time and knock on Felicia Denning's door, and at least talk to her. He was certain she wouldn't spurn him in person.

Jacob didn't believe in miracles, but he did believe Major Dance Walker had been only too happy to recommend him to Colonel Millikin for duty that would take him to Columbus, Ohio. Walker had consistently inquired how his lovemaking by letter was proceeding during the First Ohio's service in Kentucky and Tennessee, and his disappointment upon learning Jacob's correspondence with Felicia had broken off had been genuine. Jacob couldn't suppress a happy smile. The First Ohio's self-appointed Cupid was shooting arrows again.

Jacob anticipated a new dose of venom from Cam Logan and his hometown rival didn't disappoint. "Your luck and the ass-kissing from Dance Walker won't last forever, Bell. Some of the boys think you're invincible. Only a fool believes such hogwash. You should have died in that Springerville ambush that slaughtered the troopers and horses around you and left you without a scratch. There's a bullet in a grayback rifle with your name on it the same as there is for Dance Walker. I'll live to piss on both of your graves."

Jacob's temper and his tongue grabbed the lead rope before he could tighten his jaw. "Well, at least it won't be a sailor with a club that does me in."

Cam Logan cursed vehemently and blurted, "You accusing me of something, Bell?"

"Red Baker didn't run out on you. Your money is in his pockets on the bottom of the Ohio."

Cam Logan ground his teeth together. "You had any solid proof for what you're saying, you'd have me arrested."

"You're right, I don't have evidence that would hold up if I accused you of hiring a man to murder a fellow officer. So, you won't be court-martialed."

Jacob halted and looked Cam Logan straight in the eye. "I can play your game, too. I won't hire you killed. But I'm confident you'll give me an opportunity to run you out of the army, and I won't hesitate to make the most of it."

His bluff called, Cam Logan, not daring to risk unprovoked physical violence outside their commanding officer's headquarters, resorted to blustering threats, the last resort of the true bully. "Maybe the bullet that nails your hide to the wall won't come from the front. Maybe it will catch you while you're sleeping. Maybe it will ruin your wedding day. But, trust me, it will find you."

Cam Logan had plumbed the depths of the hatred one

man could bear another. Jacob didn't quail before it. "Don't miss, Cam. You won't get a second shot."

Brice Logan's son marched off cursing with each step. Jacob was surprised that even now he found it difficult to dislike Logan. In spite of his arrogance and high-handed manner, Logan was an apt student of strategy and tactics and had no fear under enemy fire. His sole drawback was a bent for harboring and nurturing an old grudge that made no sense to Jacob. He had never beaten Can Logan at anything, whether it was at cards, pursuing the same girl, or fisticuffs.

To Jacob, Cam's jealousy was akin to a never-ending tantrum on the part of a child. But then, Jacob didn't walk in Logan's boots. Maybe something unforeseen would reconcile their differences in a manner that wouldn't necessitate the death of either of them. With his next step toward his mess tent, Jacob was chiding himself for playing the eternal optimist where his fellow men were concerned. Weren't the stripes on a tiger permanent?

Fritz Howard and Sam Kite were thrilled when Jacob chose them to accompany him to Camp Chase. Aaron Spencer protested the loss of the mess's chef for a week until Jacob quieted him by explaining Corporal Howard and Private Kite had gained much experience handling loose horses at the Howard family livery stable under the tutelage of Fritz's father. Fritz tossed three days of rations in a cloth bag while Aaron helped Jacob and Sam saddle three horses.

Private LeVerne Wade showed within the hour allotted by Colonel Millikin, and the four cavalrymen departed Camp Buell at a trot. Louisville was coming awake when they reached the outskirts of the city. Downtown, the streets smelled of baking bread, wood smoke, and garbage. Merchants were rolling up window shades and stacking displays for the last of summer vegetables, potatoes, and freshly picked apples on the porches of their stores. That early in the day, there were a greater number of dogs pawing through alley trash than there were humans out and about.

In contrast to the core of the city, the waterfront was alive with activity. White and black stevedores were hastily loading freight on steam ships, passengers were lined up to board the same vessels, and a freshly recruited Union infantry brigade was disembarking from steam-powered military transports. Youthful faces yearning for the whiskers of manhood reminded Jacob that farm and small-town boys in their teens and early twenties were carrying the brunt of the western war on their thin shoulders.

Private Wade presented Jacob the necessary orders and travel vouchers, and Colonel Millikin's three remount troopers boarded the *Wheeling Star,* a passenger, freight, and mail packet of recent vintage. The bursar/ticket master accepted their military passes without hesitation. Upon spotting Jacob's cavalry tunic, spurred boots, and saber, he did, however, make a point of telling Lieutenant Jacob Bell that not a single horse apple had stained the deck of the *Wheeling Star* since its 1859 launching. Somehow Jacob maintained a sober face. He thought, *to each his own pride.*

Puffy white clouds sailed west to east, powered by a moderate wind. Jacob led Fritz and Sam to an open-air bench in the bow of the hurricane deck well away from the redundant slap of the paddlewheel and the pound of the engines. Without being asked, the bursar/ticket master sallied over with an enamelware coffeepot and three kiln-fired mugs. He filled a mug with black coffee for each his passengers, said, "I admire men with the dash to fight with swords from horseback," and retreated, leaving his steaming pot on the end of the bench.

Sam Kite chuckled and said, "Lieutenant, the folks of this old world never cease to surprise me."

Sam Kite and Fritz Howard sipped coffee while Jacob took time to read through Colonel Millikin's handwritten orders. Soon as Jacob looked up, Fritz Howard asked, "What are our plans for Columbus?"

"Our orders are pretty straightforward," Jacob answered. "We call on Major Phillip Hamtramck at Camp Chase, claim our remounts, drive them to the rail yards in east Columbus, see them loaded on cars that will be made available for them, and head back to Cincinnati."

"That's fine for the remounts. I meant what are *our* plans?"

Though Jacob knew exactly where Fritz was headed, he couldn't forgo a little teasing. "Private, I'm not following you. We have Colonel Millikin's orders, do we not? That's all we're *authorized* to do."

"Stop joshing me, sir. Unless your brain is absent without leave, you're planning to call on Miss Felicia Denning. No man with a heartbeat would allow a woman that beautiful to slip through his fingers."

"Say maybe I was to call on her, what would you and Sam want to keep your traps shut about it?"

"Well, sir, Sam and I would love nothing better than to blow the foam off a few brews at Sweeney's Pub on High Street while you're off playing Galahad to your fair lady. It's been a mighty dry haul since we shed Columbus ten months back, dryer than drought-starved thistles. My throat has a thirst water can't satisfy."

Jacob's condescending smile was returned tenfold. "All right, let's check our timetable. We dock in Cincinnati at six o'clock tomorrow evening. We'll spend the night there and entrain for Columbus on the Little Miami Railroad the next morning. At Xenia, we'll switch to the C and Z and raise Columbus in mid-afternoon. Since Major Hamtramck doesn't have a clue as to what train we'll be arriving on, I strongly suggest we wait and visit Camp Chase the following morning. Will that itinerary satisfy our collective desires and wants?"

Both privates nodded vigorously.

"Yes, sir," Sam Kite said with a guffaw. "Right up to our eye teeth."

Jacob made a mental note that physical assistance might be required to cart these two pups to bed after they "did the town" in Columbus. If they were familiar with Sweeney's Pub, they had tipped pints there with Fritz's father and not of their own accord. A visit to the Columbus Police lockup was a potential disaster he refused to contemplate.

"Sir, is the Ohio legislature in session?" Fritz Howard inquired. "I'm sure Senator Bell would appreciate your calling on him, too."

Jacob had known Fritz long enough his personal inquiries regarding members of the Bell family weren't intrusive. "Father's home in Chillicothe. He broke an ankle in a fall. He won't return to the capital until a special session convenes in November."

"I'm sorry to hear that. Sir, we haven't talked personally for weeks. What's the latest news from Jarrod?"

"Jarrod's last letter said Judah is still recovering from the bullet wound he suffered at Shiloh. He believes Judah's full recovery is months away. As for Jarrod, he's agreed to report the war for the *Cincinnati Times-Ledger* from General Grant's headquarters. His Shiloh story won him national acclaim."

"Sir, I read Jarrod's story. My father mailed me all six chapters at once. I swear he watched the battle from a balloon. He made me feel I was in the middle of it with him."

"Jarrod always had a flair for writing," Jacob said. "He loved to hear the scratch of a pen from the time he could hold one."

Fritz grasped the bursar's enamelware pot. "More coffee, sir?"

Sam Kite held out his cup, too. "Sir, you did say we'll spend tomorrow night in Cincinnati?"

"Yes, I did."

"If I may be so bold, sir, do you happen to know of a good Cincinnati pub we might visit?"

Jacob leaned back against the starboard rail of the packet boat. These two young tigers would definitely bear watching.

Jacob lingered beside the hitching post in front of the Denning family's palatial residence on tree-shaded Sullivant Avenue. He pounded dust from his sleeves and pants legs and ran a palm across his freshly shaven upper lip, jaws, and chin. The Gay Street barber hadn't come cheap and his cologne oozed a ripe, feminine smell. Better than stale sweat and grime, Jacob decided. A new uniform would have been a major boost for his appearance. As it was, the stained, threadbare tunic that had clothed him through battle and bad weather bespoke a military man of action and purpose, not the elegance and gentility of peacetime.

The setting sun cast a bright orange halo over Jacob's shoulder. He had debated which was the best hour to find Felicia at home and decided that a single woman would dine with her family most evenings. He had not pursued the gentlemanly path and forwarded a note asking permission to call on her out of fear it would go unanswered or she might reject his entreaty in writing.

His courage began to wane. His feet suddenly wanted to skedaddle. What was he doing here? Hadn't she told him she wanted nothing more to do with him when she stopped writing to him? Why should he subject himself to a face-to-face dismissal that would be harder to swallow than a bucket of hammers?

He sucked in a deep breath and willed his feet to move. He wasn't taking the coward's way out. He wasn't leaving before she told him to his face that she had no honest feelings for him in her heart, that she saw no worthwhile future for them together, that their Camp Chase kiss had been a frivolous, spur-of-the-moment show of affection that may have given him a wrong impression she regretted now, and that she was sorry she had chosen to correspond with him in a moment of weakness and indecision she also regretted.

Once at the brass-trimmed, oaken front door of the Denning home, Jacob gave his shaky will no chance to desert him. He removed his hat, seized the door's brass knocker, and gave the striker plate four hard raps to insure the home's occupants knew the stoop was occupied.

Though he heard no footsteps, the knob of the oaken door turned, and the door slowly opened to reveal a black male dressed in a ministerial shirt, frock coat with tails, short pants of the same burgundy color, silk stockings, and shoes with silver buckles. The black servant asked politely, "Whom shall I say is calling, sir?"

"Lieutenant Jacob Bell to see Miss Felicia Denning."

The servant nodded and said, "Wait here, sir, I will announce you," and closed the door.

Prolonged waiting was a skill Jacob had cultivated with considerable success. The mounting minutes slowly devoured his acquired patience. Proper manners didn't leave guests stranded at the door a second more than necessary. By now, the Denning servant could have circled the block twice. He was reaching for the doorknob, intending to make his own entry, when the knob turned from the inside.

Heart pounding, breath quickening, he braced himself for the first glimpse in ten long lonely months of the lovely creature he loved. His heart sank into his boots. What stood before him wasn't a vibrant young woman with warmth in her eyes and a welcoming smile, but a man his age wearing a precisely tailored broadcloth suit, white shirt with ruffles at neck and cuffs, and a red cravat. Blond hair spilled over half the man's forehead. His eyes were blue and his features a classic blend of rugged handsomeness and cultured refinement. The ridged cleft in his chin kept him from being the perfect choice for the subject of a Roman sculpture.

"I regret to inform you," the blond-haired man said in a carefully modulated voice, "that Miss Denning does not wish to see you."

Delivered by a potential rival in a tone implying he was of less importance than a scab on a wound that could be peeled and discarded with no fear of reprisal, the simple dismissal goaded Jacob like the pain of a red hot poker applied to the skin of his cheek. His temper boiled over in a finger snap. He found himself thinking how he could grab whoever this impertinent bastard was by the lapels of his coat, throw him aside, barge into the Denning home, and locate the person responsible for his presence at the door.

A sobering awareness of the futility of such a move struck him before he could so much as lift a finger. Did he really want to confront her, perhaps bring her to tears, all the while appearing a naïve, love-demented fool that couldn't accept rejection with the grace and maturity of a grown man?

The intentional killing of his fellow man, the stink of their bloated bodies, and the comforting of comrades condemned by the severity of their wounds made this silly charade of a romance he had chosen to enact unseemly and beneath his dignity. He stepped away from the door of the Denning home, donned his hat, and said, "Please tell

Miss Denning I wish her a most pleasant evening. Good night, sir."

He kept his pace measured and unhurried as he departed. Damned if he would display the slightest hint of the proverbial scalded hound. He'd made his decision, and he would live with it.

There was no rule, however, saying he had to like it. And he was confident as to exactly what was required to wash the bitter taste of disappointment from his mouth.

Bright sunlight hitting his face awakened him. The pound of a hammer sent blasts of sharp pain through his head. He winced and covered his ears to no avail. The hammer was inside his head. He groaned, rolled over, and buried his face in his blankets.

He tried to ignore the slam of the hammer and think. Where was he? How had he come to be naked in bed with a headache for the ages and the sour stomach of an alley drunk?

He had two vague memories. The first was of a chorus of cheers from a densely packed crowd whose uplifted hands held pint mugs dripping white foam. The second was of a blow to his shoulder and a slurred voice saying, "Keep a tight grip on him, Sam. Didn't I warn you the Bell boys are right heavy to carry?"

He threw off the covering blanket, levered himself into a sitting position, and swung his legs over the side of the bed. The banging in his head increased tenfold. He blinked his eyes to make sure he wasn't seeing things and decided that it really was his uniform, clean and pressed free of wrinkles, draped over the chair beside the bed. His stomach growled and a stark impression of having thrown up came to him.

A boot banged against the hallway side of the door.

The door of the room swung open, admitting Fritz Howard. The grinning private held a tray loaded with two steaming dishes and a china coffeepot. "Breakfast, sir. The best my aunt Francine has to offer."

The fuzzy-brained Jacob squinted and said, "What the hell happened last night?"

Fritz Howard balanced the tray on one hand, shut the door, tugged a second chair alongside the bed with a boot toe, and placed his tray on the seat of the chair. "Sir, it was a most joyous occasion. You bolted into Sweeney's, bought a round for the house, and didn't look at anything but the bottom of an empty pint for two solid hours."

Pouring a cup of coffee from the china pot, Corporal Howard handed the cup to Jacob. "I poured a little whiskey in the coffee to settle your stomach."

A grateful Jacob blew on the hot coffee and took a careful sip. "Where are we?"

"My aunt's boardinghouse on Long Street. Sam and I toted you here after you passed out. Somewhere along the way you vomited on your cheat. We undressed you and my aunt laundered your uniform, dried it over the stove, and ironed it early this morning. Sam and I thought you'd feel better if we let you sleep in."

Jacob remembered it was bright sunshine that had awakened him. "Good God, what time is it?"

"About ten o'clock. Sam and I figured if we reported to Major Hamtramck by noon, he'd most likely assume we arrived on the morning train."

Jacob nodded and laughed. "Fritz, I'll make sure you're with me on my next drunk, too."

Corporal Howard handed Jacob a slice of buttered bread. "Long as you have the money to buy, sir, Sam and I will gladly carry you home."

Though his head still hurt, Jacob's condition was improving by the minute. In big bites, he polished off Aunt

Francine's scrambled eggs, bacon, pan-browned potatoes, and porridge with milk and honey.

When Jacob finished eating, Fritz Howard set chair and tray aside and fetched his laundered long johns from the top of a corner dresser. "I'll pay your aunt whatever's due her as we leave."

"She'd appreciate that," Fritz Howard said, scooping up his tray. "Sam and I will wait for you downstairs."

Clean clothes made a new man of him. He pulled on his boots, buckled on his saber and holstered pistol, and ran his hands through his hair. He decided there was time to treat Fritz and Sam Kite to a haircut and shave, and himself a fresh shave, at the Gay Street barbershop.

He plucked his hat from the dresser and exited his sleeping room. He halted at the top of the stairs and took stock of his situation in the last few moments of privacy he would enjoy for perhaps weeks.

He'd put romantic foolishness behind him the previous evening and vowed not to dwell on what-if and what-might-have-been.

He had officers counting on his maturity, his knowledge, and his loyalty to the Union flag to carry out their orders.

He had men to command who looked to him for the leadership and encouragement they craved and needed to succeed on the battlefield.

His calling for the duration of the war was that of the soldier willing to die for his country, if necessary, to restore the Union.

Everything else was of no consequence until victory was achieved.

CHAPTER 26

War is a madness that inflicts wounds that never heal. I have watched soldiers unite under a common flag and destroy the lives of the enemy as well as the innocent caught in the path of the conflict. The intelligent soul understands the price for successfully wielding gun and saber will be paid on judgment day. I can only fight now and pray that I will be in good standing with my creator at that future moment.
—*Journal of Jacob Bell, Lieutenant, Company M,*
  First Regiment Ohio Volunteer Cavalry,
  Evening of 30 December 1862

"Seems like we drove those fifty remounts into Camp Buell just yesterday, sir," Fritz Howard said, "but we've been chasing graybacks for seven solid weeks."

Jacob slipped his pen, ink jar, and journal into a leather carrying case and stashed the case in a saddlebag. "Well, the chasing after is over. Bragg has chosen to stand and fight. He'll be on us something fierce come daylight."

Jacob Bell and the First Ohio Cavalry were encamped with the Second Cavalry Brigade composed of the First,

Third, and Fourth Regiments Ohio Volunteer Cavalry and the Fifth Regiment Kentucky Volunteer Cavalry. The Second Brigade had spent the previous week jostling with General Bragg's Confederate cavalry led by General Joe Wheeler. General Bragg's army had conceded ground and solidified their lines on the west bank of Stones River before Murfreesboro, Tennessee, and both the Blue and the Gray were preparing for the total engagement Bragg and his Union counterpart, Major General William S. Rosecrans, were seeking with the blessing and at the urging of their respective presidents.

The weather was bitterly cold. A shivering Sergeant Tom South scooted closer to the mess fire. "Lieutenant, you attended Colonel Millikin's staff meeting. Could you give us an idea of what General Rosecrans's strategy is and explain why we have all those fires burning out yonder where we have no men?"

Jacob saw no earthly reason why his mess shouldn't be aware of what General Rosecrans expected to transpire in the morning. He employed a stick for a pointer and scratched a scraggly furrow in the dirt. The mess in its entirety surrounded him with bent heads and eager ears.

"We're here on the right flank with General McCook's corps. General Thomas's corps is situated in the middle of our lines with General Crittenden's corps on our left flank near Stones River. General Rosecrans plans to strike hard with Crittenden's corps from our left, pivot on Thomas in the center, roll up the Confederate right, drive it into Murfreesboro, and capture the Rebel's ammunition and ration supplies. McCook's corps is to hold fast and occupy the Confederates to our front. We're not to attack."

Jacob tossed his pointer into the mess fire. "If you could see our lines from the sky, there are no campfires on our left flank where General Crittenden is moving his brigades into position for his morning assault. We have fires burning in the center of our lines and beyond the actual termination of our right flank in an attempt to fool the graybacks as to where our real strength is located. Everybody on board with what I've told you?"

It was nearing "Tattoo," and the military bands of both armies began playing their favorite tunes. In the crisp, windless night air, individual notes rang out sharp as the tines of a fork tapping finely spun glass. The Confederate musicians answered "Yankee Doodle" with "Dixie." "The Bonnie Blue Flag" challenged the Federal's "Hail Columbia." The upshot occurred when a band began playing "Home Sweet Home." Soldiers regardless of uniform color were suddenly singing the words together. Jacob could have become a rich man betting there wasn't a dry eye within hearing distance when the unlikely, impromptu choir of fifty thousand soldiers sang the final refrain.

"Isn't it crazy, Lieutenant, how we can sing together tonight," Sam Kite said, "and then kill each other tomorrow?"

"Sam, sometimes I still question how we were fools enough to start a shooting war with each other," Jacob said, "but we did, and a heap of people who would have preferred a peaceful solution to our differences are in the grave with more to follow as soon as the sun shows in the morning."

Jacob rose to his feet. "Gentlemen, let's grab what sleep we can. I have a hunch the graybacks will start the ball rolling mighty early. What we don't want is another Shiloh and be caught with our drawers at half-mast."

The concern for a surprise attack lingered in the back of Jacob's mind throughout the night. He awoke before first light, filled a cup with cold coffee, and sipped the bitter brew while he studied the dark horizon. The First Ohio encampment was behind Brigadier General R. W. Johnson's division on the extreme outer edge of the Union's right flank. The objective of Johnson's division was to prevent the turning of the flank by Bragg's forces. If that occurred and the Rebels overran Johnson's defenders, the way was open for a drive by the enemy to the Nashville Turnpike, the major supply artery for the entire Union army. Once in possession of the Turnpike, the graybacks could deny Rosecrans's army food and ammunition and force their surrender. The fact such a Union failure to hold mirrored Rosecrans's exact strategy for defeating his Confederate opponent on the opposite flank of his battle line wasn't lost on Jacob. Coincidence often trumped man's best laid plans.

A swirling fog, backlit by the emerging dawn, shrouded the Union camp. Here and there a few foot soldiers stirred and flames leaped at a fire or two. Other than the firing of a few Union picket rifles, which historically tended to result from jumpy nerves and were usually ignored, no warning of real consequence alerted the blue-bellies.

Gray-clad Rebel skirmishers materialized like ghostly apparitions in the cedar brakes fronting Johnson's division, hesitated until a double line of infantry marching shoulder to shoulder was a step behind them, and then the whole lot bore down on the sleeping Yankees, their dreaded Rebel yell inviting the sleeping enemy to a living nightmare of their own making.

Advancing on an extended front, the two Rebel infantry divisions simply swept through and over everything before them. Several frontline Union batteries were captured without their cannoneers firing a single round. Those blue-bellies managing to cluster behind outcroppings of rock and within clumps of cedar quickly found them themselves outflanked left and right. Facing death or certain capture, they broke for the rear, tossing away their weapons in the interest of greater speed afoot.

The experience of being rousted from their blankets by

the bawl of an officer if that were the fastest means saved the Second Cavalry Brigade. Jacob's verbal screaming of "To Horse, To Horse" was repeated in a flash by regimental buglers. Every trooper had checked his hand weapons for dry powder, filled his canteen, fed and watered his mount, positioned his saddle, saddle blanket, and bridle for a quick swing into action, and retired half expecting the unforeseen to yank him from his blankets on short notice.

The immediate need to be in the saddle galvanized the Second Brigade into a disciplined response that wasted not a precious second. A lesser reaction would have had them fighting with pistol and saber on the ground at a numerical disadvantage, negating their value as a mobile force and rendering them inconsequential.

A quick scan of the battlefield by Jacob confirmed at least half of Johnson's division was dead, wounded, or out of action. Confusion reigned and a wave of panic threatened to engulf the entire right wing of the Union army. Bugle calls to the western fringe of the fighting heralded the arrival of General Joe Wheeler and his Confederate cavalry, adding more manpower to the Rebel attack.

Though the graybacks held the upper hand in numbers, a steadfast Union officer rallied a regiment in a pile of jumbled boulders and their withering fire slowed the Confederate advance for vital minutes, allowing numbers of back-peddling blue-bellies to obey their pleading officers, turnabout, form lines, and return enemy fire before being driven back again.

The flow of the fight curved westward around the fortified boulders into a large cotton field, exposing Johnson's division to slashing attacks by General Wheeler's Rebel cavalry. The First Ohio quartered in that direction in an attempt to stay the ever-turning right flank until the Confederate tide could somehow be stemmed.

By chance, Cam Logan was riding on Jacob's left when

a horseback volley by Wheeler's cavalry riddled the front ranks of the approaching First Ohio. Jacob heard a loud grunt and the saddle next to him emptied. When he looked down, Cam Logan was sprawled among white cotton bolls holding the side of his head with blood leaking between his fingers.

A bugle blew "Recall" and the First Ohio swung about. Jacob started to turn and follow his fellow troopers. A groan from Cam Logan arrested his flight. One glance told him Wheeler's graybacks were forming up to charge.

It would probably be the death of him or a stretch in a Rebel prison camp if he failed, but he wasn't leaving Cam Logan behind. He wasn't deserting a true fighting man who had never failed his regiment. And his regiment wasn't deserting him.

Jacob jumped from the saddle. In a stroke of pure luck, the reins of Logan's horse were trapped beneath him. Jacob freed the reins and kept a tight grip on them while he grabbed the front of Logan's shirt and yanked him to his feet, a feat of unfamiliar strength that mystified him for decades.

Listening for the gallop of enemy hoofs, he shook Cam Logan and yelled, "Captain, can you hear me?"

The response was a weak, but heartening, "Yes."

"Grab your horse's mane," Jacob ordered, guiding Logan's hand until it touched the hair of the mane.

The moment Logan's fingers closed on the horse's mane, Jacob lifted his left foot into the stirrup, grabbed the back of his belt, put a shoulder under left hip, and heaved. His grip on the belt kept Logan from sliding off the horse's opposite flank.

Jacob yelled, "Grab the mane with both hands," and mounted his chestnut.

He'd done all he could for his captain. It was up to Cam Logan to have the wherewithal and the strength to stay in the saddle. Ignoring an enemy now within pistol range, he kneed the chestnut into a fast walk, glanced over his shoulder, saw Cam Logan lumped in the saddle with both arms wrapped around his horse's neck, and spurred the chestnut into a gallop as a bullets *pished* by his ears.

The recalled First Ohio had come about again to face their adversaries in front of a cedar forest, and once they recognized Jacob's plight, fired a volley to dissuade his pursuers. Jacob spied the white canvas of a Union ambulance among Johnson's regrouping division at the edge of the trees behind the First Ohio and rode straight for it. The boys of the First Ohio cheered his safe passage.

Dismounting, he helped a medic ease Logan from the saddle. The ambulance was chock full of wounded men as were the stretchers surrounding it, so Jacob and the medic propped Cam Logan against the rear wheel. The medic felt alongside Logan's head above his right ear. "I'm not a doctor, but his skull isn't broken. I think the bullet just grazed him. There's always a lot of blood with head wounds. He might be dizzy for a few days. Otherwise, he should be okay."

Jacob came to his feet and swung into the saddle. Rejoining the First Ohio, it was obvious the blue-belly situation had grown even more desperate. The Confederates had wrestled cannon forward despite the boulder-strewn terrain, the remaining grayback infantry was massing again, and Wheeler's cavalry companies were forming on the right flank for another charge. The whole right wing of Rosecrans's army was in danger of collapsing and opening a lane to the Nashville Turnpike for the Rebels.

Jacob spied Colonel Millikin in the forefront of the First Ohio. With Captain Logan out of commission, he sought new orders from his superior officer, trusting Sergeant Tom South with the men of their mess. He trotted to within hearing distance of Millikin and slowed the chestnut to a walk.

Colonel Minor Millikin was his usual composed self, assessing what strategy might yet save the day. Jacob's thinking paralleled his commander's. Millikin must act at once, or his regiment would be stampeded from the field and crushed by the overwhelming force of an enemy flushed with the smell of victory. No other officer of the Second Cavalry Brigade seemed to appreciate the dire straits confronting them, and Colonel Minor Millikin, convinced the concession of one more foot of bloody turf would be ruinous, out of necessity seized the reins of destiny.

"Private Patterson, please inform the other regiments of the brigade I would appreciate their supporting a charge by the First Ohio."

The gauntlet cast, Millikin wheeled his regiment by fours and gave the command, "Draw Saber."

There was no time to tighten girths or check the status of revolvers, for their leader rose in his stirrups and gave the command to "Charge," which was repeated to right and left the full length of the line. Racing forward under the spur, the First Ohio followed their brave and peerless commander into the jaws of carnage that might prove the death of them to the last man.

Reduced to a mere three hundred troopers by death, wounds, and sickness, the First Ohio was challenging the entire left wing of the Confederate army without support. Not a man tugged on his reins. On they galloped, striking the Rebel lines, slashing right and left, leaving a swath of blue and gray dead and wounded in their wake, slicing a line the width of the regiment in the Rebel front, penetrating clear through the enemy, forging into a melee ripe with yelling, cursing, pistol shots, flashing sabers, and horses and men struggling in a confused tangle and tumbling to earth together.

Jacob fought with every ounce of strength and will he could muster, his lust to kill the enemy negating any feeling of personal danger. A piece of scalp dangling an ear bounced off the chestnut's cheek. Spurting blood arched in red streams. A complete human head with disbelieving eyes and yawning mouth hung in the air before him. He gulped and swatted it aside.

His arm growing numb from the force of his saber blows to Rebel skulls, necks, and shoulders, he sensed the regiment's momentum was flagging as the enemy recovered from the initial shock and determined surge of their mounted attack. The push of three hundred against four thousand wasn't sustainable forever.

He heard the words he dreaded the most. "The colonel has been hit! The colonel's been hit!"

Still slashing at Rebels determined to tear him from the saddle, Jacob searched frantically in all directions. No sign of Minor Millikin. The colonel was off his horse and at the mercy of the recovering enemy.

The numbness claimed Jacob's right arm. His hand opened of its own accord and his saber slipped from his fingers. It was an awkward backhand draw but he clawed his pistol free of its holster with his left hand. He had no concern for accuracy and fired at random. The yelling Rebels gave way.

The graybacks were rapidly closing in behind the First Ohio, threatening to surround it. Jacob stood in his stirrups and scanned the battlefield to his rear. Not a single trooper from the rest of the Second Brigade was riding to assist the First Ohio. They were on their own as they had been from the outset.

The bugle notes of "Recall" reached him. He spun the chestnut and spurred him hard. The First Ohio had prevented a Union disaster by blunting the Confederate advance long enough for blue-bellies to shore up their positions, but now it was time to avert a disaster of its own.

His saber gone, his pistol clicking on empty chambers, Jacob bent low over the chestnut's neck and employed the revolver as a club. A hefty, bearded Rebel stepped in front of the chestnut, leaped, and thrust a Bowie knife at him. He warded off the meaty grayback with an elbow to the throat. His sleeve snagged the Bowie knife and left him with a minor cut on the forearm.

He saw daylight through the chestnut's ears. He was almost there, almost beyond the clutch of the enemy's grasp, when a devastating blow of unknown origin blew the chestnut sideways and off its feet. Jacob was flying upside down. He landed on his backside and bounced twice on the hard ground. Dust clogged his eyes, nose, and mouth.

At first, his whole body was numb from the impact. Then the pain in his left leg asserted itself, dominating the whole fiber of his existence, and the noise of cannons and small arms fire, the thud of hoofs, and the screams of the wounded receded into absolute silence.

Fearing death, he struggled to stay alert.

And failed.

He felt his life slipping away like a lantern burning its last drop of oil.

CHAPTER 27

He was sad the cold night rain awakened him. The nothingness of the unconscious mind had held the pain at bay. The return of his senses brought with it a raging pain that watered his eyes and made him gasp in short barks until he was out of breath. Good Lord, what had he done to deserve to die a death he wouldn't wish on his worst enemy?

He was dying, of that he had no doubt. His thinking was lucid enough between bouts of severe versus lesser pain to deduce the chestnut hadn't collided with another horse, which meant only a cannonball could have knocked the feet from under him, the same cannonball that had wreaked havoc with his lower leg. He was happy he couldn't lift his head and try to assess the damage he'd suffered. Just the thought of being a cripple gagged him.

He shivered from the cold and his teeth chattered. He was too weak to wrap his arms about his body for what little warmth they might offer. He regretted that he hadn't bled out. Now he would die alone in the dark with no one to say a forgiving word over him. He'd be nothing more than another uniformed, nameless body for a burial detail to slide into a long trench time and weather would hide from any soul that might for a some obscure reason care to look after his remains properly.

He cried a little then. The ultimate insult of war was for a man to die for his country's flag and be rewarded with an anonymous grave far from home and those who loved him, his sole recognition the listing of his name on a roster of battlefield casualties.

He senses came and went. He grew more despondent. Each woozy spell of awareness reminded him his plight remained unchanged, that he was no closer to the death he craved more desperately with each agonizing minute.

Weak yellow light attracted his eye. Cold fingers pressed against the side of his neck, and a vaguely familiar voice said, "There's a pulse. He's still breathing."

A second voice with a distinct Southern burr said, "There's little we can do for him and our wagon is nearly full."

"Didn't you say you were taking wounded from both armies under your care?"

Jacob was certain he heard the ratcheting sound of a pistol's hammer locking home. "His name is Lieutenant Jacob Bell, and I'll make it worth your while to take him with you."

The Southern voice virtually purred. "No need for the extra persuasion, sir. A coin or two in hand will guarantee your lieutenant a ride as comfortable as we can make it."

Rough hands slid under Jacob's shoulders and beneath his knees. "Careful with that right leg, Hack. We don't want to aggravate things for our new patient."

The pain from being moved was the worst yet for Jacob, and only his pathetically weak condition kept him from screaming for his bearers to leave him to die. He didn't want false hope and the continual suffering that might accompany it dangled in front of him. He had reconciled himself to a fate that would bring him peace without pain and a blissful afterlife with his maker.

But he was helpless and as easy to manhandle as an infant child.

The saving grace of being temporarily rescued against his wishes was the blissful blackness that engulfed him long before his body came to rest in the bed of the wagon taking him to an unknown destination.

He emerged from the blackness he'd come to love uncertain if he were alive or dead. There appeared to be a stone ceiling above him on which light was casting flitting shadows of human forms dancing either in celebration of good tidings or perpetrated evil. He wriggled his lower body and the resulting pain confirmed he was alive and merely suffering in a place that was neither heaven nor the fiery pit of damnation.

His probing fingers told him he was resting atop a pile of straw on a concrete floor. He slowly inched his head high enough to learn the light on the ceiling came from a pine-knot fire in a large fireplace built into the far wall of the room. He smelled the odor of burning straw. Sparks from the pine-knot fire kept igniting the straw bedding, and the flitting shadows above him belonged to two people assigned to stomp them out before they ignited a blaze that endangered the patients who lay in neat rows the length and width of the room.

A young boy pointing out expired patients as well as providing cups of water to the living ones capable of quenching their thirst discovered Jacob's eyes were open. Later, the short-bearded, bespectacled face of a rosy-cheeked individual with an open smile that bespoke warmth and concern loomed over him. "I'm Union Doctor John

Worth, and I'm glad you've pulled through, Lieutenant Bell."

With Jacob's frown, Dr. Worth lifted a cautioning finger. "You rest, I'll talk. Okay?"

Worth waited until he detected a slight nod on Jacob's part before continuing, "You're in a storeroom in Murfreesboro that was converted into a makeshift hospital after the Confederates captured me and my colleague the first day of the battle. As to your condition, I gave you one of my final morphine doses and amputated your right leg below the knee four days ago. It was a clean bone removal and we successfully tied off the arteries. Rest assured, Lieutenant, I had no other recourse. Your foot was nothing but a glob of shattered bone and torn flesh."

Doctor Worth felt Jacob's forehead. "For you, there is an upside. If infection doesn't set in, you should be up and about in a month or two."

But as a damn one-legged cripple, Jacob wanted to shout. The next second, he was glad he was hurting and too weak to get the words out. He owed Dr. Worth his thanks, not a bitter slight in return for the saving of his life.

The doctor's hopeful prognosis soured the next evening when a fever gripped Jacob and left him delirious and hot to the touch. The significance of Dr. Worth's saying he could find no sign that the fever had originated in his amputation was lost on the profusely sweating Jacob. His head ached in concert with his leg without relief. Despair set in, and the conviction he was better off dead came to the fore once more. There was a limit to how much misery a man with an unattractive future dragging around a wooden leg was willing to endure just to stay alive.

How much time passed he didn't know. Then he swore the Northern voice he'd heard on the battlefield was speaking somewhere near him. Gentle hands lifted his body, a blanket was wrapped around him, and he felt the slight give of a canvas stretcher beneath him.

His next sensation was of extremely cold air and the melting of what had to be snowflakes on his forehead and cheek. The squeal of door hinges opening floated to him. Boots pounded on a puncheon floor, and then on the hollow runners of a flight of stairs.

"Put him on the bed there," a soft feminine voice said. "We'll undress him and hand-bathe him after you're gone, and don't worry, sir, he'll have the care Doctor Worth requested."

The door of the room closed and soft bare hands stripped his clothes from him. He was too sick to be embarrassed by his nakedness in front of women he didn't know. What mattered was they smelled clean and wholesome and not like putrefying flesh, vomit, and human excrement.

The wet cloth was cool and soothing. He had to admit the two women were thorough. Not a single part of him missed out on the bathing. He was awake enough most of the time to discern one female was middle-aged with gray hair and the other a young black woman with tight curly hair trimmed close to her scalp.

He settled into a routine focused on regular doctoring and nursing care. The ever-on-the-move Dr. Worth never lingered or had much to say, but he came every other day to change the bandages on his leg and admonish him not to rush his recovery. The young black female blotted sweat from his forehead with a cotton towel and fed him broth with a spoon when he had the strength to swallow. His fever broke the third day and gradually subsided. The pain in his leg became tolerable unless he responded to an itch too quickly. The gray-haired older woman checked on him occasionally. He learned their names were Widow Browning and Miss Reba and he loved them both for looking after him virtually around the clock, and thanked them often.

He never forgot his first solid night's sleep, for when he opened his eyes Felicia Denning was seated in a chair beside his bed, reading the worn copy of *Ivanhoe* Widow Browning had provided him the day before. For a brief second, he feared he'd dreamed everything that had happened since the chestnut was blown out from under him in the devil's private purgatory and this was the final punishment—a full-blown look at the ultimate what-could-have-been—before he was dumped into the eternal fires of damnation.

But the inclusion of *Ivanhoe* was too clever for even the ruler of the nether world and neither he nor his henchmen could replicate a truly beautiful creature in such exquisite, living detail. He made no move to acknowledge her presence. Simply watching her turn pages fascinated, thrilled, and excited him. She most certainly hadn't come all this way to be his friend. And what might happen next was worth contemplating at his leisure.

He watched a slight blush spread across her cheeks. An intuitive, instinctive female accustomed to male attention, she had become aware a man was watching her without catching him doing it. Cornflower blue eyes peered at him over the spine of *Ivanhoe*.

Excited as he was to have her with him, he was at a complete loss as to how best to greet her. Nothing seemed appropriate. "Hello" was too casual and "I love you" was perhaps too bold. Thankfully, her earnest smile dissolved the tension threatening to tie his belly into hard knots.

She clutched *Ivanhoe* in her lap with both hands and said, "I hate war. It frightens and appalls me. Meeting you was the storybook tale of the girl and the handsome soldier meeting and falling in love instantly come true. Then you went straight off to fight in a real war. It made no difference that we had spent but a few minutes together, the thought of losing you was unbearable."

She paused, wet her lips, and swallowed. He waited for her to speak again. Though personal revelation was never easy, he felt she wanted him to hear her out here and now.

"I felt terrible answering your letters with silly, female gibberish. I didn't want to admit I didn't have the courage to love a man who might be killed the next hour. Then you wrote to me how horribly men had died at Pittsburgh Landing and I took the coward's way out. I stopped answering your letters and tried to forget you by seeing other men. I must have entertained every eligible Columbus bachelor in our parlor and let them wine and dine me about town nightly. And none of them appealed to me. Not a one.

"Last week, the telegram came. It told me you'd been wounded and had your foot amputated, where I could find you, and that I should come immediately."

She laid *Ivanhoe* aside, rose from her chair, walked to the bed, and sat beside him, moving very slowly for fear she might hurt him. Up close, her beauty was even more remarkable. "I cried all night over what a fool I'd made of myself. My father protested my traveling alone something awful. He pointed out you might die before I reached you. He quieted down when I told him I'd finally realized that just one day with you was better than a lifetime with any of those young bucks so terribly anxious to bed me."

She leaned over him. Her intentions were clear, but before things went any further, he had to know. "Who sent you the telegram?"

"Why Captain Cam Logan."

She saw the surprise on his face. "You didn't know it was him, did you?"

"No, I was sure it was Major Dance Walker."

"Widow Browning said the captain was responsible for

your being brought to her boardinghouse. He paid her to care for you how ever long it took for you to walk again."

The voices he'd heard while semiconscious had matched. Cam Logan was also responsible for moving him from the battlefield to Dr. Worth's hospital. He shook his head in disbelief. Only in the middle of a war could circumstances arise that would lead your worst enemy to save your life not once, but twice over. He'd never imagined he'd owe Cam Logan for anything other than the grief he might cause him. To his astonishment, he was indebted to Brice Logan's son for this wondrous creature leaning ever closer to him.

"One more question, my dear."

"Yes, but make it quick for goodness' sake."

"My wound doesn't concern you?"

Her soft laugh stirred sensations he'd forgotten.

"You're not hurt *anywhere else,* are you?"

"No."

"Then you can relax, my darling man, your Camp Chase lady will be with you forever."

Her lips were softer than rose petals.

CHAPTER 28

Hunt Baldwin was a happy man. Since his cashiering from the Union Army on charges of conduct unbecoming an officer and drunkenness, he'd scratched out a living locating prime Kentucky horses he and his bunch of cutthroats could steal and have a stand-in sell to the equine starved blue-bellies. In Glasgow, of all places, he'd spied a truly great gather—a magnificent red stallion, a seal-brown gelding, a bay gelding, and a nifty mare with a scar on her hip—in a pasture behind a barn on the northern edge of town.

He'd learned from two days of scouting that the pasture and barn belonged to Granger Huddleston, a local businessman and Glasgow's mayor. The Huddleston sawmill, smithy, gristmill, and general store closed each day at dusk and the workers went home for the evening. The night guard, if he could be deemed such by a long stretch of imagination, was a bald darkie with white sideburns dressed in denim overalls.

Hunt envisioned a post-midnight raid, a dispensing of the darkie, an opening of the pasture gate, and a non-stop drive of stolen animals to Tennessee where Federal horse buyers cared less about the origin of what they purchased.

Top-quality animals commanded top dollar, particularly if mounts for officers were being sought.

Like all men who died in the same manner, Hunt Baldwin didn't hear the bullet that snuffed out his life. It sped true from the precisely sighted barrel of a well-hidden ambusher, ripped through his chest, and fragmented his heart on contact. Body no longer controlled by brain-directed muscles, Hunt Baldwin's body slid from the saddle limp as meat on a grocer's cutting block.

It might have interested the deceased that two hours after he breathed his last on the Glasgow-Bowling Green Road, a half-breed Cherokee was seated on a stool in the corner of Granger Huddleston's smithy reloading an Enfield rifle.

"A successful hunt, I trust?" Granger Huddleston asked.

Asa Barefoot nodded and said, "He is with his proper father, the white man's devil."

EPILOGUE:
4 July 1873

Looking down the long trestle table at his family, Clay Bell decided the Good Lord had probably treated him better than he deserved. Unlike many wartime fathers such as Brice Logan, he still had his three sons after the final cannon had been fired. True, Jacob had lost a foot and Judah had been months recovering from a bullet wound. But his three boys were with him along with their wives, his grandchildren, and the whole Bell clan on this fine July afternoon, smiling, eating, laughing, and joking with him.

His daughters-in-law never ceased to amaze Clay Bell. Though they came from entirely different backgrounds—Brianna from a family rife with abuse and discord, Felicia from a home of plenty that wanted for nothing, and Lorena, the offspring of a struggling mercantile owner—they shared their doings, joys, and sorrows via constant letter writing, and, on the rare occasion he successfully arranged a weeklong family reunion, they talked as if they had grown up together in the same house. They had taken in his brother Temple's orphaned girls without being asked and provided for them until they were grown and married.

Clay Bell had been telling his friends forever that he attributed the successes of his sons to these three women. Brianna Hardin Bell had gone west with Judah and fashioned a home for his middle son after Judah discovered his true vocation was wearing a badge and enforcing the law with the help of war veteran Field Peterson as his deputy and a Cherokee half-breed jailor. Felicia Denning Bell had settled in Chillicothe with Jacob and was content being the wife of a small city lawyer and a state representative soon to be a state senator come the fall election. Lorena Gamble Bell had given her full support to Jarrod when her father-in-law and husband had jointly purchased the Cincinnati *Times-Ledger* from J. Rodgers Black, and was known at the paper's headquarters for donning sleeve garters and visor and editing copy for special editions at all hours of the night, once it was rumored while nursing her third child.

Clay Bell did have a few regrets that fine July afternoon. He had lost his lovely wife, the mother of his five children, to a fever the previous winter, and his own mother, Nadine Bell, was three years gone. Felicia and his two married daughters lived near him and tried to fill the void in his life. They watched over him now that he was a widower, retired from politics, and practicing law part-time to stay busy.

And if a fit of melancholy saddened him late at night as he lay in bed alone, he would summon forth Mother Nadine Bell's favorite adage: "My son, the love and memories of the people you meet and lose to death in this world will comfort you until you join them in the hereafter."

GREAT BOOKS, GREAT SAVINGS!

When You Visit Our Website:
www.kensingtonbooks.com
You Can Save Money Off The Retail Price
Of Any Book You Purchase!

- **All Your Favorite Kensington Authors**
- **New Releases & Timeless Classics**
- **Overnight Shipping Available**
- **eBooks Available For Many Titles**
- **All Major Credit Cards Accepted**

Visit Us Today To Start Saving!
www.kensingtonbooks.com